Charm Wars

Dan Lutts

Castine Press

Penobscot, Maine

Dan Lutts/Castine Press

P.O. 26

Penobscot, Maine/04476

www.danlutts.com

Book Layout ©2017 BookDesignTemplates.com

Charm Wars / Dan Lutts —1st ed.

ISBN 978-1-7353592-0-5

Charm World
Forbidden Lands
Rocky Strait
Mittan
The Marches
Fraedia
Caldon
Inland Sea
Caldonia
Ostica
Annatol
Anglia
Gaetan
Cyrene
Gaetania
N

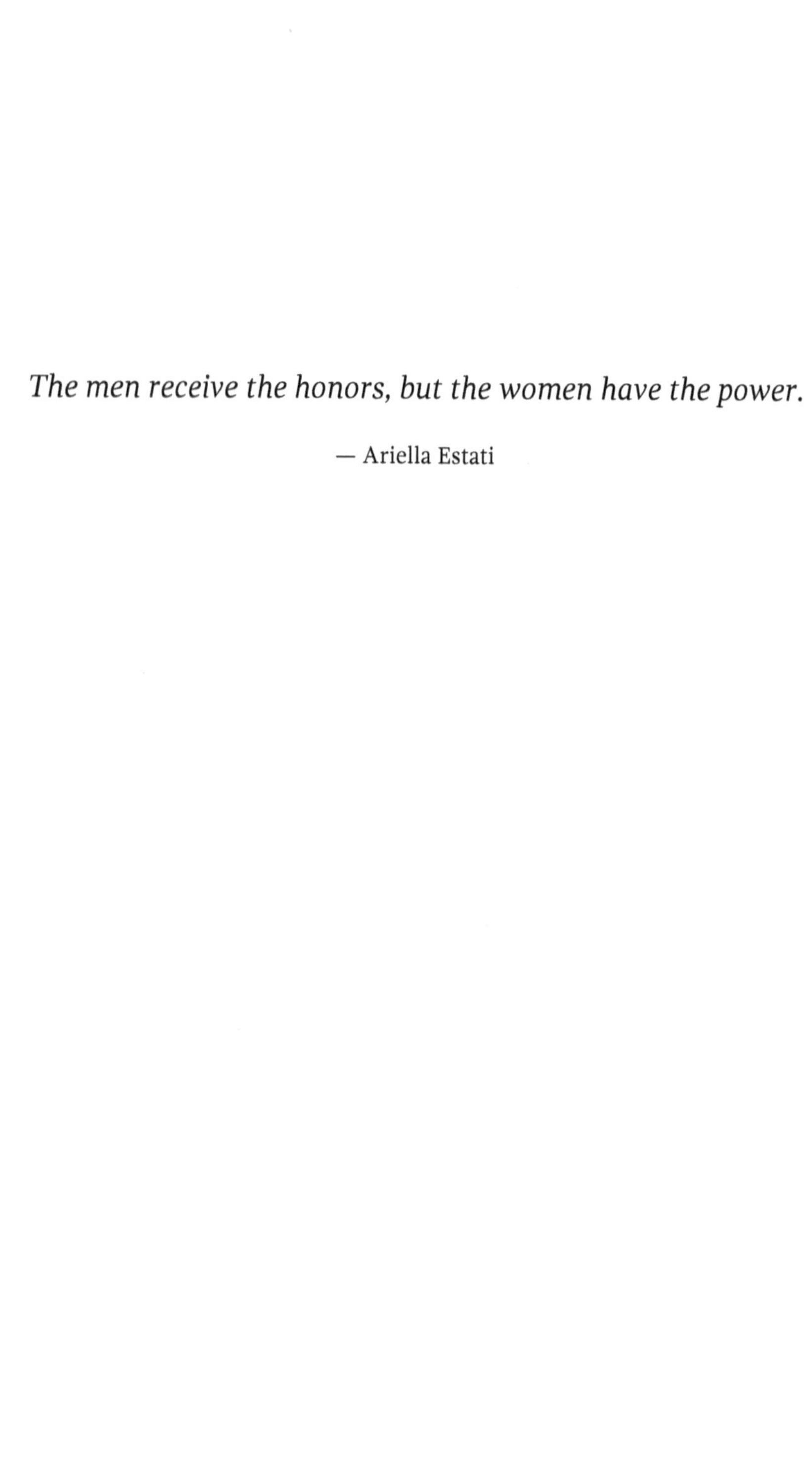

The men receive the honors, but the women have the power.

— Ariella Estati

CHARACTERS

COMMONERS AND THEIR FAMILIES
EULAND FAMILY
Sorah, Jedd's grandmother and family matriarch
Marvis, Sorah's daughter and Kald Larkin's wife
Tor, Sorah's brother
Jedd, Marvis's son

LARKIN FAMILY
Cinna, Rill's grandmother and family matriarch
Kendra, Cinna's daughter and Rill's mother
Marc, Cinna's son and Rill's father
Kald, Cinna's son and and Marvis Euland's husband
Tarri, Cinna's daughter
Rill, Kendra and Marc's son
Faith, Rill's dog

NOBLESSE AND THEIR FAMILIES
BERNE FAMILY
Jukka, Alger's father, co-chief mage, and Maude Dejune's husband
Alger, Alger's son and Shalira Estati's husband

DEJUNE FAMILY
Siema, Alyse's great grandmother, Locien Estati's wife, and family
    matriarch
Maude, Siema's daughter and Jukka Berne's wife
Pilar, Siema's granddaughter, Alyse and Mora's mother, and Degas
    Spicer's wife
Leoc, Siema's grandson
Alyse, Siema's great granddaughter and Pilar's twin daughter
Mora, Siema's great granddaughter and Pilar's twin daughter
Kate, Alyse's cousin and backwatcher

ESTATI
Ariella, Livia and Troy's great grandmother and family matriarch
Locien, Ariella's brother, co-chief mage, and Siema Dejune's husband
Yulonna, Ariella's daughter and Tolf Belkon's wife
Deuth, Yulonna's son, Adele Svagga's husband, and Garth Svagga's
    father
Shalira, Ariella's grandmother, Livia and Troy's mother, and Alger
    Berne's wife
Livia, Shalira's daughter and Ariella's great granddaughter
Troy, Shalira's son and Ariella's great grandson

SPICER FAMILY
Degas, Alyse's stepfather and Pilar Estati's husband
Isabet, Degas's sister

SVAGGA FAMILY
Adele, Garth's mother and Deuth Estati's wife
Brico, Adele's brother and Deuth's brother-in-law
Garth, Adele and Deuth's son

OTHER NOBLESSE
Cato Porta, archmage
Tolf Belkon, Yulonna Estati's husband

BACKWATCHERS AND PROTECTORS
Freyou, Dejune protector
Geoff, Dejune protector
Jade Channer, Mora Dejune's backwatcher
Magnus Roeback, Deuth Estati's backwatcher
Milco Barr, the Estati's chief backwatcher
Palquo, Dejune protector
Yall Throwstarr, Troy Estati's backwatcher

PRIESTESSES AT THE ONE GODDESS TEMPLE
Gilda, assistant chief priestess
Glenissa, elderly priestess
Jillina, young novice
Sybil Raine, chief priestess

HEALERS AND SERVANTS
Kalso, Estati head steward
Lenia, Dejune healer
Lothar, Dejune head steward

THE TWINS
Ulbra Thane, a demigod
Ulbridge Thane, a demigod

ARMY DESERTERS
Ebar
Hilbrand Wistlow
Ord

PLACES
Elustra, the afterworld
Shelar, the underworld

GODDESSES AND GODS

The One Goddess (or Divine Lady), the main deity

The Five Sisters (or the Five Weavers), weave the tapestry of life
that determines each woman's and man's life

Naela the Spinner, spins the yarn for the loom

Maela the Yarn Chooser, selects the threads that determine
a person's personality and health

Kaerla the Allotter, determines the length of a person's life

Traela the Weaver, weaves the incidents in a person's life

Gaela the Thread Cutter, chooses how the person dies and
snips the yarn from the loom to end her life

The Three Judges Three gods – two female and one male – who
judge the dead and determine whether they go to Elustra or
Shelar

Map of Caldon

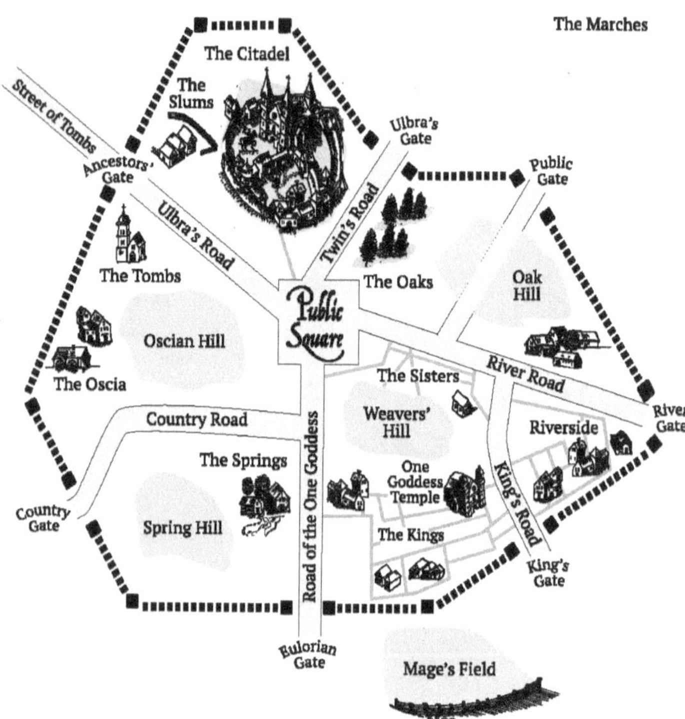

The Marches
The Citadel
The Slums
Street of Tombs
Ulbra's Gate
Public Gate
Ancestors' Gate
Ulbra's Road
Twin's Road
The Tombs
The Oaks
Oak Hill
Public Square
River Road
Oscian Hill
The Sisters
The Oscia
Weavers' Hill
Riverside
River Gate
Country Road
Road of the One Goddess
The Springs
One Goddess Temple
King's Road
Country Gate
Spring Hill
The Kings
King's Gate
Eulorian Gate
Mage's Field

N

Cougar's Lair

THE RAYS OF THE midmorning sun shining through needle-studded pine branches and naked ash and birch limbs created a patchwork of light and dark on the forest floor. Birds fluttered from tree to tree, and somewhere in the distance an owl hooted.

Rill Larkin paused by the edge of a green-and-brown thicket, his broadhead arrow nocked and his longbow half drawn. The chill, early Awakening season wind attacked his bones through the coarse wool of his heavy, dark-brown cloak. He suppressed a shiver, not from the cold but from excitement mingled with apprehension. He eyed the cougar's tracks that disappeared into the thicket of brownish bushes and scrubby, leafless trees that grew on the base of the mountain. A narrow, well-worn trail showed the cougar had come and gone that way many times before.

Jedd Euland lowered his yew longbow. "We can't use our bows in there." His words, spoken low, held a note of fear. "We should of brought hunting spears."

Rill ignored the tightening in his chest. "You know we couldn't do that," he said in a quiet tone. "My dad would skin us alive if he knew what we're doing. The spears would of been a dead giveaway."

Jedd snorted, then spoke in that slow, deliberate way that made Rill believe he thought out each word before speaking it. "He'll skin us alive anyways once we get back."

Rill shot his heavyset cousin a know-it-all grin. "Not if we bring the cougar's pelt with us."

"Even *if* we bring it with us," Jedd said, a troubled look in his brown eyes. "He told you to leave things be, remember?"

"That was two weeks ago."

"That don't matter to Uncle Marc. He means what he says. Always has."

"I don't care. That cougar killed Blaze. I loved that horse. And that damned cougar ain't gettin' away with what it did."

Jedd turned wary eyes from the undergrowth to Rill. "We can't use our bows in that thicket."

"You already said that." Un-nocking his arrow, Rill leaned the bow against a tree and placed his quiver beside it. He drew his sword, his jaw set and muscles taut. "So we'll use cold steel instead."

"Against a *cougar*?"

Rill caught Jedd's eye. "Scared?"

"No. But I got a bad feeling about this."

"I didn't come all this way to turn back now. You can stay here if you want."

Jedd blew out an exasperated breath as if he was offended by Rill's remark. "You know I won't do that. I just think we oughta be cautious."

"Don't worry. Everything will be fine."

"Where have I heard *that* before?" Rubbing his chin with thumb and forefinger, Jedd made an exaggerated show of pondering, which made Rill want to roll his eyes in exasperation. "Oh yeah. *Now* I remember. Last month when you—"

"Come on," Rill said, cutting Jedd off before he could bring up *that* embarrassing incident again. "I'll go first."

Rill stepped into the dense tangle, his outward nonchalance masking nerves twisting so tight they threatened to form a coil of rope as he forced one brown boot cautiously in front of the other.

Heaving an exasperated sigh, Jedd pulled out his sword and followed.

Rill grimaced each time a twig snapped and dried leaves crackled under their boots, or bare branches rustled against their cloaked shoulders. *We're making so much noise the damned cougar can hear us halfway up the mountain. It might even be watching us now.* Rill's heart missed a beat as he pictured the savage beast lurking nearby, ready to pounce and rip them apart with its huge claws and sharp teeth, just like it did Blaze.

The two-week-old memory that haunted Rill's mind stirred restlessly. Five years ago, a neighbor had given Rill's dad a chestnut yearling named Blaze in return for forging a sword, dagger, and other accoutrements for his daughter, who was beginning a career as a backwatcher with a noblesse Lesser Family. With his dad's help, Rill had broken and trained Blaze, who had grown up alongside him more as a family member than an animal. Rill smiled to himself as he recalled the times he and Blaze had ridden into the countryside, sometimes with Faith—the black-and-tan dog he'd rescued from the streets—racing alongside. The smile turned into a scowl as the horrific memory rose into his brain like a demon from Shelar, the Underworld. Two weeks ago, near where they'd tethered their horses today. The cougar's vicious snarls and Blaze's terrified squeals, followed by screams of pain—

The sharp crack of a twig behind him jolted Rill. *The cougar!* Rill whirled around, bringing up his sword—

Jedd leaned back fast, and the sharp blade missed his throat by a hair.

"Sorry," Jedd said, his face pale.

Rill blew out a deep, shaky breath. "I could of killed you." He waited for his galloping heartbeat to slow to a trot before he looked at Jedd, whose face had returned to its normal fleshy hue.

They nodded to each other and continued on.

When they emerged from the thicket, Rill found himself staring at a dark fissure under a gray stone ledge that jutted out above them a short spear's throw away, blocking out the sun. A loose, brownish mesh of vines grew all over the rocky mountainside, a few dead, withered leaves still attached and the rest scattered on the grassy ground beneath them. Rill frowned at the crevice. The edges weren't jagged but smooth, and the opening was almost as high as a tall woman and wide enough for a cougar to slip through.

"Whatever that is," Jedd whispered, "it ain't natural."

"It's woman-made," Rill whispered.

He started forward, but Jedd grabbed his shoulder. "Careful. There's a cougar in there."

Rill pulled free and stole toward the opening, nerves stretched to breaking, and his heart slamming so hard against his chest he could hear the impact of each beat in his ears. He stopped abruptly, just a foot from the opening, his eyes wide with astonishment. "Holy Goddess!" he said.

The vine net obscured the outline of a door whose texture and color matched the gray stone of the mountainside. But a crack from top to bottom split the door into two jagged pieces. Five long lines of deeply etched runes peeped out at Rill through the weblike openings.

Rill trailed his fingertips along the vine-covered door, dipping them in and out of the runes. "This ain't no cave. The door's metal. And mage-made!"

"Holy Twins!" Jedd said, stopping beside him. "I ain't gettin' mixed up in the affairs of no mages. Forget the cougar. Let's get outta here."

Rill spun toward Jedd, his eyes burning with excitement as wild possibilities of what might be inside tumbled through his mind, like multiple dice being shaken in a game of chance. Who knew what might turn up? "There's more than a cougar in there."

Jedd's brow crinkled into a frown, the way it always did when he thought Rill was about to do something foolhardy. "Like what?"

"Spell books, maybe. Or charms. Or staffs. Or—"

Jedd scoffed. "Dream on."

"Look," Rill said, "a mage sealed this cave and carved these runes on the door. She must of done it for a reason."

"You're obsessed with mages. It ain't healthy."

Rill swallowed an angry retort. *I'm getting tired of hearing that.*

"What if someone else finds this place?"

"Then she'll find the cougar too."

The cougar! In the excitement of this incredible, unexpected find, Rill had forgotten about it. He bit his lower lip, his resolve to find the cougar in a pitch-black cave beginning to fray. But the tantalizing prospect of discovering a treasure trove a mage had stashed inside patched his determination together. "I'm going in."

"What if magic wards are guarding whatever's in there?" Jedd said. "Wards that kill."

"The cougar's living inside. And it ain't been killed."

Jedd brushed a hand across the sandy-brown hair on the nape of his neck. "I got a very, very bad feeling about this."

"You don't hafta go in."

"You need someone to watch your back."

Rill smiled to himself. *I knew he'd come along. He always does.* "Let's go make us some light."

After fashioning a pair of torches, Rill and Jedd returned to the cave opening, where they lit the torches with flint and steel.

Ignoring the lump of dread in his stomach, Rill sidled through the gap, thrusting his torch ahead of him into the darkness. Once inside he quickly faced around, his sword at the ready. What the shimmering yellow flame revealed took Rill's breath away.

He hadn't entered a cave, but a chamber whose smooth gray walls and ceiling reflected the torchlight, like a gigantic three-sided mirror. The light gradually faded into blackness the farther it penetrated into the chamber. *This place was made by magic.* The space was about twenty feet wide and seven feet high. A line of large rectangular stone boxes on each side marched into the darkness like two files of legionaries. Rill squinted at a gloomy shape between the two files almost beyond the reflected light. The end of a larger stone box resting on a knee-high base. Rill breathed in the cold air, filling his nostrils with a faint, musky scent that must belong to the cougar.

The whisper of boots sounded behind him, and then Jedd stood beside him. The combined light of their torches rolled the gloom farther back, revealing more of the double line of boxes and the larger one in the middle.

"Look at these boxes," Rill said, his tone a mixture of excitement and awe. "I was right. This place *is* a mage's storehouse. That's why the entrance was sealed off."

Suddenly the torchlight bounced off a pair of large yellow-gold eyes glaring at them from the blackness beyond.

Rill twitched as if a blast of freezing wind had shot through him.

The mountain cat hissed a challenge at them.

Rill gripped his sword.

The cougar padded forward into the light, stopped, and hissed again—back arched, ears flat. Ready to fight.

His nerves as tense as a longbow at full draw, Rill took two cautious steps toward it.

The grayish-tan cougar gave a high-pitched snarl that ended with a yowl, and slowly stepped backward.

"It's afraid of the torches," Rill whispered.

"Let's flank it on either side, and then go in for the kill," Jedd said.

A thought swept through Rill quicker than an eye blink. *Why does that critter hafta be in here? What if I'm wounded trying to kill it? Then Jedd will hafta take me to a healer, and I won't be able to see what's inside these boxes. And what if someone else finds this place before I can return?* He stared at the cougar, his eyebrows fused together into a determined frown. *I ain't gonna take that chance.* "No," Rill said. "We'll scare the cougar off with the torches."

Jedd gaped at him as if he were crazy. "I thought you wanted to kill it."

"Later after we see what's in these boxes." Rill spoke quickly, cutting off Jedd's expressive objection. "You take the left, and I'll take the right."

Jedd hesitated and then, heaving a sigh, followed Rill's order.

Rill crossed to the boxes on his right and carefully made his way deeper into the chamber, his sword clutched in one hand and the torch held out in the other. His heart thumped a staccato beat, and his nerves stretched to snapping as in his mind he saw the cougar leaping at him, jaws wide open, and sharp pointed teeth ready to rip into his flesh. Rill booted the image from his mind.

Step by grudging step, the cougar retreated to the far wall as it turned its head back and forth from Rill to Jedd, hissing, growling, and snarling, tail swishing.

The cougar lunged at Rill.

The move caught Rill by surprise, but he instinctively thrust the flaming torch at the huge cat's snout.

Uttering a squeal, the cougar scampered backward, stopped at the wall, and hissed.

Rill stopped a few paces from the snarling cougar, his heart pounding against his chest.

Jedd came up level with him and closed the distance between them.

"Now what?" Jedd whispered.

"We'll stick the torches in its face," Rill whispered back. "The flames will frighten it, and it'll run outside." *I hope.* "I'll move in on him first. You follow."

"All right."

Rill drew a deep breath, then lunged at the cougar with a shout, thrusting the flaming torch in its snout.

The tawny cat screeched in pain.

Yelling, Jedd rushed at the cougar with his blazing torch extended.

The cougar whirled and snarled.

"Together!" Rill cried.

Shouting, the cousins thrust their torches at the wildcat.

The cougar leaped between them, raced partway to the entrance, and spun around. It gave a long, throaty snarl.

Rill and Jedd advanced cautiously, torches held forward and swords at the ready.

Slowly, one unwilling step at a time, the cougar retreated from the hissing flames. When the cat paused by the jagged entrance, Rill and Jedd yelled and jabbed their torches in unison.

The cougar scrambled outside.

Rill peered through the fissure. The cougar glared from a few feet away. Rill jabbed his torch through the opening. "Go away. Git!"

The cougar hissed one more time, then turned and trotted up the trail into the brambles.

Relief gushed through Rill, and his body sagged. He gave a shaky laugh. "We did it!"

The torch in Jedd's hand quivered. "He'll be waiting for us when we leave."

Rill sheathed his sword, his shaky hand making the blade miss the scabbard opening in the first attempt. He hoped Jedd hadn't noticed. "We'll deal with the cougar when the time comes. Right now, I wanna see what's inside these boxes."

Because of its prominence, Rill figured the middle box must be the most important one and headed for it. As he drew closer, he noticed something on the box lid that blew away, with hurricane force, all thoughts of everything else.

"By The Sisters!" he said. "This is a sarcophagus."

Carved in relief on the stone lid was the prone figure of a bearded, long-haired man wearing tight-fitting pants and a dress coat that reached halfway to his knees. The partially open coat exposed a buttoned vest that fell a hand's length past the waist. The loose material under the last square button was cut away to form an inverted V. A belt made of square links was buckled around the man's waist, over the vest, which concealed all but a large buckle and several smaller belt links. The edges of a shirt collar poked up from behind the vest. The man clasped a staff to his chest, its orb nestled under his chin and the shaft tapering into a wicked-looking point at his booted toes. Filaments covered the orb like a loosely meshed net, their ends merging into the staff. Deeply etched runes framed the figure.

Rill's gaze leaped to Jedd, who stood beside him. From the incredulous look on his cousin's face, Jedd had reached the same conclusion. "This here's—"

"A tomb! We oughtn't be here." Jedd tugged at Rill's sleeve.

Rill jerked free and ran his fingers over the smooth, chiseled stone of the effigy. "I ain't never seen clothes like these before."

"Rill," Jedd said, his tone laden with fright, "we don't belong in here."

Rill stared at the effigy as if his eyes were welded to it. "Mages don't use runes no more. And no one knows how to read them. They say the Old Mages could cast spells just with runes."

"Rill—"

"We stopped burying our dead over eight hundred years ago. We cremate them now." Realization exploded in Rill's head like a thunder clap, and he spun toward Jedd, grabbing him by the shoulders. "This tomb goes back to The Founding."

Jedd swept his arms out on either side, breaking Rill's hold. "Your fixation on mages and magic is gonna get us in trouble. Let's get outta here. Now!"

"Not yet." Rill turned toward the sarcophagus, his pulse beating fast and his hands reaching for the stone lid. "I wanna see what's inside."

Jedd yanked at Rill's wrist. "There's nothing inside except a body. A charm raider's already been here. Everything's been looted."

"We don't know that."

"For Twins' sake, are you blind? The tomb's been looted."

"Even if it was, the raider might of left some things behind."

"You're the one who knows all about mages and charms," Jedd said. "So you know the Old Mages concealed the entrances of their tombs with magic. Even I know that. But this tomb's entrance wasn't hidden."

Rill shrugged off the comment. His fingers lusted to grab the lid again and shove. "Maybe no charm seeker broke into here. Maybe . . . maybe the Concealment spell failed and a . . . an earthquake broke the entrance. We get them here, you know."

"Not in *our* lifetimes."

"It's been over eight hundred years."

"And maybe a charm seeker used a counterspell to break in here."

"Maybe," Rill said, hoping Jedd was wrong. "But if a charm seeker did break in, it was a long time ago. Otherwise that cougar wouldn't be using this for a den."

"Rill—"

"You can wait outside if you want."

"With the *cougar* out there?"

Jedd's reminder about the wildcat sent a tremor through Rill. "We'll tackle the cougar together. *After* I see what's inside this coffin."

Jedd expelled a long, resigned sigh. "If you open this and look inside, will you leave?"

"Yeah."

"All right. I'll stay. But just for this one."

After laying their torches on a nearby sarcophagus, Rill and Jedd heaved on the heavy stone lid. It took them a while before they finally eased it all the way off onto the ground and leaned it against the side of the coffin. They fetched their torches and peered inside.

Their gasps of amazement sounded as one.

Inside lay the well-preserved body of an old man with a short white beard and white hair that came down to his shoulders, his face and posture mimicking the effigy's. He wore the same style clothes as the figure on the lid, but in color—dark-blue pants and jacket and a reddish-brown vest over a white linen shirt whose collar poked out from the top of the vest. A belt of square gold links was buckled around his waist, over the vest. The staff the man clutched resembled the one on the lid. But this staff was the most beautiful one Rill had ever seen. Its color was the same reddish brown as the vest and its tapered point, which was used for close-up fighting, shone with a deadly sheen in the flickering reddish-yellow torchlight. The dark-blue orb on the staff's tip was held in place by a network of weblike silver filaments that seemed to melt into both orb and staff.

"An Old Mage," Rill murmured. "He must of been alive during The Founding. Maybe he even came over from The Forbidden Lands with the refugees during The Great Destruction."

Jedd nudged Rill's shoulder. "You've had your look. Let's go."

Rill flashed Jedd an I-told-you-so grin. "Obviously, no charm seeker's been here." He gazed at the corpse again, goose bumps sliding down his neck and back, like rivulets of ice-cold water. "He must of been powerful. I wonder who he was."

"I don't *care* who he was."

Rill gingerly reached inside the sarcophagus, removed the corpse's soft, fleshy-feeling hands from the staff, and lifted it out.

"Rill, put that back."

Rill caressed the staff with his eyes, then ran his fingers along the silk-smooth metal and fondled the blue crystal orb, like a newly smitten lover. The silver filaments had merged with the crystal to form a single glass-smooth surface. "A mage with a staff like this must of worn a powerful charm."

Rill's gaze returned to the corpse.

Jedd slapped Rill's arm. "For Twins' sake, you've gone too far. Put the staff back!"

Rill felt around the corpse's neck for a chain. When he found none, he patted down the chest. Rill examined the man's fingers, but they were bare.

"He ain't wearin' no charm," Rill said, unable to hide the disappointment. "Looks like this tomb *was* opened by a charm seeker."

"I told you so. But you never listen."

Rill scratched his cheek, a quizzical frown on his face. "Why did the charm seeker take the charm but not the staff? I would of taken both."

Jedd's brown eyes held Rill's. "But you ain't takin' the staff, right?"

Rill paused before giving a reluctant nod. "Yeah."

"And you'll put the staff back, right?"

Rill stared at the staff longingly. He pictured himself with it after he was named a mage on Name Day. The feeling of power the staff would give him. The envious looks everyone would throw at him. *I gotta have this—*

"You'll put it back, *right*?" Jedd said, his tone a command, not a request.

Rill answered reluctantly. "Yeah."

"And then we'll leave, right?"

Rill propped the staff against the sarcophagus. "After I see what's inside the other coffins." He strode toward a nearby sarcophagus.

"Rill!" Jedd said, the pitch of his voice rising toward anger.

Rill stopped at the coffin and leaned his shoulder against the lid. "Come help me."

Jedd seized him by the cloak collar, twisting the material so tight Rill choked. "You promised to look in just one."

Rill pried Jedd's fingers open, one by one. "I wanna see what's in the others."

"If I know you—and I do—you'll do more than look. You'll *take*."

"I won't. I'll be named a mage at the end of the month. Then I can come back here and take any charm and staff I want."

"You don't know you'll be named a mage."

"I feel it in my bones."

Jedd eyed Rill warily in the shadowy light and took his time to answer. "All right."

Rill grinned to himself in triumph. The stone lids of the smaller sarcophagi were lighter than the center one and easier to remove. *There's gotta be something in here I can swipe.* Beginning with the first, Rill intentionally established a pattern for their work. After they lifted the lid back on a coffin, Rill moved it into place while Jedd went to the next sarcophagus to position that lid so they both could ease it off onto the ground. All the while, Rill waited impatiently for Jedd's watchfulness to slacken.

But from the beginning, Rill encountered a mind-numbing problem that under different circumstances he'd consider a present from the One Goddess. Every coffin held the perfectly preserved body of a female or male mage in clothes cut in a similar fashion to the white-bearded mage's. Unlike the first Old Mage's corpse, these bodies wore charms and clasped staffs to their chests. The charms were beautiful—pendants and rings made from gold, silver, or bronze. Some were encrusted with emeralds, rubies, and other precious gemstones. Rill's fingers itched to filch each one. He hesitated, though, because the next charm seemed more beautiful than the previous one. He felt like a diner who couldn't choose a dish at a scrumptious banquet. *I gotta pick one,* Rill told himself over and over.

His choice finally came when they opened one of the last coffins, and found himself gawking at a large, purple, egg-shaped gemstone surrounded by eight tiny fire-red rubies on an oval pendant made of gold. *It's the most beautiful thing I've ever seen. I gotta have it.* He sneaked a peek at Jedd, whose back was to him. *Now!* Rill snatched the charm, slipped it into his belt pouch, shoved the lid back in place, and hurried to help Jedd.

"This place is a real treasure trove," Rill said as he and Jedd maneuvered the sarcophagus cover onto the ground. "If a charm seeker did open this tomb, why did she take the charm from that one Old Mage but not his staff? And why did she leave all the other charms and staffs behind? I wonder—"

"How fortunate for me she did," a voice said behind them. "And how unfortunate for you."

Rill and Jedd whirled around.

Just inside the entrance stood a skinny, middle-aged man of medium height. His gray tunic and tan pants were dirty and patched and his boots old and scuffed. Oily, unkempt hair framed his pockmarked face. In his right hand, he held a staff. The light from Rill's and Jedd's torches danced shadows across his face, making his malevolent grin appear even more evil.

A blacksmith's vise clamped Rill's chest making it hard for him to breathe. A rohan! A backwatcher or protector—either a mage or a bladeswoman or bladesman—who had been expelled by a noblesse matriarch for breaking her oath to serve and protect the matriarch's family. An outcast from society no other noblesse First or Lesser Family would touch. A woman or man who was lower even than the criminals, dagger women, and prostitutes living in Caldon's most dangerous neighborhood, The Slums.

Rill's gaze fastened on the rohan's left hand that clutched something beneath his grimy tunic.

A charm.

"Actus," the rohan mage said, his sinister smile showing he'd deliberately spoken the word loud enough for Rill and Jedd to hear.

Rill eyed the staff, his stomach paining him. The rohan had activated his charm. All he had to do now was point the staff at a target and cast a spell. Rill's gaze slid to Jedd, who appeared as rigid as a marble statue.

With exaggerated slowness, the rohan aimed the staff at the gap between Rill and Jedd, then deliberately moved it from one to the other. His lips drew up into a cruel smile, making Rill feel like a mouse being toyed with by a cat.

Rill choked on a lump of regret. *Why didn't I listen to Jedd and leave the coffins alone? We could of been partway home by now. I could of been a mage. But now I never will be.*

Slowly and deliberately, the rohan inhaled a mouthful of air and said, "Luco!"

Rill's frightened breath blended with Jedd's when the crystal burst into life, and white mage light flooded the tomb.

The rohan laughed as if he'd just watched a first-rate comedy routine as he stepped several paces forward. "Scared of a little light, boys?"

Rill's gaze jumped to Jedd. His cousin was glowering at the man, his hands balled into fists.

The rohan smirked at Jedd.

Slowly, keeping his eyes on the rohan, Rill moved his hand toward his sword's brown leather grip.

The rohan must have had invisible eyes in the side of his head. With a chuckle, he casually pointed the staff at Rill. "Foolish boy. I can kill you before your sword's half out of its scabbard."

Rill let his hand drop to his side.

"*Tsk-tsk,*" the rohan said, drawing closer. "Naughty boys charm seeking. That's a death offense. Unless you're mages, of course. Are you mages, naughty boys?"

"You know we ain't," Rill said through clenched teeth.

The rohan stepped forward a few more paces until only a staff's length separated them. "When I came across your well-fed and groomed horses a while ago, I thought that maybe their owners came from good families. Families with money. So I went looking for you. My goodness, you weren't hard to find. Not with all that racket you made in here with the cougar. Boys with horses and swords. And purses hanging from their belts." His gaze riveted itself to Rill. "And with such *interesting* things inside."

Rill's heart froze into a lump of ice as he forced himself to return the rohan's stare. *He saw me take the charm.*

The rohan flashed them both an evil smile. "So I said to myself, 'Self, I bet those naughty little boys are carrying some nice shiny gildas in their purses. Or maybe even a goldie.' You got any?"

"Why don't you come closer and find out?" Rill said. He'd tried to sound cocky, but his voice broke halfway through the question.

The rohan grinned, obviously enjoying himself. He pointed the staff at Rill. "Naughty boy. I hope you don't melt."

Terror ripped through Rill like a barbed arrowhead.

He had only moments to live.

## CHAPTER 2

Unwelcome News

ALYSE DEJUNE CROUCHED IN in a fighter's stance, a razor-sharp dagger gripped in her hand and her heart thumping madly beneath her light-green bodice. Weaponless, Kate Dejune mimicked Alyse's posture, waiting for her to attack. The two rear windows were shuttered against the cold morning air. Orange flames in the fireplace crackled like hecklers, and the twin yellow glows cast by the oil lamps on the dressing table created a pool of fidgety golden light around the girls in the gloomy bedroom.

Kate leaned toward Alyse, balancing herself on the balls of her feet. "Come on. Stab me—if you can."

Frustration reared inside Alyse despite her efforts to stomp it down. They'd been knife fighting since after breakfast, and she still couldn't close the gap between them for a death blow. She took a deep, determined breath, then lunged at Kate with the dagger.

Kate sidestepped and jeered. "You can't touch me with that thing. Try again."

Alyse cursed under her breath as she slowly circled Kate. Every time she tried to close in for a thrust, Kate danced away.

"Come on!" Kate motioned Alyse forward with cupped fingers. "Don't think of me as your backwatcher. I'm your enemy. I'm here to kill you—"

Alyse feigned a knife thrust.

The move must have surprised Kate because she stood in place as if frozen.

Got you! Alyse stepped in for the kill.

Kate spun away, seizing Alyse's wrist at the same time, and twisted.

Sharp pain shot through Alyse's wrist as she stumbled. The knife clunked against the bedroom's mosaic floor. In the scuffle, Alyse's foot struck the dagger, sending it skidding across the flat, multicolored mosaic stones to the fireplace. The pommel clunked against the brick hearth extension.

Kate released Alyse's wrist. "I used this trick on you before. You should've stocked it away in your head."

"I will."

"You'd better. You're defying your matriarch by learning self-defense. So if you're going to learn, then learn."

"Great-Grandmother Siema's rule is stupid."

"It's not just her rule. It's every matriarch's."

Alyse's eyes burned with indignation. "Noblesse women shouldn't have to rely solely on their backwatchers for protection. We should be allowed to defend ourselves. The men can. So why not us?"

"I agree," Kate said, pushing back long strands of black hair from her forehead. "Otherwise, I wouldn't be risking my position here by teaching you."

Alyse watched her wiry, hazel-eyed cousin cross to the fireplace. The flames were burning low, allowing the sharp, cold air of early Awakening season to invade the room again, raising small chill bumps on Alyse's shoulders. Kate added a couple of logs to the fire, scooped up the dagger, and returned.

She shook her head as if perplexed. "I don't know why you have so much trouble with knife fighting. You certainly can throw the dagger well."

Alyse pinched a fold of her silk dress's dark-green skirt. "I could do better if I didn't have to wear *this*. It gets in the way of my legs."

"You have to learn to fight in your everyday clothes." Kate pointed to the dress and then to her own Dejune lightweight wool livery of tan tunic with red trim and tan pants tucked into dark-brown leather boots. "You have yours and I have mine."

Alyse pulled a face at Kate even though she knew her cousin spoke the truth.

Kate handed her the dagger hilt first. "I think we'd better work more on the basics. And figure out some techniques to get your fighting legs more used to the skirt."

Alyse and Kate repositioned themselves.

"All right," Kate said. "Come at—"

Three quick raps sounded on the bedroom door.

"That's Lothar's knock," Alyse said.

"Give me the dagger."

Alyse thrust the knife hilt first at Kate, who slipped it into the drawer of the dressing table. After smoothing down her skirt and light-green silk bodice, Alyse opened the door to greet the family's head steward.

"Lady Siema requests your presence in the matriarch's chamber," Lothar told her.

Through years of practice, Alyse kept her face expressionless upon receiving an official summons to a matriarch's council. "Thank you, Lothar. Tell her I'll be right there."

The steward inclined his head. "Very well, Lady."

"I wonder what my great-grandmother wants," Alyse said after Lothar left.

Kate shrugged. "Maybe she's having your mother divorce Degas Spicer. That seems to be the only time she summons you and Mora to a matriarch's council. When she has your mother divorce your latest stepfather."

A sudden weariness flooded into Alyse that made her want to sit down, elbows on the dressing table and head in her hands, and weep from frustration. "I hope not. Four stepfathers in nine years is more than I can bear. Besides, I like Degas. He treats me nicely, unlike my previous stepfathers." Alyse heaved a resigned sigh. "Well, there's only one way to find out."

Alyse threw a yellow cloak of finely spun wool over her shoulders to ward off the chill that the fireplaces never seemed to dispel completely in the larger open spaces of the house during this time of year. The bedroom door opened directly onto the family area. Alyse had taken only a few steps when movement to the left caught her attention. The cloaked backs of two girls, one with chestnut hair just like Alyse's and the other brunette, were walking toward the door that opened onto to the courtyard in the rear of the family compound. The bottom of the chestnut-haired girl's red silk skirt swished in time with her steps. The brunette's pace matched her companion's. Her swishing, dark-brown cloak ended at her calves, exposing legs encased in tan pants tucked into dark-brown boots.

Alyse's twin, Mora, and Mora's backwatcher, Jade Channer.

Alyse stopped short and watched her sister and Jade disappear into the courtyard. *If Great-Grandmother is going to announce Mother's divorce, why didn't she summon Mora too?* The question bubbled in her mind like a hot spring, sending boiling streams of anxiety through her body as she walked across the family area to the matriarch's chamber, which shared a wall with the formal dining room. *Something serious must be happening that includes me and not Mora. But what?*

Alyse stopped abruptly a staff's length from the thick, black oak door as realization burst into her mind. *Great-Grandmother knows Kate's been teaching me self-defense.* That would be just like Siema because she always had it in for Kate. Alyse recalled how Siema had expressed outrage when Kate's mother, who belonged to a distant, ne'er-do-well family in the Dejune clan, had married a commoner mage. He'd had ambitions of using the marriage to get elected to the Magesterium and founding a commoner-noblesse family. Unfortunately, they'd both died in a tragic accident, leaving Kate an orphan. Siema had been pressured by the Dejune clan matriarch to take her in. Alyse had hit it off with Kate immediately. She'd even foiled Siema's plan to make Kate a scullery maid by insisting she be her lady's maid. Later she'd convinced Siema to make Kate her backwatcher too. The memory made Alyse's lips lift into a smile. Few people could get Great-Grandmother Siema to change her mind after she'd made a rock-hard decision.

But who could've snitched on us? The answer followed the question instantly. *Mora.* Bitterness turned Alyse's belly sour. *Most twins aren't just sisters but close friends as well. But not us.*

Alyse closed the distance to the door as she fished for excuses that would save Kate from Great-Grandmother Siema's wrath but couldn't find any that Siema would accept. *I'll bear the brunt of it. After all, I'm the one who asked her.* But as Alyse's backwatcher, Kate was responsible for protecting Alyse. And that included preventing her from breaking centuries-old traditions. Noblesse girls do *not* defend themselves. Their backwatchers do. Alyse scraped angry tears from her eyes with her fingertips—anger not at trouble caused by Mora or Siema but by herself.

With nervous fingers, Alyse smoothed her bodice and skirt, straightened her shoulders, and knocked.

Siema's sharp voice pierced the dense wood like a spearhead. "Enter."

Filling her lungs with an extra-deep breath, Alyse opened the door and stepped into the large, windowless room that formed the heart of the Dejune compound. Her gaze snapped to the skinny, wizened, old woman sitting in the ornately carved matriarch's chair on a dais that took up the back part of the room. Ever since she was a child, the Dejune women had hammered into Alyse's head that generations of Dejune matriarchs had sat in that black oak chair. Including the current one, Siema Dejune, who peered at her through gray, frosty eyes while she pushed her straight-handle cane between her knees against the skirt's folds of her brown embroidered dress.

Involuntarily, Alyse's eyes shifted to the ancient fresco on the wall behind Siema. The scene showed the Five Sisters who determined every aspect of a person's life, creating her or his fate. The large oil lamp suspended from the ceiling over the dais illuminated every detail. The first Sister, Naela the Spinner, spinning the yarn for the loom. The second, Maela the Yarn Chooser, selecting the threads whose thickness and colors determined the person's personality and health. The third, Kaerla the Allotter, drawing lots to determine the length of the yarn, which fixed the number of years in the person's life. The fourth, Traela the Weaver, weaving into the tapestry the incidents that made up the person's life. And the fifth, Gaela the Thread Cutter, who chose how the person died, waiting with scissors in hand to snip the yarn to free the tapestry from the loom, ending the person's life.

A coiled snake of anxiety formed in Alyse's belly. She can't expel Kate. Kate would become a rohan. Alyse's gut writhed in pain as an image of her cousin, backwatcher, and best friend being ejected from the family compound in disgrace rose up in her mind like a horrid nightmare. Kate would become a rohan or, if she were lucky, perhaps a dagger woman, one of the loathed assassins for hire living in The Slums—

Siema rapped her cane's silver-covered tip on the black oak floorboards. "Come, child. We're waiting."

Two large oil lamps suspended from the black oak beams in front of the dais cast harsh yellow light on four straight-back chairs set in a row facing the dais. The left two seats were empty. Two women, one with dark-brown hair and the other with gray-streaked auburn hair, sat in the chairs to the right. Pilar and Maude Dejune, Alyse's mother and grandmother respectively. The flames in the fireplace crackled and popped as if chiding Alyse for disobeying a long-standing matriarchal rule by asking Kate to teach her self-defense.

Siema waved Alyse forward, impatience fused into the motion.

Projecting a self-confidence she didn't feel, Alyse strode to the chairs as if she were the face of innocence and began to settle into the empty seat beside her mother.

Siema crooked a shriveled finger at her. "Come here, child."

The serpent started to uncoil in Alyse's stomach.

Stopping before the first of the three steps leading up to the dais, Alyse faced her great-grandmother. The serpent unwound faster.

Siema folded veined, wrinkled hands over each other on the cane handle and smiled at Alyse. "I have wonderful news."

Huh? The serpent vanished, and was replaced by a thick cloud of confusion that swirled through Alyse's mind. Wonderful news? *Then it's not about Kate and me.* Relief dispelled confusion. She beamed at Siema. "What's the news?"

"You're getting married."

Alyse's mind went blank, and she stood as if paralyzed. "I . . . I'm *what?*"

"I'm nearing the end of my life," Siema said, her tone indicating she could care less about Alyse's dumbfounded reaction. "Soon I'll join our ancestors. Your great-grandfather, Locien Estati, will join his ancestors too. Which of us joins them first, only Kaerla the Allotter knows."

Alyse put a trembling hand to her suddenly parched throat. "Who am I marrying?"

Siema ignored the question. "Since before The Great Destruction, for almost two thousand years, the Dejunes and the Estatis have been allies. We keep our alliance intact through the bond of marriage. My death or Locien's will sever that bond. So we must form a new bond before the current one breaks—"

"*Who* am I marrying?"

Siema slowly ran the forefinger of her top hand back and forth along the back of her lower hand gripping the cane's handle. "Troy Estati."

"No!"

Behind her, Pilar and Maude gasped. In front of her, Siema peered through slitted, viperlike eyes. "Explain yourself."

Alyse struggled desperately to pull together her scattered thoughts. "I . . . I'm only fifteen."

"I was *fourteen* when I married Locien," Siema said in a hard, even tone. "Next week you'll be *sixteen.*"

Siema's unexpected retort unsettled Alyse.

"It's not as if Troy's a stranger, dear," Pilar said. "You've both known each other all your lives. You used to play together as kids."

"The same goes for Mora," Alyse said. "And I happen to know that she likes Troy. And that she would marry him if—"

Siema banged her cane against the floorboards. "Out of the question. You're the firstborn, so you marry first."

"But Mora was born only moments after me."

"Correct me if I'm wrong, child. Does 'after' mean 'before'?"

"No. But not every noblesse family requires its firstborn child to marry first—"

Siema slapped Alyse's words away. "This family does. And we have since we were made noblesse two thousand years ago in Euloria."

"Times change, Great-Grandmother. You can set a precedent. Other First Families have."

Siema opened her mouth to respond but Alyse cut her off.

"Livia Estati is firstborn. She's still single. But you want to marry me to her brother, Troy. And he's *second* born."

Siema wrinkled her nose as if she'd just smelled a dead skunk. "Livia is an exception. A disgrace to her family. And no, there will be no precedent set in this house."

"But—"

"Even if I wanted to marry Mora to Troy, I can't because he insists on marrying you. And the Estatis have the bargaining power in our alliance, not us."

"But—"

"Are you defying me?"

Yes. "No."

"Good." Siema fingered the bun of white, stringy hair on the back of her head while her gaze seemed to turn inward in thought. After a long stretch of time, she gave an almost imperceptible nod as if she were agreeing to something after an internal dialogue with herself. She bent toward Alyse, timeworn hands clutching the cane's handle. "As firstborn, you're third in line to become matriarch—after your Grandmother Maude and your mother, Pilar."

Alyse wondered if that was why she and Mora didn't get along. Because Mora wanted to be matriarch but couldn't because she'd been born just a few moments too late. She looked past Siema to the image of Traela the Weaver on the fresco. *I wish you'd reversed the timing of our births.* "Yes, I know that."

"You also know our status as a First Family is declining," Siema said.

Alyse knew that too. Year after year, she had watched the numbers of household staff decrease. Cooks. Scullions. Gardeners. Stable hands. Work women and workmen. Everyone still called Lothar the chief steward. But Alyse recalled when there were three other stewards who had served under him. Over the years they had vanished, one by one, without explanation. But hardly any protectors and backwatchers had disappeared. After all, even a declining First Family had to keep up appearances, which was measured in backwatchers, protectors, and clients.

Clients. Guilt at her selfishness for not wanting to marry Troy seeped into Alyse's gut like stagnant water. Clients drove a First Family's status. "Leoc was *such* a disappointment," Grandmother Maude often said of her younger brother. Every time her grandmother said that, Alyse wanted to block her ears because she didn't like to hear her beloved uncle belittled. Alyse knew what Maude meant though. Uncle Leoc might be the famed Commander of the Eastern Legions fighting against Caldon's mortal enemy Gaetan, but he wasn't a mage. And only a First or Lesser Family who had a male mage sitting in the Magesterium could have clients. Four generations had passed since the last Dejune mages, Anglia and Angelo Dejune, had been born. Anglia had been the last Dejune archmage and Angelo had been the family's last magestrate.

For four generations, the Dejune receiving hall had remained empty of clients attending their morning greeting to their Dejune patron and accompanying him down The Citadel into the Public Square for the Magesterium session. And for four generations no death mask of a Dejune chief magestrate had been added to the family's substantial collection of death masks in the tall black oak cupboard behind the receiving chair. All her short life Alyse hadn't thought much about the empty receiving hall or the vacant receiving chair or the closed cupboard doors. Until now. *Why should I feel guilty for wanting to live my own life instead of following a narrow, pre-*

scribed path?

Siema's lean fingers danced a staccato beat on the arm of her chair, making sharp *tap tap tap* sounds. Alyse had never seen her great-grandmother so hesitant before. Siema's fingers slowed to a stop, and she focused on Pilar and Maude.

Alyse glanced over her shoulder. Just in time to see her mother and grandmother give what appeared to be reluctant nods to Siema.

Siema's gaze swung to Alyse. "You're third in line of succession. So it's proper you be let into the matriarch's secret." Siema's knuckles turned white as she gripped the cane handle tighter, apparently in reaction to what she was about to say. "We've lost almost all our *magetas*—the prestige that makes us a First Family."

Alyse sucked in a surprised breath. *How could I be so blind?*

"Our family needs mages, magestrates, chief magestrates, and clients again," Siema said, the pained tone in her voice showing her distress. "Only our alliance with the Estatis gives us what little *magetas* we have left. And the Estatis keep renewing our alliance because we have the Sister charm."

Alyse knew all about the Sister charm. Everyone in Caldon did. Originally the Sister charm belonged to the demigoddess Ulbra Thane, who had bequeathed it to the Dejunes for adopting her illegitimate daughter by Meurdar Dejune. Caldonian society was matrilineal, which meant that children took the mother's name, not the father's. The adoption turned the custom on its head, making the girl a Dejune. Possessing the Sister charm increased the Dejune's status among the First Families. It was the second most powerful charm in existence, less potent than the lost Elder charm but more potent than the demigod Ulbridge Thane's Brother charm. In the thousand years since Caldon's founding, only a few Dejune archmages had been powerful enough to access the Sister charm's potent spells. And Anglia Dejune was one of them.

Siema's chair creaked as she changed positions and spoke in a tone that held a hint of fear. "If the Estatis should learn our secret, they might not renew our bond of friendship."

"What secret?"

Siema's flint-gray eyes locked upon Alyse's. "If you reveal this secret to anyone, I'll expel you."

The threat made Alyse's stomach clench tight. "I'll tell no one."

Siema swallowed as if to postpone disclosing the secret. "We can't access the charm vault."

For a moment, the dais seemed to spin, making Alyse dizzy. When she was younger, Alyse had tried several times to sneak into the family's charm vault at one end of the passageway under the family library. The door handle had always refused to turn. She'd known where Great-Grandmother Siema kept the key. Once, nerves quivering as if she were walking a narrow path on a high cliff, she'd filched the charm vault key and sneaked down through the hidden trapdoor into the passageway and gone to the charm vault. She'd inserted the key into the lock and turned right, and the tumblers had clicked into place. But when she'd turned the handle and pushed, the door had refused to budge as if it were glued in place. Alyse's mind went blank for a moment. Then realization smashed into her brain, forcing her eyes to pop wide open.

"Someone put wards on the door." Alyse paused. "Anglia."

Siema nodded. "Anglia cast special wards on the charm vault door that only a very powerful archmage can cancel with the Peer charm. Unfortunately, she didn't anticipate it would take this long to produce a powerful Dejune archmage. No one did. You're the fourth generation. And our time is almost up."

The shocking revelation made Alyse's core turn cold. It took a short time for her to recover. "Why don't you ask Great-Grandfather Locien to cancel the wards? He's our ally. He's a powerful archmage. And he wears the Peer charm."

Siema's face crinkled into a mask of disgust. "And show him our weakness? Foolish girl. You should never trust an ally with such knowledge. They can turn on you in a heartbeat. Ours will if they learn this secret."

"So that's why you wear the Peer charm," Alyse said. "Because there's no archmage in our family to cancel the wards. And you're waiting for one to be born who can."

Pushing herself to her feet with her cane, Siema pulled out a dark-blue, tear-shaped gem surrounded by a scalloped silver frame from behind her bodice and dangled it by its silver chain. "Yes. I told Locien I wore the charm because I coveted it, even though I'm not a mage. He believed me and vowed to keep the secret. I believe he has . . . so far."

"But there's more, isn't there?" Alyse said.

"Yes." Siema tucked the charm behind her brown bodice and eased her body into the chair, using the cane to steady her herself. "As you know, only three Peer charms exist. The Estatis had two and we had one. But ours was stolen by the Gaetanian illusionist, who murdered her brother, Angelo, when he was making an offering at the family sepulcher on Street of Tombs. When I became engaged to Locien, Anglia demanded that the charm be included or she'd cancel the wedding."

"Because she was going to cast the wards," Alyse said.

"The archmage who cancels them will need the Peer charm." Siema thumped the floor with her cane, and urgency laced her words. "But time's running out. Some of our allies have already deserted us. Only our bond with the Estatis is stopping the others. If our family goes through one more generation—*your* generation, Alyse—without producing an archmage, the Estatis will abandon us. So will all our other allies. And the House of Dejune will fall."

Alyse stared wide-eyed at her grandmother while the shocking disclosure twirled dizzily in her mind. She blinked, bringing the room slowly into focus, turned her head, and saw Pilar and Maude staring intently at her. The sight made Alyse's pulse beat faster. "Let me get this straight. You want me to marry Troy so I can give birth to an archmage who can cancel the wards Anglia cast on our charm vault."

Siema nodded. "Yes. Preferably a male archmage so he can resume our family's vacant seat in the Magesterium."

"That's a heavy expectation."

"But not unrealistic," Siema said. "Troy was named an archmage last year. And he comes from a long line of powerful archmages, including his uncle, Deuth. Ulbra Thane's blood runs in your veins. So marrying you to Troy is bound to result in an archmage. A powerful one."

Alyse forced her head into a nod, clenching her jaw so tight her cheek muscles bulged at the thought of being forced into a loveless marriage.

Siema's lips bent into a thin smile. "That's a good child. You must put your family's needs above your own. You'll understand that when you sit in this chair."

I don't want to sit in that chair. Let Mora. I want— An idea dropped into Alyse's mind as if a gift from the One Goddess Herself. *I can delay the marriage. That will give me time to come up with a plan to avoid it.* "Umm . . . there's one thing."

Siema's white eyebrows furrowed. "Oh? What's that?"

"My Name Day Celebration is at the end of the month. If I'm named a mage, I won't be able to marry Troy until after my fledgling training."

"I've already considered that."

Alyse's budding hope wilted.

"Here's what's going to happen," Siema said in a firm voice. "You'll be engaged to Troy. The announcement will be next week, on yours and Mora's sixteenth birthdays, at a banquet to be held here. At the end of the month, you will attend your Name Day Celebration. Understood?"

Alyse forced her head to nod.

"If you're named a mage," Siema said, "the wedding will be postponed until the end of your fledgling training. If you're not named a mage, you will marry Troy shortly after Name Day. Understood?"

Alyse forced three foul-tasting words from her mouth. "Yes, Great-Grandmother."

Alyse waited for dismissal, knowing the meeting was over and eager to escape the loathsome room.

Siema readjusted her position in the matriarch's chair. "After Name Day, you will become an adult and a citizen. You will put away your dolls and other childish things. And you will stop those useless

Eulori lessons with Priestess Sybil."

Alyse strove to keep her anger from appearing on her face.

"Those lessons are a waste of time," Siema said. "Goddess alone knows why you want to learn a dead language that no one uses anymore."

Alyse squeezed her mouth shut to prevent objections from bursting through them like sharp-pointed daggers.

"I only agreed to the lessons for Leoc's sake. He was so insistent that you learn to read, write, and speak it." Siema shook her head disapprovingly. "My, how your uncle dotes on you."

Alyse's eyes slid to the ancient ornamental loom next to Siema's chair that had stood there for generations. Just as the Five Sisters' loom on the fresco behind Siema symbolized that they controlled the warp and weft that made up the tapestries of everyone's lives, Siema's loom symbolized that she controlled the warp and weft that made up the tapestries of every Dejune in her family and every retainer, including Kate. The urge to take an ax and chop the hideous loom to pieces possessed Alyse as if she had been taken over by a demon from Shelar. She had no ax. But she *could* kick the ugly old thing off the dais onto the floor. Alyse resisted the impulse, clenching her hands into fists.

Using her cane, Siema pushed herself to her feet. Pilar and Maude stood up too. Siema raised her veined right hand in the matriarch's benediction, index finger in the air, while daughter, granddaughter, and great-granddaughter bowed their heads.

"May the blessings of the Dejunes—past, present, and future—be with you always."

While Pilar and Maude stayed behind to speak with Siema, Alyse forced herself to walk out of the room at a normal pace. She strode through the family area, past Kate's bedroom door, and into her own adjoining bedroom. Alyse was halfway across the room when the connecting door between the bedrooms opened, and Kate walked in.

"I was about to ask how things went," Kate said. "But I see by your expression they didn't go well. Do you want to talk about it?"

"Not about everything," Alyse said. "Because if Siema found out, you and I both would be expelled."

"Sometimes your great-grandmother can be overly dramatic."

"Not this time. But I can tell you this. . . ." Alyse filled Kate in about the engagement with Troy Estati. "It makes me furious because I don't have any control over my life. I'm expected to marry Troy. I'm expected to be named a mage, hopefully an archmage. And I'm expected to give birth to a child—preferably a male and an archmage—who will take our family's seat in the Magesterium."

Kate gave a low whistle and put a hand on Alyse's shoulder. "You're in a real bind."

"Yes. I'm expected to do the three things I detest most. Practice magic. Marry against my will. And give up my Eulorian studies. And yet I can't bear the thought of being expelled. That's worse than dying."

"What will you do?"

Alyse shook her head in dismay. "I don't know. I don't want to marry Troy—or anyone else, for that matter, unless I love him. But I don't want to be expelled. I wouldn't be buried with my ancestors. And my spirit would wander forever between the Underworld and the Afterworld."

Resolution tangled with despair, and Alyse didn't know which would win the struggle.

## CHAPTER 3

Charm Seeker

RILL AND JEDD STOOD before the grungy rohan as immobile as the double row of sarcophagi behind them in the dark crypt. The only light came from the blazing white crystal on the rohan's staff, the two torches lying on the lids of a pair of coffins, and rays of early afternoon sunlight sneaking through the tomb's opening, which the rohan's body partially blocked. The tomb's gloom matched Rill's mood.

Rill flicked his gaze from the crystal to the rohan's pockmarked face resting under a tangle of greasy copper hair. Thoughts flashed through his mind faster than a storm of hailstones. His dad teaching him to forge his first knife. His mom baking his favorite dessert of pears with sweet white wine for his last birthday. Cutting temple school to stand in the Public Square with his friends so they could gawk at the magestrates, surrounded by their clients and backwatchers, approaching from all directions to attend a Magesterium meeting. Scratching his dog Faith's belly while she lay on her back wriggling with delight in the courtyard of his—

I ain't goin' out without a fight. Rill reached for his sword.

Before Rill's fingers touched the leather-wrapped grip, Jedd lunged at the rohan.

The rohan swung the crystal at Jedd. "Venta!"

An invisible force slammed into Jedd, hurling him backward until he was gulped up by the blackness. A heartbeat later a *thud* sounded, followed by a grunt of pain.

Shock paralyzed Rill. Then his fighting instincts, created through years of practice, kicked in. He whipped out his sword and swung at the rohan.

The rohan deflected the blade and slammed his staff against Rill's side.

Rill staggered into a coffin.

The rohan chuckled.

Fear tied Rill's stomach into a knot. The rohan was toying with him.

The rohan beckoned Rill forward. "Come at me, sonny."

Rill didn't take the bait to charge the rohan impulsively. Instead, he feinted with his sword, seeking an opening.

The rohan struck at Rill's head.

Rill dodged and slashed again. But instead of slicing through cloth and flesh, the blade's keen edge struck the staff. The force of metal on metal reverberated up Rill's arm, almost making him drop the sword. Rill swore to himself. Like charms, staffs were made of an indestructible metal. As he backed away, Rill glanced at the sword. The meager light revealed a small nick in the blade's edge.

Use the flat of the blade against a staff, not the edge. Rill muttered a curse. How many times had he been told that? And he forgot it in his first real fight.

Cackling gleefully like a demented demon, the rohan struck again, head-side-head-center-leg-head-shoulder with eye-blinking speed.

Rill moved backward, fending off each blow. And with each step, his panic increased a notch. Many mages relied on their staffs solely for casting spells, preferring to kill from a distance, and left the close-up fighting to bladeswomen. But some mages savored the thrill of using their staffs as quarterstaffs in one-on-one combat. Unfortunately, this shabby man was one of those.

Running feet slapped against the stone floor.

Rill hesitated, distracted by the sound.

The rohan shifted his stance toward the noise as Jedd shot out of the darkness and attacked him from the opposite side. The rohan parried his sword.

Rill thrust at the rohan.

The rohan's staff moved at lightning speed, blocking Rill's blade with one end, striking at Jedd's with the other. To Rill, it seemed as if they were fighting two rohans instead of one.

By now, Rill's sword arm was getting tired. Sweat ran down his forehead, and his breath came out in ragged gasps. He risked a quick glance at Jedd. His cousin appeared just as spent. Rill strained to keep panic at staff's length. Jedd's uncle, Tor Euland, had trained Rill and Jedd in sword fighting, and both cousins considered themselves skilled swordsman. But with a sinking feeling in his gut, Rill realized they were outmatched by a grubby, pock-faced, down-and-out rohan.

The rohan spun toward Rill.

Jedd slipped his blade under the rohan's open guard. But the opening was a feint. The rohan knocked Jedd's sword aside and shoved the crystal into his belly. Jedd doubled over as air whooshed out of his lungs. With a mirthful cackle, the rohan cast a Wind spell on him, which sent Jedd skidding back across the rocky floor into darkness again.

Rill swung at the man, a cry of rage bursting from his lips.

The rohan struck Rill's wrist with his staff.

Sharp pain tore up Rill's arm like a ripsaw, and his sword clattered on the ground. Rill drew his dagger.

The rohan knocked it from Rill's hand and forced him backward step by step until Rill bumped into a sarcophagus.

The interplay of flickering torchlight and darkness made the rohan appear like an evil spirit come up from Shelar. "My my, this has been fun," the rohan said, not the least bit winded. "But all good things must come to an end."

Panting, Rill glared defiance and threw himself at the rohan.

The rohan spun away and tripped Rill with his staff.

Rill fell hard onto the ground.

The rohan pointed the orb at him. "Incenbolt."

Fear clogged Rill's throat. He squinched his eyes shut, ready to die.

Nothing happened.

Rill's eyes flew open.

The mage was gaping at the crystal, disbelief on his face. He cast the spell again. "Incenbolt."

Still nothing happened.

"There's more than one way to stick a pig," the rohan said. A sharp, thin blade sprang out of the staff's butt.

Rill scrambled across the stone floor for his sword, gripped it, and rolled over. His heartbeat battered his ears.

The rohan struck his staff against the blade, sending the sword spinning. Looming over him, the rohan raised his staff to thrust its blade into Rill's chest.

Something whizzed overhead past Rill and slammed into the rohan's chest.

The mage staggered backward, and his staff clattered upon the stone floor.

"You forgot about me!" Jedd said, stalking out from the shadows.

Feebly, the rohan clutched the knife hilt with both hands and tried to pull out the half-buried blade. Jedd walked up to him, cupped his hands over the rohan's, and shoved the dagger hilt deep. The rohan let out a low "ugh," staggered backward, and collapsed to the ground.

Jedd helped Rill to his feet. "You all right?"

"Yeah. But I'll tell ya. I sure thought I was a goner." Nausea climbed the walls of his stomach. "Thanks. We should both be dead."

"I know. If his spell hadn't failed, he'd be standing here looking down at *our* bodies." Jedd stared openmouthed at the corpse, his face chalk white even in the gloom. "I . . . I ain't never killed a man before."

"It was him or me."

"I know, but . . . I . . . I think I'm gonna be sick."

Jedd stumbled behind a sarcophagus and threw up, his retching sounds going on and on. Gritting his teeth against his own queasiness, Rill slipped his hand under the rohan's tunic and groped for a chain. When his fingers touched the links, he pulled a bronze charm out and over the man's head.

"What're you *doing?*"

Rill spun toward the voice.

Jedd stood in front of the sarcophagus, an outraged expression on his still-pale face.

"Taking his charm." Rill shoved the charm and chain into his belt purse, on top of the Old Mage's. "He don't need it no more."

"You promised not to take any charms."

"From the coffins." Even as he spoke, Rill's conscience pinched him, but he ignored it. "This one's not from them."

"Damn it, Rill." Jedd held his arms straight at his side, fingers opening and closing. "Charm seeking—and that's what you're doing—is a capital offense unless you're a mage. Can't you get that through that thick skull of yours?"

"Relax," Rill said. "Everything will be fine. I'll be named a mage at the end of the month at my Name Day Celebration."

"You don't know that. Few mages are named. I certainly wasn't last year at my mine."

"I will be."

"In your dreams."

"I ain't dreamin'."

"You're so obsessed with becoming a mage, it's scary."

"You wait and see." Rill patted his belt purse. "Then I'll. come up with a story about how I found them, and legally claim them as mine."

Jedd made a derisive snort. "That ain't a smart move. Noblesse families control their mages' charms. You know that. If you have your own charm, you won't find no patron. Unless you join the legions or the sea service. But then you'll hafta turn your charm over to your commanding officer."

"If I have a powerful charm," Rill said, "I'll find a patron. The matriarch of a powerful First Family, not a Lesser Family. She'll want me for the charm."

"She'll kill you for the charm."

"I suppose Uncle Tor told you that."

Jedd nodded emphatically. "He served a matriarch who did just that. Killed the mage and took his charm but made it appear as if a rival family had done it."

"You're just trying to scare me," Rill said. "But it won't work. Everything will be fine. You'll see."

"'Everything will be fine,'" Jedd mimicked. "Don't you ever get tired of saying that?"

"Nope."

Jedd brushed by Rill, pulled the dagger from the rohan's chest, and wiped the blood off on the man's dirty tunic. "Come on. We gotta get outta here."

"What—and leave his body behind?" Rill said. "It's gonna rot and attract all kinds of critters into here." A savage snarl echoed inside Rill's skull that sent his pulse galloping. "Even the . . . cougar."

"I forgot about him," Jedd said.

"We'll deal with the cougar when the time comes." Rill prodded the rohan's corpse with his boot. "We hafta bury him somewhere far from here. Otherwise, if someone finds him, she might discover this place."

"Yeah."

"And whatever you do, don't tell no one what happened. If our matriarchs find out, or our moms—"

Jedd rolled his eyes as if Rill had just made the dumbest statement he'd ever heard. "Tell me something I don't already know."

Together they womanhandled the rohan's body through the tomb's entrance. After concealing the opening with branches, they lugged the corpse along the path through the thicket. A short distance beyond the clearing, they discovered the cougar's body, its side burned through by a Fire spell. Relief tumbled through Rill because now they didn't have to face the beast. He wanted to stop and stare at the corpse but Jedd, apparently overly eager to finish this distasteful business, pushed him to move on. It took them a while to circle around the side of the mountain, lugging the heavy corpse, before they found a secluded, rocky area.

"We'll cover the body with rocks," Rill said, nodding at a hollow between two boulders.

By the time they'd hauled enough huge stones to cover the corpse, Rill's arms were aching despite the hours he'd put in developing them by working in his dad's forge.

Rill reached down to take hold of the rohan's legs, but Jedd stopped him with a hand on his arm. "When we're done here, let's go back and put his charm in the tomb. Then you can go through the motions of 'finding' it when you're named a mage."

"I'm gonna hide it in my dad's smithy," Rill said. "I have a hidey-hole there that he don't know about." Jedd opened his mouth to say something but Rill cut him short. "How can I cast a spell when I ain't got no staff?"

Doubt loitered in Jedd's brown eyes, unwilling to leave.

Rill patted Jedd's arm. "Relax. Everything's gonna be fine. Trust me on this."

Power of Centering

AFTER KATE LEFT, ALYSE paced back and forth across her bedroom's mosaic floor in the semidarkness while images from the matriarch's council kept barging into her mind like unwelcome visitors, causing conflicting emotions. Anger at being put in a situation in which whatever decision she made would hurt her. Guilt over not wanting to help stop her family's decline. And frustration at not being able to choose her own husband like the commoners could or to live the kind of life she wanted.

Alyse expelled a deep breath of frustration. She ached to write the history of Euloria and early Caldon, but whenever she mentioned it, her mother, grandmother, or great-grandmother would scoff at her because it was the men who wrote the history—based, of course, on what the women told them. Their opposition had forced her to do the research in secret. She also wanted to have nothing to do with magic, and now her Name Day Celebration was fast approaching, and the family expected her to be named a mage. She frequently prayed to the One Goddess that she wouldn't be named one.

Magic. It had destroyed Euloria, and now with this ages-long war with Gaetan, magic was destroying Caldon as well with coalitions of First and Lesser Families vying for dominance and staging charm raids on their enemies. Fortunately, she had never experienced a charm raid on her family's compound and she hoped she never would. She balled her hands. *Why can't I be my own woman?*

Alyse glanced around the murky bedroom, the *snaps, crackles,* and *pops* from the angry flames in the fireplace bursting like explosions in her ears, and felt the walls squeezing in on her. She flung her yellow cloak around her shoulders and hurried outside into the chilly rear courtyard.

Near the back gate, Alyse found Kate practicing knife fighting with a young female protector named Freya, whose long, brown hair was tied into a ponytail. She stopped beside another young protector, Geoff, who was watching them with folded arms. Alyse liked both protectors because their friendliness toward her seemed genuine and because they were Kate's friends. She returned Geoff's welcoming smile, then watched the sparring.

Kate and Freya circled each other, feigning with their daggers, but neither was taken in by the other's ruses, and both appeared to be evenly matched. Alyse was transfixed by their maneuvering, and she made a silent vow to become as good a knife fighter as them. But if she married Troy Estati, she'd not only be trapped in a loveless marriage bound by ancient rules that forbade her to learn knife fighting, but she'd not be able to research and write history. And if she ever became the family matriarch—*good Goddess, no!*—she'd be locked into a tiny cage like a captured bird from which she could never escape.

Turning, Alyse fled into the house past startled servants in the family area and shut herself in her bedroom. The quivering flames in the fireplace hardly dispersed the gloom. She leaned back against the door, overwhelmed by despair at her fate. *What can I do? Who can help me?*

The answer, when it crept into her mind, was so obvious she wondered why she hadn't thought of it sooner. Priestess Sybil Raine. And with the chief priestess's name came her constant injunction to "Center yourself to control your emotions."

It had been weeks since Alyse had centered herself, and now the need tugged at her. After lighting a finger lamp and taking a key from the dresser drawer, Alyse left the bedroom and started across the family area to the library, which was on the other side between Maude's and Pilar's bedrooms. Kate fell into step beside her.

"Geoff told me you seemed upset."

"I was. But I'm dealing with it."

Kate nodded at the finger lamp. "The archives?"

"Yes. Want to come?"

Alyse and Kate went into the library. The window shutters were closed against the cold afternoon air, keeping the room in darkness. The floor tiles were squares with circles in the center. Alyse didn't need the dancing yellow lamplight to show her the way to the tile with the special embedded circle. She knew the path by heart. She lifted up the circle to expose a ring bolted into the wood. When she pulled the ring, the square tile and the section of oak floorboards beneath it rose soundlessly on oiled hinges to reveal a square opening leading down into blackness. The light from the finger lamp illuminated the top part of a narrow staircase that disappeared into the darkness.

Alyse led the way down the stairs. When her foot touched the bottom step, soft-white mage light winked on. The light rolled out along the floor like a processional carpet, revealing a tunnel, and continued until it stopped at a thick iron-bound door of solid oak at the far end. The Dejune charm vault. Leaving the finger lamp on the bottom step, Alyse followed the mage-lit path, with Kate keeping step beside her. She stopped at another door partway along the corridor and unlocked the door with the key.

Mage light flooded the room when Alyse crossed the threshold. She eased out a deep sigh of serenity. Already the tension, anger, and sense of hopelessness were ebbing from her body like an outgoing tide.

The Dejune Family archives.

Every time Alyse entered the archives, the two walls containing open floor-to-ceiling cupboards stuffed with ancient scrolls made her feel as if she had just walked into a candy store. She had discovered the archives when she was ten. For generations, though, no one had come down there except to deposit contracts and other legal papers. A few years ago, she had come across a scroll written in Eulori. The ancient, undecipherable writing on the parchment had sparked her interest in learning the language of the Old Ones and the history of the times before The Great Destruction in The Forbidden Lands and during the early years of Caldon's founding. She had sent a letter describing her marvelous find to her beloved Uncle Leoc, who was in The Marches with his legions fighting Gaetan and its allies Mittan, Fraedia, and Ostica. He had written back encouraging her to learn Eulori and suggested she ask Priestess Sybil, who was an expert in the language, to tutor her. His encouragement made Alyse feel closer to him than to anyone else except Kate.

Later Leoc had written her that he thought some of the scrolls actually dated back to before The Great Destruction, which had set Alyse's insides vibrating with excitement. But she had never discovered any. Only ones written after Caldon's founding, before Farnish had gradually replaced Eulori as the modern-day language of Caldon. A few scrolls were in the Common Tongue, the language of diplomacy, but Alyse wasn't interested in those.

As usual, Kate headed for the third wall whose shelves held old books and boxes filled with commonplace documents—letters, contracts, bills, receipts, and other family-related records.

Alyse pulled out a straight-back chair and sat down at the large oak table in the middle of the room. Doubt nibbled on her ear. She had stopped performing the deep-breathing exercise to balance herself several weeks ago and now wondered if she could still do it successfully. Last year she had fled to the One Goddess Temple in tears after an emotionally trying time with the family. Priestess Sybil had taught her the exercise. It had taken some time for Alyse to master it. Since then she had performed the exercise so often that her mind and body could relax and merge into one and open themselves to the living force of the goddesses and gods almost immediately. Until she had stopped practicing.

Alyse inhaled a deep breath. *Here goes.*

She folded her hands in her lap, shut her eyes, and began breathing deeply in and out.

As if in answer to Alyse's doubt, divine energy flowed into her solar plexus, which was the seat of her being, and fanned out to the seven other chars—crown, eyes, throat, heart, hands, pelvis, and feet—and then left her body and returned to the goddesses and gods. All the while, though, her solar plexus continued to drink in more divine power in a continuous flow until she achieved a calming equilibrium.

Alyse had no idea how much time had passed before she opened her eyes, breaking the link with the divine power. Her lips curled up into a smile. She felt relaxed, aware, and strong and was no longer upset by her impending engagement or by the other problems that, a short time ago, had appeared insurmountable.

Alyse stood and stretched.

Kate glanced up from a document she'd been reading by the shelves at the third wall. "Feeling better?"

"Oh yes."

Alyse stared at the rows of cupboards that were jammed full of scrolls. A long time had passed since she had discovered a scroll written in Eulori. How wonderful it would be to come across one now. So far, she'd unearthed some letters, stories, and even a poem. But her greatest find, just half a year ago, was a journal written by a Dejune a hundred years after The Great Destruction. Her flesh tingled at the prospect of turning up another one.

Going to a section she hadn't explored yet, she pulled scroll after scroll from its cubicle, gently unrolled the first part using the round wooden handles at each end to scan the beginning to see if it was written in Eulori or Farnish. She searched through the first column of cupboards from top to bottom without finding any in Eulori and was partway through the second column when Kate called to her.

"Hey," she said, "I didn't know Siema bought a couple of farms."

"We don't own any farms. Only our villa."

"Not anymore. She bought two farms. One six years ago and the other four years ago." Kate waved a pair of parchments at Alyse. "Here are the bills of sale."

Alyse went over and took the documents from Kate. She scratched her head. "That's odd. No one's ever mentioned this to me. Maybe whatever is raised on the farms is being sold at the public markets and is what's helping to keep the family afloat financially."

"Maybe the information's only for the ears of the Dejune women in a matriarch's council," Kate said.

"Probably." Alyse handed the parchments back to Kate. "I'll be allowed to attend matriarch's councils next week, when I turn sixteen. Then I'll learn about the farms."

Alyse returned to the cupboard, pulled out scroll after scroll, and placed them on the table as disappointment nipped at her because they were in Farnish. When she'd emptied the cupboard, she gazed at the scrolls piled on the table while she rubbed the back of her neck in discouragement. *I can't expect to find one in Eulori right off. Maybe the next cupboard . . . or the one after that.*

Alyse started returning the scrolls. But the end of the wooden handle on the next-to-last one struck something that prevented it from going all the way in. Alyse pulled the scroll out and stuck it in again, but something still obstructed it. Making an irritated sound in her throat, she pulled all the scrolls out, placing them back on the table, and reached inside. Her lips parted in surprise when her fingers touched a metal rod. She explored it with her fingers. The rod was the length of her middle finger and the diameter of her forefinger. *What's this for?* She peered into the cupboard, but the rod was hidden in the shadows.

"Kate," Alyse said, "would you bring the finger lamp from the stairs."

"What's going on?"

"I'm not sure. But I need to see inside here."

When Kate returned with the finger lamp, Alyse lifted the shivering flame up to the opening and peered inside.

Kate looked in too. "What's that?" Kate asked.

Alyse frowned at the rod. "There could be a secret compartment behind this cupboard."

"And that thing opens it?"

"Maybe. Let's see what happens."

Gingerly, Alyse pushed the rod forward toward the back of the cupboard, but the rod wouldn't move. She pushed up. Still nothing. But when she pushed down, something behind the cupboard clicked, and a section of cupboards swung slightly outward. Alyse pulled it the rest of the way open.

"Holy Sisters!" Kate muttered.

Alyse stepped toward the opening, but Kate pulled her back and took the lamp. "It could be booby-trapped. If it is, I'll be the one to spring it."

Alyse hated it when Kate deliberately put herself in danger for her sake but knew it was pointless to argue. After all, protecting her *was* Kate's job. So Alyse followed Kate through the opening.

They entered a small room. Nine large metal boxes sat on the floor arranged in stacks of three. A thick coating of dust covered the lids of the top ones, and dust had formed a carpet on the floor.

"Looks like no one's been in here for generations," Kate said.

Alyse traced a finger through the dust on a lid. "Because no one comes down here anymore. They've probably forgotten this room exists."

"Whatever's inside these boxes must not be worth much," Kate said.

"Or worth a lot. Why else would they be hidden in a secret storage room?" Alyse opened the lid of the first box and peered inside.

Her mind went blank, and she staggered into Kate from dizziness. Kate put a hand on Alyse's elbow to steady her.

"What's wrong?"

"N-nothing's wrong."

"A bunch of metal cylinders," Kate said, brushing up beside her and squinting inside.

"I don't believe it!" The words came from Alyse's mouth in a whisper.

"Don't believe what?"

"They're talking tubes."

Kate peered at her in bewilderment. "Huh?"

"From Euloria." Alyse jumped up and down with excitement. "From before The Great Destruction. Priestess Sybil showed me one a couple of years ago. The refugees took some with them when they fled across the Rocky Straight."

"You've never told me about talking tubes."

"Because Priestess Sybil told me it was our secret. Now it's your secret too. Talking tubes are so rare hardly anyone remembers them."

Kate opened another box, exposing more talking tubes. "I don't think they're rare anymore." She paused, then said, "They talk?"

Alyse nodded, her insides vibrating like a tuning fork. "They contain information and messages. Like scrolls and books do. Only the words are spoken instead of written."

"I've never heard of such a thing."

"I told you . . . they're rare. But they were common in Euloria."

"And they actually speak to you?"

"Here," Alyse said, "I'll show you."

She lugged the opened box into the library and set it on the table. Gingerly, she took out a metal tube and clasped it in both hands as if she were holding a newborn babe, making sure her palms were firmly around the metal. "You hold it like this."

Several heartbeats later, a voice spoke in a foreign tongue.

"Holy Weavers!" Kate said in an awe-filled voice. "But I can't understand a word she's saying."

"Because she's speaking Eulori."

"What's she saying—"

Waving Kate to silence, Alyse listened intently as the long-dead person spoke. For a brief moment, the room spun as recognition pierced Alysc's brain. "Oh my Goddess, it's Ulbra Thane!"

Kate leaned in closer.

Time slipped away, and Alyse felt as if she were living not in the present but in a past moment while goose pimples raced up and down her spine in continuous competition with one another. Finally Ulbra stopped talking, but Alyse kept hold of the tube. Moments later, Ulbra spoke again, but from the beginning. Reverently, Alyse placed the cylinder on the table. As soon as the metal broke contact with Alyse's hands, Ulbra's voice ceased.

Alyse felt light-headed as she looked at Kate. "It . . . it was as if I were in Euloria. During The Great Destruction. Ulbra said the Atlanders had finally breached the city walls. She and Ulbridge had raided the Charm Repository and gathered a group of refugees. She and Ulbridge were going to hold off the enemy long enough for the refugees to escape through the gate on the other side of the city."

Kate looked at her with a stunned expression. "Was this before she got pregnant by Meurdar Dejune?"

"Years before. She didn't have her affair with him until after Caldon was founded."

Kate reached for another cylinder from the box, then hesitated.

"Go ahead," Alyse said. "It won't bite."

Kate took out the tube and wrapped her palms around it. This time a different woman's voice spoke. The cousins listened in silence.

"What's she saying?" Kate asked.

"She's talking about Rasa Gaetani, the last queen of Euloria. She took the throne name of Caldonna the Third."

Kate shrugged and replaced the tube. Unlike Alyse, she wasn't much interested in history. Kate chose another cylinder at random. A man began speaking.

"What's he saying?"

Alyse inhaled a shuddering breath as spots danced in front of her eyes. "Put it down! Make it stop."

Kate released the tube as if it had seared her hands. The tube clunked onto the tabletop. "What's wrong?"

It took a lot of effort for Alyse to calm her rattled thoughts. "Look. We have to keep these talking tubes secret."

"Why?"

"Because they contain powerful information that could be misused if it gets into the wrong hands. And the Dejunes and other First and Lesser Families are the ones who would misuse it. On one another."

"Seriously?"

"Yes."

"All right." Kate nodded at the tube she had dropped. "But what makes that particular one so special?"

Alyse hated herself for not confiding the secret to Kate. But she had no choice. "I can't say right now. I have to listen to all of if it." She caught Kate's eye. "Alone."

"All right." Kate turned to leave.

Alyse seized her wrist and gave her an imploring look. "Remember. You can't tell *anyone*. If Siema should find out—"

Kate removed Alyse's hand. "I told you I'll keep your secret. We're best friends. And if you were a backwatcher, we'd be sword sisters."

After Kate left, Alyse closed the door and returned to the desk. A jittery sensation grew in her belly as she picked up the talking tube with trembling hands and listened to the speaker.

"Each magic point in your body determines the kind of magic you can use to cast a spell. In this exercise, you will use Kinesi magic, which resides in your pelvis. Kinesi power allows you to manipulate objects. In this exercise, you will perform one of the easiest and most basic uses of Kinesi magic. You will move a small object.

"Begin your breathing exercise to go into the magic state. Open yourself to the power of the magic plane. Let its energy flow into your solar plexus and from there out to the seven other magic points in your body: crown, eyes, heart, throat, hands, pelvis, and feet. Now let your own personal energy merge with the magic power into a continuous circle of personal and magic energy. Know that this merged energy is the basis of your magic power. Know that this energy is yours to control.

"You will use Kinesi magic. Concentrate on your pelvis. Feel the power there. It is yours to control. Select a small object. Focus your full attention on it. Now . . . visualize that object in another location—"

Alyse dropped the cylinder as if thorns had suddenly sprung from it and pricked her palms. *Oh my Goddess! This is the same exercise as the centering one I did. I . . . I wasn't just calming myself. I was accessing the magic plane.*

Alyse's mind rebelled against the frightening implications of what she had been doing for the past year. Only mages could access the magic plane—and then, only through their charms. From everything she had heard about spellcasting, the process involved a tug of war between the mage's personal energy and the magic plane's energy, with disastrous consequences if the mage lost the contest. Yet the instructor talked not about a struggle between the two forces but of them blending into one.

Alyse peered at the cylinder lying in front of her on the oak table. Did Priestess Sybil know her centering exercise was a variation of the one performed by the ancient Eulorian mages to access Kinesi magic?

Alyse hesitated, then settled back in the chair, closed her eyes, and began the deep-breathing exercise again. When she reached a state of equilibrium between the two energies, she opened her eyes. To her surprise, the power continued cycling through her body. She focused on the talking tube and pictured it sliding to the other side of the table.

The cylinder moved.

Alyse gasped in wonderment.

## CHAPTER 5

Aunt Talia's Visit

THE SUN WAS CLIMBING high in the afternoon sky by the time Rill and Jedd turned onto Street of Tombs that led to Ancestors' Gate. Rill's gaze wandered among the jumble of sepulchers that lined the road and stretched beyond both sides of the city wall. The sight always took his breath away. He picked out the lavish monumental crypts that belonged to the most powerful First Families such as the Dejunes, Estatis, and Porti.

Rill reined in his horse and shifted his eyes reluctantly to where the Larkins' humble vault was hidden in the distance behind a cluster of unpretentious crypts that belonged to other commoner families. Then he sought out the ancient commoner tomb he had stumbled upon a few years ago. It was hidden behind a taller crypt a short distance from his family's vault.

The weather-beaten tomb belonged to a single man whose name had been worn smooth over time. Like the man's name, the elements had almost erased the inscription. *When you pass by, stranger, think of me. I strove to make something of myself, but failed.* Rill didn't want to end up like that unfortunate man who now was known only to his ancestors. *I'm gonna become noblesse. I'm gonna make something of myself. And when I do, my Larkin tomb will be by the side of this street, large enough for everyone to see, no matter where they stand.*

"Come on," Jedd said, his fingers dancing a quick step on the pommel of his saddle. "Our parents expected us home long before now."

Rill pressed the heels of his boots against his horse's flanks and continued on, with Jedd keeping pace. They rode at a slow walk through Ancestors' Gate into the city and onto the worn cobblestones of Ulbra's Road, which was bordered by The Slums and The Tombs neighborhoods. Even though the sun shone brightly down on him, apprehension nibbled at Rill as he passed by the tenements and storefronts on The Slums side. He knew his reaction was foolish because nighttime, not daytime, was when the honest Caldonians feared venturing into The Slums' dark streets and alleyways. They passed by pedestrians wearing gray mourning ribbons on their coats or tunics and by storefronts and apartment windows displaying the ribbons too. The signs of families mourning for daughters and sons and wives and husbands killed in battle. Caldon's eternal war with Gaetan affected even the city's most loathsome inhabitants.

The Citadel, the highest of Caldon's Five Hills, loomed up in front of Rill. He eyed with envy the magnificent houses and compounds that dotted the sides and crest of the hill as he followed the roads that led around The Citadel toward the Public Square. Only the oldest, most powerful, and wealthiest noblesse families lived on that hill. Their ancestors had fled The Great Destruction with The Fraternal Twins, Ulbra and Ulbridge Thane, and had built the fortified settlement on The Citadel's summit that had expanded into today's walled city-state of Caldon. His heart ached with longing. *I'm gonna live up there one day.*

When Rill reached the side street that cut between The Citadel and the back of the Public Square, he and Jedd eased their horses into the throng of pedestrians, riders, and litters carried by liveried noblesse servants. Before long, Rill reached the Old Market, whose open-air stalls had occupied the rear and eastern side of the square for hundreds of years. Scents of cooking meat from food vendors' stalls wafted through the air. Rill pulled his horse up short to avoid a woman hurrying home with a slab of cooked meat wrapped in old parchment. Because fire was a constant threat in all the neighborhoods, where most tenements were made of wood, landlords forbade their tenants from having fires, even for cooking. So the food stalls did a thriving business year-round. Rill felt lucky he did live in a stand-alone house made of bricks, with a hearth and beehive bake oven beside it, and a mom and aunt who cooked delicious meals.

Partway along the eastern side, Rill swung onto River Road, which ran between Oak Hill and Sisters' Hill, through River Gate, and ended at the commercial docks and the bridge over the Euloria River. Finally, he reined right and plunged into the maze of nameless, narrow streets between Sisters' Hill and the imposing city wall of brick-faced concrete blocks. This was Rill's neighborhood, The Kings.

The street wasn't wide enough for the cousins to ride abreast. Before Jedd could fall back behind him, Rill clasped his shoulder. "Remember our story. What happened back there can't get out."

Jedd bobbed his head in agreement.

Rill plowed a path through the human traffic, his horse's hooves clattering on the cobbles. Dogs barked in streets spotted with smelly horse manure and dog poop. Babies cried in the arms of shopping mothers whose older children carried the goods they'd bought. Rill spotted more gray mourning ribbons on people's clothes. Dilapidated tenements three stories high blocked out the sun, throwing the road into perpetual shadow. On narrow, gray-brick sidewalks, owners of run-down first-floor shops stood at outdoor stalls hawking their wares or dickering with shoppers. Shabby buildings leaned against one another, and even the alleys that cut between them seemed dingy and uninviting. Shouts and peals of laughter from wine shops and eateries pummeled Rill's ears.

After several twists and turns, Rill passed the neighborhood's One Goddess Temple with its large cobblestone courtyard, sanctuary, and House of Healing. With Jedd trailing behind him, Rill went through a tangle of streets until they reached a wider, more prosperous cobble road and sidewalks lined with tenements—many with well-maintained shops on the first floor—and free-standing houses.

Some had gray mourning ribbons on their windows. Well-to-do merchants and craftspeople lived in this area. Eventually, Rill went by the brick, three-story tenement Jedd's grandmother and matriarch, Sorah Euland, owned, whose façade had been freshly whitewashed. Using money he'd accumulated as one of Caldon's most sought-after backwatchers, Tor Euland, who was Sorah's son and Rill and Jedd's uncle, had purchased the building as security for the family if he should die in service. The investment had proved wise.

At the end of the next block, two houses shared a waist-high plastered-brick courtyard wall. The *tap tap tap* of wooden mallets against chisel butts came from the farther house, which bordered an intersection. The place belonged to a monument maker. He was busy sculpting raised-relief figures into a nearly completed gravestone while his three workers were shaping marble blocks. Tombstones, statues, and obelisks in various stages of completion were scattered across the courtyard, which was coated with marble dust and chips.

The nearer courtyard enclosed a modest single-story house made of yellow-stucco-covered bricks and a sloping clay-tile roof painted red. Smoke curled lazily up into the air from the kitchen chimney, and a large pile of seasoned firewood was stacked near the front door, whose red matched the red of the roof tiles. A blacksmith shop with an attached stable, both with brown-painted pine sides and roofs and a horse enclosure, took up the right-hand side of the courtyard.

Rill and Jedd turned their horses into the nearer courtyard.

Their horses' hooves had barely clattered on the cobblestones when a medium-sized, black-and-tan mutt dashed out of the stable, barking excitedly. Rill dismounted, knelt, and hugged the dog, laughing as it licked his face.

"Hello, girl." Rill scratched behind the dog's ears. "I'm just as happy to see you too."

Jedd dismounted. "What's this, Faith? No welcome for me?"

Dutifully, Faith brushed against his brown-booted legs.

The front door of the house opened, and Marc Larkin's heavily muscled figure filled the doorway. He still had on the soiled pants and smudged, sweat-stained linen shirt with rolled-up sleeves that he wore while working at the forge. He strode toward the boys.

"'Bout time you got back, Rill," Marc said, his brown eyes narrowed in annoyance. "Aunt Talia's here. And she's been waiting for you all afternoon. Take care of your mounts. Both of you. Then come inside." He nodded at Jedd. "Your mom and grandma are here too."

Marc strode back toward the front door.

Oh great. Rill mentally rolled his eyes as he walked his horse toward the stable. Aunt Talia. His mother's . . . what? Sister? Cousin? Friend? Or was she related to his father? Rill actually had no idea what Aunt Talia's relationship was with his family. She spoke like a rich, educated commoner and wore expensive clothes that she concealed beneath a shabby cloak as if she were ashamed to be seen in The Kings wearing them. And she always brought gifts, often pricey delicacies or exotic foods the family could never afford to buy. Whenever Rill asked who she was, the answer was always the same: Aunt Talia was a family friend who had "married well."

If he was puzzled by Aunt Talia's relationship to the family, Rill was even more puzzled by his parents' relationship to each other. Caldonian society was matrilineal. Kinship passed through the woman. When a couple married, they retained their own last names, and their children received the mother's last name. The husband lived with the wife's family. Yet both Rill's parents, Kendra and Marc, shared not only the same family name but also the same mother—which made them brother and sister. But Caldonian law forbade such incestuous marriages. Rill figured out early on that one of his parents must have been adopted by Grandma Cinna, the family's matriarch.

An adoption like that didn't surprise Rill. Legally, a person who had been expelled by her family could be adopted by another family and given the adoptive family's last name. The adoption didn't establish a blood tie until the next generation, which left the adopted woman or man free to marry within her new family. Such adoptions rarely occurred because an expulsion branded the person as an undesirable. And how could either of his parents ever have been an "undesirable"?

Rill often wondered which of his parents had been adopted. He had broached the question to Grandma Cinna, but she had told him curtly to mind his own business. Once he had even worked up the nerve to ask Jedd's grandmother. Grandma Sorah had told him to speak to Grandma Cinna about it. Fat chance of her telling. What secret about his parents were the two matriarchs hiding?

Last year an incident really stirred Rill's curiosity. He'd been going by his parents' closed bedroom door when he'd heard his father say, "Talia." He'd stopped and put his ear to the door.

"She can't keep comin' here the way she does," his father had said in a worried tone. "It's too dangerous. They're sure to find out."

"We can't stop her," his mother had responded. "She's like Rill. Got a mind of her own."

"If her brother discovers—"

A pot had clattered heavily to the floor in the kitchen, followed by Grandma Cinna's scream. Rill had dashed into the kitchen to find his grandma holding an arm scalded by boiling water from the fallen kettle. He'd started to take hold of her wrist to look at the injury just as his parents had rushed into the room. And he'd always wondered what his father had been about to say.

With that thought still in Rill's mind, he and Jedd entered the stable with their horses. Rill removed the saddle and blanket and brushed down his horse while questions about Aunt Talia kept teasing him. His stomach churned at the prospect of seeing her again because the adults always acted weird whenever she visited. Every so often he would notice her eyeing him in a funny way—as if she were taking his measure—when she thought he wasn't looking. Sometimes when he entered the room unexpectedly, the adults would break off their conversation as if he had caught them by surprise speaking about some forbidden topic. Other times when he was in the room, he suspected the adults were speaking to one another using code words.

Rill sneaked a look at Jedd. Rill had deliberately placed his horse by the loose piece of pine floorboard by the wall that concealed his hidey-hole. And all this time he'd kept an eye on his cousin, who'd started brushing down his horse on its far side, facing Rill. Now Jedd moved to the other side, putting his back to Rill.

Now or never! Rill silently pulled up the floorboard and stuffed the two charms into the hole. Then he gingerly pressed the wood back into place and returned to his brushing.

When he and Jedd finished, Rill wiped the road dust from his boots with a dirty rag. Then, bracing himself for the impending meeting, he headed for the house, Jedd matching his pace beside him. When Rill's hand touched the door latch, a pitiful whining sounded behind him. Rill turned. Faith was sitting on the cobbles eyeing him woefully.

Rill opened the door. "Come on, girl."

Jedd held back, letting Rill go ahead of him, after Faith.

Rill stepped into the dusky, shuttered kitchen. Warm air infused with delicious aromas from a stew, simmering in a cast-iron kettle hanging from a fireplace crane over the flaming hearth, greeted Rill, making his stomach growl. A tray containing loaves of sourdough bread Rill's mom, Kendra, had baked sat cooling on the pine table near the hearth that she used for preparing food for cooking. Kendra had a habit of taking bread to less-fortunate neighbors, or neighbors who had just lost daughters or sons fighting with the legions in the east, the Sharp Teeth Mountains in the west, or with the sea service. Kendra's and Marc's younger sister, Aunt Tarri, turned to smile at him from the hearth, a gravy-coated wooden spoon in one hand and the kettle lid in the other. A pair of oil lamps created an oasis of shimmering light around the adults, who were sitting on either side of the long oak trestle table in the center of the room. Red-burnished clay wine cups were in front of them.

Aunt Talia sat between Rill's grandma and his mom on the far side. When she saw Rill, the lips in her homely, diamond-shaped face turned up into a warm smile that canceled out the reproachful looks Cinna and Kendra fired at him.

Grandma Sorah and Jedd's mom, Marvis, whose backs were to the door, twisted around on the trestle bench to look at the tardy arrivals.

Marc stood behind Kendra, his thumbs hooked over the top of his pants.

Rill's gaze latched on to the large, canvas-wrapped bundle tied with string lying on the table near an almost-empty glass wine bottle. Aunt Talia had brought the wine, of course, because neither the Larkins nor the Eulands—or most other Kings dwellers—could afford bottled wine.

Aunt Talia stood, dark-blue eyes sparkling, and opened her arms wide. "Oh, Rill, I'm *so* glad you returned before I left."

Rill stepped into the embrace, feeling some loose strands of her shoulder-length hair tickle his nose, and resigned himself to the customary peck on the cheek. "How are you, Aunt Talia?"

"Fine." Her glance swept him up and down from his thick, wavy, deep-red hair, whose color matched his mom's, to his scuffed brown boots. "My, how you've grown since the last time I saw you."

"Umm, yeah. My mom feeds me a lot."

"Because he never stops eating," Jedd said.

Turning with a laugh and a smile, Aunt Talia hugged Jedd. "And Jedd. I can't see one without the other, can I?"

"Guess not," Jedd said, grinning.

Faith barked and sidled up against Aunt Talia, who knelt and kissed her on the forehead. "I've already welcomed you once. Are you starved for affection?"

Faith barked happily, then settled herself by the hearth.

Kendra nodded at the package. "Your aunt brought you something."

Rill look at the nondescript bundle with renewed interest as Talia handed it to him. Whatever was inside was soft but contained a core of hardness.

"Thanks, Aunt Talia."

Rill set the parcel back on the table, slit the string with his dagger, and opened the canvas. He stared blankly at the contents for a moment, and then euphoria burst inside him when his mind registered the dark-blue cloak made of soft wool—the kind of cloak only the rich could afford. The cloak enclosed something soft and something hard. His hands trembling with eagerness, Rill unwrapped the blue wool. Inside, he found—

Rill's and Kendra's responses collided with each other.

"Holy Goddess, Aunt Talia—thanks!"

"Talia, no! You've gone too far. I won't permit it."

Rill suppressed a yelp of surprise at the beautiful white linen shirt and the chestnut-colored cotton vest, short jacket, and pants the cloak had concealed. Underneath the clothes, he discovered a pair of black boots made of soft, expensive leather. Like the cloak, they were clothes only the rich could afford.

Ignoring Kendra's protest, Aunt Talia smiled at Rill, her blue eyes shining in the soft lamplight with a mixture of warmth and pride. "It's for Name Day."

"Talia!" Kendra said sharply, with a violent shake of her head that made her red shoulder-length hair whip against her face. "I forbid it!"

Kendra's "stop or else" reaction was one that always made the other family members cease whatever they were doing and pay attention. But to Rill's astonishment, Aunt Talia ignored his mother. Calmly unfolding the shirt, she held it up to Rill's chest and pointed at the pronounced V in the neckline.

"This is your naming shirt. It's the same as the ones the sons of noblesse and rich commoners wear. The Naming charm will fit inside the V and rest against your skin. It will be in plain view. So now you won't have to humiliate yourself by taking off your shirt to let the audience see the charm's decision."

Gratitude for this mysterious woman surged through Rill like an in-rushing tide.

Kendra shot to her feet. "You have no right to give him those clothes."

Talia faced Rill's mother, her back as rigid as her expression. "I have every right. He's a Larkin. And I won't see him humiliated by people who think their sons are better than yours."

Marc spoke, his voice low but firm. "Actually, Talia, we ain't decided yet if he'll participate in Name Day."

Rill's heart froze.

"That's right," Kendra said.

Talia's gaze snapped to Grandma Cinna, who nodded in confirmation.

The kitchen became so still that a pop from the hearth fire seemed to explode in Rill's ears. "Ain't I got a say in this?"

The adults ignored him.

Talia turned her head to Marc. "You can't be serious."

The firm set of Marc's jaw under his short copper-colored beard said he was. Talia glanced across at the Euland women. "Do you agree with this?"

"Yeah," Sorah responded.

Marvis nodded grimly.

Aunt Talia brushed aside a stray lock of ginger-colored hair, the brisk motion betraying irritation. "If Rill doesn't take part in the Name Day Celebration, he won't become a citizen. That's the law. You all know that."

Marc's expression turned sour. "Name Day. The only reason for Name Day's so the damned noblesse can find more fools who think that being mages'll give them an entryway into the ruling class. Instead, they're being used by the noblesse to maintain their control of the state."

"That ain't true," Rill said. "Name Day gives everyone the chance to become a mage and—with luck and sponsorship—to become noblesse."

Kendra folded her arms over her chest. "Name me the last commoner mage who became noblesse."

"Makel Syndow."

Kendra dismissed Makel with a scoff. "That was three generations ago. The game's fixed against you and every other commoner. The noblesse will never open their ranks to one of us."

"They will to me."

Turning to Talia, Kendra jabbed a finger at Rill. "See? That's why we're questioning whether to let him participate. He's so foolish he believes their lies. If we let him, he'd follow the noblesse around like a lovesick puppy."

"He already does every chance he gets," Marc muttered.

"He's headstrong and reckless too," Cinna said. "Goddess knows what would happen if he became a mage."

Rill ground his teeth as he pictured himself returning here after he'd become noblesse. How his folks would grovel and suck up to him. "I'll be sixteen next week. Then I'll be an adult and can do whatever I please. I *will* celebrate Name Day, and you can't stop me."

Cinna rose slowly to her feet, her heavyset figure looming up like a demon from Shelar in the lamplight. She brushed her fingers through her gray, white-speckled hair, then cast a long, icy look at Rill. "I'm your matriarch. I'm the one who makes the decisions for this family. If you defy me, I'll expel you. Then we'll see how high and mighty you are."

"You'll become less than a citizen," Kendra added. "Less, even, than a rohan."

Marvis straightened on the bench, her jaw muscles visibly tense. "I still can't believe you wanna become one of *them*. They're the ones that killed your uncle."

Kald Larkin. Rill's parents' brother, who had died before Rill was born. And the father Jedd had been too young to remember. The man rarely talked about in his presence yet the one person both Larkin and Euland adults revered almost as if he were a demigod. He'd been conscripted along with so many other Kings dwellers to fight in the centuries-long war against Gaetan. And been killed in a faraway country. In all of Rill's fifteen years of life, neither family had ever skipped making offerings to Uncle Kald at the Larkin's family sepulcher on Ancestors' Day. "Maybe his wandering spirit will somehow find its way home," Grandma Cinna always said wistfully. But Rill doubted it would.

A sudden thickness clogged Rill's throat, and he lowered his eyes. "I . . . I know, Aunt Marvis."

"The noblesse deprived me of a husband and Jedd of a dad. Your grandma of a son. Your parents and aunt of a brother."

"I know, Aunt Marvis. But—"

A spoon struck the floor by the hearth with a wooden clatter. Faith jumped up with a sharp *yap*. Rill spun toward the sound. Tarri Larkin stood glaring at them, mahogany eyes blazing and nostrils flaring.

"Killed him?" She uttered a short, bitter laugh. "The noblesse murdered him. Conscripted him as spell fodder because Marc stood up to them. Now my baby brother's lying in an unmarked grave in a foreign land." She heaved a racking sob. "His spirit's doomed to wander between the Underworld and the Afterworld because he wasn't buried here with his ancestors."

Marc wrapped a comforting arm around her shoulder. "Killed. Murdered. It don't make no difference which. My little brother's just as dead."

Aunt Talia appeared flustered by the way the conversation had changed focus, which was unusual because Rill had never seen her rattled before. "Well . . . umm . . . our discussion has gone rather far afield. We were talking about Rill's participating in the Name Day Celebration. Perhaps we should return to that."

"Yeah," Kendra said. "Maybe we should."

A heavy blanket of silence smothered the room.

Rill looked from his parents to his grandma. "What do I hafta do to change your minds?" He spoke the words with a touch of truculence in his voice that paled compared to the anger roiling in his belly.

Kendra's deep-blue eyes drilled into his. "You can't change our minds because we ain't made them up yet."

Rill resisted the urge to slam his fist on the tabletop in frustration. "Then what do I hafta do for you to decide to let me participate?"

"Change your ways," Kendra said. "Come home right after temple school."

"I will."

"No more hanging out in the Public Square to gape at the noblesse, and no more nonstop babbling about mages and magic."

Rill hid a jubilant grin. A few weeks under the family's yoke of discipline would be worth the sacrifice. *Once I become a mage and get a patron, I'll have cut myself free of them.* "All right."

"No more—"

"Fact is," Marc said, scratching his jaw through his beard with calloused fingers, "a few weeks of model behavior ain't gonna change nothin'."

Rill felt as if he'd been punched in the belly as his father's laconically spoken words threatened to shred his plan.

"Oh, come now," Aunt Talia said. "Give Rill a chance. He's only a boy."

"He'll be a man next week," Marc said.

Aunt Talia put a hand on Kendra's wrist and spoke in a pleading tone. "Then do it for my sake, if for no one else's."

Kendra bit her lip, then looked at Marc who put up his hands as if to ward her off. "I'm the father. It's the mother who makes the decisions."

"No," Cinna said. "It's the matriarch." She turned to Aunt Talia, her expression softening. "For your sake, I'll wait and see how Rill behaves."

Rill's legs threatened to buckle from relief. *I'll become the model son if that'll convince them.*

"Aunt Talia's putting her trust in you," Cinna told Rill sternly. "You'd better not betray it 'cause you ain't gonna get another chance."

"You can trust me," Rill said, ignoring a pang of guilt.

Aunt Talia opened the window shutter and peered out at the darkening sky. "I should be going. I've stayed later than I intended."

She made ready to leave.

"You forgot something." Cinna took the clothes, folded them into the cloak, and rewrapped them in the canvas. She offered the bundle to Aunt Talia. "Rill still can't accept these because I still ain't made no decision yet."

Aunt Talia accepted the package reluctantly.

Turning to Rill, she put a finger under his chin and tilted his head so their blue eyes met. "I know you'll do as you said. But no matter what happens, Rill Larkin, you're just as good as any noblesse boy."

Her comment set Rill's pride spinning. Yet, at the same time, his conscience jabbed him. He ignored the uncomfortable sensation. *I'll do whatever it takes to become a mage. I swear by the One Goddess I will.*

## CHAPTER 6

Miscast Spell

RILL'S FIRST OPPORTUNITY TO to keep his promise happened the next afternoon when school let out at the One Goddess Temple. Rill never had a chance to get to know any of the girls in his immediate neighborhood very well. Whenever he showed an interest in one, the same thing always happened. Grandma Cinna would take him aside and tell him the girl's matriarch had complained he was spending too much time with her. The matriarch had no objection to Rill, of course. It was just that the matriarch wanted to wait till after Rill's Name Day Celebration before she decided whether or not she would let the girl continue to see him.

The first time Grandma Cinna had said it, Rill's mind had stopped dead. He'd blinked rapidly at his grandma, not believing he had heard correctly, before he had forced the question from his mouth. "Why me?"

Grandma Cinna had shrugged. "I've told you more than once to be satisfied with the life you got. But no. You're dead set on becoming noblesse if you're named a mage. And I've told you to keep those thoughts to yourself. But no. You gotta yell it to the whole neighborhood."

Dismissing her comment, Rill mentioned his lifelong dream to another girl he liked. When Grandma Cinna pulled him aside to tell him the girl's matriarch had complained about his interest in her, resentment singed Rill like flames from his grandma's hearth. "So I said it to someone else. Plenty of other kids from here get named mages on Name Day. A few even get to become backwatchers and protectors."

"But no kid from here who's named a mage has ever gotten a patron. The matriarchs of the First and Lesser Families don't want them. Those kids get conscripted into the legions or the sea service instead 'cause the noblesse hate us Kings dwellers."

"It ain't fair," Rill said.

A pained look came into Grandma Cinna's eyes as if she knew how Rill felt. "Maybe. But this is what Traela the Weaver wove into your tapestry of life. And you gotta live with it."

So Rill hunted in other places for a girlfriend. Selina came from a different part of The Kings and attended temple school with him. And—Holy Sisters!—she was just as obsessed about the noblesse, mages, and magic as he was. After temple school, they often would go to the Public Square together, sometimes with a bunch of school chums, to watch the noblesse parading around with their retinues of clients and backwatchers. Other times, when the Magesterium was in session, they'd goggle at the building's red-marble-faced exterior and wonder aloud to one another what the magestrates were debating about inside.

Oftentimes, Rill would vow to get himself elected to the Magesterium after he became a mage. "When I'm elected, I'll become a new mage and enter the ranks of the noblesse commoners. I'll marry a noblesse girl. She'll live in my compound, not hers, on The Citadel. Our sons and daughters will be Larkins. And they'll be noblesse." He would pause. "I'll need a powerful patron to sponsor me though." Then he would force a smile when he thought how difficult that would be. "But I'll find one."

Each time his declaration made Selina pout. "It ain't fair," she would say, "that commoner boys who are named mages at their Name Day Celebrations can become noblesse and commoner girls can't. And it ain't fair we can't become magestrates, neither."

Rill would simply shrug. "That's the way the One Goddess set the world up."

But now Rill had to toe a thin line. So when school got out that afternoon and Selina suggested they go to the Public Square, Rill refused.

"I can't," Rill said. "I gotta go right home and help my dad in the smithy. If I don't, Grandma Cinna won't let me attend my Name Day Celebration."

Gripping his hand, Selina pulled him to the side of the temple, out of sight of the courtyard. "I don't wanna go alone."

"I'm really sorry. But I gotta go help my dad. You'd do the same if you was in my fix."

"Just for a little while?" Selina asked in a whiny voice.

"No. I gotta—"

"What can I do to change your mind?"

"Nothing."

In response, Selina pushed her body against Rill's and kissed him passionately, thrusting her tongue into his mouth.

Rill shoved her away. "Stop it!"

"Why? You always like it when I do that."

"I told you I gotta go help my dad."

Selina pouted, then reached for him again.

Rill shoved her back against the marble wall.

"Oww!" Selina rubbed her shoulder. "That hurt." She sulked. "You ain't fun no more."

"I gotta go." He strode away, leaving her sulking.

For the next week after that, Rill continued to keep his promise. He attended school and ignored the entreating looks Selina lobbed at him. And every day at the smithy, Rill immersed himself in his work. He even listened intently while his dad explained various techniques to use. His change in attitude impressed Marc, who told him that a true blacksmith understood not only how to use a particular method but why. "Keep this up," he said, "and you'll become a first-rate blacksmith." Rill basked in his father's seldom-given praise.

All the while, Rill had been apprehensive about his sixteenth birthday celebration. He feared that his family might ignore it or, even worse, spend the time harping on how he had to do better if he wanted to attend his Name Day Celebration. His anxiety proved groundless. When he got up that morning, everyone wished him a happy birthday. In the evening, the Eulands came over for dinner, and Cinna made a toast welcoming Rill to adulthood and gave him a new sword Marc had fashioned in secret. Jedd gave Rill a new long-bow he had crafted from fine yew and a sheath of broadhead arrows.

"I have another sheath almost finished," Jedd added. "I'll bring it by in a few days."

"You'd be better off as a bowyer or a fletcher than as a backwatcher," Marc told Jedd. "Cobb the bowyer taught you well. You got a real talent for crafting bows and making arrows."

Jedd thanked him for the compliment and said, "I appreciate all Cobb's done for me after Uncle Tor died. And I make decent money. But I got real talent with the sword and dagger too. Uncle Tor saw to that. And I wanna follow in his footsteps . . . if only I can find a family that wants to take me on."

A couple of days later, Rill was working in the smithy by himself. It was one of the three private days in Caldon's eight-day week when schools and many shops and businesses were closed. No state business was conducted, and families generally spent time together or met with friends, neighbors, and relatives. Rill hadn't finished his previous day's project and had volunteered to complete it today.

Despite Rill's efforts to reform, the thought of the two charms he had hidden in the hidey-hole constantly burned in his head, like a pair of red-hot coals. Today they grew hotter and hotter with every clang of his cross peen hammer against the wrought iron on the anvil until Rill couldn't stand the torture any longer. Putting the hammer aside, he went into the stable. The place smelled of leather, dung, and urine. He went to his hidey-hole by the wall, lifted up the loose piece of pinewood, and pulled out the two charms.

He just wanted to look.

He took out the charms and placed them on the floorboards. The rohan's bronze charm was just ordinary looking. But the oval, gold pendant beckoned to him as if it were controlling him with a Compulsion spell.

He picked up the charm.

"Rill, what're you doing?"

Startled, Rill jumped to his feet. "Nothing. I wasn't doing nothing."

Jedd stood holding a sheath of broadhead arrows. His gaze sprang from the rohan's charm on the floor to the Old Mage's charm in Rill's hand. Outrage flared in his eyes. "You told me you only took one."

Rill's throat tightened, making it difficult to get words out. "Well, I—"

"Lied."

"Well . . ." Rill raised his chin defiantly. "So what if I did?"

"You told me you wouldn't take no other charm."

Rill batted the accusation away with his hand. "I'm gonna be named a mage at the end of the month. So what difference does it make how many I took?"

"You got no way of knowing you'll be named a mage."

"No? Well, there's one way to find out." Rill slipped the Old Mage's charm around his neck and tucked it under his tunic.

"What're you doing?"

"What does it look like?"

"You're crazy!"

"Relax. Nothing's gonna happen. Everything'll be fine—"

Jedd flung the sheath upon the floorboards. "I'm getting real tired of hearing you say that."

"I'm only gonna activate the charm. If I can do that, then it'll prove I'll be named a mage."

"You'll be named an idiot," Jedd said. "What if something bad happens? Your folks will find out about the charms. And then we'll hafta tell them about finding the tomb and me killing the rohan."

"No we won't. We'll just say we came across the rohan in the mountains. He tried to kill us. And we found both charms on him."

"Rill—"

"Be quiet so I can concentrate."

Jedd lapsed into sullen silence.

His stomach muscles quivering, Rill put his hand to his tunic and arranged the back of the charm firmly against his chest. He closed his eyes and emptied his mind of everything but the charm. Like every kid in Caldon, he knew the word to activate the magic.

"Actus."

He twitched when a weird sensation began flowing through his body. Magic energy! He did a joyful dance in place. "I did it! I activated the charm. I'll be named a mage." Rill grinned at Jedd. "I told ya so."

"That's great. Now deactivate it."

Rill found the sensation of the energy coursing through his body addictive. He didn't want it to stop. "No, no. Wait." He turned to a harness hanging on the opposite wall.

"Rill, what're you doing?"

Rill pointed his finger at the harness.

"Rill, don't cast a spell!"

"Will you calm down? I ain't got no staff. So nothing's gonna happen."

"Some mages don't need staffs to cast spells."

Rill scoffed. "As if I'm one of them. Now be quiet."

Jedd made an angry sound in his throat but said nothing more.

Rill sucked on his lip, thinking. What had that rohan said when he'd cast the spell? Incenbolt. That was it. Stretching out his arm, he pointed his forefinger at the harness.

"Incenbolt."

In less than a heartbeat, energy sped through Rill's body and down his arm. A thin streak of orange-red fire shot out of his index finger and struck the wood next to the harness. Instantly, the dry wood exploded into orange-red flames.

Jedd's body struck Rill's, and both boys tumbled onto the floorboards. In a panic, Jedd scrambled to his feet and raced into the blacksmith shop. He ran back with the water bucket Marc used to quench hot metal from the forge and hurled its contents on the fire, which was ravenously eating into the wood. But as soon as the liquid touched the flames, it turned into steam.

"Holy Twins!" Jedd cried, his face as white as long-dead ashes. "What are we gonna do now?"

Rill pushed himself onto his knees as the energy continued surging through and out of his body. *The energy flow was supposed to stop flowing after I cast the spell.* Panic gripped Rill by the throat. It wasn't just the magic energy that was gushing out but his own life force as well.

"Jedd, help!" he cried. "I can't stop the energy."

"Deactivate the charm!"

"I don't remember the command!"

Sudden dread overwhelmed Rill. He looked at Jedd, whose image was wavering as if it were a ghost. "Jedd—"

Then blackness engulfed him.

## CHAPTER 7

Betrothal Party

ALYSE SAT AT HER cherrywood dressing table in a white linen shift while Kate ran a hairbrush through her long chestnut tresses. Flames crackling in the fireplace and wavering in the oil lamps burning on either side of the vanity encircled her with a ragged patch of light, but the gloom surrounding the light matched Alyse's bleak mood. Faint, rasping music from the receiving hall forced its way into the bedroom like an intruder. Nausea gnawed at Alyse's belly. She glanced at Kate's reflection in the vanity mirror.

"Maybe you could tell them I'm sick. I am, you know. I feel I could throw up at any moment."

Kate smiled sympathetically at Alyse's image. "Then your mother would be here in an instant to drive you out. Or worse, your grandmother would come."

Alyse made a face. "Yech! Then I'd really be sick."

Both girls laughed.

The door burst open, and Alyse's mother, Pilar, strode across the mosaic floor in a whirlwind of red silk damask. She stopped by the dressing table. "Aren't you ready yet? Most of our guests have already arrived, including the Estatis."

Alyse stomped on a waspish retort. "I'm almost finished."

Pilar turned on Kate. "And you, Kate. Your job is to see that Alyse is ready on time."

"I'm doing my best, Lady Pilar," Kate responded mildly.

Pilar tapped Alyse's shoulder. "Get out there fast."

Kate helped Alyse into the dark-blue gown, whose color matched Alyse's eyes, adjusted the silk damask folds so they fell properly, and laced up the back. After slipping her feet into a pair of blue leather shoes, Alyse went to the full-size mirror and appraised her image in the lamplight. Her lips drew up into a thin smile. The high bodice made her look prim and proper. *Good. The last thing I want is to appear enticing to Troy.*

Kate came up behind her and held a pair of dangle earrings up to her ears.

Alyse squinted at them in the mirror. "No. I want something that makes me look demure." In the end, Alyse settled on a pair of blue stud earrings that matched her gown.

"Ready?" Kate asked.

Alyse nodded, her heart fluttering nervously. "I wish you were coming with me."

Kate's lips grew into a slow smile. "I'm glad I'm not."

Alyse punched Kate's shoulder playfully. "Traitor."

"Sometimes being a lowly servant has its rewards."

Alyse hugged Kate and left.

Outside, Alyse leaned against the bedroom door and closed her eyes as flames hissed like hecklers in the large fireplace in the family area. She couldn't put off her appearance forever. She opened her eyes. She still had trouble recognizing the family area, the part of the house where her family lived. But this was the only space large enough to accommodate the number of guests at the formal dinner.

Drawing her shoulders back, Alyse strode past white-linen-covered tables that were set with elegantly engraved, silver place settings and goblets made of handblown glass and candelabra whose candles created islands of light throughout the room. A servant, who had just climbed down from a stepladder after lighting the candles in the last of the chandeliers, inclined his head as she went by. Alyse had never seen the normally dim room so radiant before. She wished her own thoughts could be as bright.

She paused involuntarily at the threshold to the receiving hall, startled by a sight she'd never seen before—the huge, normally empty chamber jammed with people and buzzing with voices. In the left rear corner of the torchlit hall, musicians were blowing into recorders and plucking and sawing at lutes and fiddles, their feet tapping time to the lively music. No one appeared to be listening.

Alyse scanned the room and picked out some of the families present. Dejune. Estati. Spicer. Berne. Svagga. But instead of seeing people, she saw strands of an intricate political web that connected the Dejunes with their allies among the First and Lesser Families. *How many of these families have come only because of our alliance with the Estatis?*

"Your pardon, Lady," Lothar said, coming up beside her. "Lady Siema awaits you."

Alyse's stomach roiled inside her as she glanced left. Wearing her best lavender silk gown, Great-Grandmother Siema occupied the receiving chair on the dais in front of the cupboards containing death masks of past Dejune chief magestrates, her cane parked between her knees in the folds of the skirt.

Great-Grandfather Locien Estati's gaunt, stooped body seemed lost in the smaller chair that was set back a foot from hers to reflect his status as her husband. He scratched his bald head that was ringed by a turf of white hair. The exposed section of the silver chain that held his powerful Overlord charm concealed beneath his white shirt glittered in the torchlight.

The positions of the two chairs on Siema's left side mirrored hers and Locien's. An elderly woman with a boxy figure, and straggly white hair arranged in a bun, sat in the matriarch's seat watching Alyse through dark-blue eyes under thin, white eyebrows. Ariella Estati, Alyse's future mother-in-law.

Ariella's grandson, Deuth, lounged in the other chair, which was set back a foot, his legs crossed. He was impeccably dressed in his customary white linen shirt, finely woven gray vest, black woolen pants and short coat, and highly polished black leather boots. Because Ariella's husband had been killed in a charm raid a few months ago, Deuth was acting as her "substitute matriarch's spouse" for the occasion. Deuth fingered the silver chain holding the Estati's remaining Peer charm, and sent Alyse a warm, welcoming smile.

Siema motioned to Alyse, impatience etched into every crease and cranny on her face. Alyse hurried to her great-grandparents and future in-laws.

"There's no excuse for being late," Siema said. "Especially at your own betrothal party."

"Oh, come, come, Lady Siema," Deuth said, brushing back wayward strands of his cinnamon-colored hair. "Don't be too harsh on her. I'm sure she's nervous. I was at my betrothal party."

Ariella wrinkled her nose. "'Nervous' hardly describes what *you* felt."

Siema shooed Alyse off. "Circulate. Meet your guests."

Alyse spotted Troy's parents—Deuth's sister, Shalira, and her husband, Alger Berne—talking with some guests at one end of the rectangular drain pool in the center of the hall. Alyse liked Shalira and her easygoing, scatterbrained husband. But her stomach churned at the thought of approaching them because they'd start talking about how wonderful it would be to have her as a daughter-in-law.

Alyse's eyes darted to the buffet table where her current stepfather, Degas Spicer, was talking to Deuth Estati's wife, Adele Svagga. Alyse hastened to greet them.

"There you are," Degas said. "We were beginning to think you weren't going to attend your own betrothal party." He patted the back of her hand. "I'm glad to see you here."

"You would've shown more sense if you'd stayed away," Adele said.

Degas shot her a scandalized look. "What a horrid thing to say."

Adele shrugged.

Disgust for this loathsome woman crawled over Alyse's skin, but she kept her expression neutral. The hatred between Deuth Estati and Adele Svagga was talked about openly all over the city, along with their frequent, tempestuous love affairs.

"Lord Brico isn't coming?" Alyse asked.

"No," Adele responded.

"That's too bad." Inwardly Alyse rejoiced. Adele's brother—a short, swarthy mage who had a reputation for never forgetting insults—gave her the willies whenever he was around.

Alyse chatted briefly with Degas, Adele, and a few other guests who drifted to the buffet, then she wandered over to the family shrine by the front door where Troy's older sister, Livia, was chatting with Deuth and Adele's son, Garth Svagga. Alyse usually kept clear of Livia, who had a reputation for being wild and causing scandals that brought Ariella's wrath down on her, usually with no effect. But greeting them would postpone her talking with Shalira.

When Alyse stopped in front of them, Livia had just said something to Garth, ending her words with a snide smile. Garth choked on a mouthful of wine. *Oh, gross! But he's just the type of boy Livia's attracted to.*

"Congratulations on your betrothal," Livia said.

Garth rolled his eyes suggestively. "Looking forward to your wedding night?"

Livia's dark-blue eyes fired sparks at him. "Why don't you shut up."

Even as Alyse dismissed Garth's comments with an apologetic grimace to Livia, she compared Shalira's two children. Short, voluptuous Livia with her dark skin, blue eyes, and curly, shoulder-length black hair seemed mismatched to tall, handsome, light-skinned Troy with his blue eyes and mop of short-cut, reddish-brown hair. Not even his misshapen nose detracted from his good looks. Alyse wondered, and not for the first time, if the rumor was true. That Deuth, in a rage over one of Livia's scandals, had punched Troy in the face when he'd tried to defend her from Deuth's wrath. According to the rumor, Deuth also refused to allow a healer to reset Troy's broken nose. Alyse dismissed the rumor as she heaved a mental shrug. She'd seen stranger family combinations than the Estati siblings.

Livia tapped Garth's wrist. "Why don't you get some food at the buffet table."

"Huh?

"I want to talk with Alyse, girl to girl."

After Garth left, Livia twisted a curly black lock around a finger while she leveled a frank look at Alyse. "I understand you're a bit . . . reluctant . . . about marrying my little brother."

"I really don't think that's any of your business. It's between the matriarchs."

"Everything that involves Troy involves me." Livia stepped closer, eyes hard and a hint of anger in her voice. "I don't want to see him hurt."

Alyse's first instinct was to leave. But she paused as realization slid into her brain. *Maybe we're not so different, Livia and me.* She settled her shoulders, determined to confide in her. "I don't want my life dictated to."

Livia's blue eyes softened, making her features more attractive. "Oh?"

"I want to be . . . more like you. Independent. My own woman."

For just a moment, Livia's lips trembled. Then her jaw clenched. "Be careful what you wish for. Life's always brighter from the outside looking in."

She turned and walked away.

Alyse watched Livia approach the buffet table, slap a hand on Garth's shoulder, and say something that set him to laughing. *Stupid me. Why did I say that to her? Now she told Garth. And that's why they're laughing. Dumb, dumb, dumb.* She blew out an exasperated breath as her gaze sought out Shalira Estati by the draining pool. Alyse squared her shoulders. She couldn't put off greeting her any longer.

"You look resplendent this evening, Alyse," Shalira said, her blue eyes radiating friendliness.

Shalira's husband, Alger Berne, nodded vigorously. "Yes indeedy."

Shalira pushed a loose strand of cinnamon hair back in place. "Both Alger and I are happy for you and Troy."

"Yes indeedy," Alger said. "And we're looking forward to your wedding too. I know Siema is going to make it a blowout affair." He put his hand to the side of his mouth and said in a conspiratorial whisper, "But no one's supposed to know that."

"Why don't you circulate around," Shalira told Alger. "I want to talk with Alyse woman to woman."

Alyse groaned to herself as Alger walked away. *More pressure on me to marry Troy.*

Shalira's expression turned serious. "I know you're not happy about getting married. I wasn't either, when I was told to marry Alger. But I grew to like him. We're happy together. And we have two fine children."

"Your brother certainly isn't happy with *his* wife," Alyse said.

"There were extenuating circumstances regarding the marriage."

"Such as?"

Shalira waved the question away. "That matter's in the past. It's been dealt with, and there's no point in bringing it up again because that will just stir up bitter memories. What I'm concerned about is the present. You and Troy." She touched Alyse's arm. "Please don't go into your marriage expecting it to fail. Be positive. Help make it work."

"The way Deuth helps make *his* marriage work?"

Shalira pursed her lips in disapproval. "Neither Deuth nor Adele wanted their marriage to work. So it failed." Shalira squeezed Alyse's shoulder. "But Troy wants his to work. And you should too. Because if you don't, your marriage will be just as loveless as my brother's. I don't want that to happen to you or to Troy. So what do you say?"

Shalira's appeal made Alyse feel as if her world were shrinking and closing in around her, smothering her. She stood up straight, arms at her side, muscles tense, and hands balled into fists. "I wasn't consulted about this marriage. I was *ordered* to marry Troy. No one has the right to determine my life but me—"

"We don't determine our fates," Shalira said. "Our matriarchs do."

Alyse shook her head. "No, not our matriarchs. The Five Sisters. They weave the events of our lives into our tapestries of life. And I refuse to believe that marrying Troy is woven into mine."

For a moment, Shalira's eyes focused inward and tears appeared. She blinked the tears away. "You're going to have a hard road to travel if you buck your great-grandmother."

"It's my road and I'm prepared to travel it."

Shalira opened her mouth to say something, hesitated, then sighed and walked off.

Moments later, Alyse's mother, Pilar, approached her. "Why aren't you with Troy? You should be greeting your guests together."

"Because I haven't seen him."

"Have you tried looking for him?"

Before Alyse could answer, Troy walked through the door from the family area with Mora leaning on his arm. Alyse gasped, shocked by the sight of her twin in a low-cut gown that exposed the lacy top of a sheer, black breast band. Mora had darkened her eyelashes and eyelids, applied a heavy layer of red ocher to her cheeks, and painted a thick concoction containing red henna dye on her lips. Torchlight made her diamond earrings sparkle. She hung on Troy's arm, openly flirting with him.

Alyse's lips curled back in disgust. "What's Mora doing dressed like a . . . a whore?"

"What *you* should be doing," Pilar said. "The wife's role is to seduce her husband into supporting her family, not his. Remember, Troy's first loyalty is to the Estatis. Just as yours is the Dejunes. You must undermine his loyalty. Bend him to your will without his knowing it. And remember . . . he'll try to do the same to you." Pilar shoved Alyse toward Mora and Troy. "Go to Troy. If you'd been doing your daughterly duty, Mora wouldn't be with him now."

Gluing on a happy face, Alyse headed for Troy and Mora. Just before Alyse reached them, Mora giggled at something Troy said.

Troy smiled at Alyse. "Hi, Alyse. I'm glad you finally decided to join us. I kept thinking about you."

Mora wrapped an arm around Troy's and squeezed it. "We were in Uncle Leoc's *bedroom*—"

"Looking at his war trophies," Troy said, untangling Mora's arm from his. "But I was anxious to get back here to see you. You weren't anywhere in sight when Mora suggested we see the trophies."

Mora's lips compressed into a tight line.

"Well," Alyse said, "I'm here now."

"How *nice*," Mora said, shooting her a sour look.

Troy massaged the back of his neck. "I suppose you're excited about the banquet?"

"That's one way of putting it," Alyse said.

Troy turned to Mora. "I enjoyed looking at the trophies. But now I want to talk to Alyse."

"Of course," Mora replied stiffly. "Don't let me detain you two lovebirds."

Alyse watched Mora cross to join Livia and Garth. Livia greeted her with a happy shriek and a hug, while Garth grinned cynically. *They all deserve one another.*

"What do you want to talk about?" Alyse asked.

Troy linked arms with her. "Let's go someplace where we can be alone."

Alyse unlinked her arm. "Where?"

"In the back garden."

"Outside. Why?"

"Because I want to talk with you in private. And because I think it would be good if both our families saw us disappear together. You know. The happy couple wanting some time alone before the big announcement."

He linked arms with her again. When she tried to pull free, he drew her arm back. "We need to talk."

After fetching a cloak from her bedroom, Alyse accompanied Troy into the peristyle that surrounded the garden. Overhead, a full moon hung in the night sky, a glowing island surrounded by a sea of twinkling stars. To the left, chatting voices and the aroma of cooking meats and sauces wafted toward them from the kitchen that shared a side wall with the peristyle. Those smells overpowered the ones from the stable set against the high granite wall on the right that surrounded the compound.

In the garden, green shrubs grew in intricate patterns, and flowers had begun to push their way up through the earth in their annual awakening of life. An ornamental fountain with a marble statue of a girl holding a pitcher stood in the middle of the garden. Water streamed from the pitcher into the basin. The sounds of talking, singing, and hearty laughter drifted to Alyse from the rear courtyard. Off-duty Dejune protectors and backwatchers were socializing with the guests' backwatchers. The same fraternizing, Alyse knew, was going on in the front courtyard as well.

Several Dejune protectors were patrolling the wall walk on the stone rampart surrounding the compound. Festive times like this made a noblesse family particularly vulnerable to a charm raid.

Alyse and Troy sat down on a stone bench by the pool. Troy scratched his deformed nose, then raked his fingers through his hair while he collected his thoughts. He appeared ill at ease, which surprised Alyse because Troy was a replica of his uncle—a man full of self-confidence. Troy faced her, his lips twisting into a lopsided smile.

"I understand you have reservations about our marriage." He gave an awkward laugh. "It seems to be an open secret. To everyone but me, that is. Mother informed me this morning."

"I didn't mean to embarrass you. It's just that . . ." Alyse's voice faltered.

"Go on," Troy said. "You can tell me face-to-face. You seem to have told everyone else behind my back."

Alyse folded her hands in her lap and stared at them. "It's just that, well . . . I don't want a traditional marriage that's made for political expediency. Just to keep political alliances intact. Where wives and husbands have no feelings for each other. Your uncle's supposed to live at the Svagga compound. But he hardly spends any time there. I don't want that in my marriage."

"Neither do I. And we don't have to let it be that way with us."

"How do you know that?"

"Because I love you." Troy smiled uncertainly. "I've loved you ever since we were kids. And like you, I don't want a frigid, loveless marriage like Uncle Deuth's. I want a wife who loves me."

A dull, heavy feeling formed in Alyse's chest. *Why did I have to be born first? Why not Mora instead? Then she'd get to marry him.*

"If I love you and you love me," Troy said, "the marriage is bound to work."

Eyes downcast, Alyse fingered her skirt, dreading the words she was about to say. Then she met Troy's eyes head-on. "The fact is, I don't love you."

"That's not true."

Alyse went completely still, stunned by Troy's audacity. "Are you telling me I don't know my own feelings?"

"Yes."

Alyse jumped up and swung around to face him. "You presumptuous—"

Troy pulled her back upon the bench. "Do you think I didn't know what Mora was up to when she maneuvered me into your uncle's bedroom? But I went along with it for one reason."

"What was that?"

"To see your reaction when you saw us together. You were jealous. Which means you have feelings for me—"

Alyse wrested free of Troy's grip and started to rise to her feet again. "You arrogant—"

Troy pulled her back down and laughed. "Your reaction just proved my point."

"It proved nothing. For your information, I was disgusted at Mora's dressing like a slut." Alyse peeled Troy's fingers from her arm. It felt as if they were glued to her skin.

Troy's lips blossomed into a self-satisfied grin. "I don't believe you."

He reached for her arm again, but Alyse batted his hand away and slid to the far end of the bench. "The only feelings I have for you is as a friend."

Troy's grin faded, and his face turned serious. "Can't friendship lead to love?"

"No," Alyse said with a quick shake of her head. "I want to love the boy I marry *before* I marry him, not after. And love doesn't always come after marriage. Just look at your uncle and Adele."

"They're the exception."

"They're the rule." Alyse slid closer to Troy and put a hand on his wrist. "Mora loves you. Why not marry her?"

"Because it's you I love." Troy squeezed her wrist as he said the words. "Besides, your great-grandmother demands that the firstborn marry first."

"Too bad your matriarch doesn't require the same. Then Livia would be the one under fire, not me. But no one wants her."

Troy's face darkened like a thundercloud, and for a split moment Alyse feared he might attack her. "Don't you *ever* speak about Livia that way again."

"I'm sorry. I only meant—"

"I know what you meant. And we aren't talking about Livia. We were talking about us."

Alyse shifted on the bench to face Troy, her muscles tense. She could feel the pulse hammering in a vein on her neck. "Then let's finish the conversation. Three points. One. I don't love you. Two. I'm going to marry for love. Three. I won't settle for less. Period."

Troy rose from the bench and towered over her, blue eyes flashing angry sparks. "Yes, let's finish the conversation. Two points. One. You're marrying me whether you want to or not. And two. You'll learn to love me. Period."

Troy yanked Alyse to her feet and forcefully linked arms with her. "You and I are going back inside. Put a smile on your face so our parents will think we came out here to enjoy each other's company."

He half dragged Alyse toward the entrance to the family area. "You'll learn to love me. Because your family's survival depends on it."

Alyse stumbled to keep pace as her thoughts swirled around in her head so fast she couldn't keep track of them. This was a side of Troy she'd never seen before. He had forced her to make a choice. But how could she live with herself if she hurt the family by refusing to marry him? Yet how could she live with herself if she did marry him?

Alyse gulped down a sob as they entered the family area. Were the Five Sisters weaving an unhappy marriage into her tapestry of life?

Or were they weaving her expulsion from the family with a hard life to follow?

Rill's Punishment

LIKE A SWIMMER PUSHING himself up from the bottom of a deep, murky lake, Rill made his way from darkness to light. Feeling gradually returned to his body. He lay prone, his head resting on something soft, but he lacked the energy to move or think.

"He's coming 'round."

His mom's voice dislodged a mental barricade that sent frightful memories tumbling into Rill's mind like an avalanche of boulders cascading down a mountainside. His eyelids snapped up, and he lurched into a sitting position. Gentle hands pushed him back down. Two faces hovered over him: Kendra's and Jedd's.

Kendra released her grip on his shoulders. "Take it easy, Son. You've been through a lot. Stay with him, Jedd. I'll tell the others he's awake."

Rill glanced around at the familiar surroundings of his gloomy bedroom. A fire crackled softly in the fireplace near the bed. Flames from a finger lamp on his dresser bounced off the mirror to strengthen the lamp's light. His quiver full of arrows hung on a wall peg between his bow bag and sheathed sword.

Rill plucked at the heavy woolen blanket covering the top sheet. "What happened?"

"You almost killed yourself," Jedd said sharply. "*That's* what happened. I told ya to leave well enough alone."

"Next time I'll listen to you."

Jedd snorted. "I've heard *that* before."

"I mean it this time."

"And I've heard that before too."

Rill closed his eyes. Even the short conversation had taxed him. A chill snaked down Rill's spine as, in his mind, he pictured the flames devouring the wood and the panicky horses banging their iron-shod hooves against the stalls. After a long while he opened his eyes again. "Did . . . did the stable burn down?"

"No."

Rill blew out a weak sigh. The horses were safe. "What happened after I passed out?"

"I pulled the charm off your neck. Then Aunt Tarri and I carried you in here while Uncle Marc and Aunt Kendra put out the fire."

Astonishment gave Rill the strength to prop himself up on his elbow. "How'd they manage that? Mage fires are almost impossible to put out except with magic. Otherwise you gotta wait till it burns itself out."

"It was just getting started. So they were able to do it. Wasn't easy though. And the fire did do some damage."

"But it was mage fire," Rill said. "So the neighbors know—"

"Nothing. No one saw the flames. Only the smoke. Uncle Marc told them coals from the forge started the fire. He's got the worst of the damage patched already."

Rill eased himself down on the bed. "How long have I been lying here?"

"A couple of days. You were in a bad way. I fetched Priestess Sybil. If it weren't for her, you'd probably be dead." Jedd's face darkened. "But you're in trouble. *Real* trouble."

Normally Jedd's words would have sparked a response. But Rill was too exhausted to care. "What about you?"

"I'm in trouble too. For not stopping you."

"What did you tell them about the charms?"

"What we agreed to say. That we took them off a rohan we

killed."

"And?"

"They believed it."

Thank Goddess for that at least.

For the next three long days, Rill stayed in bed. His family made sure he ate properly and wasn't disturbed. Even though no one mentioned what he'd done, he could tell by their stern looks that the fire and the charms would be brought up soon. He hoped he could talk his way out of the trouble, like he had managed to do with all the other sticky situations.

On the fourth day, Rill was allowed to get out of bed and go to breakfast. He entered the kitchen apprehensively, fearing the kind of reception he would receive. A couple of dirty earthenware mixing bowls sat on the pine preparation table near the hearth. The flames crackled angrily as if reprimanding him. The family sat at the oak trestle table staring at him with grim expressions.

He moved toward his parents, but Grandma Cinna motioned for him to sit by the corner end next to her. She filled a brown earthenware bowl with porridge and handed it to him.

The adults ate in oppressive silence, which made Rill lose his appetite. He toyed with his porridge, making trails in it with his wooden spoon, dreading what would come after the meal.

When breakfast ended, Grandma Cinna stood up and motioned to Rill. "Come into my bedroom. I got something to say."

Sour bile rose in Rill's throat. He balled his hands into fists, digging the nails into his palms to keep his mind off throwing up as he reluctantly followed his grandma toward her bedroom, which also served as her matriarch's chamber, just off the family room. The rest of the family walked behind him, making Rill feel like a condemned prisoner going to his execution.

Three low wooden stools were near Cinna's bed, the middle—the matriarch's stool—was slightly in front of the other two. Grandma Cinna settled her large-framed body on the matriarch's stool while Kendra and Tarri sat on the others. Marc took up a position by the closed door, arms folded, and brown eyes frosty.

Cinna motioned for Rill to step forward, and she grimly took a small wooden box from Aunt Tarri, opened the lid, and tipped the box toward Rill. "Explain these."

Guilt caused a spark of defiance. "Jedd told you about them."

"I wanna hear the story from you."

"In the mountains we met up with a rohan. He tried to kill us. We killed him instead. And I took his charms." Rill wanted to look away, but he forced himself to maintain eye contact while the guilt wormed its way up and down his spine.

"He wore them both?" Cinna asked.

"Just the bronze one. The gold charm was in his purse."

"You're lying." Kendra shot to her feet, anger blazing in her dark-blue eyes. "A rohan would never have a charm like the gold one. Tell us how you got it."

"I told you. From the rohan."

"Liar! You—"

"Quiet, Daughter," Cinna said, her eyes still on Rill.

Rill wished he'd listened to Jedd and left the charms in the Old Mage's tomb and then gone back for them after Name Day. But it was too late now, and he wouldn't admit his guilt. "I already told you the truth."

Cinna held Rill's eyes for a long, long time. Finally, her shoulders sagged, and sadness crossed her face. "Very well. Have it your way." She rose from her stool and faced Rill. "Rillyan Larkin, you stole them charms. Your blind lust to be a mage put our family in great danger. It's a capital offense for anyone but a mage to seek or possess a charm."

Rill shivered as if a cold wind had blown through the room. His folks only called him by his whole first name when they were severely angry with him.

Cinna's jaw tightened, and her brown eyes had a winter chill. "You turned sixteen, but you ain't legally an adult yet. Not till the last day of the month, on Name Day. If your theft is discovered before then, it won't be you that pays the price, but me. And your mom. And your Aunt Tarri. With us women dead, there won't be no female left to carry on the Larkin line. Our ancestors will cry out, but there won't be no one to hear them or to honor them on Ancestors' Day. The Larkin family will end with you."

Her last words touched home. Who would remember Uncle Kald? Or his mom and dad? Or Grandma Cinna or Aunt Tarri? His cheeks flushing with shame, Rill lowered his gaze to the floor.

"Look at me!" Cinna said. "To make matters worse, you *used* the charm. You actually cast a spell. Without training. And look what happened. You almost killed yourself. You came near to burning down the stable and the blacksmith shop as well. The horses too. You almost destroyed our family's livelihood. And if your parents hadn't gotten the flames under control when they did, the neighbors might have found out you were practicing magic."

Rill swallowed to moisten a suddenly parched throat but his mouth had gone dry too. *She's gonna expel me.* His heart slammed against his rib cage, seeking a way out.

"Fire," Cinna said. "That's the one thing everyone in Caldon fears the most. You know that. Most of the tenements are made of wood. Many of the houses too. Once started, a fire could wipe out an entire neighborhood. Other neighborhoods too. Maybe even the city. Yet you cast a Fire spell. What recklessness!"

Cinna stepped toward him while Rill's heart struck harder to break free. "The Larkin women have met in a matriarch's council to discuss what's gotta be done. This is my decision."

Rill held his breath, dreading to hear his grandmother's next words.

"I ain't gonna expel you from the family," Cinna said.

Rill closed his eyes as he nodded.

"But you ain't gonna take part in your Name Day Celebration."

Rill froze in place while his stunned mind processed what his grandma had said. Then anger burst into fire inside him.

"So you ain't gonna become a citizen," Cinna said. "But you'll remain a Larkin. In time, you will take over the family smithy business as planned. And there ain't gonna be no more thought of mages and magic."

Rill backed away, hands out to ward her off as anger devoured him in its crackling flames. "You can't do this. I got the power. I showed that in the stable."

Cinna's brows narrowed. "You showed you ain't to be trusted with that power."

"I cast the spell without a staff. With just my fingers."

"We know that."

"I can become someone important," Rill said. "Someone powerful. I can become noblesse."

"All the more reason to nip that ambition now," Cinna said. "Before you cause worse harm."

Rill backed away more. "You ain't gonna stop me from being named a mage."

"You know there ain't no appeal from a matriarch's decision. I've told you what's gonna be. It's your duty to obey."

"And if I don't?" Rill thrust his chin out.

"Then I *will* expel you."

Anger exploded into rage, consuming Rill like a forest fire out of control. He strode to the door, then spun around to face his grandma. "Expel me if you want. But I *will* be a mage." He stormed out, slamming the door behind him.

## CHAPTER 9

Happy News

ALYSE SPENT MOST OF the day after her betrothal party in her bedroom enveloped in a cocoon of melancholy. She split the time between lying on her bed in semidarkness, head on the feather pillow, staring at the ceiling, and looking out of the unshuttered windows at the bleak sky and watching dingy-white clouds scud across in the wind.

You'll learn to love me. Because your family's survival depends on it. Troy's words ran through her head on an endless loop, making guilt gush through her. What right did she have to marry for love when doing that could ruin her family? Yet what right did her family have to make their survival depend on her unhappiness? Alyse begged the One Goddess several times to get her out of the marriage but had received no sign that She had heard. The lack of response increased her despair.

"Oh, why wasn't I born a commoner?" Alyse said the next morning when Kate stopped by to see how she was doing. Alyse was sitting at her dressing table sharpening her dagger on a honing stone in the thin light streaming through the bare windows, oblivious to the chill sneaking in with it. "Their lives are so much easier than ours."

"Be careful what you wish for. Their lives are just as difficult, but in different ways." Kate paused and nodded at the dagger. "You're not going to stick Troy with that, are you?"

The absurd and unexpected question made Alyse's mind go blank. She blinked a few times, and then broke into a laughing fit. Kate laughed too. Finally, Alyse put a hand on her aching chest as she got her breathing back under control. She wiped laughter tears from her eyes with her palms. She grinned at Kate, who was wiping tears away too. The laughing fit from Kate's outrageous question had finally dispelled her gloom.

"No," Alyse said, still a little breathless. "But I'm not going to marry him."

Kate sat down beside her on the cherrywood bench, her expression serious. "How are you going to get out of it?"

"I'm going to play along with them for a while. Something might come up to get me out of it."

Kate responded with a *harrumph.* "That's a pretty lame plan."

"Right now it's the only one I've got."

"And when it comes time to take your wedding vows?"

Unease crept into Alyse's mind. She'd never put her own private vow into words. She straightened her shoulders and looked Kate in the eye. "Then I'll run away."

Kate's brown eyebrows knit together in concern. "Siema will expel you."

"Expulsion is better than being forced into a marriage I don't want."

Kate put a hand on Alyse's arm. "When you decide, let me know, and I'll go with you."

Love for Kate gushed through Alyse like an unstoppable river. She blinked away tears of gratitude and feared she'd burst out sobbing if she spoke. So she hugged Kate in a close embrace.

Later that morning, Alyse's spirits were brightened when a letter arrived for Siema from Alyse's beloved uncle, Leoc Dejune. For the rest of the morning and into the afternoon, Alyse waited impatiently for her great-grandmother to share the letter's contents with the family. At last Siema called the family together and announced that Leoc had arrived at their country villa for a few days on state business.

Alyse's heart danced a pirouette. She wished Uncle Leoc could come directly to their home on The Citadel, but, of course, he couldn't because the Magesterium had an an aversion to allowing soldiers into the city. And Uncle Leoc was a soldier—Commander of the Eastern Legions assigned to The Marches in the east to fight Gaetan and her allies—and active-duty soldiers were not allowed to leave their assigned areas. Sometimes the Magesterium gave high-ranking officers like Uncle Leoc permission to return for special reasons, but they were forbidden to pass through the city gates. Punishment for a common soldier who broke that rule was severe: a dishonorable discharge and loss of citizenship. But the penalty for a general was worse: loss of his magerium, the authority to command, and permanent exile.

"We'll leave tomorrow morning," Siema announced.

Alyse couldn't wait to tell Kate the wonderful news.

Leoc Dejune, Pilar's younger brother, was the most famous general in Caldon. For the past six years he had been stationed at The Marches, an imprecisely defined area along the eastern border that separated Gaetan's two client states, Fraedia and Mittan, from Caldon. Gaetan was Caldon's archenemy. Last year Leoc had defeated Mittan and turned it into an ally. Now their combined legions were pressing Fraedia from both sides, like a nut between the jaws of a nutcracker. But so far, the nut had proved too hard to break open.

Alyse had hardly seen her uncle during all that time. Even when he had been wounded in battle against the Fraedians, Leoc had insisted on recuperating in camp instead of at the family villa. "A commander must stay with her legionaries," he'd written in his letter, informing Siema of his wound and subsequent decision. His most recent visit had occurred shortly after his recovery when he had come to receive an official accolade for his conquest from the Magesterium. The magestrates, accompanied by a throng of well-wishers, had gone to the Dejune villa in the country to honor him. Leoc had left early the next morning, and Alyse could still recall her disappointment while she'd watched him ride away.

Alyse missed her uncle. She missed his kindness, his laughter and humor, and his larger-than-life presence. And she lived on the memories of the wonderful times the two of them had spent together in her earlier years. For Alyse and Mora's sixth birthday, Uncle Leoc had hired a troupe of actors to perform a comedy for them. And when they'd turned seven, he'd given them matching yearlings. The recollection always made Alyse smile. Mora had turned her nose up at her yearling, wanting to have nothing to do with the "ugly, foul-smelling thing." But Alyse had been thrilled with hers. Leoc had taught her how to ride, and until he had been given his magerium, both of them—despite Siema's objections—had taken rides into the countryside together, unaccompanied by backwatchers.

After dinner Alyse went into the family archives to center herself. Since discovering the talking tubes, she had followed those instructions instead of Priestess Sybil's. In spite of her aversion to magic, the ancient exercise gave her a stronger sense of calmness and control over herself. She also liked the idea of listening to Eulori being spoken by an Old One—an actual Eulorian who'd been dead for a thousand years—and of performing the very same exercise they used to do.

At the end of every session, Alyse moved the box a little farther along the tabletop using Kinesi power. Tonight something marvelous happened when she ended the session. To her astonishment, the box skidded across the table, onto the floor.

That night Alyse went to bed delighted with her expanding Kinesi power and eager to see her uncle.

###

The next morning, wrapped in warm woolen cloaks to protect against the early morning cold, the family set out for the Dejune villa. Alyse went on horseback, riding the now-grown yearling Uncle Leoc had given her. She was looking forward to seeing a smile of pleasure on his face when he recognized his birthday gift to her. Kate accompanied her on the horse Mora had rejected. Siema and Locien traveled in a litter carried by liveried servants, while the rest of the family shared a passenger wagon pulled by four mules. A picked group of backwatchers and protectors accompanied them on foot. Kate's friends Freya and Geoff, along with a mage named Palquo, were in the party.

This year Great-Grandfather Locien and Grandfather Jukka were co-chief magestrates. Because Jukka was presiding chief magestrate this month, the nine dynamae walked on either side of the wagon along the dusty road. These official state bodyguards in black tunics and pants—five male mages with black-orbed staffs and four male bladesmen with swords sheathed in black scabbards—escorted the presiding chief magestrate whenever he was on official state business. They accompanied Jukka today because Leoc had come to the family villa in his role as Commander of the Eastern Legions.

The procession made its slow way down The Citadel, skirted the Public Square, and left Caldon through the Country Gate. Once outside, Alyse reveled in her freedom, riding ahead with Kate. As the sun climbed toward midmorning, the sky grew brighter, and the air became balmy, and everyone shed their woolen cloaks in what was becoming an exceptionally warm day for early Awakening season. What traffic the procession encountered was light, mostly people on foot or a few farmers riding in two-wheeled carts loaded with firewood or leading mules with panniers stuffed with preserved foods going to neighborhood markets in the city. On the small farms that dotted the countryside, men, women, and children tilled their fields, mended fences, and went about their daily chores. Alyse considered these scenes of rural life idyllic and wished she could live at their villa year-round.

In the late morning, when she and Kate were ranging ahead of the little caravan, she spotted a ramshackle farmhouse just off the road. Paint was peeling off the barn, and one of its double doors hung askew. A cow was gazing forlornly over rickety fence rails at a disturbing sight that raised Alyse's hackles. She reined in her horse and shaded her eyes with her hand to watch. Three men with cudgels were forcing a family out of their farmhouse. An elderly man, who must have been the farmer, was shouting at them, but the distance was too great to make out his words. Two women, a gray-haired one, who was around the same age as the farmer, and the other, who could have been their daughter, were screaming at the men too. Three small children clutched the young woman's skirt, sobbing.

One of the men, who was tall and brawny, shoved the farmer to the ground and kicked him in the side.

"What's going on there?" Alyse said.

"Looks like they're being evicted," Kate responded.

Alyse's pulse sped as if it were racing in a hundred-yard dash as she saw the man kick the aged farmer again while he was trying to regain his feet. "Those men are thugs."

She pressed her heels against her horse's flanks and galloped up the road to the farm.

Kate chased after her.

Alyse drew rein in front of the group. "What's going on here?"

The two shorter men glanced uncertainly at the brawny one. He blew out a dismissive breath, apparently unimpressed with Alyse's expensive clothes and Kate's Dejune livery and the sword on her belt. "None of yer damned business. So butt out, girlie."

Alyse moved her horse closer to him. "I'm making it my business."

The man shook his cudgel at her. "I'm gonna tell ya just one more time, girlie. Butt out!"

Standing in the stirrups, Alyse put on her noblesse mask and used her most imperious tone. "Do you know who I am?"

The man answered with a sneer. "I don't give a rat's ass who you are."

"You had better give a 'rat's ass,'" Alyse told him. "Because I'm Lady Alyse Dejune, great-granddaughter of Locien Estati, co-chief magestrate of Caldon. Granddaughter of Jukka Berne, co-chief magestrate of Caldon. And niece of Leoc Dejune, Commander of the Eastern Legions."

Kate put her hand on her sword's leather-wrapped grip. "And I'm her backwatcher."

The tall man swallowed hard while his companions exchanged apprehensive glances.

Alyse nodded curtly at the leader. "I asked what's going on here."

"We're evicting 'em, Lady," the man replied, his tone now respectful. "For not repaying a loan they took out from my patron."

"They're stealing our farm!" the older woman said, her voice shaking with outrage as she helped the old man to his feet. "That's what they're doin'."

The farmer nodded, his wrinkled face flushed with anger. "That's right. My two sons was conscripted, and we had trouble workin' the farm without 'em."

"Don't let those two fool you, Lady," the man said, pointing his cudgel at them. "The farmer's wife here took out a loan and put up the farm as collateral. She couldn't repay the loan. So now we're possessing the place. It's all legal."

"It's criminal!" the younger woman shouted, the trembling children still clutching her skirt. "If my husband was here—"

The leader turned on her. "He ain't here. And a good thing for him too 'cause if he tried to interfere—"

The sound of feet slapping against the dirt road sounded behind Alyse. Palquo, puffing from the workout, stopped beside her and leaned on his mage's staff to steady himself while he caught his breath.

"Lady Alyse, Lady Siema orders you to return immediately."

"In a moment. After I—"

"She said *immediately*." Palquo lowered his voice. "She's very angry with you for interfering here without permission."

Palquo's words must have carried to the leader because his deferential attitude vanished. His lips bent into a jeering smile. "You'd better run along, *Lady*."

Kate moved her horse up to the man and kicked him hard in the belly.

The man stumbled backward with an *oomph*, dropping the cudgel and doubling over.

"And you'd better keep a civil tongue," Kate told him.

Alyse cast a worried glance at the farm family. *I'm sorry I can't help you.* Then reluctantly turning her back on the unfortunate family, she left while resentment at Siema's untimely intervention churned in her stomach.

Siema gave Alyse and Kate a tongue lashing for getting themselves and the family involved in something that was none of their business. And, even worse, for interfering with the lawful execution of a contract.

"From now on," Siema concluded, her flint-gray eyes hopping angrily from Alyse to Kate, "you both stay with us."

Grudgingly, Alyse kept pace with the caravan.

## CHAPTER 10

Politics of Marriage

SHORTLY AFTER NOONTIME, THE procession turned onto a narrow side road that led past fields of grazing cows, sheep, and goats and of rich farmland being tilled by Dejune tenants. Before long, the green ornamental fir trees that surrounded the fishpond near the villa loomed up ahead at the bend, blocking the sight of what lay beyond. When they rounded the turn and the family villa appeared in the distance, excitement coursed through Alyse's veins at the anticipation of seeing Uncle Leoc.

The blue-plastered, stone-walled villa with its sloping, red-tiled roof was larger than the Dejune compound on The Citadel but had a much smaller staff that made for a more casual lifestyle, which Alyse enjoyed more than the stuffy one in the city. On one side of the villa, multicolored perennials were pushing through the ground in Siema's flower garden, while on the other side, the tall green hedges that formed the outer wall of the huge hedge maze were neatly trimmed. Freshly painted outbuildings—including stable, smithy, workshops, and smokehouse—stretched out behind the house. As the party approached the villa, the household staff filed outside and lined up by the front door to await the arrival of the matriarch and her family.

Alyse's heart did a hand flip when Uncle Leoc, dressed in a casual, loose-fitting red tunic and brown pants, limped along behind the servants and placed himself in front of them. Her gaze went to the now-healed left leg, which bore one of several wounds he'd received in his final battle against the Mittanians. When she'd come here to witness him receiving the accolade from the Magesterium for his victory, her heart had ached to see his most visible wound. Leoc, though, seemed oblivious to his disability. So did the women. After the accolade, noblesse and commoner women had flocked around him like a gaggle of geese until the presiding chief magestrate had sent his dynamae to rescue him.

Leoc's weather-beaten face broke into a warm smile as he stretched out a hand to help Siema out of the litter. "Grandmother Siema, it's so good to see you."

While her uncle was greeting the rest of the adults, Alyse and Kate dismounted. Passing her reins to Kate, Alyse joined her sister. Irritation flashed across Mora's face when, instead of turning his attention to her and Alyse, Leoc smiled at Kate and greeted her as "Cousin Kate." A flush of pleasure colored Kate's cheeks. Leoc was the only Dejune adult who made it a point to publicly recognize her connection, distant though it was, with the family.

Leoc turned to Alyse and Mora, smiling at them in that warm, kind way that made Alyse want to grin back until the corners of her lips ached. "You both have grown since my last visit. You've become women."

"We've turned sixteen," Mora told him, thrusting her chest out proudly. "Our Name Day Celebration is next week."

"I'm sure you'll both be named mages. The family needs more of them."

"We need them in the men," Siema said, "not in the women." She sniffed disdainfully. "*You* certainly disappointed us on Name Day."

Laughing off the insult in his normal easy manner, Leoc took Siema by the elbow and guided her toward the front door. "Now, now, Grandmother. We mustn't discuss family matters in the open." He lowered his voice so Alyse could barely hear his next words. "Especially in front of the servants. You never know which one's a spy."

Siema snorted.

The villa staff had everything prepared for the family's arrival. Alyse's bedroom, which connected to Kate's, had been aired out; her bed was made up with newly laundered linen sheets and a warm woolen blanket; a small pile of kindling was neatly stacked by the fireplace. The windows were unshuttered to let in the warm afternoon air and sunlight.

After freshening up, Alyse joined the rest of the family in the dining room. The pair of windows in the outer wall were open, and the afternoon sunlight flowing through them brightened the room. Bouncy, yellow flames from oil lamps set strategically throughout the room added to the light, chasing the remaining shadows away. The sideboard groaned with silver platters stacked with cold grilled meats, vegetables, fruits and cheeses, along with plates of various pastries, and jugs of different wines. Dispensing with the servants, everyone helped themselves to the food. Afterward, they went into the courtyard to take advantage of the day's remaining warmth and settled into a cluster of comfortable chairs.

While the women chatted with one another and Mora played with a gray-and-white kitten, Alyse listened half-heartedly to the men discuss Leoc's campaign against Fraedia. Locien, Jukka, and Degas were all impatient for him to conquer the Fraedians so he could move against Ostica, whose defeat would bring him to the Gaetanian border.

Alyse wasn't that interested in military talk but did notice that her uncle spoke in general terms, without providing any specific information.

"After you defeat Gaetan," Jukka said during a lull in conversation, "maybe you can replace Geraldo Afrius as Commander of the Western Legions and break through the Sharp Teeth Mountains to Annatol. We've been fighting the Annatolians almost as long as we have the Gaetanians."

"Geraldo is a fine commander," Leoc said. "If he can't break through those mountain passes, neither can I." When Jukka opened his mouth to respond, Leoc cut him short. "So much for military matters." Then Leoc went and sat down beside Alyse.

Abandoning the kitten, Mora scurried over to join them. She immediately launched into a monologue about her goings-on, talking mostly about petty things and her hope for a marriage alliance with a powerful family. Leoc listened attentively. When Mora finally paused for a breath, he turned to Alyse.

"What's going on in your life?"

Alyse shrugged. "Nothing much."

"Nothing much!" Mora said, a glint of jealousy in her eyes. "Do you know she's going to marry—"

"Troy Estati? Of course I do."

A baffled expression pasted itself on Mora's face. "What . . . how did you know?"

Jukka chuckled from a nearby chair. "Your uncle's not Commander of the Eastern Legions for nothing. He has his spies and informers everywhere."

"Besides," Locien added with a laugh, "Siema wrote to him a few weeks ago that she was planning to do it."

Leoc returned his attention to Alyse. "You're going to marry an Estati to keep our alliance intact and that's 'nothing much'? It's really a big deal."

Alyse strove to put a light tone in her voice. "What's there to say? Marrying to keep our alliances intact is what we Dejune women do."

"She resisted the marriage," Maude said. "Can you imagine that? The ungrateful girl."

"Grandmother had to threaten expulsion," Pilar added. "To my own daughter. The shame of it. Our ancestors must be rolling over in their tomb."

Mora's eyes flew open, then narrowed into slits when they shifted to Alyse.

"That's all over and done with," Leoc said, a note of irritation in his voice. "So there's no need to bring up the matter again. She's going to marry him. So be happy and have done with it."

Siema responded with a *harrumph* to his words and then announced that the journey had worn out her tired old bones, and she was going to take a nap. Locien said he was tired too, and left with her. Alyse, taking their departures as an excuse to escape, informed everyone she was going out to take some air.

For a little while, Alyse wandered around the grounds. She bumped into the head gardener, who was getting ready for the Awakening planting, and spoke with him about his plans. Afterward, she meandered into the stables and ended up chatting with the stable boy, and together they watched an adorable little colt who had been born the previous week. Alyse knew her mother would scold her if she were caught socializing with the outside staff, but she didn't care. She liked the people who worked at the villa and they, in turn, appeared to like her.

The *clang, clang, clang* of hammer against iron on an anvil came from the blacksmith shop. Alyse paused near the door, wondering if she should interrupt the blacksmith at his work for a brief chitchat. The last time she had come to the villa, he had shown her how to make a nail, and she still kept it in a little box on her dressing table at home. Before Alyse could reach a decision, Mora stalked up to her. Anger swirled in dark clouds across Mora's face.

"I don't believe what I heard," Mora said.

Alyse had expected a reaction from Mora as soon as Maude had opened her big mouth. "Oh? And what was that?"

"That you don't want to marry Troy."

"That's old news. Grandmother shouldn't have brought it up. I'm marrying him." Alyse hated herself for stringing Mora and the rest of the family along. *At least she'll get to marry Troy if I run away. There. I've said it again. Run away. Get used to thinking the words. Then it'll be easier to do.*

"That's not fair." Mora jabbed a finger in Alyse's chest. "I love him. I'd marry him in a heartbeat. But *you're* marrying him, and you don't even want to."

Alyse feigned a resigned sigh. "We don't marry for love, Mora. You know that. We just do what we're told."

"But I love him. I'd do anything to keep our families together. *Anything.*"

Alyse kept silent. What could she say?

"Goddess damn you!" Mora said. "If I were born a heartbeat sooner, I'd be the one marrying him."

I wish you were. Despite herself, Alyse experienced a twinge of sympathy for her sister. "If it's any consolation, I asked Great-Grandmother to let you marry him instead, but she refused."

"I hate you!"

Mora slammed her fist into Alyse's stomach. Alyse clutched her belly, the breath wooshing out of her lungs, and she doubled over in pain. Mora pulled her arm back for another punch but someone grabbed her wrist.

"That's enough," Kate said.

"Butt out of this, *Lady's Maid!*" Mora spat out the title as if it were a piece of filth.

Kate held on to her wrist.

"Let go of me," Mora said. "Or I'll tell Great-Grandmother Siema."

"Tell her what?" Kate said. "That I did my job as your sister's backwatcher by preventing you from harming her?"

A new voice startled all three girls. "She told you to let her go, Lady's Maid."

Jade stood a few paces away. She wore no sword, but her hand was on the hilt of her dagger. "Everyone says you're good," Jade said, drawing her knife and moving toward Kate. "Maybe we should see just how good you are."

Stepping back, Kate held her hands up, palms out. "I won't fight you. It's against our oath to the family."

"I won't tell anyone," Mora said quickly.

Alyse stepped between the two backwatchers. "But I will."

Jade pulled back slightly and glanced at Mora.

Alyse shoved Mora toward Jade. "Take her and leave."

Mora flung a look of hatred at Alyse, then stomped off with Jade.

"Phew," Kate said. "That was a nasty little scene."

"Yes it was," Alyse said, rubbing her sore belly. "Thanks for stepping in. But I'm afraid you've made enemies of Mora and Jade."

Kate shrugged. "They've both disliked me for a long time."

After Mora and Jade disappeared, Alyse asked Kate to give her some space alone. Kate agreed reluctantly and headed for the stables to check out the colt.

Alyse resumed her wandering and eventually ended up by the entrance to the hedge maze. When she had first ventured into the labyrinth as a child, she had become lost among the confusing paths divided by tall green hedges. In a panic, she had burst into tears, sobbing for help. Each time she recalled the memory, she also remembered the relief that had flooded through her when Uncle Leoc had appeared and asked why she was crying.

Choking out the words, she said she didn't know her way back. Leoc laughed and told her if she let fear control her, she would never find her way out. "Think rationally about the problem," he said. "Here's what I'd do if I were lost." Then he led her out through the maze, breaking branches as they went, and explained how he was using the branches as markers to show him where they'd been. The next day she returned to the labyrinth and refused to come out until she had mastered its puzzling twists and turns.

Now Alyse walked to the center of the maze and sat down on the granite bench whose surface had been worn smooth by generations of Dejune rumps. Bringing her knees up under her chin, she wrapped her arms around her legs and focused on the bushy green wall in front of her. Emptying her mind of all thoughts, she lost herself in her Eulorian centering exercise.

All of a sudden, Leoc's voice broke her concentration. "So there you are."

Blinking, Alyse glanced up as her inner focus wavered.

"Sorry," he said, standing a few paces away. "I didn't mean to startle you."

It took Alyse a moment to turn her attention outward. She smiled warmly at him. "That's all right."

Leoc returned the smile. "Daydreaming?"

"Ah . . . yes."

Leoc sat down beside her. "But not about your wedding."

"Umm . . . no."

"Are you going to go through with it?"

Alyse avoided his eyes. "Of course," she said.

"You're lying."

Alyse sensed her face flushing as guilt pricked her chest.

"Don't worry," Leoc said, patting her arm. "I won't tell anyone."

"Is it that obvious?"

"To me. But understandable."

"What do you mean?"

"Most Dejunes don't mind being told what to do." Leoc gave Alyse such a loving smile that it set her body tingling. "But not you. You want to strike out on your own. To live your own life instead of having to do 'what's best for the family.'" Leoc mimicked Siema's voice.

Alyse laughed.

Leoc's brown eyes sparkled at her. "I think you're actually going to discover some way to get out of the marriage."

Before Alyse could respond, he took her hand in his, covered it with his other hand, and gave a gentle squeeze. "Even when you were very young, I saw a remarkable quality in you."

"You did?"

"Yes. That's what makes you so special to me. Because it's a trait I wish I had."

"What? You're the Commander of the Eastern Legions. You're brave and fair and honest. I don't have traits like that."

"Do you remember when you insisted that Kate be your lady's maid instead of a scullery maid?"

"Yes," Alyse said, the old memory stirring outrage even now after so many years. "To treat a blood relative that way. Even a distant one from a disgraced family—"

"That's what I saw," Leoc said. "The courage to take a stand. To be your own woman and to go your own way regardless of the consequences."

Alyse stared at him, openmouthed.

Leoc's lips curved into a sad, lopsided smile. "Surprised?"

"Thunderstruck."

Leoc released her hand. "Have you ever wondered why I've managed to stay single for so long?"

"Yes, and I've used you as a role model. If you can oppose Great-Grandmother's pressure to marry, so can I."

Leoc burst out laughing so hard tears flooded his eyes. "Oh, she's put a lot of pressure on me."

"What's so funny about resisting her pressure?"

"What's so funny is that you have it backward. I didn't resist her pressure. I don't have the courage to do that. I relish my position as Commander of the Eastern Legions too much to resist Grandmother Siema's orders."

Alyse blinked in astonishment. "What are you talking about?"

"Siema ordered me *not* to marry."

"What do you mean?"

Leoc fixed his brown eyes on the neatly trimmed green hedge in front of him as if he were collecting his thoughts. "Right now there are only three Dejunes she can marry off. You, me, and Mora. Right?"

"Yes."

"And there are more than three important First Families we need to have marriage alliances with. Normally, that wouldn't be a problem. But right now, for certain . . . reasons, it is a problem."

"Because our family's power and fortunes are in decline," Alyse said.

"Ah, so you know."

Alyse nodded. "It came out during Great-Grandmother's lecture on why I have to marry Troy."

"Then you also know that maintaining the Estati alliance is of prime importance to us."

"Yes."

"That's why Siema wants to marry you to Troy first. Because the Estati alliance is our most important one. Then she marries Mora to our second most important ally. Of course, she'll first have to decide which family that is. But that leaves several other powerful families we need to keep as allies. I know some are being courted by the Traditionali. And the Commonali have already peeled off a couple of the Bernes' allies."

Leoc rearranged long strands light-brown hair to cover the premature bald spot on his head. "So that's where I come in. Siema dangles me in front of our remaining allies like a lure among a school of fish. A lure the fish snap at but can never quite get hooked on."

Alyse fumbled for her voice as the shocking revelation sank into her mind." Why, that's awful. I never knew."

Leoc smiled ruefully. "I command thousands of legionaries. I have power and riches. Women throw themselves shamelessly at me. But I can't marry. Who knows? I might have to remain single for the rest of my life. Our great-grandmother is the one who'll decide that. But I do what she tells me because if I don't, she'll have the Magesterium revoke my magerium. She might even expel me. After all, 'The men receive the honors but the women rule.'"

Alyse watched the fluffy, white clouds scudding across the brilliant blue sky while she bit her lip, working up the nerve to share her decision. *I can trust Uncle Leoc with my life. So why not with my secret?* She readjusted her position on the stone bench. "If I have to marry Troy, I'm going to renounce the family."

Leoc shook his head, frowning. "That's a momentous decision. One that can destroy your life."

"Or make it better."

"That seldom happens. So think carefully before you act."

Alyse made strong eye contact with Leoc, her face a mask of determination.

"Uh-oh," Leoc said. "I know that look." The levity of his tone couldn't conceal the concern behind it.

"I am *not* going to marry Troy. I'd rather be a beggar in the street than an Estati bride."

"Don't be so rash. For my sake if not your own."

"I mean what I say."

Leoc frowned, as if in thought, and then squared his shoulders. "All right. I'll make a deal with you."

Alyse eyed him suspiciously. "What kind of deal?"

"If you decide you won't marry Troy—"

"I'm *not* going marry him."

"All right. When you decide it's time to announce your decision to the family, don't. Run away instead. To my camp."

"To The Marches?"

Leoc nodded. "That's where my legions are."

Alyse's heart beat faster at the enormity of his suggestion. "But that's almost a two-week journey from here. Through unknown country. For me, anyway."

"You're the girl who just threatened to live in the street as a beggar. And now you're afraid to travel to The Marches?"

His words were like a distant voice as Alyse's mind grappled with how she could ever manage such an enterprise.

Leoc must have read her thoughts because he patted her wrist. "I'm sure Kate will go with you. Together you can make it."

Alyse chewed on her lower lip while she pondered the possible weaknesses to Leoc's plan. "If I run away, Great-Grandmother will guess where I'm going. She'll send people after me."

Leoc nodded. "True. But you'll have a lead on them. And once you enter my camp, you'll be safe."

"But Great-Grandmother is our matriarch. If she orders you to send me back, you'll have no choice. Otherwise, the Magesterium will revoke your magerium. You just told me so yourself."

"*If* I refused her order not to marry," Leoc said. "Yours is a different situation. After all, she still has Mora whom she can marry to Troy. Besides, once your defiance becomes public knowledge, I don't think many First Families will be that interested in marrying their sons to you. You're much too headstrong." He said those last words with a smile. "Besides, I'm a hero. The Conqueror of Mittan. And I'll have my legions at my back."

"You'd use your legions to protect me?"

"No," Leoc said with a laugh. "But in the field, I hold the magerium. That gives me sole authority in The Marches and in the lands I conquer. Not even the Magesterium has the legal authority to give me orders while I'm in my province. They can only advise."

"Unless they revoke your magerium."

"I think both our allied and enemy families will think twice before doing that. Not after I defeated Mittan."

"Because replacing you might jeopardize winning the war?"

"Yes." Leoc fussed with his hair and the bald spot again. "Your staying with me will give Grandmother Siema a chance to cool off. I'm sure I can negotiate an arrangement with her that will satisfy you both."

"What kind of arrangement?"

Leoc shrugged. "How should I know? It hasn't been made yet." He put a finger under Alyse's chin and tilted her head so their eyes met. "So how about it? Are we agreed?"

"Yes."

"Good."

Alyse laughed happily, her cares falling away for the first time in days, and wrapped her arms around Leoc. How she loved this wonderful man. "I feel better already."

## CHAPTER 11

Battlefield News

THAT EVENING ALYSE SLIPPED into the dining room. The window shutters were partially closed to the evening breeze, which was growing chillier. Torches in sconces along the walls whispered softly, their shimmering yellow light reinforcing the golden glows from the oil lamps on the dining table. Everyone else had already started eating.

Alyse went to the silver warming pans on the sideboard and loaded her plate with spicy mutton stew that she ladled over rice, a heap of mixed vegetables, and wheat bread baked that morning. Then she settled into the empty straight-back chair beside Mora who ignored her, while Leoc greeted her with a smile from across the large oak dining table.

The small talk was convivial and lighthearted. The women gossiped about the more outrageous goings-on in the other families, while the men tossed in comments now and then. None of the noblesse's antics appeared to surprise Leoc. Not even the current scandal involving the Dench Family, which was the talk of Caldon.

"Can you believe it?" Siema said to Leoc. "Kelsys Dench rejected his family—"

"A good noblesse family too," Maude added.

"And was adopted immediately by the Raecip Family." Siema

sniffed disdainfully. "Commoners."

Leoc took a sip of watered red wine. "Kelsys is clever. I'm sure he did it for a reason."

"They say he's sleeping with his sister," Pilar said.

Siema's forkful of carrots, beets, and broccoli paused halfway to her mouth. "Pilar, not in front of the girls."

Mora rolled her eyes, her foul mood apparently cured by the prospect of juicy gossip.

Alyse perked her ears, eager to hear more. She loved spicy gossip just as much as Mora.

"Kelsys doesn't deny it," Pilar said, motioning Leoc to pass the glass carafe of watered red wine.

Leoc's eyes sparkled mischievously at her as he handed her the carafe. "Kelsys probably started the rumor himself to get people like you all worked up."

"Well, I never—"

"Please let me finish," Locien said. "Two of my spies told me Kelsys wants to be made a defender of the people. An office only a commoner can hold. That's why he got the Raecips to adopt him."

Jukka banged his fist on the table, rattling the dishes. "He wants to destabilize the government by vetoing laws passed by the Magesterium. It takes just one defender's veto to do that."

"Someone's got him in her purse." Locien wagged his fork at Leoc. "But whose purse is it? That's the question."

"Kelsys will become a problem only if he gets elected," Leoc said. "I think all the factions will band against him—Noblessari, Traditionali, and Commonali alike—because he'll pose a threat to the established order if he wins."

"I agree," Siema said. "We've never had a problem getting our candidates elected or blocking our enemies. All it takes is a few well-placed bribes. I'll get to work on it."

"See?" Leoc said with a grin. "The problem's already solved."

Leoc took a long sip of wine. As soon as he put the goblet back on the table, his expression turned serious. "But we have another problem besides Kelsys. A much more serious one that won't be so easy to resolve."

"That's right, Siema said. "Leoc asked me to summon a matriarch's council after dinner to discuss it. The men will attend as well. Leoc wants to apprise us of the problem before he reports to the Magesterium when they come here tomorrow."

Alyse exchanged an excited glance with Mora.

"Not you two," Siema told them. "Just the adults."

Mora's lips tightened into a thin line. "I'll be an adult next week."

"Hopefully, by next week, you'll start acting like one," Siema retorted.

After supper, the adults scattered in different directions and Mora stalked off. Alyse went searching for Kate and found her in the kitchen eating at a long trestle table with the household staff. She paused in the doorway taking in everyone's good-natured banter and laughter. The cook noticed her and muttered something. The conversation ceased, and the staff stood and faced her. Crossing the threshold, Alyse apologized for interrupting and asked Kate to come with her. When they were alone, Alyse told her about the matriarch's council. "Whatever Uncle Leoc is going to say must be important if the men were invited," she concluded.

"You're not thinking of eavesdropping, are you?" Kate asked.

"Don't be silly," Alyse said. "Of course I am."

Kate traded roguish grins with her. "Well, in that case, I guess I'd better go along to watch your back."

Alyse often spent time in the library during her stays at the villa. So no one paid them any attention when she and Kate went inside. The windows were shuttered against the cool night air, but the light of the oil lamp Kate placed on the table created a shimmering, pale-yellow circle in the darkness. The gloomy shapes of bookshelves and scroll cubicles surrounded the girls on three sides, and the faint images of a fresco decorated the fourth—the wall the library shared with the matriarch's chamber.

The three sconces on the wall between the two rooms must have been installed generations before the fresco was painted because the unknown artist had incorporated them into her painting. A few years ago while Alyse was reading, Kate had discovered that one sconce concealed a spy hole. Alyse and Kate speculated that the peephole had been made by a husband or servant to keep her own family informed about the Dejunes' conversations when they were meeting in a matriarch's council.

While Kate locked the door, Alyse placed a footstool beneath the middle sconce. Stepping on the stool, Alyse pressed a hidden button, and the sconce swung outward, revealing a small hole that was level with her eyes. Alyse peered through the tiny opening.

Torches in sconces lit up the matriarch's chamber. Everyone was sitting in a semicircle of straight-back chairs facing the dais. Siema sat in the matriarch's chair, her cane tucked between her knees while Uncle Leoc stood by the bottom step, facing the rest of the family. His voice came faintly to Alyse through the peephole.

". . . to you first before I report it to the Magesterium," Leoc was saying. "Something disturbing is happening on the battlefront. It's too sensitive for me to put in a dispatch or to have a messenger deliver orally. That's why I've come in person to speak to the magestrates." Leoc paused to sweep his gaze across the family. "Magic is failing."

Alyse's stunned reaction matched her family's. For the longest time, no one spoke.

"Failing." Siema echoed Alyse's thoughts. "What do you mean by 'failing'?"

"When our mages cast spells," Leoc replied, "nothing happens. Then, after a while, the magic returns and the spells work."

"You said 'sometimes.' How many times?"

"Twice last month and once this month . . . so far."

"How often does this failure last?"

"The first two times, not very long. Once during spellcasting practice and again while instructing new recruits." Leoc pursed his lips. "But the third . . ."

"What about the third?" Siema asked.

"It happened two weeks ago and lasted from noon till early afternoon. During battle."

"By The Sisters!" Locien said. "I don't believe it. How—"

Siema silenced him with an upraised hand, then nodded at Leoc. "Go on."

"We'd discovered a weak point in the Fraedians' lines. At a salient, a part that projected out at an angle. My mages spent the better part of the morning softening up the whole front to keep the enemy in doubt about our real target, the salient."

Locien blew out an impatient breath. "That's basic tactics. Get to the point."

"My legionairies attacked the salient. Swordswomen and archers first, followed by lesser mages to protect them. Spells and counterspells flew back and forth like arrows. The legionairies took an enormous beating and almost reached the salient. They would have taken it too. Except . . . the magic suddenly stopped."

Alyse imagined a crowded, bloody battlefield with death-dealing spells speeding back and forth. And then to suddenly have that chaos cease.

"What happened next?" Siema asked.

"The Fraedians repulsed us," Leoc replied. "My legionairies broke and ran."

"Cowards," Jukka muttered.

Leoc spun toward his father. "Those 'cowards' are some of our finest legionairies. They endure privation and death every day, so people like you can sleep peacefully in their beds at night."

"Obviously they're not doing their jobs—"

Siema banged her cane on the dais floorboards. "That's enough!" She motioned to Leoc. "Continue."

"We formed our lines in front of our camp," Leoc said. "Just as our lines were about to break, the magic suddenly worked again, and we repulsed the enemy."

Maybe the One Goddess is answering my prayers and will put an end to magic. That thought gave Alyse a delightful tingle in her chest.

"In the end," Leoc said, "both sides' positions returned to where they'd been before the attack. I negotiated a truce so we and the Fraedians could remove our dead from the battlefield."

"So things are at a stalemate again," Siema said.

"Yes."

"If magic is failing," Degas said, "no mages in Caldon have noticed it."

Locien rubbed his fingers on his chin. "It could be that till now the failures have been so short that no one's noticed."

"Forget about who's noticed the failures," Leoc said. "We need to find out what's causing them."

"The charms?" Degas said.

Leoc shook his head. "If it were the charms, they wouldn't all fail at the same time. The problem must be in the magic plane. That's where the charms get their power. And we don't know anything about the magic plane except how to harness its power through the charms."

"This is serious," Jukka said, his tone ominous. "If the magic should fail completely—"

Siema banged her cane on the dais. "Fail? It can't fail. Our entire way of life—our power—depends on magic."

The adults exchanged worried glances. It was Locien who put their thoughts into words.

"If magic fails, so will our power to rule."

Alyse silently moved the sconce back into place and stepped down from the stool. *I hope the magic does fail. Then one of my problems will be solved.* But when her feet struck the floor, reality slammed. Great-Grandmother Siema was right. Their way of life did depend on magic.

And the adults would do everything in their power to prevent magic from failing.

## CHAPTER 12

Defiance

WEARING HIS BEST TUNIC, pants, brown boots, and cloak, Rill slipped out the back door instead of doing his before-breakfast chores. By the time his parents noticed him missing, it wouldn't matter. He'd be long gone, and they'd never guess where to look for him. Maybe they'd assume he'd left early for temple school. Whatever they thought, he couldn't care less.

From early to midmorning, Rill loitered by the edge of the Public Square, nerves pulling his heartstrings tighter than a mandolin's as he worked up the nerve to execute his plan. Every so often his eyes drifted to the Magesterium building of red-faced marble that beckoned to him like an enchantress. His destiny lay there. At last he spotted activity on the cobble-paved road on the far side of the square that led down from The Citadel. Tiny figures of men in black boots, pants, and cloaks, and gold-trimmed black tunics surrounded by throngs of other figures. The magestrates with their backwatchers and clients. As the processions approached the Public Square, other black-clothed men and their entourages descended from the four other hills and emerged from neighborhoods to congregate in the Public Square.

Rill noticed one magestrate, a tall, gaunt man with a crown of whire hair set on his bald head, ambling down from The Citadel with his entourage. Locien Estati, co-chief magestrate and one of the most powerful men in the country. Rill eyed the other magestrates enviously as they promenaded around the square, trailed by their retinue of clients, greeting and chatting with one another, or negotiating deals with political allies and enemies, or granting impromptu audiences to well-heeled supplicants. *If my plan works, I'll be a magestrate one day.* Rill ignored the taunting voice in his head that said his appeal would fail because Grandma Cinna, his matriarch, had final say in this particular matter.

Before long, a short, portly magestrate with gray, close-cropped hair joined Locien. His cortège accompanied him, along with the nine dynamae. Jukka Berne, this month's presiding chief magestrate.

Rill stared. *If only I could approach him. Tell him my story. The Magesterium has the power to overturn tradition. Like the one that says a matriarch's word is final.* Rill expelled a bitter breath. Jukka would laugh him out of the square. But a judge. He had the power to set legal precedent and appeal a ruling to the Magesterium. Even a matriarch's. At least that's what one of the boys in his magestrate-watching group had told him once. Unfortunately, the boy had added that it hadn't happened in several generations. But Rill had to try.

Yet the outrageousness of his scheme still made Rill hesitate. *If you don't move now, you'll never make it happen.* Drawing in a deep lungful of breath, Rill gathered his courage and started walking.

He looked at the white marble-faced building far ahead set between the Magesterium and the Hall of Naming and strode past the merchants' booths that surrounded the Public Square. He hardly noticed aromas of meats sizzling on food vendors' grills and the cries of merchants hawking their wares. He savagely tugged free when a peddler selling religious trinkets plucked at his sleeve. He went by the Treasury building, passed under the stony gazes of the Statue of Ulbra and Ulbridge Thane, and walked by the gigantic complex of the Mother Goddess Temple, whose high priestess oversaw the smaller One Goddess Temples that served each of the city's nine neighborhoods.

His destination loomed up ahead—the Law Court.

Rill went up the white marble steps and through the open doorway. Unlike the partitioned interiors of other public buildings, the Law Court's was an open space enclosed by four walls and a roof. Dust motes danced in the bright morning sunlight shining through the large windows. Throughout the vast interior, noblesse and commoners—individually and in groups—were speaking with judges. Rill found it easy to pick out the judges because they wore blue pants and red vests over white linen shirts and held staffs topped with red orbs. The multitude of voices merged into an incoherent jabber.

Rill walked his gaze to a judge who was chatting with a nearby commoner, and chewed on his lip, wary of annoying the judge by interrupting his conversation. Just then, an elderly judge emerged from a nearby group and passed in front of him.

For a brief moment, Rill hesitated, heart thrumming from fear. Now or never. "Excuse me, Judge," he said, his words coming out in a rush.

The judge scanned Rill from head to foot. Rill had the uncomfortable feeling in that brief moment that the judge had assessed his background, wealth, and the potential political advantages of listening to him. Rill's face grew warm. *I'm just a commoner boy and shouldn't even be here. Only adults are allowed.* He booted the self-defeating thought from his mind. He half expected the man to move on, but to his relief, the judge waited.

He'd rehearsed his appeal countless times. *This'll work. Don't think. Just talk.* Rill launched into his appeal about wanting to bring a case to court against his matriarch. But before he was halfway through, the judge motioned for him to stop.

"To be brief. Your matriarch forbids you from taking part in the Name Day Celebration, and you want me to intervene. Right?"

Hope wrapped itself around Rill like a warm blanket. The judge was actually paying attention. "Yes, Lord."

But the blanket turned ice cold when the judge shrugged indifferently. "Sorry, boy. There's nothing I can do. Your matriarch's decision is final. You'll just have to accept it and get on with your life."

"There must be some way to—"

"There's *no* way. Your matriarch's ruling is law. You know that. And you should be ashamed of yourself for wasting my time."

The judge turned to leave.

Rill's pent-up anger at his grandma and parents—and now this uncaring judge—exploded in a volley of red-hot words. "I didn't ask to be a blacksmith's son. And I don't wanna be a blacksmith. I wanna be a mage."

The judge halted abruptly, turned, and cocked his head inquiringly at Rill. "You're a blacksmith's son?"

"Yes, Lord."

"From what neighborhood?"

"The Kings."

"Who's your matriarch?"

Rill's heart knotted painfully as, too late, he recognized the fatal defect in his scheme. The noblesse hated his family for turning the Kings dwellers against them. "Cinna Larkin."

"And your mother is Kendra Larkin," the judge said, frowning.

Rill resisted the urge to look down at the floor. Throwing his shoulders back, he met the judge's disapproving look with defiant ones. "Yes."

Rill struggled to not open his mouth in astonishment when the judge did something unexpected. Instead of dismissing him, the judge rubbed the side of his cheek with a forefinger. "Well," the judge said at last. "I still can't do anything for you. After all, your matriarch is acting within her rights."

Anger seasoned with frustration crossed Rill's face, and he started to turn away, but the judge stopped him with a hand on his shoulder. "You look like a fine, strapping boy who would make a good citizen. And it would be a shame to deny you the opportunity to become one. And to become a mage, if that's woven into your tapestry by Traela the Weaver."

Rill's body stiffened in anticipation.

The judge nodded as if pleased with himself. "So I'll tell you what I'll do. Jukka Berne is the presiding chief magestrate this month. You know who he is?"

"Of course."

"He might be interested in your case. After all, Caldon's at war, and we need every mage we can get."

Renewed hope sprung roots in Rill's chest. *I ain't gonna be a legionary. I'm gonna be a magestrate and a commoner-noblesse.* But Rill figured it best to keep that part of his ambition unspoken.

"Tell him Judge Gabe Fortis recommended you to him and strongly suggested he listen to your story." He whispered in Rill's ear, "And make sure you speak with him in private."

After thanking Judge Fortis, Rill hurried outside. Jukka was conversing with a pair of fellow magistrates near the Magesterium. A dynama thrust his black-orbed staff in front of Rill's chest.

"You have no business here, boy."

"I do have business here," Rill replied respectfully, while his instincts yelled for him to shove past the man and dash up to Jukka. "Judge Gabe Fortis sent me to speak with Presiding Chief Magestrate Jukka Berne."

The dynama studied him distrustfully. "Haven't I seen you before? Yes. Yes, I have. With that group of bratty kids that's always hanging out around here. What did they do—dare you to speak with the chief magestrate?"

"No. I'm telling the truth. Judge Gabe Fortis—"

The dynama shoved him backward with his staff. "On your way, kid. And tell your friends your ruse didn't work."

Rill flung a desperate glance at Jukka who was still in deep conversation with the two magestrates. He had to catch Jukka's attention.

"It ain't no ruse," Rill shouted. "Judge Gabe Fortis told me to see Presiding Chief Magestrate Jukka Berne. You can turn me over to the City Watch if I'm lying."

Jukka turned toward the dynama. "What's going on there?"

Rill spoke before the dynama could answer. "Judge Gabe Fortis sent me to see you, Lord."

Jukka studied him through hazel eyes while his gray-brown eyebrows plunged into a quizzical frown. "Whatever for?"

"'Cause of my problem."

Jukka tilted his gray-haired head to the side like a bird. "A problem? What problem?"

Rill looked pointedly at the two magestrates with Jukka. "He told me I gotta tell you in private."

"This sounds intriguing," Jukka said as he waved the magestrates away. He turned to Rill. "Now, let's hear your problem. And it had better be a good one."

Keeping his voice low, Rill told him his story.

Jukka listened, his lips gradually flattening, until Rill finished. "There's nothing I can do. You should know that. You've just wasted my time." Jukka beckoned a dynama to come over. "You need to be taught a lesson you won't forget."

Rill's heart jumped up his throat, forcing words to fly from his mouth. "Judge Fortis thought that too. Until I told him my matriarch is Cinna Larkin."

A mixture of shock and surprise swirled across Jukka's face. "Cinna Larkin! You're . . . you're the blacksmith's son?"

"Yes, Lord."

"And you're so opposed to your matriarch's decision that you came here to appeal it?"

"Yes, Lord."

Jukka became silent, his expression turning inward, and Rill pictured wheels spinning inside Jukka's mind. At last Jukka smiled thinly. "You know what you want and you take it. I like that quality in a man. The person you want to see is my colleague, Locien Estati."

"Thank you, Lord."

"Go tell him—" Jukka shook his head. "No, by Goddess. I'll take you to him myself." Seizing Rill's wrist, Jukka dragged him toward the group of noblesse and powerful commoners, who surrounded Locien. Jukka's stout body moved faster than seemed possible, and his dynamae scurried to overtake him. When the dynamae pushed the onlookers aside, Locien turned his stoop-shouldered body to his son-in-law with raised brows.

"Such a dramatic entrance," Locien said dryly. "Are the

Gaetanians attacking?"

"Worse," Jukka replied with a dramatic hand flourish. "An injustice has been done to this poor boy that must be made right."

His hand still clasping Rill's wrist, Jukka pulled Locien aside, well out everyone else's hearing, and described Rill's predicament.

Locien's reaction mimicked Jukka's initial one. "Why the fuss? His matriarch is well within her rights."

The corners of Jukka's lips pressed into a smile. "His matriarch is Cinna Larkin."

Locien's white bushy eyebrows rose as if reaching for the creases in his forehead. "Oh." Then, after a pause, he met Jukka's expectant look with a thoughtful frown. "Yes. You're right. His matriarch *has* done him a great injustice—denying him the chance to become not only a citizen, but a mage."

Jukka nodded. "My thought exactly. I think this is an injustice you might want to rectify personally."

Locien smacked his fist into his palm. "Definitely! Caldon is at war. We need mages now more than ever. And a boy who shows such determination shouldn't be denied the opportunity to become one, no matter what his matriarch says."

"I agree," Jukka said. "And he's prepared to do whatever it takes. Even if it means bringing his case before the Magesterium."

Locien turned to Rill, brown eyes blazing with indignation. "Your chance will not be denied. Do you know where my family lives?"

Rill's heart leaped for the sky. "Yes, Lord."

"Good," Locien said, squeezing Rill's shoulder. "Go there and speak with my sister, Lady Ariella. Tell her what you told me. In the meantime, I'll send a note informing her of my decision and the reasons behind it. I'm sure she'll agree with me."

"Thank you, Lord," Rill said, resisting the urge to embrace him. "I'll not disappoint you."

Locien smiled at Rill. "Oh, I'm sure you won't."

Then Locien chuckled and exchanged a knowing look with Jukka. But Rill was too excited to pay much attention to the silent communication. Excitement percolated through his veins. His plan had worked.

So far.

Intervention

RILL STRODE UP THE cobblestones of Citadel Road under the warming noontime sun to the crest of the hill where many wealthy and powerful First Families lived in a confusing sprawl of fortresslike compounds. Turning left, he walked past grand homes concealed behind thick stone ramparts three times higher than a woman and separated by wide gaps of open land. Rill knew where the Estatis lived. He had been there several times with his friends to gawk at the Estati compound. And he'd been chased away just as many.

But this time he had a legitimate reason for going.

Rill stopped at the Estati compound. To the far left, he could see distant buildings and streets—parts of The Slums, Caldon's most disreputable neighborhood that, over hundreds of years, had slowly crawled like a slug up to the base of The Citadel. The thought of that sordid neighborhood sent an icy finger raking down his spine.

He turned his attention to the compound facing him. This fortress was more imposing than its neighbors, and its rough granite walls were higher and more ancient too. On either side of the heavy, metal-bound gate stood two protectors—a bladeswoman and a mage—wearing the black, purple-trimmed Estati livery. Rill politely told them that Lord Locien had sent him there to speak with Lady Ariella.

The bladeswoman opened a small window in the left half of the gate and spoke to someone. Moments later, that side swung inward.

Rill stopped involuntarily on the granite paving stones just inside the compound and, mouth wide open, stared at what had always been concealed behind the lofty walls. A barracks was in either corner of the front wall, its roof level with the wooden walkway that ran along the four inner sides of the wall. A protector stood watch at each corner while others patrolled the wall walk. Off-duty protectors lounged by the barracks basking under the sun, reading, writing letters, gambling, and gossiping. Just a spear's throw in front of him stood a formidable two-story house built from thick granite blocks. The first floor was a solid surface, broken only by a front door and unshuttered windows. Narrow archers' slits pierced the granite on the second-floor level.

After searching Rill for weapons, the bladesman led him to the front door and pulled on the bell rope. An elderly, heavyset man whose bald crown was surrounded by a sea of thinning gray hair opened the door. He wore a short black coat and pants, a purple vest, and black shoes. Obviously, he was the steward.

"Kalso," the bladesman said, "Lord Locien sent this boy to see Lady Ariella."

Kalso motioned for Rill to enter, then asked him the nature of his business. Rill replied that Lord Locien had ordered him to speak directly to Lady Ariella, and no one else, about a private matter.

"Wait here," Kalso said and left.

The golden sunshine that filtered through the drain hole in the roof above the catch basin revealed a large rectangular room. The receiving hall. All thoughts of his desperate mission slipped away as, mouth wide open, Rill turned in a slow circle, gulping in the sights like a man dying of thirst guzzles water. A shrine on each side of the front entrance, one dedicated to the Estatis' ancestors and the other to the family's personal goddess. The ornamental receiving chair stood on a dais on the other side of the room. As the current Estati magestrate, on the morning of each public day, Locien Estati returned here from the Dejune compound and sat in that chair to receive his family's commoner clients, who afterward escorted him to the Public Square.

Then Rill ogled the tall brown-oak cupboard with at least twenty rows of closed doors behind the chair. The ancestral cupboards. He'd never seen any before. But everyone in Caldon, from child to tottering old man, knew what they were. Each cupboard contained the beeswax death mask of an Estati male who had held the chief magestrateship. The huge number of cupboards proclaimed not only the Estatis' prestige and power but also the family's antiquity.

When I become chief magestrate, my receiving hall will have its own cupboard of ancestral death masks. And mine will be the first.

Rill's eyes leaped to the single larger cupboard above the others, centered squarely in the middle. Goose bumps raced across his shoulders. That lone cabinet had to be the one that held Ulbridge Thane's death mask. Ulbridge had married into the Estati Family after Caldon was founded and had bequeathed his Brother charm to them. Rill knew about the Brother charm. Everyone in Caldon did. That legendary charm, the third most powerful in existence, formed one pillar of the Estatis' power. Few families would dare go against anyone who possessed the Fraternal Brother's charm. Enthralled, Rill crossed the frescoed floor to the cupboards and stretched up his arm to touch the top door.

"I wouldn't do that if I were you," a voice said.

Rill whirled around, his face flushing from guilt.

A short, buxom girl wearing an embroidered gray silk gown stood near the entrance to one of the side rooms, her dark-blue eyes signaling disapproval. She appeared to be in her mid-to-late teens. She twisted a finger around a lock of curly black hair that framed her heart-shaped face.

Rill eyed the golden links that disappeared behind the bodice of her V-neck dress. A charm, he knew, dangled at the end of the chain.

She smiled at him, making her homely face attractive. But Rill's throat went dry because he had the uncomfortable feeling she was eyeing him the way a cat would a mouse it meant to tease to death. Even though he'd never seen her before, he knew who she was.

Livia Estati.

The girl whose outrageous behavior scandalized not just her own family but all of Caldon.

Rill licked his lips nervously.

Slowly and provocatively, her eyes fastened to his, and she ran her tongue across red-tinctured lips. "And you are?"

"Umm . . . L-Larkin, umm . . . Lady. R-Rill Larkin."

Livia closed the gap between them and placed a hand against Rill's chest. He could feel the warmth of her palm through his tunic.

Livia laughed teasingly. "You look like a scared rabbit."

Rill froze, and his face, neck, and ears felt as if they were on fire.

"Because he thinks he's your prey," an amused voice said.

A boy of average height with short cinnamon-colored hair and wearing dark-brown woolen pants and short jacket, which partially concealed the light-brown vest and white linen shirt, stood in the doorway to the family area. The boy had been dressed the same way the few times Rill had seen him in the Public Square with Deuth or Locien Estati. Although the newcomer bore little resemblance to Livia, he was her younger brother, Troy.

Troy stopped beside Livia and gave Rill the once-over. "What have we here?"

"A boy named Rill Larkin."

"Son of a tradesman by the look of him."

Livia patted Rill's cheek, which made him flinch. "Oh . . . I think he's kinda cute."

Troy gave a mocking laugh. "You think every boy you meet is 'kinda cute.'"

She ran her fingers lightly up and down Rill's neck and held his eyes with hers.

The cat was about to pounce. Panic paralyzed Rill, and to his astonishment, he found himself wishing he hadn't come here.

Livia slowly moved her hand to his chest and smiled seductively. "Because I have universal tastes." Then, puckering her lips, Livia threw a kiss at Rill as she moved away.

Rill's tense muscles went slack. Then, gathering his wits together, he faced Troy. Nothing could be as bad as what he'd just gone through with Livia.

Troy inspected Rill with arrogant eyes. "What's your business here, boy?"

"I'm here at the request of Lord Locien Estati," Rill said, Troy's arrogance stirring courage in him. "I'm to speak with Lady Ariella in private."

Troy stepped forward. "I'm an Estati, and you'll state your business to me."

"In that case, you must be Lady Ariella. My . . . I never woulda known."

Livia snickered.

Anger reddened Troy's face. "I'll teach you to mind your manners."

Fear shot through Rill when Troy clutched at something beneath his shirt. His charm!

Just then a tall, middle-aged woman, with a body shaped like a pear, entered the room. Her face, like Livia's, resembled a heart but was surrounded by straight red hair streaked with white. "Troy, mind your manners. You're an Estati, not a common street thug."

Anger sped across Troy's face but was gone when he turned to the woman. "Yes, Grandmother," he said meekly.

The woman brushed past her two grandchildren. Turning to Troy, she said, "Leave us." Then she snapped her fingers at Livia as if she were a servant. "Make yourself useful for a change. Go polish a charm or something."

Rill's gaze hopped to Livia. She was blinking back tears while at the same time gritting her teeth as if she were ashamed of showing emotion. Then he caught Troy sending his sister a sympathetic look.

The woman spun toward Rill. "I'm Lady Yulonna Estati," she said. "Our matriarch, Lady Ariella, sent me here in her place. I understand you have a private message from Lord Locien. You can give it to me."

"Yes, Lady." Rill told his story.

When he finished, Yulonna observed him thoughtfully as if he were an insect under a magnifying glass. "So you're the blacksmith's son," she said, more to herself than to Rill. "And you want to be a mage. This might prove interesting."

Yulonna called Kalso and ordered him to fetch her daughter. A short time later, Kalso returned to report that Lady Shalira was indisposed with one of her migraine headaches.

"Where's my son?" she asked.

"I believe Lord Deuth is at the Svaggas', Lady."

Lady Yulonna harrumphed. "He picked a fine time to visit his wife. Send someone to fetch him." She turned to Rill. "You'd better wait here until it arrives. After my mother, Lady Ariella, reads it, she'll decide what to do."

Yulonna summoned a servant, who ushered Rill into a small room off the receiving hall.

Sunlight spilled through the single, partially shuttered window, illuminating several polished cherrywood chairs and a pair of small, square tables with unlit oil lamps on them. The servant left, closing the door behind her.

# # #

Deuth Estati strode along the red-brick sidewalk toward his family's compound with long, purposeful strides, his shadow chasing to keep up.

Magnus Roeback, his tall, gray-haired protector mage, kept pace beside him.

Deuth welcomed Grandmother Siema's summons home with the same relief that gushes through a drowning man when his head unexpectedly pops up above water. He hated his infrequent visits to the Svagga compound because they meant he had to spend time with his wife, Adele. Goddess, how he loathed the woman.

And the thought of Garth, their pimple-faced son, made Deuth's stomach twist in disgust. He thanked the One Goddess that Garth was a Svagga and not an Estati and that the kid wouldn't pollute the Estati bloodline.

Livia's pollution was more than enough.

Deuth passed walled compounds of allies and enemies and nodded courteous greetings to noblesse he passed, friends and foes alike. Civility should always be foremost in daily life, at least on the surface. Things had been peaceful lately. Only one charm raid on an Estati ally in the past eight months, and that one from an enemy Commonali family that lived on one of the other Five Hills. At least that's what Deuth's spy had reported, having been planted in the household of his longtime nemesis, Cato Porta, who led the Traditionali faction in the Magesterium.

Deuth frowned to himself as a vague suspicion crept through his mind like a fugitive trying to avoid capture. Wily old Cato could have turned her into his own spy and was using her to further one of his foul schemes against his—Deuth's—family. Yet her information had always been reliable. So far, anyway. Deuth made a mental note to check her out and wished he'd thought of it sooner. You can never be too certain of people, even those you trust.

He stopped to let a funeral cortège of family members, clients, and professional mourners pass by, everyone wearing mourning gray. The matriarch hugged the urn containing her grandson's ashes close to her chest. He had died fighting against the Annatolians in the Sharp Teeth Mountains. The stalemate there had been going on for generations, and Geraldo Afrius, the current Commander of the Western Legions, was having no more luck battling his way through the rugged passes than his predecessors. The matriarch's grandson was one of the fortunate few whose corpses were brought back home to be buried in their family tombs so their spirits wouldn't wander.

The procession paused for Deuth to say a few comforting words to the matriarch. Afterward, as he waited respectfully for the mourners to pass by, Deuth focused his eyes on the Temple of the Sister perched on the other side of the road.

The bright afternoon sunshine bouncing off the polished white marble façade made him squint. The centuries-old temple contained Ulbra Thane's tomb. The Dejunes had her Sister charm. Goddess, how he'd love to get his hands on it. Their fortunes were ebbing.

Perhaps Grandmother Siema will tire of the alliance. Then I'll get my chance. He smiled to himself at the thought. That'll make up for Ulbra's great crime against my family.

As soon as Deuth passed through the front door into the receiving hall, Kalso, the head steward, told him Lady Ariella wanted to see him immediately in the matriarch's chamber. Deuth found her on the dais fiddling with her ornamental loom. He chuckled to himself. She couldn't weave or spin wool if her life depended on it.

"Hello, Grandmother," Deuth called out, tossing her a jovial smile.

Ariella glanced up from her loom, a grin splitting her wrinkled face. "The blacksmith's son is here."

Deuth's mind blanked out, and he stopped short as if the soles of his black leather boots had suddenly become coated with a strong glue. "Huh?"

"The blacksmith's son is here." Ariella smirked at him. "Begging for our help."

"Are you serious?"

Ariella picked up a parchment sitting on her cherrywood matriarch's chair.

Deuth flew up the steps, snatched it from her, and read the words hastily scribbled across the note, each letter burning itself into his brain as if it were on fire. Deuth looked up from the note to Ariella, his eyes wide with disbelief and his mind still reeling from the scheme's brazenness.

"Grandfather wants us to *champion* him?"

"You have a problem with that?" Ariella asked, a crafty light twinkling in her dark-blue eyes.

"Not at all." Deuth grinned at her. "In fact, I think I'm going to enjoy this."

Ariella cackled. "We'll play him like a mandolin, plucking the strings to the melody we want."

Deuth couldn't wait to start plucking.

# # #

For Rill, time crawled along on the back of a snail while he sat in the dim sunlit room waiting for something to happen. One part of him wished time would speed up so he could put his fluttery nerves to rest. But another part of him sent coils of dread snaking through his belly as he pictured himself being booted from the compound to the jeers of the watching protectors for wasting the Estatis' time.

Lord Locien wouldn't of sent me here if he didn't intend to help me. Rill hoped that were true. But he was "the blacksmith's son." And the noblesse hated his dad for turning the Kings dwellers against them. Maybe this is all a trick, and they ain't really gonna help me. They just wanna make me look like a fool.

Finally, around midafternoon, rapid footsteps approached the room. Rill's eyes snapped to the door while his pulse raced. He held his breath, nerves tense.

A tall, slender man with ear-length, cinnamon-colored hair walked in. His white shirt was of expensive linen and the black coat, gray vest, and black pants were made from finely spun wool Rill's family could never afford. "Rill Larkin," the man said. "The blacksmith's son."

"Y-yes, Lord."

"I'm Deuth Estati."

Rill leaped to his feet, knocking over the chair, and bowed his head. "Lord."

Deuth smiled, then waved an elegantly manicured hand at the overturned chair. "Please be seated."

Embarrassment burned Rill's face as he fumbled to right the chair. He'd just made himself look like a fool in front of this great lord. He wanted to run off but perched on the edge of the seat instead.

If Deuth noticed, he gave no indication of it while he positioned another straight-back chair to face Rill and sat down. He casually crossed his legs. "Lady Ariella told me about your problem. But I'd like to hear about it from you in your own words."

After drawing in a deep breath, Rill related his predicament as accurately as he could.

Deuth ran a finger back and forth along the soft, black leather of his boot. "Now, why would your matriarch and your parents not want you to attend your Name Day Celebration?"

The image of orange-red flames eating into the walls of the stable blazed up in Rill's mind. He viciously stamped it out with a mental foot. "I . . . I don't know, Lord."

Deuth smiled encouragingly at him. "Of course you do. If I'm to help you, I must know the truth."

"Well . . . they ain't got no use for mages or noblesse. But you must already know that."

"I do. And now they're taking out their own prejudices against the ruling class by denying you the chance to become a citizen and a mage." Deuth shook his head disapprovingly. "That's very selfish of them."

Deuth's last statement shattered a dam of pent-up anger in Rill, releasing a torrent of words. "It is. I don't wanna spend my life pounding iron on an anvil. I wanna make something of myself. I wanna be a mage. I wanna be noblesse—"

Irritation swept across Deuth's face, which caused a spasm of fear to convulse in Rill's heart. *I shouldn't of mentioned noblesse.* "Forgive me, Lord. I overstepped myself. I didn't mean no offense."

"And no offense taken," Deuth said, his features softening. "If my grandmother had denied me the opportunity to become a mage, I'd be just as angry—no, *outraged*—as you." Deuth squeezed Rill's wrist. "I share your anger. In fact, the whole Estati Family shares your anger at the injustice your matriarch and your parents did to you."

Elation drummed in Rill's chest while gratitude for this wonderful man and his matriarch sprang up like a geyser from his heart. "Thank you, Lord."

"Lady Ariella is impressed by your determination," Deuth said. "Most boys in your situation would simply obey their matriarch's decision. But not you. You know what you want and you go after it."

Rill basked in the praise. "Thank you, Lord."

"I do have one question though. Does your determination have any limits?"

"None."

"Even if it means getting the Magesterium involved?"

Rill felt as if someone had just squeezed the air out of his lungs. "The . . . the Magesterium?"

Deuth nodded curtly. "A matriarch's decision is law. It would take a decree of the Magesterium to change that. And such a ruling is not to be taken lightly. My family won't put itself out on a limb for you simply to have you saw it off from under our feet. So I ask again . . . does your determination have any limits?"

Rill eyed Deuth with hard purpose. "None. I'll do whatever it takes."

"What happens if you aren't named a mage?"

"That won't happen."

"Feeling cocky?"

"No."

"Sounds that way to me."

He'd cast a spell without a staff. With just his finger. "It's the truth."

Deuth stared intently at Rill, then his lips curled up into a smile. "Who am I to question such resolution?"

Deuth stood, and Rill hastily shot out of his chair, almost knocking it over again.

Deuth clapped Rill's shoulder, propelling him toward the door. "Come along, Rill Larkin! Let's go see your family. We have a surprise in store for them."

Rill's body tingled with anticipation. The Estatis had championed his cause. Now all things were possible. He suppressed a giddy laugh of delight. He couldn't wait to see the expressions on Grandma Cinna's and his parents' faces when they saw him enter the courtyard alongside Deuth Estati.

## CHAPTER 14

Charm Raid

A DEAFENING EXPLOSION SHOOK the back courtyard.

Alyse jerked into a sitting position in bed, her heart frozen and her mind whirling in confusion.

Kate's connecting door with Alyse's burst open. The meager flame from the finger lamp Kate held illuminated the sword and dagger buckled over her white cotton nightshift. "Get up! We've been attacked."

Alyse scrambled out of bed, fear billowing up her throat, expanding with air until she almost choked.

Wild shouts, clangs of swords clashing, and voices crying in pain attacked her ears through the partially open window shutters. Alyse's mind turned as blank as a parchment sheet. She strained to recall where she had put her dress. No! There wasn't time to grab the dress because the cardinal rule had been drummed into her head since childhood. If the compound is attacked, go to the safe shelter *immediately* because even a moment's delay could end with her death if the raiders quickly overwhelmed the family's defenders.

Kate eased the door open and peeked into the family area.

Her heart hammering in her ears, Alyse peered over Kate's shoulder.

Servants were racing through the family area lighting torches set in sconces along the walls to provide light for the defenders if the raiders should make it into the house. Backwatchers were sprinting toward the adults' bedrooms on the side opposite Alyse's to escort the other family members to the safe shelter.

The ring of sword against sword and ear-piercing cracks of spells and shouts of attackers and defenders moved into the peristyle garden just outside the family area.

Another blast shook the front courtyard.

"Come on!" Kate said.

They ran toward the dining room. Before they'd covered two spear lengths, the door to the garden burst inward with a deafening roar that made Alyse's ears ring. A huge wood splinter whizzed by Alyse's head as attackers charged into the family area.

"Back!" Kate cried. "Into the bedroom."

They dashed inside. While Kate locked the door, Alyse closed and bolted the window shutters, then took the dagger from her dresser drawer and unsheathed the blade.

A sharp burst, followed by something crashing onto the floor. Booted feet pounded and swords clashed.

"Jade! Oh, Goddess—no! Help! Somebody, help!"

Alyse's breath caught in her throat as she imagined her sister being hacked to pieces by the raiders. "Mora!" She charged toward the door.

Kate yanked her arm so fiercely that Alyse almost lost her footing. "We have to help ourselves."

Shouting raiders raced past their door toward the receiving hall.

"Listen," Kate said, her voice tight with urgency. "We don't need to worry about the mages. They have to see their targets to cast spells. As for the bladeswomen, the door's only wide enough to let in one or two at a time."

Alyse's nerves twitched as if they were being pricked by dozens of sharp-pointed pins. She gulped a deep breath that reached the bottom of her lungs, and nodded. She wouldn't get out of this if she panicked.

Kate stoked the hearth to create a low flame, then drew her

sword. "If they come in, let *me* do the fighting. Use your dagger only to defend yourself, and don't hesitate to strike. Understand?"

Alyse's fingers tightened around the dagger's leather-wrapped grip. The weapon, puny though it was, gave her strength. "Yes."

Kate extinguished the finger lamp. Alyse waited tensely in the shadows near the hearth while the sounds in Mora's room subsided.

"The other's in here."

An earsplitting blast blew the door off its hinges.

A woman wielding a sword rushed over the shattered wood.

Kate cut her down.

A man and a woman leaped over the body. Kate met them face on, parrying their blades with both sword and dagger. The fight took them toward the sleeping alcove. Alyse beat down the urge to attack the raiders while their backs were to her.

A mage stepped over the body sprawled by the door. "Give me a clear cast!" he shouted.

The two attackers split apart, exposing Kate to full view.

The mage pointed his staff at her.

Horror sealed off Alyse's throat, threatening to choke her. *Don't hesitate.* Kate's injunction sliced through her brain like a knife cutting through bonds.

Alyse screamed and charged the mage.

Whirling, he swung the staff at her head.

Alyse ducked and plunged the dagger into his chest.

The mage dropped the staff and staggered backward.

Alyse scooped up the staff and smashed his skull with the orb.

He fell to the floor, dead.

Breathing hard, Alyse retrieved her dagger and turned toward the three shadowy figures battling. Part of her mind was mesmerized by Kate's deadly skill—the first time she had ever seen her cousin fighting for real. The other part was terrified one of the raiders' swords might slip through Kate's guard because Kate was maneuvering to keep the attackers away from her.

A murky figure in the doorway blocked the torchlight from the family area. A bladeswoman holding a bloodstained sword.

Firm determination empowered Alyse. She had killed the mage, and she could kill her too.

Alyse lunged at her, and the bladeswoman spun, seized Alyse's wrist, and twisted.

Pain pierced Alyse's wrist as the knife rattled on the mosaic floor.

The woman kicked the weapon aside. "A noblesse girl fancying herself a fighter," she said, her voice laden with contempt. "You're lucky we're under orders not to harm you. You'd be *so* easy to kill."

The raider turned to join the fighting.

Snatching up her dagger, Alyse flung it at the woman—just the way Kate had taught her. The bladeswoman let out a sharp cry when the blade struck her in the back with an audible *thump*. Her body went rigid. "Bitch," she said.

Alyse seized the mage's staff and swung it at the woman, who stumbled backward. Rage gave Alyse added strength.

"I'm the bitch you don't want to meet!" Alyse rammed the orb into the raider's belly.

Dropping her sword, the raider clutched at the staff.

Alyse walked steadily forward, forcing the bladeswoman to stumble backward toward the fireplace. When the bladeswoman was a foot from the bricks, Alyse lunged at her.

The raider screamed as the impact of the dagger's pommel against the bricks forced the blade to go hilt deep into her body.

Alyse drew back the staff.

The bladeswoman collapsed to the floor.

A cry of triumph behind her burst into Alyse's brain.

A sword clattered on the floor.

Alyse whirled around and gasped. Kate was staggering backward in the gloom.

The bladeswoman lunged at Kate with her sword.

At the same time, the bladesman swung his sword at Kate's neck.

Kate caught her balance and feinted toward the woman with her dagger.

The man's sword missed Kate's neck but cut into her side. She reeled sideways.

The woman moved toward Kate, sword raised for the fatal blow.

Kate slipped under the woman's guard and stabbed her in the chest.

The woman dropped her sword and leaped at Kate, wrapping her arms around Kate's and pinning them to Kate's sides.

"Kill her, Yon!" the woman yelled as she fell, pulling Kate down with her.

Yon hesitated, waiting for an opening to use his sword.

The bladeswoman maneuvered herself on top of Kate. She lifted Kate's head by her hair and banged it against the floor tiles.

Kate cried in pain and drove her dagger into the raider's stomach.

The woman twitched, let out a long sigh, and collapsed upon Kate.

With a grunt of pain, Kate shoved the body off. She climbed shakily onto her hands and knees and shook her head.

Yon drew back his sword to strike Kate's neck.

An uncontrollable shudder blew through Alyse like a freezing wind. Kate would be killed!

## CHAPTER 15

Confrontation

AS HE WALKED THROUGH the shadowy maze of narrow cobblestone streets in The Kings alongside Deuth Estati, anticipation made Rill's pulse beat faster while dread created a sour taste in his mouth. He imagined a fiery confrontation with his folks when they saw him with Lord Deuth. His mom's temper, which she kept under tight wraps, would explode like a volcanic eruption. He'd seen it happen just once, and he'd lost a night's sleep reliving the scene over and over in a set of horrible nightmares. And the disapproving looks his dad and grandma would give him . . .

The vision made Rill's stomach churn as if it were being stirred up, like a pudding in a mixing bowl. He swallowed a deep breath. Lord Deuth had told him not to worry, but doing that was difficult. If the fireworks resulted in his attending Name Day, though, it would be worth it.

Rill sneaked a look over his shoulder at the two backwatchers who accompanied them. One was an arrogant young bladesman with straw-colored hair named Yall Throwstarr. The other was a tall, middle-aged mage called Magnus Roeback whose gray, shoulder-length hair, gray beard and mustache gave him the appearance of a wise old man.

Rill thrilled at the way Kings dwellers stepped out of the group's way, some hastily and others sullenly, onto the gray, clay-brick sidewalks. Curses and angry murmurs pursued the small band. The realization that they feared Lord Deuth sent a rush of power coursing through Rill.

As Rill walked down his own street, the *clang, clang, clang* of hammer on iron grew louder the nearer they came to his house.

Rill threw Deuth a quizzical look when, instead of entering the courtyard, Deuth stopped just outside the entrance.

Faith must have heard them arrive because she raced into view from around the far side of the stable. But instead of going to Rill, she stopped in the middle of the cobbled courtyard and growled, teeth bared, ears forward, and hair raised.

"What's gotten into you, girl?" Rill said. "It's me." He stepped toward her.

Deuth took hold of his arm. "We wait." He nodded to Magnus.

"Kendra Larkin!" Magnus shouted.

The pounding of hammer on anvil stopped abruptly, and Marc emerged from the smithy, a cross peen hammer in his hand. His brown eyebrows lifted in shock when he spotted Rill, then plunged into a deep scowl when he shifted his gaze to Deuth and the backwatchers. He stopped beside the snarling dog. "Faith, stand down."

Faith's growls died away, but she kept angry eyes on Rill's companions.

Marc flung Rill a withering look. "So *that's* where you disappeared to. Can't say much for the company you keep though."

Deuth's lips formed into a mocking smile. "I've brought your son home, and that's all the thanks I get?"

"It's more than you deserve."

Deuth looked beyond Marc to the house. "I came to see your wife."

Marc stepped toward him so only a few spear lengths separated them and waved the hammer at Deuth as if it were light as a feather. "You can deal with me."

Deuth shrugged as if treating with one was good as treating with the other. "May we enter your courtyard?"

"Ain't my permission to give."

Deuth nodded at the cross peen hammer. "You gained quite a reputation in the legions using that hammer of yours. Against the enemy when your camp was overrun. You can throw that thing fast as lightning and strike a target at fifty paces, or so I'm told."

"I've killed my fair share of Gaetanians with it." Marc looked pointedly at Deuth. "Including mages."

"The mages must not have been very powerful."

"They were just as powerful as you. Some maybe more."

Deuth burst out laughing. "Are you actually claiming you can hit me with that hammer before I can cast a spell on you?"

Marc nodded, his face dead serious.

"That's pure brag."

Marc hefted the hammer. "I'd wager this against your staff any time."

Deuth's face brightened. "Are you issuing me a challenge?"

"If that's what you want."

"To the death?"

"To the death."

"Accepted!" Deuth said with a grin. "Shall we meet inside your courtyard?"

"In the street. 'Cause you ain't got permission to enter. And keep your damned backwatchers out of it."

Deuth turned to Yall and Magnus. "You heard him. This is between me and the blacksmith."

Fear gripped Rill by the collar as he pictured his dad's hammer striking Deuth in the face. He—Rill—would lose his champion and his only chance to become a mage. But his dad . . . even if it were a fair fight, the noblesse wouldn't stop until they got him executed. "It's true," Rill told Deuth. "I seen my dad throw. Quicker than a blink, he can hit the target. He—"

Yall clamped a hand on Rill's shoulder. At the same time, Marc shot Rill a reproving look. Magnus and Yall moved to the opposite gray-brick sidewalk, Yall dragging Rill with him.

Faith bared her teeth while she growled low, ears pinned back. She started forward.

Marc put his free hand on her neck. "Faith, stand down!"

Rill struggled and kicked to free himself from Yall's viselike grip towing him backward. He had to stop it! Then Magnus's hand latched on to Rill's other arm, fingers digging into his flesh through the tunic's coarse wool. Rill's head spun dizzily as he saw his dream shattered. And his dad. How could his family and ancestors forgive him if he caused his dad's death? Rill squeezed his eyes shut, then opened them. He didn't want to watch but had to anyway. His heart pounded painful sledgehammer blows against his chest.

Curious neighbors, who had congregated nearby, retreated into their homes and shops. A few came back out with longbows, swords, and cudgels.

"Stay out of this!" Marc shouted. "This is between me and Estati."

Deuth walked backward into the middle of the now empty cobblestone street, then gestured for Marc to leave the courtyard.

Marc started forward, and Faith moved with him, her throat still rumbling. "Faith, stand down!" Marc said.

Giving one last growl, as if in protest, Faith stopped, her black-and-tan body stiff and her eyes fastened on Deuth like rivets.

Marc headed toward the street again.

"Marc Larkin, don't you dare take another step!" Body taut and her dark-blue eyes blazing with fury, Kendra Larkin marched across the courtyard to her husband. "What in Goddess's name are you doing?"

Marc shot her a mystified look as if she'd just asked a really dumb question. "Why . . . challenging him to a duel. It's about time we rid ourselves of him."

"And create more problems with the noblesse. As if we don't have enough with them already."

"But it would of solved one of 'em."

Kendra rolled her eyes in vexation. Then her fiery gaze swept across Deuth and the backwatchers and settled on Rill. "What are you with them for?"

Throwing back his shoulders, Rill returned her look with a challenging one. "I—"

"Came to us to appeal your matriarch's decision," Deuth said. "The one that denied him a chance to participate in his Name Day Celebration. That's what he's done."

Kendra's scowl wavered as if her mind were having trouble digesting the meaning of Deuth's words. "He *what?*"

"You heard me," Deuth said. "May we enter?"

Kendra glared at him. "Only you and Rill," she finally responded, her tone rasping like one of Marc's files. "Not the others."

"Agreed. Just keep that damned dog away from me."

Kendra motioned to Faith, who sat down beside Marc and watched Deuth through hostile eyes.

Deuth beckoned to Rill.

Rill hesitated, intimidated by his mother's fury. Then, with an effort, he shrugged off the emotion the same way he'd brush a bug from his shoulder. Ain't my fault he's here. It's hers.

Kendra nodded curtly to him, then pointed at a spot beside her. Rill went to it, forcing his feet to move at a normal pace like Deuth's.

"State your business," Kendra told Deuth.

Deuth sent her a smile that didn't go beyond his lips. "As I said. Rill came to my family and appealed your . . . umm . . . *mother's* decision to not allow him to attend his Name Day Celebration."

"There's no appeal from a matriarch's decision. You know that as well as I."

"That's true. Unless her decision threatens the welfare of the state."

Kendra snorted contempt. "He's no threat. You'll have to come up with a better excuse than that."

Deuth made an exaggerated show of tapping his chin and gazing up at the sky as if he were pondering, then smirked at her. "Then how about this? We're at war with Gaetan and also stalemated with the Annatolians in the Sharp Teeth Mountains. Our enemies outnumber us in in swordswomen, archers, and cavalry, and we outnumber them in mages. Unfortunately, the number of children in

Caldon with magic power has been declining. So the state needs every mage it can find to refill the ranks of the fallen. To prevent a child from attending her Name Day Celebration puts the state at risk. It also aids and abets the enemy. Therefore, denying a child the opportunity to show herself to have magical powers should be a capital offense."

"Should, not would." Kendra pointed to the street. "Get out. And take your two thugs with you."

Cynical amusement danced in Deuth's blue eyes. "Oh, not so fast. Your son appealed to Jukka Berne, the presiding chief magestrate. Jukka referred the matter to his colleague, Locien Estati. I'm sure you've heard of *him*." Deuth said that last sentence with a sneer. "He's my grandfather. Turns out my grandfather took a personal interest in Rill's welfare. He's also deeply concerned about Caldon's survival and our diminishing number of mages. So he's prepared to propose a law to the Magesterium."

Deuth paused expectantly, obviously awaiting a response, but Kendra just glared at him. Deuth cleared his throat.

"The law will make it a capital offense to forbid a girl or boy from attending her Name Day Celebration. Punishable by death. Applicable to both the matriarch and the parents. The law will take effect retroactively—to the beginning of this month."

The color drained from Kendra's face. "You wouldn't dare."

"Try me," Deuth said, his voice sharp as flint. "My family and our allies control the votes in the Magesterium. If we want the measure to pass, it will."

A murderous light blazed in Kendra's eyes as she balled her hands into fists, her fingers clenched so tight her knuckles turned white, and her breathing came faster and faster.

Deuth's face turned pale.

Rill's stomach shot up into his throat, forcing his mouth open. He'd seen his mom angry before. Mostly at him, and he often feared her reaction if she discovered some of the things he'd done. But his response to her anger now was different. Not fear, but terror. Watching her made his skin prick all over.

Kendra stepped toward Deuth. "I'll teach you to harm my son!" Kendra said, enunciating each word. She pointed at Deuth's chest.

Deuth jumped back as if his foot had been scorched by fire.

Rill held his breath, eyes bolted to Deuth and his mom. His frayed nerves told him to run, but his frozen muscles held him in place.

"Kendra!" Marc yelled.

Marc's shout shattered Kendra's rage. Her body twitched, then her shoulders sagged, and her arm sank to her side. She gulped in deep, ragged breaths.

It took a long moment for Deuth to regain his composure and for normal flesh tone to return to his face. He tugged at the hem of his black short jacket, then he made an exaggerated show of picking an imaginary piece of lint from the sleeve.

"Yes, Kendra. Listen to your husband." Deuth's lips flattened into a thin, taut line. "And now listen to me. I'm authorized to speak for the Magesterium. Defy the will of the people, and the state will enforce it."

"'Will of the people.'" Kendra spat the words. "That's a joke."

Deuth opened his mouth to respond, but someone else spoke first.

"Ain't no joke."

Stern faced, Cinna Larkin strode across the cobbles and stopped beside Kendra. "They've left us alone 'cause we've left them alone."

Kendra turned her smoldering blue eyes toward her mother. "The noblesse have gone too far this time. I won't tolerate it. Neither will the Kings dwellers."

"Won't tolerate what?"

"Allowing—"

"Rill the chance to become a citizen and a mage." Cinna shook her head, sadness claiming all her features. "No, Kendra. The Kings dwellers ain't gonna rise up to protest something as trivial—"

"Trivial!" Kendra said. "I won't let the Goddess-damned noblesse—"

"You *will* let them." Cinna pulled up her heavyset body straighter and folded her arms across her ample chest. "We can't fight the

Magesterium on this."

"We can," Kendra said, leaning in toward Cinna. "We—"

"Can't protect Rill all his life." Cinna reached for Kendra's arm, but Kendra bent it away. "Rill's gotta make his own way in the world. And we ain't got no choice but to let him. He's gotta learn from his mistakes."

"Even if they prove fatal?"

"Only the Five Sisters know if that'll happen."

"No!"

Cinna's eyes narrowed into slits. "You forget your place, Daughter. The decision ain't yours to make. It's mine. Rill *will* attend his Name Day Celebration."

Kendra's body became as rigid as one of the monument-maker's raised-relief figures next door.

Cinna stepped toward her and tapped a finger on her chest. "Say it."

Kendra worked her jaw as if she found movement difficult. Then her shoulders slumped. "Rill . . . will . . . attend his . . . Name Day Celebration."

"Good," Deuth said in a cheery tone. Then his voice hardened. "But remember. Rill is under my family's protection. So he'd better be there."

"He will be," Cinna told him.

Marc hefted his hammer. "Now, get outta here before I change my mind about using this."

Deuth and the backwatchers left without another word.

Rill's lips stretched into a slow smile as his eyes brushed across his parents and grandmother. His mom was holding on to his dad as if without his support, she would fall. And Grandma Cinna's thickset body was rigid as a quarterstaff.

Then Rill's shoulders slumped from exhaustion, and he yearned for something to lean against. Despite all the roadblocks his parents and grandma had thrown up against him, he had succeeded. He was the victor, not them.

Cinna's face turned as dark as a thundercloud. "You foolish boy.

Just look at what you've done."

"I told you," Rill said, too tired to inject defiance into his tone. "I'm gonna be a mage, and you ain't gonna stop me. But no. You wouldn't believe me—"

"Oh, we believed you all right." Kendra pulled away from Marc. "Your stupid, mindless action in the stable showed us that. And now you walked straight into the Estatis' hands. You've opened a whole new bag of troubles for yourself and for us."

"Like what?"

Kendra started to answer, but Marc interrupted. "The Estatis are our personal enemies. Now they're gonna use you to get back at us."

Cynicism toward his parents and grandma spun itself around Rill and gave him courage through his tiredness. "See? You can't tell me. So you came up with a feeble excuse like that. I'm gonna be a mage. I'm gonna start my own noblesse-commoner family. And no one's gonna stop me."

Cinna heaved a weary sigh. "What's done is done. And there ain't no changin' it."

Rill trailed his glum-faced folks inside. He wanted to shout his joy to the whole neighborhood. He was on his way to becoming a mage and noblesse. Nothing could stop him now.

## CHAPTER 16

Aftermath

RAGE EXPLODED INSIDE ALYSE. "No!" She stretched her arm toward Yon.

Like a tidal wave, energy from the magic plane surged into Alyse's solar plexus, cascaded into her pelvis, sped down her arm, and burst out of her palm.

An invisible force swept Yon off his feet and flung him against the wall. His head smacked the plaster-covered bricks with a sickening *crack,* and he crumbled to the floor.

Alyse gaped at Yon's dim figure and the dark mess of brains and blood pooling on the colored mosaic stones. Her mind scrambled like a crazed woman to understand what had just happened. A tremor shook her body as realization grew in her brain like a poisonous mushroom.

Kinesi magic!

The bedroom began spinning like a child's top, and Alyse breathed faster and faster. Her legs wobbled. She put a hand on the wall to steady herself while images of her practice sessions in the family archives flickered through her head. Oh, Goddess above, what have I done? She gulped down a huge mouthful of air. Steady yourself. You've got to steady yourself. Then she forced her lungs to work more slowly. Gradually, like a top losing its momentum, the room slowed to a stop.

Kate climbed unsteadily to her feet.

Thankful for the new focus, Alyse rushed to her and clasped her shoulders to keep her stable. "Are you all right?"

"I've felt better," Kate said in a shaky voice.

The dwindling flames in the fireplace gave just enough light for Alyse to spot two dark stains spreading out on Kate's white nightshift. "You're bleeding. You need a healer."

Kate motioned to her sword lying on the floor a few feet away. "What I need is my weapons. The fighting's not over."

"It is for you."

It took all of Alyse's strength to keep Kate upright as she helped her to the bed in the sleeping alcove. Kate lay down with a groan. She pressed an arm against her side wound and a hand on her chest wound. Dark blood seeped out from both places, merging into one huge bloody splotch on the nightshift before soaking the blanket.

Alyse yanked Kate's bloodstained dagger from the belly of the woman Kate had killed, dashed to the wardrobe, flung the door open, and tore a nightshift off the hanger with such force that it sent the hanger dancing crazily. She lost all sense of time as she worked at a madwoman's pace cutting makeshift bandages with the dagger. Two large squares, which she folded into smaller ones, to place over the wounds and two long strips to wrap around Kate's chest to keep the squares in place. Alyse's muscles twitched with Kate's grunts when she pulled the strips tight before knotting them.

Expelling a deep breath of relief, Alyse lit the finger lamp and put it on the night table beside the bed. Her body sagged, weary from the ordeal, and she yearned to lay down beside Kate and fall asleep. Instead, she sat on the bed near Kate's feet, put her elbows on her upper thighs, and rested her head between her hands. She had to stay awake with the dagger beside her in case raiders came in again.

Alyse awoke with a start, horrified that she'd dozed off. She cocked an ear. The cacophony of fighting seemed to be fading.

Two shadowy figures darted through the damaged doorway.

Alyse leaped to her feet, fingers gripping the dagger's handle.

They'll have to kill me to get to Kate.

The intruders glanced around, spotted her, and headed toward the bed.

Alyse crouched into a fighter's stance, muscles tensed to snapping. She focused on the dark forms as if her world had just narrowed until those two enemies were the only things that existed.

"Lady Alyse," a woman's voice said. "Are you all right?"

Alyse's muscles sagged in relief as she recognized Kate's friend, Freya. "Yes. But Kate's wounded."

As the pair came closer, Alyse recognized Geoff.

"Is it serious?" Geoff asked as they stopped by the bedside.

"Bad enough," Alyse said.

"I can still fight if I need to," Kate grumbled.

Freya ran her eyes over Kate's bandages and the bloodstained bed. "Not from the look of you."

Kate licked her lips as if her mouth were dry. "Weren't you guarding the rear gate tonight?"

Geoff nodded. "They took us by surprise. A Concealment spell."

Kate gave them both an anxious look.

"We have to go," Freya said. "There're still raiders at large. We just wanted to see if the two of you were all right."

Kate stared at the empty doorway after they left. "It's going to go hard on them."

"What do you mean?" Alyse asked.

"The raiders blasted their way in during their watch. It'll go hard for everyone who was on duty there. Siema will make examples of them to make sure everyone else will be on sharpest alert in the future."

"That's silly," Alyse responded. But a shadow of doubt formed in her mind.

A while later, the din of fighting petered out, and all the voices Alyse heard belonged to her family's protectors and backwatchers.

Kate stirred, then propped herself up by her elbow. She motioned at the dead mage with the smashed skull, the female raider lying near the hearth with Alyse's dagger in her back, and Yon's body sprawled out on the mosaic stones like a child's ruined doll. "You did that?"

"I couldn't just stand by and let them kill you."

A tired smile spread across Kate's lips. "You saved my life." She pointed to Yon's broken skull. "How did you do that?"

Alyse plucked at her bloody nightshift, wishing she could fade into the shadows. Drawing in a deep breath, she gazed at Kate, whose hazel eyes staring back at her were filled with concern. She wet her dry lips. "I . . . I'm not sure. I wanted to get him away from you. And then the Kinesi power just . . . well, it just came. All by itself."

"Kinesi power?"

"Yes. It's centered in your pelvis and lets you move objects. I've been practicing with it for my breathing exercises. But I've only been able to move a small box . . . until now."

"You're talking about magic," Kate said, awe etched into every crease of her face. "You used magic! Without a charm."

Alyse's body trembled as she recognized she would have to face the frightening implications of what she had done crash down on her like an avalanche. She *had* worked magic, which was impossible to do without a charm. And without casting a spell either. Fear made her choke on her words.

"I-I'm sorry—"

"No. Don't be sorry. I'm thanking you. You saved my life."

"Kate," Alyse whispered, caught up in the weird fear that someone might overhear. "I'm frightened."

Degas Spicer ran into the room, almost tripping over the corpse in the doorway. The white glow from his staff's crystal threw back the darkness. "Alyse, are you all right?"

Alyse grasped Kate's wrist and spoke low. "Tell no one."

Kate nodded.

"Yes," Alyse said as her stepfather stopped by the bed.

"Kate, you're wounded," Degas said.

He stepped toward her, then froze when he noticed Yon's smashed skull. "Goddess in Elustra! Who did that?"

"I did," Kate said before Alyse could respond.

Degas's eyes shifted to her, wide as a wine cups. "How?"

"Can't really explain it." Kate winced. "He was going to kill Alyse. I just . . . went berserk and flung him against the wall."

"Well done, girl," Degas said. "Well done. I wish we had more backwatchers like you. Poor Jade."

Alyse became aware of faint sobbing from Mora's room. "What about Jade—and Mora?"

"Jade's been gravely wounded. Mora's all right, but . . . incapacitated."

"What do you mean 'incapacitated'?"

"Degas!" a voice called out from the family area. "Degas, where are you?"

"In Alyse's bedroom!" Degas shouted.

Jukka Berne dashed through the doorway, jumping over the corpse at the threshold. "Siema's dead, and Locien's badly wounded."

The two men raced out. Alyse chased after them.

The broken door to her great-grandparents' bedroom dangled from a hinge. Lenia, the family healer, bent over Siema's body sprawled on the bed. Maude and Pilar flanked her on each side. A patch of blood surrounded a charred hole in Siema's nightshift. A Fire spell.

Alyse drew in a breath to scream in horror, then blew it out. She clenched her hands into fists, the nails biting into her palms. *I'm not weak. I can handle this.* She turned to Degas. "Where's Great-Grandfather?"

"In your Uncle Leoc's bedroom." Degas put his hands on Alyse's shoulders and looked at her, concern drawing his brows together. "What's happened is horrible. But you're a Dejune. And soon you'll become an adult. So it's time you took up an adult's duties. See to Mora. Then tend to the dead and wounded." He pushed her into the hall. "Act calmly in front of the servants and retainers. Now, go!"

Alyse strode across the family area, striving to project an outer calm that belied her inner agitation so she could project authority. Only now did the violence and carnage of the attack strike home. The torchlight grudgingly exposed shady figures of the dead and wounded sprawled on the floor in pools of blood. Some of the injured were making such pitiful cries that Alyse wanted to plug her ears with her fingers. The walls were charred by Fire spells. Furniture was broken and overturned. Doors were shattered or hanging askew. Oddly enough, Alyse didn't see any wounded raiders, only dead ones. Her foot tripped on something, but she managed to keep her balance. She looked down. A severed arm. Her stomach heaved, but she grit her teeth and kept going.

When Alyse entered the bedroom, she heard Mora sobbing in a corner. Jade lay unconscious on the floor, her nightshift sodden with blood. Corpses of two men clad in nondescript clothes lay near her. Kneeling beside Jade, Alyse felt her pulse still beating, but weakly. She ripped Jade's nightshift down the middle. Red blood streamed from a vicious chest wound and a deep slice in her arm. Alyse took a clean cotton nightshift from Mora's wardrobe to bandage the wounds the same way she'd done Kate's. Afterward, she stood and assessed her work. The makeshift bandaging should hold until Lenia could tend Jade.

Alyse frowned at Jade as an odd thought crept across her mind as if it had just emerged from a hidey-hole. She had bound Kate's wounds and now Jade's. But listening to the soul-ripping cries of the wounded made her feel that wrapping bandages around their wounds was inadequate. She wished she could *heal* them. Really make them whole again. But that required magic, and she wanted nothing to do with magic.

Mora's wailing shattered her thoughts.

Alyse knelt beside her sister. "Mora," she said, touching her shoulder. "It's all over."

"Jade's dead!"

"Jade's alive." Alyse stood and held out her hand. "Come on. We have wounded backwatchers and protectors who need help."

Mora batted the hand aside. "Get away from me!"

Alyse hesitated, wondering what Siema would do. She'd take charge. Turning her back on Mora, Alyse strode out of the room and found the head steward. "Lothar, how many of our people have been killed and wounded?"

"Eleven killed, Lady. And twenty-one wounded."

Alyse was staggered by the figures but kept her dismay under wraps. "And the raiders?"

"Twenty-three. All dead." He paused, a mystified expression on his face. "They killed their wounded who couldn't escape with them. I saw it myself. One of them was running by one—a woman—near the rear garden. She said, 'Remember our pact. Kill me.' He finished her off, then continued running."

Alyse gulped down foul-tasting bile that had gushed into her mouth as if from a fountain. She threw back her shoulders. I'm a Dejune. "Lothar, send messengers to the Estatis, the Bernes, and the Spicers. Tell them what's happened, and ask them to send their healers here right away."

"Yes, Lady."

She touched his arm as he turned away. "And send someone to fetch Priestess Sybil as well. We can use her help."

"Not her," Lothar said. "Your grandmother won't allow it."

Alyse put her hands on her hips. "I was put in charge here. Do as I say!"

"With all due respect, Lady Alyse, not in this case. I know Ladies Maude and Pilar will support me in this."

Alyse ground her teeth in frustration. "Then go."

After Lothar departed, Alyse ordered all the wounded to be taken into the family area and for mattresses to be brought for them to lie on, turning the hall into a temporary house of healing. She also had the corpses carried to the rear courtyard and separated by retainer and raider. Finally, she visited the injured, speaking to each person by name and examining their wounds to identify the more serious cases, which she would have the healers tend to first. Alyse was just finishing up with the last retainer when her mother stopped beside her.

"How's Great-Grandfather?" Alyse asked, rising to her feet.

"Not good, but Lenia is doing what she can."

"We should send for Priestess Sybil."

Pilar's nostrils flared. "I'll *not* have that woman in this house." She gestured at the wounded retainers. "Tell me what you've done so far."

Alyse told her.

"You've conducted yourself well." Pilar glanced around as if she'd noticed something for the first time. "Why isn't Mora here?"

"She's upset because Jade was seriously wounded."

Pilar squeezed her lips together in disapproval. Turning, she crossed the family area with long strides. Alyse hurried to catch up. Pilar knelt beside Jade and examined her wounds. "Who bandaged her?"

"I did," Alyse said.

"What about Kate?"

"She's wounded too. I bandaged her up as well."

Pilar smiled her approval, sending ripples of pride through Alyse. "Good work." Kneeling next to Mora, Pilar touched her shoulder. "Mora, the fighting's over. Everything will be all right."

"But Jade—"

"Will recover."

Mora sniffed and looked at Pilar through puffy, tear-filled eyes. "It . . . it was horrible."

"For all of us." Pilar helped Mora to her feet. "Now, be strong like your sister. She didn't sit in a corner weeping when Kate was wounded. She made herself useful. You must do the same."

Mora lobbed a fierce glare at Alyse that Pilar didn't notice. But Alyse did, and she knew Mora would hold the comparison against her.

# # #

Maude stepped into her new role as family matriarch immediately, establishing order from chaos. She instructed Pilar to set things straight in the rear courtyard and Mora to clean up the front courtyard. Alyse's cheeks warmed with pleasure when Maude complimented her for the initiative she'd shown in separating the dead retainers from the wounded ones and for turning the family area into a temporary house of healing. She told Alyse to continue tending the wounded. Alyse was thankful for the task because it kept her mind off the unexpected and horrifying way she'd used magic.

Some of the retainers began lugging the raiders' corpses from the house into the rear courtyard but Grandmother Maude raced up to them and ordered them to leave the bodies where they were. She told Lothar to give Mora the same message in the rear courtyard and Pilar in the front courtyard. "And also tell Lady Pilar to see me *immediately*," she added.

Then Maude began searching the raiders like a crazed woman, not caring about staining her hands and dress with their blood. Alyse watched her with mystified eyes, wanting to ask her why she was doing that but knowing she'd earn a sharp rebuke in return.

Alyse had hardly returned her attention to her patient when she heard rapid steps approaching from the rear courtyard.

"What's wrong?" Pilar asked.

Maude drew Pilar close and spoke rapid words in a tone so low Alyse couldn't hear.

Pilar's mouth dropped open with a stunned look on her face. "No!"

"Search the front courtyard!" Maude said, her tone near panic.

Pilar raced toward the receiving hall as Maude resumed her frenzied search of the dead raiders' clothes.

Alyse resumed replacing a blood-drenched bandage on her patient, her mind half on her task and the other half on Maude and Pilar's odd behavior. Her hands stopped as if paralyzed, the long strip of cloth at one-and-a-half wraps around the man's chest, and realization pierced her brain. Great-Grandmother's Peer charm! The raiders stole it. The Estatis would be furious when they find out. She hoped she wasn't there when they did.

Before long, a grim-faced Deuth Estati arrived with the Estati healer and a small group of protectors. Troy and Livia accompanied him as well. Alyse went to greet them.

"Where's my grandfather?" Deuth demanded.

Alyse directed him to Leoc's bedroom. Deuth and the healer

headed there, but Troy hung back, obviously wanting to speak with her. Livia stayed too, as if she didn't want to visit her grandfather without her brother beside her.

"I've been meaning to see you," Troy said.

Why does he have to come now in the middle of all this? "Troy, I'm sorry, but I'm busy," Alyse said, unable to keep the annoyance from her voice. She waved a hand at the wounded backwatchers and protectors on mattresses scattered throughout the floor. "I have to tend these people before they die from their wounds."

"We have to talk about our marriage. You've avoided me every time I've tried to meet with you."

Anger burned inside Alyse's stomach like a blazing fire. She scraped him with her eyes, not caring if Livia was privy to the scene. "You threatened my family if I didn't agree to the marriage."

"I meant that as a motivator."

"I don't love you, Troy, and even if I did, a threat isn't a motivator. You're just like your Uncle Deuth. Throwing your weight around because you've got so much power and prestige." She pushed her face closer to his. "And you know what? It told me our marriage would be just like your Uncle Deuth's and Adele Svagga's. That's not what I want."

Troy's laugh matched his arrogant expression. "You don't have a choice. Unless you want to be expelled."

Alyse pulled herself to her full height and locked eyes with him. "I'd rather expulsion than marriage."

"You're not serious."

Livia jabbed Troy's shoulder. "Leave it, little brother. She needs to work, and we need to see Great-Grandfather Locien."

Troy turned abruptly and left with Livia, his back stiff with fury.

Frustration bubbled in Alyse's chest as she returned to work—and flinched at an angry shout from Uncle Leoc's bedroom.

"Stay out!"

Deuth stood in the doorway blocking Troy and Livia.

"I want to see Great-Grandfather," Livia said.

Deuth thrust a finger in her chest as if it were a spear. "He loathes the sight of you." Deuth reached for Troy. "Only you," and then drew Troy into the bedroom.

Turning, Livia stumbled toward Alyse. In spite of her dislike for her, agony blossomed in Alyse's heart. "Livia, I'm so sorry."

"Oh, that's all right," Livia said with feigned nonchalance. "Great-Grandfather's always hated me. They all do, you know. Except for Troy and my mother. Everyone told me not to come. But I thought, well . . . now that he's on the edge of death, maybe he'd relent and make amends. But I guess he's not afraid of facing the Three Judges."

Impulsively, Alyse hugged her.

Livia returned the embrace, then pulled back and stroked Alyse's arm. "But what about you? What you went through must have been horrific. Are you all right?"

"I am. But . . ." Alyse paused, her suddenly tight throat making speech difficult. "Kate was seriously wounded."

Livia brushed a wayward strand of chestnut hair from Alyse's cheek and tucked it behind her ear. "I'm so sorry—"

"Aleena . . . Aleena . . ." The pitiful voice of a protector in blood-stained livery and lying on a pallet cried above the whimpers and groans of the wounded.

Livia turned to Alyse, distress swirling on her face. "What?"

"He's dying. And he's calling out to his sister."

"There's no one to comfort that poor man in his last moments?"

The protector's heart-wrenching call had affected Alyse too, making her feel guilty about leaving retainers, some whom she'd known all her life, to die alone. She swallowed a sob that welled up in her throat. "We have no more healers. Ours and yours are with Great-Grandfather Locien. So we have to see to the living and not the dying."

Livia's expression hardened. "What's his name?"

"Aleen."

Livia crossed to the pallet, knelt, and took Aleen's hand in both of hers. "Aleen, I'm here."

Joy lit Aleen's face like a glowing sun. He expelled a breath, and then his hand went limp.

Livia crossed his hands over his chest, closed his eyes with her fingertips, and stood. She gazed down at him for a long time. Then, pivoting on her heel, she approached Alyse with quick purposeful steps. "How can I help?"

The surprise of Livia's request, along with her abrupt change in demeanor, paralyzed Alyse's vocal cords. Livia, who always seemed so intent on shocking everyone with her scandalous behavior, was acting *so* out of character. "Why, you can do what you just did. Comfort the ones who are dying. And give hope to those who will live."

From time to time, Alyse glanced from her work to check on Livia. What she saw made amazement spin through her mind as if this Livia were a totally different girl from the one she'd known. To each patient, Livia demonstrated both compassion and cheerfulness. She tenderly eased the last moments of the dying and even wrote a short farewell letter for a backwatcher who dictated to her and promised to hand deliver it to his mother. Livia bantered and joked with the wounded as if they were longtime friends and actually had one of them laughing so boisterously that Alyse had to ask her to move on to someone else because she feared the patient's wound might burst open. Whatever the reason for the transformation, Alyse hoped it lasted because this Livia was one Alyse could be friends with.

Finally, the Berne and Spicer healers arrived and began treating the wounded. The sight of them working snapped the tension that had been stretching Alyse's nerves taut for so long. Alyse wanted to wilt into a chair and let relief flow into every nook and cranny of her body. Instead, she continued caring for her own patients.

Around midmorning, while Alyse was changing the dressing on a badly wounded protector, Lothar informed her that Maude required her presence in the rear courtyard.

The sky was gloomy, like her thoughts, and the air cool. Thick, jagged pieces of oak and metal—the remnants of the rear gate—were scattered over the granite paving stones.

Alyse's heart missed a beat at the line of bloody raiders' corpses stretched out side by side on the paving stones, their heads touching the first row of thick granite blocks that formed the outer defensive wall.

The family's allies were clustered nearby, talking in low tones. Deuth and Troy Estati. Degas Spicer. Jukka Berne and his son, Alger, who was married to Deuth's sister, Shalira. Like an outcast, Livia stood apart, ignored by everyone. Indignation at the way the adults had ostracized Livia boiled in Alyse's belly. And after the way Livia helped our wounded retainers. Alyse deliberately planted herself beside Livia and exchanged smiles with her.

Mora, her face pale, stood beside Pilar and Maude by the corpses.

Maude motioned for Alyse to join them. "You girls will become adults next week," she said. "But last night's attack requires you to assume those roles earlier. So I'm including you in our consultations." Turning to her allies, Maude waved a hand at the bodies. "Do you recognize any of them?"

"Look closely, Livia," Deuth said. "The way you throw yourself at everyone—men and women alike—regardless of their status, you're bound to know some of them."

Livia's face flushed, whether from anger or embarrassment, Alyse couldn't tell. But Livia joined Pilar and the men as they went from one corpse to the next studying their pallid faces.

Maude glared at Mora who remained in place. "You too."

For a moment, Mora hesitated. Then her green eyes turned hard as emeralds, and wordlessly she went from body to body. A couple of times she scooched down, took a pale chin between her fingers, and twisted the head to get a closer look. Alyse wondered why. Not one of the corpses was familiar.

"Well?" Maude said after everyone had finished.

"I know that one," Deuth said, prodding a man's leg with the toe of his highly polished black boot. "His name was Darg. He was a minor mage in our household." Deuth leveled a reproving look at Livia, who returned it defiantly. "But he proved to be . . . unreliable. So we withdrew our patronage last year."

Maude summoned protectors to remove the corpses. "Burn them like trash and scatter their ashes to the wind, so they'll wander for all time between Elustra and Shelar and never find rest."

She led everyone out of hearing range of the on- and off-duty protectors and the ones disposing of the bodies.

"What charms were the dead mages wearing?" Deuth asked.

"Nothing important," Maude replied. "Just low-level warrior ones. They'll add nothing of value to our inventory."

"Perhaps whoever sent them thought the attempt might fail," Degas said. "So instead of putting their most powerful charms at risk, they sent these mages with low-level ones."

"Or maybe they thought those charms suited the task," Deuth said.

"We need more than speculation." Maude ran her upper teeth back and forth across her lower lip as if she were working up the nerve to do something. "I'm summoning a matriarch's council. The men are to attend as well. So are my granddaughters. Livia and Troy are excluded."

Alyse and Mora followed the adults into the matriarch's chamber. A fire was already blazing in the hearth, and the oil lamps were burning, creating an area of light surrounded by shadow. The semicircle of four straight-back chairs were in front of the dais for the women. Alyse was keenly aware of the empty one beside Pilar, which had been Grandmother Maude's. Now Alyse watched Maude climb the dais steps as if she were carrying a heavy burden on her back and settle herself in the black oak matriarch's chair. The men stood near the crackling fireplace.

Maude wet her lips and glanced uneasily around the room, her gaze quickly sweeping over the men by the hearth as if she were preparing herself for something unpleasant. "They stole the . . . Peer charm."

Triumph felt bitter in Alyse's mouth. She had been right.

"Good Goddess in Elustra!" Degas said. His brown eyebrows jumped, then dove into a scowl. "And Locien's charm?"

"It's safe," Maude answered. "He always hides it at night, and the raiders fled before they could find it."

"Thank the One Goddess," Deuth said. Then he looked at her in puzzlement. "Are you telling us the raiders actually made it to your charm vault, canceled the wards, and broke in? Because if you are, I saw no indication of it."

Maude's Adam's apple bobbed as she swallowed. "It wasn't in the charm vault. Siema was . . . wearing it."

Deuth stepped backward in shock, stumbling against the hearth extension. "*Wearing* it! My grandfather never told me she was doing that."

"Perhaps he thought it was none of your business."

Deuth's blue eyes boiled with anger. "It *is* my business. That charm's been in my family since The Founding. Your family had its own Peer charm once. But seven generations ago you let a Gaetanian thief—"

"Don't you lecture me!" Maude shot to her feet. "I know both charms' histories just as well as you."

"Yes," Deuth said, marching up to the dais steps and glaring at Maude, his arms stretched at his sides like poles and his hands balled into fists. "And ever since then, generation after generation, your matriarchs have hounded ours to include our second Peer charm in the wedding contracts. We finally gave in when my grandfather married Siema—and suddenly the charm's stolen."

"Not 'suddenly.' Siema's been wearing it ever since their wedding night. For over sixty years."

"I don't care how many damned years she was wearing it. The charm was stolen. Because Siema didn't value it enough to keep it in your charm vault." Deuth paused to take a breath. "What in Goddess's name ever possessed Siema to wear it? She wasn't a mage."

"She thought the charm would be safer on her than in the vault."

"We should never have given you the charm."

Alyse tensed as she sat in the chair. "Our status as a First Family is declining." Great-Grandmother Siema's words echoing in Alyse's mind caused a shroud of impending doom to smother her, making it difficult to breathe. The secret's out. Now the Estatis will break their alliance with us for losing the charm. Then the shroud blew away like clouds scattering in different directions, making her muscles relax. If they break our alliance, I won't have to marry Troy.

"Oh, please, please," Alger Berne said. "We can fling recriminations at one another till the sun goes down. But let's not. What we have to do is find out who's behind the raid."

"Alger's right." Jukka went up to Deuth and drew him away. "Quarreling won't accomplish anything."

Deuth ran his fingers through his wavy cinnamon-colored hair. "You're right. What's done is done. Our families have been allies for far too long to let this matter, serious as it is, come between us."

His words brought gloom back to Alyse.

"I agree," Maude said, a hint of relief on her face. "So now what?"

"Obviously," Deuth said, "we have to find out who's behind the raid."

"Won't we learn that when whoever stole the Peer charm begins to use it?" Alger asked.

"That might not happen for years," Pilar said. "We need to know now."

"That's right," Maude said. "But finding out is going to prove difficult. Except for Darg, those corpses are all nameless faces."

"What was in their belt purses?" Deuth asked.

"Nothing that could identify them," Maude replied.

"There's more," Alyse piped up, amazed by her own audacity as everyone's eyes turned to her. "Lothar said the raiders killed their wounded before they fled."

The adults gasped in unison.

Degas shook his head in disbelief. "Goddess in Elustra! A death pact. I can't think of a single protector who would agree to one, no matter what Family she served. Those people must be fanatics."

Alyse tried to imagine Kate doing what the raiders had done. Kate would give her life to save Alyse from an attack. But Kate was a backwatcher. They didn't get involved in charm raids. Only protectors did. Would Freya or Geoff agree to a death pact if they went on a charm raid? Mentally, she shook her head. That would take their oath of fealty too far.

Jukka put a fresh log on the flames in the fireplace. "They served someone. The question is, who?"

"Not a family in Caldon," Degas said.

"Maybe a client state," Deuth said. "We still allow their ruling classes to have a limited number of charms and mages so they can manage their people."

Degas flicked the words away with a snap of his fingers. "They're even less likely to have retainers *that* devoted."

Deuth swore under his breath. "They served *someone*."

"Rohans?" Mora said.

Everyone looked at her as if she were insane.

"I mean, why not?"

"Because their only loyalty is to themselves," Pilar told her.

Maude banged her hand on the arm of the matriarch's chair, making Alyse jump. "Enough talk. We need an action plan. I propose that each of our families put word out on the street that we're looking for information about the attackers. And that there will be a huge reward for anyone who gives us a tip that leads us to whoever was behind it."

Everyone murmured their assent.

Alyse didn't consider Maude's suggestion much of an action plan. After all, the likelihood seemed to be that the raiders had come from outside Caldon. *Maybe they're Gaetanians.*

"There's something I want everyone to witness." Maude raised her voice. "Lothar, bring in the oath breakers."

The door opened, and the head steward entered.

Freezing cold roiled in Alyse's stomach and spread throughout her body to the tips of her hands and feet. Oath breakers? What's she talking about?

Freya, Geoff, and Palquo walked behind Lothar. All three were unarmed, the mage without his staff and the protectors without their swords. Palquo's face was pale, but Freya's and Geoff's wore angry expressions. Behind them marched five armed protectors.

Skirting the four chairs, Lothar conducted the three protectors to the dais, while their escort stopped a short distance away. "Lady Maude," Lothar said, "I've brought you the oath breakers."

Alyse's brain spun in confusion a the sight of the three protectors. Then it came to a jerking halt when she recalled Kate's words after Freya and Geoff had left her bedroom. "It's going to go hard on them." She stirred restlessly in her chair. This was insane.

"You three were in the rear courtyard on guard duty with the others when the attack occurred." Maude spoke the words as an accusation, not a question.

Palquo's body trembled and his hands shook. "Yes, Lady."

"Correction," Freya said, folding her arms across her chest. "We're the only ones on guard duty who *survived* the attack."

Geoff nodded emphatically. "And we fought just as hard as the others to protect your family. We upheld our oaths, just as those who died upheld theirs."

"You broke your oaths," Maude said. "You swore to protect my family. Yet you failed to stop the attack or to warn us in time to prevent the raiders from entering our house."

"They were protected by a Concealment spell," Palquo said, rushing his words together. "We didn't know they were at the gate till they destroyed it."

Maude rose from her chair, her body stiff with anger. "You're a mage. You should have detected the spell."

Palquo shrank under her stare. "Please, Lady. The spell was a higher level than my charm. Years ago, when I asked for a higher-level one, you told me I had to settle for this one."

The charm vault! The matriarch's chamber seemed to spin round and round in Alyse's mind, throwing her off-balance. We couldn't give Palquo a higher-level charm because they're locked in our charm vault, which no one can access. She peered keenly at Maude as the room settled and knew Maude couldn't say anything that might reveal the family secret. Grandmother Maude was setting an example to protect the secret. Alyse fought the urge to scream at her grandmother and demand that she not use the three loyal protectors as pieces in a game of strategy. Instead, she stared at them, wanting to share their suffering.

"You failed to keep your oaths," Maude said.

"No!" Freya dropped her arms to her sides and balled her hands into fists. "We broke no oath. We gave you our loyalty, just as the others on guard duty did."

"There were seven of us on duty at the back wall when the attack began," Geoff said bitterly. "But we had the misfortune of surviving. You're holding that against us out of spite."

"Not one of you three has a single wound," Maude said.

"Is it our misfortune that we were the better fighters?" Freya asked, head lifted and gray eyes spitting defiance.

Alyse's heart beat against her rib cage like a savage beast wanting to burst free. She bounded out of her chair. "No!" Pilar reached for her wrist to pull her back down, but Alyse batted her hand away. "Freya and Geoff fought along with everyone else. They came to my bedroom during the fighting. To check that I was all right. Then they joined in the fighting again. They're *loyal*."

Jumping to her feet, Pilar clutched Alyse's shoulders and forced her down on her seat.

"Enough!" Maude said, slicing her hand through the air. "You broke your oaths to my family. So we withdraw our patronage from you."

Palquo dropped to his knees and stretched his arms. "Please, Lady. I've served you faithfully for over fifteen years."

Two of the escorts hauled him back up.

Stepping down from the dais, Maude ripped the charm off from around Palquo's neck and shook it angrily in front of his face. "The Dejunes lent you this charm because you swore an oath to protect us. Now we take back our charm."

"Show mercy to me. Don't make me a rohan."

Alyse tried to stand again to protest, but Pilar hauled her back down. She watched, horror welling like a rising sea, as Maude formally expelled Freya, Geoff, and Palquo. Maude ended the expulsion by saying, "Go patronless forever and never return to our family again."

After the protectors had escorted the three out, Maude motioned for Alyse to stand. Alyse could tell that her grandmother was so furious that she was going to rebuke her in front of their allies. Arms as her side, she clenched her fists, determined to stand like a deeply rooted tree against the fierce wind of Maude's fury.

"Don't you *ever* oppose me in front of our retainers again," Maude said, her tone seething. "Do you understand?"

"Yes, Grandmother."

"If you—" An insistent rap on the door interrupted Maude, and she hurled an irritated glance at the closed door. "Enter."

Lothar burst in and rushed to the dais steps, his face drained of color. "Lord Locien. He's . . . dead."

## CHAPTER 17

The Euloghe

HER NERVES STRETCHED PAINFULLY tight, Alyse hurried along the gray, traffic-worn cobblestones of River Road, which ran from the Public Square to River Gate and then toward the docks, mariners' shops, taverns, and brothels by the water. She pulled the hood on the coarse woolen cloak she wore, when visiting The Kings, farther over her head. Not as protection from the cold—the early Awakening season sun was exceptionally warm this morning—but as protection from being recognized. True, chances of anyone she knew seeing her were slim, but she couldn't take any chances.

The cries of butchers, wine merchants, street food sellers, and other shopkeepers peppered her ears from all directions as she hurried past wooden tenements, shops, and corner shrines on either side. She excused herself as she elbowed past the men and women who were shopping and chatting on the gray-brick sidewalks and the kids who were playing in the road. She wrinkled her nose at the stench from garbage piled in alleyways and from dog poop and horse droppings littering the road. Oak Hill rose up on her left and Weavers' Hill on her right. Not long now before she took the right-hand street into The Kings.

Alyse's stomach churned sickeningly at the thought of how, in the past eight days that made up a Caldonian week, her world had turned upside down, dumping her upon the shore of a frightening, unknown realm. The unaccustomed weight of the long-bladed dagger sheathed on her hip and the pressure of the shorter knife strapped to her thigh, under her rough woolen dress, felt strange. So did venturing outside the compound by herself—let alone into The Kings—for the first time in her life, behind her mother's back and without a backwatcher. Alyse thanked the One Goddess, as she had every day since the attack, that Kate's wounds were healing nicely. She wished Kate were with her now. Yet it would be several more weeks before Kate could resume her backwatching duties, so Alyse had to go by herself. She didn't trust anyone else to escort her to the One Goddess Temple on this particular mission.

When she reached the familiar road into The Kings, Alyse started down the weblike network of streets that would take her to the only person who could help navigate her to safety.

Eight days lost. And all the while she had been champing at the bit, like a racehorse impatient for the starter's call, to gallop at breakneck speed to Chief Priestess Sybil Raine.

During the first six days, Alyse couldn't think of a legitimate excuse to leave home while Great-Grandmother Siema's embalmed body had lain in state in the receiving hall for all the women from the extensive Dejune clan and from their allied families to view. On the sixth evening, Alyse had witnessed Siema's cremation on the funeral pyre. The next morning, she had helped Maude, Pilar, and Mora gather Siema's ashes, then watched Maude enter the family mausoleum on Street of Tombs to place the urn alongside the ones containing the ashes of previous Dejune matriarchs. Yesterday, the eighth day, Alyse had attended the lavish public funeral the Estatis had celebrated in the Public Square for Great-Grandfather Locien. Today the Estatis were gathering Locien's ashes to place in an urn beside the other Estati chief magestrates' urns in their family's sepulcher. Alyse thanked the One Goddess she didn't have to attend because that would have meant a ninth day lost.

Alyse broke into a quickstep when she spied the white marble-faced edifice of the One Goddess Temple looming up, like a haven from her troubles, at the end of the final block. She half ran across the large courtyard—brushing by devotees and ignoring vendors behind stalls asking her to buy cooing white doves from cages, votive candles, and relics—took the six marble steps up to the porch, two at a time, hurried through the open pair of oak doors, and ran into the outer sanctum. Her hastiness earned her a disapproving glare from a woman in a red long-sleeved dress with a blue-scalloped neckline and matching blue sash. A priestess. Her sharp words, "Alyse Dejune, show some respect!" made Alyse slow down a bit. Alyse hastened along the left wall of the outer sanctum and went through the door to the wide passageway that connected the temple to the House of Healing. Priestess Sybil's office was halfway down the hall, just before the library.

Alyse found Sybil working at her desk in her book-lined office. A small statue of the One Goddess in her red dress with yellow-scalloped neckline and yellow sash knotted around her waist stared at Alyse from a niche behind Sybil.

Sybil glanced up in surprise from the parchment she'd been writing on. "Alyse." She set aside the quill pen, moved from around the desk, and hugged Alyse.

Affection for this tall, heavyset woman, dressed just like the statue, diffused through Alyse.

"I'm sorry about your great-grandparents," Sybil said. "And about so many others." Sybil put a hand on Alyse's arm. "I also heard that Kate was wounded. Is it serious?"

Alyse pulled away. "Yes. But she's recovering."

Sybil went to the door and scanned the passageway. "You came without a backwatcher?" At Alyse's nod, Sybil continued. "You shouldn't have done that, especially after what just happened."

"I didn't have any choice," Alyse said. "I had to see you without my family knowing." Nausea churned in her stomach and dread froze her vocal chords. She stood facing Sybil, her heart beating rapidly.

Sybil's silver eyes filled with concern. "Something horrible has happened." She positioned two chairs to face each other, eased Alyse into one of them, and then sat down opposite her. Leaning forward, she took Alyse's hand in one of hers and covered it with the other. "Whatever it is, I'm here to listen and help."

Alyse pulled in a shuddering breath. "I . . . I killed someone. During the attack. He was going to kill Kate."

"It's a terrible thing to kill someone. But under the circumstances—"

"Using Kinesi magic."

Sybil's eyes bulged, and her hands convulsed, sending a stab of pain through Alyse's fingers and wrist. She released Alyse's hand and sat back. "How . . . how did you learn that kind of magic?"

Haltingly, Alyse explained how she had discovered the talking tubes and listened to one that described how to access Kinesi magic and how she had moved the box. "I kept accessing the magic to move the box. I thought doing it was fun, even if I was using magic." She recounted the attack and how she'd killed the bladesman named Yon to save Kate's life. "And I used the magic without a charm or staff," she concluded, the words almost sticking to her mouth. "I didn't even cast a spell. It just . . . happened."

Sybil looked as if Alyse had punched her between the eyes.

Alyse wanted to flee from the room and keep running until she stumbled to the ground from exhaustion. "Say something—*please!*"

"This is very, very serious," Sybil told her.

"You're frightening me."

"You should be frightened because some people will perceive you as a threat to the state."

"How can I threaten the state? I'm just a sixteen-year-old girl."

"It's the Kinesi magic. Only a euloghe can access it."

Alyse tilted her head, mystified. "What's a euloghe?"

"Someone who has the magical powers of the Old Ones—the early Eulorian mages. Before they began using charms and staffs."

"The scrolls and books I've read haven't mentioned them."

"That's because little was written about them." Sybil adjusted her position on the chair. "In fact, most people have forgotten euloghi ever existed. A few do remember though. Mostly among the First

Families. But they keep the knowledge to themselves."

"Then how do you know about them?"

"Because the knowledge has also been passed down to certain One Goddess priestesses through the generations. They're called Memory Keepers."

"And you're a Memory Keeper?"

Sybil nodded.

Confused thoughts spun around in Alyse's head like a child's top. Her dark-brown eyebrows plunged into a frown. "But . . . why am I a threat? I'd think the noblesse would give their eye teeth to find someone who had the Old Ones' powers."

"It's not quite that simple." Sybil fingered her braided bun of gray hair while she gathered her thoughts. "In the early days of Euloria, before the wars with Atland, only a few Eulorians could access the magic plane and cast spells. They didn't need charms or staffs to work their magic either. Often their ability was passed down within families, from one generation to the next. Then the wars began. Euloria was a little country, with few legions and few mages. Atland was a large country with numerous legions but far fewer mages than Euloria."

"Like Caldon and Gaetan," Alyse said.

Sybil nodded. "In the first war, the Atlanders almost defeated the Eulorians. Only the mages' spells prevented that from happening. But the Eulorians lost many soldiers and most of their mages in the conflict. If a second war broke out, they knew they'd be defeated."

"What does all this have to do with me?" Alyse asked anxiously.

Sybil tapped Alyse's wrist. "Patience. I'm coming to that. To defend themselves in a second war, the Eulorians needed more mages. They knew that some Eulorians had the potential to access the magic plane but not the ability. They also knew that some people had an aptitude for one type of magic over the other types. So the Eulorians created the charms and staffs and devised a way for the charms to access the magic plane. Each charm used the power of a single char and held specific spells whose levels varied depending the charm's power. The spells were channeled through the staffs. Like using a longbow to shoot arrows."

"And the Naming charm?" Alyse asked.

"Its purpose is to identify the char that its wearer has the greatest ability to control."

"But archmages can access all the chars," Alyse said. "And some, like Cato Porta, don't need staffs to cast spells. They can use their fingers, like . . ."

"You?"

Dread sent chills crashing through Alyse's body like heaving ocean waves. *Is she saying I'm a euloghe? Goddess, I hope not.* "Y-yes."

"That's because archmages come close to being euloghi. But they're not."

"Why?" Alyse asked, petrified at hearing the answer.

"Because they can't access Kinesi magic." Sybil lowered her voice as if fearful someone might be listening on the other side of the closed door. "Only a euloghe can do that. Unfortunately, when you kept performing the Kinesi exercise and moving the box, you kept strengthening your Kinesi power."

Alyse pounded her chest with a fist. "Why me, of all people?"

"Because Ulbra Thane's blood runs through your veins. She was one of the most powerful mages who ever lived. She had an illegitimate daughter with Meurdar Dejune, don't forget. And Meurdar was a powerful mage too. You inherited their powers."

"I don't want their powers." Alyse's gaze shifted to the door, and the urge gripped her to run off, but dread nailed her to the chair.

"The First and Lesser Families control access to the charms and staffs," Sybil went on relentlessly ignoring Alyse's horrified reaction. "By controlling that access, they control the state. *You* threaten that control because you don't need a charm or staff to cast spells. But the noblesse have a problem."

"W-what's that?" Alyse forced the question, horrified and curious at the same time.

"Most of the rules and theories of magic died with the Old Ones," Sybil replied. "The noblesse don't have that knowledge. They know how to make magic work but don't understand why it works. The euloghi have the potential to discover that knowledge."

"By having a Memory Keeper teach them."

Sybil ignored Alyse's comment. "That's why the euloghi threaten the families' dominance. Because they can work all eight types of magic without charms and staffs." Sybil paused. "And whenever a euloghe is discovered, usually at the Name Day Celebration, she's killed."

Terror wrapped itself around Alyse like the thick coils of a python. She sprang up, knocking the chair backward. "I'll never do the char exercise again. They'll never know."

Sybil stood to face Alyse, her expression bleak. "It's too late for that."

"Why?"

"Because you've awoken your euloghe power. Now either you learn to control it, or it will control you."

Alyse's hand went to her mouth, stifling a gasp of horror. *I want to have nothing to do with magic. And now I'm caught up in it. Goddess help me.*

"And because the Naming charm will identify you as a euloghe," Sybil continued relentlessly, her silver eyes staring at Alyse. "The charm has eight points. One for each char. Seven, all but the top one, light up for a potential archmage. But all eight light up for a euloghe. When that happens, the Name Master declares the celebrant an archmage. Shortly afterward, she has a fatal accident. Often during fledgling training. And her death allows the noblesse to maintain control of their magical powers."

"I'll run away," Alyse said.

"You'll do no such thing," Sybil retorted.

"I have no other choice."

"You do."

"What's that?"

"You can let me teach you how to block all but one of your chars when the Naming charm accesses them."

Alyse shot her an incredulous look. "Are you serious?"

"Totally."

"Why not teach me how to block them all? Then I'll be named a nonmage."

"That's impossible. The charm will sense your power. The Name Master will realize what you're doing, and that you're a euloghe."

Alyse's breath came in short gasps. Sybil waited for Alyse to get her breathing under control.

"You know the eight forms of magic," Sybil said. "Mind Bending. Illusion. Shape-Shifting. Healing. Warrior. Natural. Transmutation. And Kinesi. You choose which one you want left open."

Alyse creased her brow in thought. All magic was offensive and could be used in combat, which repelled her. Except for one. She recalled her satisfaction helping the wounded family retainers after the charm raid. She'd wished she could heal them instead of just bandaging their wounds. But true healing required magic. Now her life depended on learning one form of magic. And what better type than Healing? She smiled at Sybil, her mind at peace with her decision.

"Healing magic," she said. "I want to be a healer."

"That's the heart char. The charm will name you a healer on Name Day." The corners of Sybil's mouth dropped into a frown. "There is one problem though."

Alyse's insides quivered. Just when a solution was offered, it was suddenly whisked away. "What's that?" she asked, and held her breath, fearful of the response.

"You're going to marry Troy. But custom forbids that you not marry for as long as you're training to be a healer."

Alyse wanted to dance and sing praises to Priestess Sybil for devising a plan for saving her from being named a euloghe. And as a healer, she also could make a difference in people's lives. She hid a secret grin. After training, she and Kate could escape to Uncle Leoc's camp in The Marches. She would be able to repay him by healing his sick and wounded legionaries.

"Oh," Alyse said, "I think I can handle that."

## CHAPTER 18

Strangers Meet

CARRYING TWO CANVAS BAGS, Rill entered Cobb the bowyer's shop. The store was on the ground floor of the tenement Sorah Euland owned. A counter near the back ran most of the width of the room, stopping at the door to Cobb's living quarters. Yew longbows of varying heights, draw weights, and lengths of pull were displayed on the wall behind the counter alongside shorter composite bows. Tubs full of arrows with different arrowheads—barbed, leaf-shaped, swallowtail, blunt—dotted the floor by the left wall, their white feathers sticking up like the blossoms of deadly long-stemmed flowers. Quivers, bow gloves, bracers, and other accessories hung from hooks along the right wall.

Rill greeted Cobb, who sat at his workbench by the windows on the left, shaping a length of yew into a longbow with a drawknife. Sunshine from the right-hand window highlighted a pile of trimmed white goose feathers on the workbench where Jedd sat attaching the feathers to a shaft with black fletching string. A stack of nocked and feathered shafts without points lay nearby.

Rill plunked the smaller bag on Jedd's workbench with a *clunk*. "Here's the curved broadheads you ordered."

"At last!" Jedd said. "Now I can finish making these arrows." He nodded toward Cobb. "He's been badgering me for them all week."

"'Bout time they arrived too," Cobb said but with a smile that showed he wasn't serious.

Jedd pointed at the larger sack slung over Rill's shoulder. "What's that?"

Rill jiggled the bag, which gave off metallic clangs. "Hinges for Priestess Sybil. She's replacing the ones on the temple door. My dad just finished forging them, and I hafta take them to her. Wanna come?"

Jedd fingered his bag of broadheads, then glanced inquiringly at Cobb.

"He won't be gone for long," Rill told Cobb. "Besides, my dad keeps me so busy in the smithy when I'm not in school that I hardly get a chance to see Jedd."

Jedd sent Cobb a pleading look.

Cobb smiled. "Off with the both of you."

Rill went with Jedd to the Eulands' apartment on the top floor so Jedd could fetch his dagger. Then they went out to the street and headed for the One Goddess Temple, weaving around Kings dwellers who were chitchatting on the gray brick sidewalks and in the cobblestone streets and avoiding laughing little kids darting around people's legs, playing.

"Are things any better with your folks?" Jedd asked, stepping aside for someone passing by on horseback.

"With Grandma Cinna and Aunt Tarri," Rill replied. "And my dad's gotta talk to me 'cause we work together in the smithy. But my mom . . . she still hardly speaks to me at all."

"She'll come around."

Rill kicked at a stone, sending it flying over the cobbles past a man's leg. "Ain't likely 'cause this morning Aunt Tarri found a package by the front door. The clothes Aunt Talia gave me for Name Day."

Jedd gave a low whistle. "That must of stirred up a thunderstorm with your folks."

Rill rolled his eyes skyward. "More like a volcanic eruption. With my mom, anyways. She insisted we throw the clothes away. But

Grandma Cinna put her foot down. Said I could wear them."

"That must of made Aunt Kendra furious."

"Sure did. She said not even the One Goddess would make her attend the Celebration. Dad said he won't go neither." Rill choked on a lump that burned hot in his throat. "And I was at the point where I thought he might."

Jedd touched his shoulder. "I'm sorry about that. But at least Grandma Cinna and Aunt Tarri are going. That's something."

"Yeah. Ain't it now." Sad memories of the past few days made Rill's shoulders slump. Jedd must have sensed his gloomy mood because he didn't try to continue their conversation.

They passed through a poor section of The Kings where shop awnings and taller tenements threw the narrow street and sidewalks into day-long shadows, and they wove around Kings dwellers chatting and laughing with one another until at last they reached the road that led to the temple. Up ahead, an island of white marble rose majestically out of a choppy sea of dilapidated tenements, shops, taverns, brothels, and corner shrines. Worshipers, many dressed in scruffy clothes, clustered in the temple courtyard buying white doves held in large cages, votive candles, and religious objects from vendors at wooden stalls. Men, women, and children mounted the six white marble steps, worn smooth by hundreds of years of worshipers' feet, to the temple porch and disappeared through the open double doors while others emerged and descended the stairs.

Partway along the road, Jedd touched Rill's arm. "I think we got trouble."

"What do ya mean?"

"You notice the people hanging around here?"

"No."

"Then take a look."

Rill glanced around. Cloaked women and men loitered silently on both sidewalks. Their hoods were pulled over their heads, concealing their faces. Rill slowed his pace to look while he switched the bag of hinges to his other shoulder. A vague, unsettling sense of foreboding pressed down him like a leaden weight. "They don't act like Kings dwellers."

Jedd nodded toward a side street. "More are coming out of there."

One of the newcomers adjusted the front of her cloak. The two sides parted just a bit—and revealed the knob of a club.

"Holy Sisters!" Rill said. "Did ya see that?"

"Yeah. She's got a weapon."

"They ain't Kings dwellers. That's for sure."

Rill and Jedd exchanged worried looks.

"I got a bad feeling about this," Jedd said.

"Me too. We gotta warn Priestess Sybil. Something terrible's about to happen."

Rill and Jedd quickened their pace. When they reached the edge of the temple courtyard, Rill cast a last look over his shoulder and spotted a teenage girl with long, black hair striding past the loiterers toward the temple.

The wind caused by her long, decisive steps made her dark-blue cloak flutter out behind her. She wore commoners' clothes—tunic, pants, and boots. But the sword and dagger buckled around her thin waist made him stop and stare. One of the idlers leered at her, then said something to his companions as she passed by, and they burst out laughing. Another gripped her arm.

Quicker than an eye blink, she spun toward him while she whipped her dagger straight up from its sheath. The pommel struck the man so hard under the chin that Rill heard the impact of metal against cracking bone. The man staggered backward. His companions guffawed. The black-haired girl continued toward the temple.

"Wow!" Jedd said. "I gotta learn that move."

Rill felt like saying the same thing. Instead, he said, "Let's go. We ain't got no time to waste."

They trotted across the courtyard and followed the worshipers up the temple steps. Men, women, and children of all ages filled the outer sanctuary. Some, holding doves they had purchased in the courtyard, waited their turn to enter the inner sanctum and approach the One Goddess. Others were in small memorial alcoves along both sides, lighting votive candles to honor their ancestors or to request a favor from the Divine Lady. Fragrant scents from the candles wafted through the air.

From the inner sanctuary came the melodious hymns priestesses were singing to the One Goddess, along with the cooing of doves and the flutter of wings as devotees released their birds into the air. The doves circled above the worshipers' heads before escaping through the windows high in the yellow walls. At the far end, the tall statue of the Divine Lady, resplendent in her long-sleeved red dress with its yellow-scalloped neckline and yellow sash, smiled beneficently down on Her children.

His heart galloping like a wild stallion, Rill hurried to Priestess Sybil's office. The door was invitingly open. But, to Rill's dismay, they found the office empty. Rill and Jedd exchanged anxious looks.

"We gotta find her," Rill said.

They double-timed it back to the outer sanctum.

"There's Jillina," Jedd said, pointing to a young woman near the entrance to the inner sanctum, who wore a novice's yellow long-sleeve dress with a red-scalloped neckline and matching red waist sash. "Let's ask her."

Before he could respond, Rill noticed the black-haired girl in the blue cloak entering the outer sanctum. She grimaced and put a hand on her side under the cloak.

Jedd plucked at Rill's sleeve. "Come on."

Jillina welcomed the cousins with a smile. "Rill and Jedd—"

"Novice Jillina," Rill said. "Where's Priestess Sybil?"

"In her office."

"She ain't there."

"I'm looking for Priestess Sybil too," the black-haired girl said, stopping beside them.

Jillina's face radiated surprise. "Kate, what are you doing up from bed? You shouldn't—"

"Please answer my question," Kate said. "It's important."

Jillina hesitated, then said, "Have you tried the inner sanctuary? Or the House of Healing?"

Kate muttered an unintelligible response and marched toward the inner sanctuary. Rill and Jedd scrambled after her. When they caught up beside her, she had almost reached Glenissa, an elderly, gray-haired priestess who was blessing a dove before the worshiper released it into the air. The trio stopped in front of her. Despite his urgency, Rill wavered about interrupting the priestess in the middle of a blessing. But Kate had no such problem.

"Priestess Glenissa, I must see Priestess Sybil immediately. It's *urgent*."

"Kate," Glenissa said, blinking in astonishment. "What are you doing up?"

"Forget about that. Please answer my question."

Glenissa made a *tsk-tsk* sound. "Is your task so urgent you must interrupt the One Goddess's blessing?"

"Yes." Kate's face crinkled with pain, but she recovered almost instantly.

Glenissa excused herself to the worshiper and took the three teens aside. "What's so serious that you had to interrupt me?"

"A mob's on their way here to attack the temple," Kate said.

Glenissa pulled a face at them. "You must be mistaken."

"She ain't," Rill told her. "Me and Jedd saw 'em too."

"You don't have much time," Kate said. "I'll warn Priestess Sybil, and you evacuate the temple."

"I can't evacuate the temple just on your say-so," Glenissa said. "You could be mistaken."

"She ain't," Rill said.

Glenissa bit the inside of her cheek. "Disrupting the temple like this. That's something only the chief priestess can do."

"She will," Kate said. "Just tell us where she is."

Glenissa's gaze walked pensively across the three serious faces. She set her jaw. "She's in the archives."

Glenissa left. But instead of returning to the devotee in the inner sanctuary, she strode toward the temple door.

"Where's the archives?" Rill muttered to Jedd, who shrugged.

Apparently Kate knew because she hurried toward the corridor leading to the House of Healing. Rill and Jedd followed her. She led them through the long, wide hallway, passing Sybil's office and the library, until they reached a narrow staircase that led below ground level. Oil lamps set in niches ran down the length of the right side of the stairs. Only the bottommost lamp was lit, its wavering, yellowish light revealing the beginning of a dark, narrow passageway. Kate rushed down the steps, taking two at a time. Partway down, she paused and put a hand to her side.

"Are you all right?" Jedd asked, touching her shoulder.

"Yes," Kate replied. When she reached the bottom step, she picked up the lamp and strode along the passageway to a closed door. She opened it and stepped inside.

Rill and Jedd piled in behind her.

Two silent, motionless figures sat across from each other at a table. An oil lamp was between them, its low flame barely illuminating their faces: Priestess Sybil and an attractive teenage girl with chestnut hair dressed in commoners' clothes. The tableau lasted less than a heartbeat.

Startled, Sybil rose from her chair. "Kate!"

Sybil's action made the chestnut girl blink as if she were disoriented at being plucked out of a trance. "Kate," she said, her face registering surprise. "What are you doing here? You should be in bed."

"And you should be at home, Alyse," Kate said, affection mixed with reproach. "And I've come to fetch you there. "

Alyse looked abashed. "How did you know I was here?"

"It was obvious. To me, anyway."

Alyse stood up. "I know Mother's going to be furious with me. But I had to come."

"Your mother's fury is the least of your worries right now," Kate said.

Sybil looked at Rill and Jedd. "What are you boys doing here—"

"There's a mob forming." Rill switched the bag of hinges onto his other shoulder. "On the way here we saw—"

"They formed on River Road," Kate said. "I passed them on my way here. I heard them talking. They're going to attack the temple. Some of them have already gathered in the street outside."

Anger swirled across Sybil's face.

Alyse turned to Sybil. "You should call for the City Watch—"

Sybil shook her head. "The city watchers can't help. They're only authorized to guard the city gates and the Public Square. Plus search for deserters from the legions and the sea service."

"We'll stay and help defend the temple," Jedd said.

"Yeah." Rill's stomach was all aflutter as images of him fighting valiantly against overwhelming odds whirled through his mind. *I'll be a hero.* He wished he'd brought his sword along.

Sybil's next actions mimicked those of a legion officer giving orders on the eve of a battle, a side of her Rill had never seen before. "Rill, go home and tell your dad what's happening. He'll call out the neighborhood watch. Jedd, you protect Rill. Alyse, go home with Kate." Sybil shooed all four out the door. "Hurry!"

Rill ran along the corridor and took the stairs two at a time up to the hallway, his heart racing as fast as his feet. The others nipped at his heels. He ran toward the inner sanctum. Kate came up beside him, matching his pace. Jedd, Alyse, and Priestess Sybil's rapid footfalls chased after theirs. As Rill approached the door to the outer sanctum, panicky cries erupted from the temple. By the time he'd passed through the doorway, a small group of cloaked intruders with clubs and swords were racing through the inner and outer sanctums. Shrieking, terrified worshipers were streaming out of the inner sanctum, and worshipers in the outer sanctum were piled up at the double doors struggling to push their way through the people ahead of them. From outside in the courtyard came screams and shouts and the splintering sounds of vendors' wooden stalls being smashed.

"It's too late," Sybil said. "They're already here."

A mob of women and men wielding clubs, swords, and daggers beat and sliced their way through the crush at the doorway. Crying in panic, the worshipers turned back and scattered throughout the temple. Some invaders chased them, batting and slashing at them. Others dashed into the alcoves and overturned votive tables. Silver and brass candleholders fell to the ground. Votive candles were knocked free, and rioters stomped on them.

Nearby, a brawler slammed a club against an old man's head, smashing his skull.

"Bastard," Kate muttered, and drew her sword.

The rioter's eyes snapped to her weapon, and he ran off to find easier prey.

Jedd unsheathed his dagger.

A club-wielding attacker knocked a woman to the ground.

Jedd charged the man, who swung at him. Jedd ducked under the club and stabbed him in the belly.

Kate regarded him with sudden respect when he returned with the club. Then she tripped a man who was chasing a child and ran her sword into his chest. "Where'd you learn that?"

Jedd blocked a man's sword with his club. The blade bit into the wood. Jedd kicked him in the groin. The man doubled over. "From my uncle," Jedd said, pulling the sword from the wood and then whacking man on the head with the club. "He was one of the best backwatchers there ever was."

"What was his name?"

"Tor—"

Kate parried a woman's blade. Dropping her sword, Kate stumbled and put her hand to her side.

The woman swung at her.

Jedd knocked the blade aside. Before he could follow through, the woman fled.

Jedd moved toward Kate, concern on his face. "You're wounded."

"I'm all right." Kate wiped her hand, which was concealed beneath her cloak, on her tunic. She grimaced as she picked up her sword. "Your uncle. He's not Tor Euland, is he?"

Jedd nodded, pride shining in his eyes.

Kate grinned at him. "I'm honored to be fighting beside you."

"Kate and Jedd," Sybil said. "You're not to fight unless you absolutely have to. Your job is to protect Alyse and Rill." She pointed back to the way they had come. "Your best chance is to leave by the kitchen."

Sybil started toward the center of the melee.

Alyse took hold of her wrist. "You can't go there. You'll be killed."

Sybil removed Alyse's hand. "This is *my* temple. My job is to protect it and the people who worship in it. Whatever happens to me is the will of the One Goddess."

Then she strode toward the fracas.

"Rill, here." Jedd tossed him the captured club.

Rill caught the club, then looked around the outer sanctuary, fear clawing at his chest. Rioters were everywhere. Five attackers wielding bloody swords and clubs chased worshipers away from the passageway to Sybil's office and the House of Healing and then stationed themselves in front of it.

"We're cut off from the hallway," Rill said.

"We can't go out through the main entrance," Alyse said. "The hallway is our best chance to escape."

Rill's mouth threatened to drop open when she drew a long-bladed dagger from beneath her cloak. *She has gumption. Nothing at all like Selina.* He gripped the club firmer, then realized with a jolt that he was still holding the sack of hinges in his other hand. *I'll put them to good use.*

"Rill . . . Alyse," Jedd said as he drew his dagger for two-handed fighting. "We're your shields. So stay behind us."

He and Kate ran toward the five raiders guarding the corridor entrance, Rill and Alyse following behind.

Some raiders tried to intercept them.

Kate felled one with her sword.

Jedd sliced a man in the side. Then he blocked a woman's sword, ducked under her guard, and stabbed her with the dagger.

Surprised by the unexpected resistance, the remaining attackers scattered.

Rill wanted to burst into giddy laughter. He swallowed the urge. "Now's our chance!" he said. "Run for the—"

"Look, there's some!" a voice yelled to their left.

Eight or ten rioters peeled off from a group and charged toward them. Three club-wielding men led the pack. Ducking under one man's cudgel, Jedd ran his sword into his chest.

Beside him, Kate quickly dispatched the other two.

Three more, brandishing swords, stepped over the bodies. Her expression hard as granite, Kate drew her dagger for two-handed fighting. Then, as if they'd communicated a silent signal to each other, she and Jedd launched an attack at the same moment. They battled fiercely, parrying and thrusting and protecting each other's backs so smoothly that, to Rill, it seemed as if they'd been functioning as a team for years. But as soon as they downed one opponent, another took her place. Grudgingly, Jedd and Kate gave ground, taking one backward step after another under the relentless weight of the assault, forcing Rill and Alyse backward toward the hallway.

"Rill," Jedd shouted, "the passageway. Get going!"

Rill threw a quick look over his shoulder. The entrance was still clear.

But then several raiders rushed by. They skidded to a stop and glanced toward him.

Fear walked up Rill's spine on icy feet. They seemed ready to attack. He readjusted the heavy bag of hinges on his shoulder.

The raiders sprinted toward them.

A woman with a cudgel was in the lead.

Rill swung his bag at her. The bag struck her in the face with a bone-cracking *smack*. Rill whirled around to face the next attacker.

But Alyse had ducked under the woman's club and stabbed her in the stomach.

Rill threw the bag of hinges at another assailant. When he ducked, Rill lunged at him with his dagger, opening a deep gash in his side.

Dropping his sword, the man staggered.

Before Rill could finish him off, Alyse thrust her knife into the man's back. The man fell to the floor, nearly dragging Alyse with him before she could pull out the blade.

Rill scooped up the man's sword.

A heartbeat later, Kate was there engaging the others, leaving Jedd to fight alone. Pulling off her cloak, she whipped it across an opponent's face, distracting her. She skewered a second attacker, then blocked another's sword thrust. A large, wet stain on the side of Kate's tunic drew Rill's attention. The gasp of dismay from Alyse told him she'd noticed it too.

Kate flung a quick, desperate look at them. "The way's open. Go!"

"Kate, no!" Alyse screamed. "Your wound's reopened. You can't stay. We'll leave together or not at all."

Kate deflected a thrust and staggered a few feet backward. "Do as I say!"

Alyse hesitated, her face drained of color.

"Come on!" Rill said and seized her hand.

Alyse struggled against his viselike grip. "No!" She appeared to fumble for words. "Gaela the Thread Cutter. It can't be Kate's time. Not today—"

Frustration at Alyse's reluctance churned in Rill. "They're putting their lives on the line so we can escape." He ran, dragging her with him. "Do you want them to do that for nothing?"

Together they sprinted along the hallway, past Sybil's office.

Rill stopped short when a sudden thought popped into his mind. He released Alyse's hand. "We can't go into the courtyard through the House of Healing. There's probably raiders still there."

"Through the kitchen." Alyse ran past the stairway to the archives and stopped by a closed oak door. "Through here."

Rill's first thought was that the staff had locked the door. But when Alyse tried the latch, the door opened and they rushed through. The room was deserted. They raced out the back door into a tiny courtyard that bordered a narrow, curbless street. The buildings on the other side loomed over them like ogres. Rill paused to catch his breath. Alyse did the same.

Faint shouts and screams came to Rill from the front courtyard. He glanced up the road. A woman and a man raced toward them. The man was gripping a small boy and girl by the wrists, almost dragging them over the rough cobbles. He stumbled when he neared Rill. Fortunately, he released his grip on the children before he hit the ground.

"Get the kids and keep going!" he shouted to the woman.

She snatched the children's wrists and continued running.

The man clambered to his feet and looked at Rill and Alyse, his eyes so wide his irises seemed to be floating in white. "They're coming this way. Run!" He sprinted after the woman and children.

Heartbeats later, raiders burst into view, howling like a pack of crazed wolves.

"Look!" One of them pointed at Rill and Alyse. "Don't let them escape."

Rill seized Alyse's hand and ran.

## CHAPTER 19

Sounding the Alarm

ALYSE RACED ALONGSIDE RILL, her shoes slapping against the gray cobbles. Fear of capture leaped off Alyse's back when their pursuers stopped chasing them after Rill plunged into a shadowy rabbit warren of narrow streets. But fear of becoming lost quickly replaced it as she became disoriented by the unfamiliar roads, buildings, shops, and tenements because she had never ventured deeper into The Kings than by the single route she knew to the One Goddess Temple. So she stuck close to Rill, her heart careening out of control because she feared getting lost in a neighborhood that had a reputation for hating the noblesse.

She followed Rill down one street after another in a confusion of twists and turns, shoving past Kings dwellers walking home with baskets of groceries, selling foods and goods from outdoor stands, and gossiping on street corners. In a small nook of her mind, Alyse found it bizarre that all these people were going about their daily tasks while just blocks away a mob was creating mayhem at the temple. And Kate . . . Alyse strove to keep worry about her at bay.

Rill spread the alarm as they went.

"To arms!" he yelled as they dashed through the streets. "The One Goddess Temple's being attacked."

Before long, Alyse's legs threatened to give out from beneath her and a red-hot knife seared her lungs with every breath. She stopped and hunched over, hands on knees, gasping.

Rill jostled her elbow impatiently. "Come on! We can't stop now."

"I can't take another step until I catch my breath," Alyse rasped.

"Then I'll go on alone." Rill hesitated. "What about you?"

"I'll find my way back to the temple."

"You might get killed."

"I'll take my chances."

Rill wavered, his expression betraying his eagerness to be off but also his reluctance to abandon her. He heaved an exasperated sigh. "You're just as stubborn as me. Can you walk?"

"Yes.

"We'll walk while you get your second wind. Then we'll run."

They alternated between walking and running until they came to a long, wide cobblestone street with modest, well-maintained tenements, houses, and shops. Rill went several blocks before he turned into an enclosed courtyard that shared a waist-high wall with a monument-maker's home and workshop. On the other side of the wall, two young men, probably apprentices, were polishing marble slabs. Alyse caught the faint smells of hay and horse manure from the longer part of a wooden L-shaped building on the right side of Rill's courtyard. Wisps of smoke curled into the air from the chimney in the nearer, shorter section. The building had to be a stable and a blacksmith's shop. A pair of horses gazed curiously at Alyse from inside a rectangular enclosure of split-wood rails near the building. A yellow one-story house with a red door that matched the red of the roof tiles took up the entire width of the opposite end of the court-yard.

Rill angled toward several adults clustered near the horse enclosure who were facing an agitated man in his early twenties. Sweat rolled down the man's face and he was panting for breath. He was speaking animatedly to a tall man with a coppery beard and hair who wore a leather apron and held a heavy-looking, short-handled hammer as if it were a stick.

A short, slender woman stood beside him, listening intently to the speaker. The long, flame-red hair that framed her heart-shaped face and her dark-blue eyes matched Rill's. Next to her stood a heavyset, older woman who wore her gray, white-streaked hair in a matronly bun and a square-faced woman with shoulder-length, brownish-blonde hair. Two other men, one wearing a butcher's bloodstained apron and the other a middle-aged man holding a stoneworker's mallet, completed the group.

A black-and-tan mutt sat on the cobblestones between the blacksmith and the red-haired woman. As soon as Alyse and Rill entered the courtyard, the dog barked joyfully and bounded toward them.

"Not now, Faith," Rill said and ran by the dog.

The disruption caused the adults to turn toward Alyse and Rill. Rill approached them. But Alyse, overcome by sudden shyness and a feeling of vulnerability in this strange environment, hung back.

"Dad, Dad!" Rill cried. "Call out the neighborhood watch. The temple's being attacked."

Everyone looked at Rill in astonishment.

Except for the red-haired woman. Her dark-blue eyes focused on Alyse. And it might have been Alyse's imagination, but a glimmer of recognition sparked in the woman's eyes. But the reaction disappeared as quickly as it had come.

"See, Marc?" the young man said to the blacksmith. "I told ya so."

Marc turned to Rill. "Tell me what happened, Son."

In a breathless rush of words, Rill began jabbering until his father put a beefy hand on his shoulder.

"Stop and take a deep breath. You ain't makin' no sense."

Rill paused and with effort got himself under control. Then he described what had happened more coherently.

"Who're the attackers?" the red-haired woman asked Rill sharply.

"Don't know."

"Were there mages with them?"

"Didn't see none."

"Where did the raiders come from?"

Rill stamped his foot in frustration. "Mom—"

"They assembled on River Road beforehand," Alyse said, stepping forward. "Then they went to the temple as a group. Some gathered near the temple courtyard ahead of time."

Rill's parents exchanged worried glances.

Marc massaged the back of his neck with a calloused hand. "Who's behind it? If we knew that, we'd know the reason for the attack."

"Could be a ruse," his wife said. "If everyone left this part of The Kings to defend the temple, we'd leave ourselves vulnerable."

"Now, Kendra," Marc said, a trace of censure in his voice. "Why would they wait all these years to move against us? Besides, they promised to leave us alone."

Anger rose like crackling blue flames in Kendra's eyes. "What's a promise to *them*?"

"Mom . . . Dad," Rill said, "what're ya talking about? Who promised to leave you alone? And why?"

"Do we go or not, Marc?" the butcher asked impatiently.

"We can't not go," Marc replied. "But we can't take no chance it's a ruse, neither." He turned to the butcher. "Sound the bell to call out the neighborhood watch. I'll take half of them to the temple. The other half stays in the general area to keep an eye on things."

The butcher hurried off to carry out Marc's order.

"I'll get my sword," the monument maker said and headed for the adjoining wall.

"Me too," Rill said.

He started for the house, but Kendra caught his arm. She nodded toward Alyse. "What's *she* doing here?"

"Raiders were chasing us," Rill replied. "So I brought her here." He tried to wrest free of Kendra's grip. "I gotta help defend the temple."

Kendra's blue eyes glared. "You brought her. So you're responsible for her."

From somewhere nearby, a bell tolled.

Before long, the monument maker returned with his sword. The two apprentices, eyes wide with excitement, accompanied him. They both carried clubs. Soon the butcher returned, grim faced and armed with a sword. Then other men and women began trickling in, weapons in hand and passions aroused, asking why the alarm was sounding.

I shouldn't have left Kate. Worry ate into Alyse's gut like a ravenous wolf while in her mind Gaela the Thread Cutter lurked beside Kate's tapestry of life with her scissors. Alyse touched Marc's sleeve. "My friend Kate's at the temple. With Rill's friend Jedd. They stayed and fought so we could escape." Alyse choked on a sob. "Kate's got a side wound that's bleeding badly. Oh, *please* help them."

"If they're alive," Marc said grimly, "we will." He went into the house.

Worry seeped into every nook and cranny of Alyse's mind. Everything depended on Rill's father and his neighbors. On how quickly they would act and how hard they would fight. But so much time had passed since she had left the temple.

Sudden fear clenched her heart, making her gasp.

Kendra noticed Alyse's reaction. "What's wrong?" she asked.

"N-nothing," Alyse replied.

But she'd lied. Something *was* wrong. She'd had a terrifying premonition that fulfilled her worst fear. Today, perhaps even this moment, the Five Sisters would complete Kate's tapestry of life. Today Gaela the Thread Cutter would snip the yarn and remove Kate's tapestry from the loom.

Today Kate would die.

## CHAPTER 20

Kendra's Secret

BY THE TIME MARC came out of the house with his sword, fifty or sixty armed Kings dwellers, both women and men, were milling in the courtyard and the street, their voices babbling with excitement. Marc still carried his hammer. He hefted it as if deciding whether or not to leave it behind, then nodded to himself and kept it.

He hugged Kendra, who kissed him lightly before he pulled away.

"Be careful," she said softly. "I don't want to lose you."

Marc's lips spread into such a loving smile that Alyse's heart ached to be its recipient. And Kendra returned a smile just as loving. A hard lump formed in Alyse's throat, making it difficult to breathe. *They had married for love.* Her soul ached to trade places with Kendra. To give and receive genuine, heartfelt love to someone like Marc who wanted to be with her, sharing good times and bad times. Inseparable. Together forever.

Marc turned toward the Kings dwellers. "Those of you designated to stay behind, keep alert. The attack might be a ruse. As for the rest of you, let's go!"

Giving a ragged cheer, half of the Kings dwellers started up the road.

Two women dashed into the courtyard as Marc jogged out. Alyse studied them. They had to be mother and daughter because both had similar oval faces, medium builds, and brown eyes. But the younger one's long hair was light brown, while the older woman's had turned mostly gray.

"Is it true?" the older woman asked, stopping in front of Kendra. "The temple's being attacked?"

"Yes," Kendra replied.

The younger woman's glance darted around the enclosure, worry carved into every line of her face. "Where's Jedd?"

The swallow Rill took was audible to Alyse's ears. "He's at the temple, Aunt Marvis. Defending it."

"Goddess in Elustra!" Marvis said and clapped a hand over her mouth.

"What's he doing there?" the older woman asked.

Rill explained how Jedd had gone with him to deliver some hinges to Priestess Sybil and how a band of thugs had attacked the temple.

"You didn't stay with him?" she said, her words edged with reproach.

Rill looked shamefaced. "Grandma Sorah, he sent me away."

Alyse's indignation sparked. "Jedd stayed behind to buy time for Rill and me to escape. My friend Kate stayed with him to help." Alyse choked on a sob. "Her wound reopened. I saw it before we left. She . . . she'll bleed to death."

I'm sorry," Sorah said. "I didn't know."

"Let's go into the house," Kendra said.

Everyone went into the kitchen and sat down at the larger trestle table. The dog, Faith, settled near the crackling hearth. Kendra poured watered wine for everybody and then sat down across from Alyse. To Alyse, it seemed that Kendra's blue eyes, which had been so soft and loving when gazing on her husband such a short time ago, were now a pair of blue ice cubes.

Cinna, who was the Larkin matriarch, introduced the other women to Alyse. Giving only her first name, Alyse said she was the daughter of a merchant from another neighborhood. Afterward, Rill and the women lapsed into silence, apparently thinking about Marc and their neighbors now battling at the temple.

Alyse joined them in silence, her mind centered on Kate. *This can't be her time. She survived the charm raid. She can survive this too. Besides, Jedd will protect her.* Kendra's words, spoken with exaggerated politeness, broke into Alyse's thoughts. She looked at Kendra in surprise. "What?"

Kendra sent her a smile that reached only to the tips of her lips. "I asked what brought you to the temple today?"

Cinna and Tarri exchanged wary glances, and Alyse detected an ominous change in the mood among the women. She frowned to herself, puzzled. What was behind Kendra's hostile attitude? "Priestess Sybil is tutoring me in Eulorian history. I went for a lesson."

"Oh? And why is a *commoner* studying Eulorian history?"

"Because the history of Euloria is the history of us all. Commoner and noblesse alike. And, if you must know, my parents disapprove of me studying it."

"Oh, I'm sure they do," Kendra said, her voice laced with malice. She leaned forward to say something else, but Cinna put a hand on her arm.

"Careful, Daughter."

Kendra's glance drifted to her mother, and the two women held each other's gaze. Alyse discerned an invisible tug of war going on between them. Cinna must have won because Kendra's shoulders sank. Cinna smiled at Alyse—

The door burst open, and Marc dashed into the kitchen.

"Marvis," he said, "Jedd's been wounded."

Marc's gaze turned to Alyse.

Her heart iced over as Gaela the Thread Cutter rose in her mind like a horrible apparition.

"Kate was wounded too," Marc said. "I'm afraid she's . . . dying."

"Oh, Goddess, no!" Alyse cried. She raced out of the house into the street, then stopped and frowned in confusion at her unfamiliar surroundings.

Then Rill was beside her. He grabbed her wrist. "This way!"

Hand in hand, they sprinted up the street. In her mind, Alyse saw

Gaela the Thread Cutter snipping the last strand of yarn from Kate's tapestry. The image filled her with such horror that she found herself outpacing Rill, and only his hand in hers slowed her down. Partway along the next block, Rill pulled her to a stop in front of a tenement.

"In here," he said. He barged through the entryway and raced upstairs to the third floor.

Alyse followed so close at his heels that she stumbled into him when he stopped abruptly to open the door opposite the staircase. They entered a long hallway running left and right lit by oil lamps in wall sconces.

Marc came up behind them.

Alyse spun around to face him. "Where's Kate?"

"In Tor's bedroom," Marc said as Kendra and the other women burst through the doorway. "I'll take you to her."

Alyse followed Marc and Rill along the left-hand corridor, the other women chasing at her heels like hounds after foxes. Three closed doors lined the right side. Rill disappeared through the next-to-last door. Sorah and Marvis went in after him.

When Kendra began to follow them, Marc wrapped his rough fingers around her arm. "You need to come with us."

Kendra froze as if glued to the wood floor planks. Then slowly she turned to face him, her features set in dreadful expectation.

"Please," he said.

Kendra's face became so deathly pale it seemed to Alyse that Kendra should have been wrapped in a winding sheet. And her hand gripped Marc's so hard that her knuckles turned as white as her face. But she went with Marc into the last bedroom. Alyse had the unsettling feeling that, somehow, Kendra could make the difference between Kate's living or dying.

Alyse followed them into the bedroom. Coldness formed in her chest and then spread to her arms and legs her when she saw Kate lying on the bed, her face deathly white and her slashed tunic soaked with drying blood. She could barely see Kate's chest rising and falling with every shallow breath.

Kendra's chin quivered. "She has the pallor of death on her. No healer can help her now. Not even Priestess Sybil."

"I know that," Marc said. "Priestess Sybil told me herself."

"Let her slip into Elustra, the Afterworld, and be with the One Goddess."

Marc shook his head. "No. You can save her. You have the power."

"I vowed to the One Goddess never to use my powers again."

Kendra turned away.

She flinched when Marc gripped her shoulders and twisted her back so her tormented blue eyes met his hard brown ones. "Kate deliberately took a sword meant for Jedd. She saved his life. I was there. I saw it."

Kendra uttered a strangled cry like a tormented animal. "There's nothing I can do. Let her cross over."

"At least *look*, Daughter."

Alyse started at the unexpected voice behind her. Cinna's voice. Rill's grandmother and his Aunt Tarri were standing behind her.

Kendra ripped free of Marc's grasp and glared at Cinna, her breath coming in rapid, shallow gasps. "Oh, you intend me to do more than look. Doesn't my vow 'never again' mean anything to you? It did when I took it."

Marvis Euland elbowed her way between Cinna and Tarri. "Kendra," she said, her voice as hard as the marble in the monument-maker's courtyard, "you hafta prevent her from crossing over. She saved my son's life."

Kendra covered her ears and rocked back and forth on the balls of her feet.

Marvis marched up to Kendra and pulled her hands down to her sides. "I lost my brother, Tor. That left only my son, Jedd—"

Kendra clutched at her red hair with both hands, making Alyse fear she would pull it out by the roots. Then Kendra released it and turned to Tarri. "I traded my life for one life already. You, of all people, know that. Why must it now be for two?"

Tarri's mouth opened and closed, but no words came out. To

Alyse, it seemed as if Kendra had made an accusation that Tarri couldn't refute. She wondered what it could be.

"Jedd's son is Kald's son," Marvis said, relentless as a wolf closing in on its prey. "Your *brother's* son, Kendra. That girl received her death wound saving your brother's son. Is death her reward?"

Kendra pressed her fist against trembling lips and backed away from Marvis.

Marvis stepped forward. "By saving her life, you won't trade one for another. You'll give back a life."

Kendra turned to Cinna and spoke in a tormented voice. "Mother, tell me what to do."

"I can't, Daughter," Cinna responded gently. That's a decision you gotta make yourself. But I do think that in this one case, the One Goddess will forgive you for saving Kate."

Kendra stood like a child lost in the woods, undecided which direction to go.

"Kendra," Marc said, kneeling at Kate's beside, "she's slipping away. You gotta make a decision now."

An anguished sob racked Kendra's body and her shoulders sagged. Then, her face turning grim, she gulped down deep, ragged breaths, and straightened. She appeared to be in control of herself again. She turned to Alyse. "Leave us."

"No," Alyse said. "I left Kate once, but I'll not leave her again. Not while there's hope."

"*Kendra.*" Marc said her name in a tone laced with an urgency Alyse had never heard before not even during the charm raid. "She's slipping."

Kendra's hard, cold eyes turned to Alyse. "I know who you are, Alyse Dejune."

The statement shook Alyse from her head to the soles of her shoes.

"But can I trust you to never tell what you see happen here?"

"Yes, yes," Alyse responded. "I'll keep whatever secrets you want. Just save Kate."

"*Kendra!*" Marc said. "She's stopped breathing."

Horror made Alyse freeze as still as the Statue of the One Goddess in Priestess Sybil's temple. Then her body quick thawed, and she started toward Kate's bed.

Cinna's hand clamped on her arm like a vise. "If you love Kate," Cinna told her, "don't interfere."

Kneeling beside the bed, Kendra placed both hands on Kate's bloody chest and stared intently at them. A hush descended on the room. Alyse watched Kendra remain in the pose for what seemed like an eternity, her nerves fraying like ropes stretched beyond the breaking point. Even after sweat broke out on her forehead and her body began to tremble, Kendra didn't change position. Alyse winced when Kate's arms and legs twitched. Kate let out a sharp gasp. Then she groaned. Relief gushed through Alyse like water suddenly released from a dam into a dry riverbed.

Exhausted, Kendra let out a weary sigh and climbed shakily to her feet. "She'd crossed over to the Afterworld. But I managed to bring her back. She came willingly, though, because she didn't want to leave Alyse."

Alyse rushed to Kate's bedside, knelt, and laid her head on Kate's chest, oblivious to the blood on the tunic. "Thank you, thank you," she murmured over and over. She glanced up at Kendra, chill bumps sliding down her neck and spine as her fears about Kate slid away into oblivion, and the enormity of what Kendra had just done exploded in her brain. "What kind of magic was that?"

Her shoulders drooping from exhaustion, Kendra shot her a bleak look. "Just remember your oath, Alyse Dejune."

"You did the right thing, Daughter," Cinna said, draping an arm over Kendra's shoulder.

Kendra shrugged off the arm. "For what—breaking my oath?"

"You did it just this once," Marc said. "And for a good reason."

Kendra laughed bitterly. "Yes. 'Just this once.' That's how it begins. And there will be another 'just this once' for another 'good reason.' And then another."

Marc and the women eyed one another uneasily. An awkward silence ensued, until Marc cleared his throat as if reluctant to disrupt the tableau. "We should take Kate and Alyse back to the temple and put them in Priestess Sybil's care. It'd be better if they were found there than here."

Gratitude for Kendra and what she had done for Kate expanded in Alyse's chest until she thought it would burst. She turned to Kendra. "I owe you such a great debt that I'll never be able to repay it in full."

"You owe me nothing," Kendra said. "Because I didn't do it for you. Just remember your oath. Because if you break it, you'll wish you hadn't."

Kendra's unexpected response made Alyse's gratitude fizzle. Puzzlement replaced it. What did Kendra fear if people learned about her extraordinary healing powers? And how had she gained them? Alyse wished she knew. Because she could use those powers herself to become a powerful healer.

Another thought replaced it. Kendra must be hiding some dark secret.

Alyse wondered what it was.

## CHAPTER 21

Name Day

ALYSE ENTERED KATE'S SHADOW-ENSHROUDED bedroom. Kate was lying in bed, propped up by pillows and reading a book by the light of an oil lamp. The single window was shuttered against the early Awakening morning season chill, and a fire burned in the fireplace, its flames crackling merrily.

"Well," Alyse said, twirling a pirouette across the mosaic floor, "how do I look?"

Kate examined Alyse's dark-blue gown in the dim light, her eyes running up and down from the modest neckline, just low enough to make the Naming charm visible, to the matching blue shoes on her feet. "You look beautiful."

"You should see Mora's gown," Alyse said, allowing just a trace of disapproval into her voice. "Bright red with an immodestly low neckline. She says she wants to make sure the back of the Naming charm makes contact with *all of* her skin."

Kate chuckled as she put a finger between the pages she'd been reading to act as a bookmarker. "The boys will be attracted like flies to flypaper."

Alyse eased herself down on the bed, careful not to jounce the mattress. "I wish you could go."

"Same here. Even if they don't allow backwatchers inside the Hall of Naming, at least I could've waited outside."

Alyse ran a hand affectionately along Kate's arm. "How are you feeling?"

"Better." Kate smiled. "Lenia stopped by little while ago to check on me. She's pleased with how well I'm recovering."

"That's good."

Kate flipped the book over and laid it on the bed. "You know, I never told you this. But there was a time . . . and this is really, really weird . . . but for a time I thought I was dead."

Alyse felt as if Kate had just punched her in the stomach. She strained to turn her shocked expression into a curious one. "What makes you think that?"

"Well, I felt as if I was drifting away toward darkness. And I felt sad about it because I was leaving you and didn't want to. But I couldn't do anything about it. So I kept drifting toward that darkness. Then I heard someone's voice—a woman's—calling my name. There was a struggle . . . a tug of war . . . and I felt myself being pulled back and forth. Finally, the voice said, 'You can't have her yet. I won't let you.' Suddenly I was free. And the next thing I knew, I was here in bed with you looking down at me."

Alyse's chest tightened. She wished she could tell Kate how Kendra had defied the Five Sisters and pulled her back from the Afterworld, her tapestry of life somehow placed back on their loom. But she had sworn an oath to never tell. Alyse considered her silence and the guilt linked to it a small price to pay for Kate's life.

Kate adjusted her position in bed. "Do you know yet who attacked the temple?"

"I overheard Grandmother and Grandfather talking about it," Alyse said. "The Magesterium had Ianna Caymoore, the mindbender, question some of the raiders who were captured. They came from other cities. From neighborhoods equivalent to The Slums. Someone hired them. A different woman or man in each city. The raiders thought the recruiters might be ex-legionaries or sailors because of their military bearing."

"Not too helpful," Kate said, frowning. "Why would anyone want to attack the temple?"

"Beats me. Maybe—"

The door opened and Pilar walked in. She nodded at Kate, then turned to Alyse. "It's time to go."

Alyse's insides quivered with anxiety as she followed her mother into the receiving hall. Pilar stopped near the receiving chair. Mora was already waiting there in her brassy red gown. Their stepfather, Degas Spicer, and their grandfather, Jukka Berne, stood by the door to the front courtyard.

Jukka had become sole presiding chief magestrate until the Magesterium chose a replacement to serve out the rest of Locien Estati's term. Jukka's nine dynamae were clustered near him, waiting to escort him down The Citadel to the Hall of Naming.

Grandmother Maude, dressed in her best silk gown, left Jukka and planted herself in front of Alyse and Mora. Her sharp gray eyes stepped from granddaughter to granddaughter. "Be sure to sit in the front row. Prominent families should always be in prominent view."

"Yes, Grandmother," Alyse said.

Mora rolled her eyes when Pilar and Maude turned to answer Jukka's call to hurry or they'd be late.

Maude waved to let him know she'd heard, then turned back to her granddaughters. "Do us proud. Both of you." She blew out an exasperated breath. "Leoc was *such* a disappointment when he wasn't named a mage."

Alyse bridled at the criticism of her beloved uncle. It took all of her willpower to swallow an angry retort.

Pilar took over as if she and her mother were partners in a tag-team match. "Alyse. Can you imagine how frightened we were for you? We had no idea where you'd gone. It's a good thing Kate thought of checking at the temple."

Alyse mentally rolled her eyes. She'd already apologized several times for sneaking off, but her mother and grandmother kept harping like a pair of dogs that wouldn't let go of their favorite bones.

Maude nodded in vigorous agreement. "If it weren't for Kate, you probably would've been killed. Your thoughtless action jeopardized our hopes to revive our family's declining fortunes."

"And our alliance with the Estatis," Pilar said.

Maude's gaze turned frosty. "You think only of yourself, not of your family. Alyse, how can you be so selfish?"

Both of you see me only as a pawn to be shuffled around on a board. How can you *be so selfish?* Alyse wished she could spit those words at Maude but knew doing so would only bring more trouble.

"Maude," Jukka called impatiently, "if we don't leave now we'll be late."

Maude waved an acknowledgment, then turned to Alyse. "If you're named a mage, I'll lift the restrictions I put on you for sneaking off to the temple."

"I'll do my best," Alyse said. Her gut lurched in her belly like a ship being pounded on a stormy sea. Priestess Sybil had shown her how to trick the Naming charm, a feat Alyse still thought was impossible. But she had to believe in herself. That she could make the Naming charm name her a healer.

Because failure would bring death.

Hers.

# # #

A delightful warmth spread through Rill's body as he put on the Name Day clothes Aunt Talia had given him. The sensation wasn't caused by the golden sunlight dancing through his bedroom window but from his mom's unexpected change of heart to attend his Name Day Celebration. She'd told him last night. She and his dad would attend, along with Grandma Cinna and Aunt Tarri. Rill had feigned astonishment. But he'd been waiting for the past two days for the announcement, expectancy stretching tighter each day like a wire nearing its breaking point.

Three nights ago, he had passed by his parents' closed bedroom door when he'd heard his mom speak his name. She should have lowered her voice, but she sounded so deeply engaged in tense conversation with his dad and grandma that she probably didn't realize she was speaking so loud. So, of course, Rill had put his ear to the door.

"Yeah," Marc had said. "We gotta protect him. He's untrained. And you know what he'll be named."

"I won't let that happen," Kendra said. "Not to my son. We have our disagreements. But he's flesh of my flesh. Blood of my blood."

"Are you certain you can do it?" Cinna asked.

"Yes."

Marc spoke hesitantly. "But . . . what if . . . what if Traela the Weaver ain't woven what you're gonna to do into his tapestry? What if She's woven that he ain't a eulo—"

"And what if she's woven that he is and that I protect him?" Kendra said, her voice so sharp Rill pictured his dad flinching. "By doing this very thing?"

"What will he be named if you gotta intervene?" Marc asked.

"An archmage," Kendra replied. "He needs all the magic possible to protect himself from our enemies."

"But what about your vow?" Cinna asked.

"I broke it once already for someone I didn't know," Kendra had snapped. "Do you think I won't break it again for my own son?"

Stunned, Rill left, fearing they might discover him at the door if Grandma Cinna or one of his parents decided to leave just then. He went outside, Faith padding beside him, and by the time he reached the stable he wondered if he'd imagined the unbelievable exchange instead of actually hearing it.

How can my mom influence the Naming charm? That's impossible. But no. He *had* heard her say it. And his dad and Grandma Cinna had acted as if she were stating a fact.

That night at supper, his mom had announced that she and his dad had changed their minds. Rill had done such a great job of acting surprised that afterward he'd figured he could become a professional actor.

"Let's go, Rill," Marc said.

Kendra stopped Rill before he reached the door. She put a hand on his shoulder and fixed him with a stern look. "Remember what I told you earlier. When Cato puts the Naming charm around your neck, turn and look me in the eyes until the Naming charm makes its decision."

Rill nodded. "They'll stick to yours like they was nailed on."

His mom gave him a tight smile in return.

They walked to River Road and then turned left and headed for the Public Square. Soon they joined a trickle of early arriving celebrants and their families heading toward the white marble-faced Hall of Naming near the Law Court.

A portly, gray-haired man in the black tunic and pants with silver trim of a Magesterium servant stood on the multicolored fresco floor just inside the antechamber. He waved the adults toward the center double doors that pierced the back wall. "Noblesse sit in the left center isle," he said. "Commoners sit on the right center isle."

Other Magesterium servants, shouting like city criers, kept saying, "Noblesse candidates through the far left door. Commoner candidates through the far right door."

His heart beating a rapid pitter-patter, Rill gave his name to the Magesterium servant sitting behind a desk by the far right door. The man, who was called a "names keeper," checked *Rill Larkin* off a list on the desk. Then Rill went through the doorway into a huge semicircular amphitheater filled with oak benches and settled himself on one partway down next to the aisle.

A happy beam of sunlight shone down on him from a high window. A premonition that he'd be named an archmage, for sure. Rill hugged the thought to himself. Today was the first day in his journey to become noblesse.

Like a bumblebee drawn to a flower's nectar, Rill's gaze flew to the jeweled casket sitting on the table in the middle of the dais in front of the semicircle of benches. The overhang of the red velvet cloth covering the tabletop was emblazoned with four large gold letters: MACP—*Magesterium and Caldonian People.* Two armed city watchers in gray pants and gray, red-trimmed tunics stood on either side of the ancient, iron-bound oak box.

Rill's heart quickened. That tiny chest held Caldon's most important treasure.

The Naming charm.

A babble of nervous and excited voices elbowed their way into Rill's thoughts as adults settled into their benches in the two center sections reserved for families. His parents, aunt, and grandma had left early to get seats up close. "So you can see my eyes clearly," his mom had told him. Now Rill saw them sitting in the third row, behind the benches reserved for the sole chief magestrate and other officials.

Rill waited, tapping his fingers impatiently on his leg, wishing time would speed up so Cato could put the Naming charm around his neck.

Soon the trickle of candidates and their families turned into a flood. Rill's gaze wandered across the rapidly filling benches. His heart jumped against his rib cage when he spotted two chestnut-haired girls walking down the aisle of the noblesse candidates' section. One wore a dark-blue gown with a modest neckline. The other wore a gown red enough to match his own flame-red hair, with a daringly low neckline that allowed the top of a black breast band to peek above it. Physically the girls were mirror images of each other. Both were medium height and wore their chestnut hair piled up, leaving their necks bare for the chain of the Naming charm. And they both had the same face.

Alyse's face.

Rill felt as if he'd been hit on the head by one of his dad's heavy rounding hammers. Alyse was noblesse! And a twin. What luck. She was in debt to him three times. For rescuing her from the temple. For giving her refuge in his home. And for his mom helping her friend Kate recover from her wounds.

He looked at the twins again as they sat down in the middle of the first row. His eyes jumped back and forth from one to the other in confusion.

Which was Alyse?

# # #

"Do you think the boys will notice me?" Mora asked, tugging at the lacy top of her black breast band.

"I don't see how they can't," Alyse replied, straight faced. She hugged the joke to herself. Mora's target was the noblesse boys sitting behind her, not the commoner boys sitting across from her on the other side of the amphitheater.

Mora nudged Alyse. "There's a boy who's noticed me. He's a commoner though. But look! He's practically leaning out of his seat gawking."

Alyse ignored her. She was sick and tired of her sister's vanity.

Mora gave a snide laugh. "He can't take his eyes off of me." She prodded Alyse again. "Look!"

Reluctantly, Alyse looked—straight at Rill Larkin. Their eyes fastened on each other's as if they had been locked together with his father's hand-wrought bolts. Images of how he'd rescued her from the temple raiders tumbled through her head in a jumble of pictures that had no chronological order. She chewed the inside of her lip. *I owe him and his family a huge debt.*

Mora's petulant voice scattered the images as if blown away by a strong wind. "Why is he looking at you instead of me?"

Alyse blocked out Mora's voice. Would the Naming charm reveal that Rill had the same incredible healing power as his mother? Or maybe Kendra was keeping it a secret from him. Why had she vowed never to use her power again when her magic could help so many people? Kate was living proof of the good Kendra could do. But Kendra could do more than heal. She could pull someone back from the Afterworld. Kate had died, yet now she lived. The thought sent awe rippling through Alyse. *I've never heard of that happening before.*

Mora broke into Alyse's thoughts with an elbow jab. "Look! He's smiling at you."

Alyse's eyes met Rill's . . . and she returned the smile.

Mora opened her mouth for some kind of retort.

But her reaction became stillborn when the door behind the dais opened, and a wrinkled old man, whose bald top of his head appeared like an island surrounded by a sea of white hair, stepped through. His out-of-fashion coat, vest, and pants hung from his body like laundry drying on a clothesline. Even if she didn't already know his identity, Alyse would have known who he was instantly. Just about everyone in Caldon could recognize the eccentric Name Master. Cato Porta, the leader of the ultra-conservative Traditionali faction. He'd been elected chief magestrate four times. And he was reputed to be one of the most powerful archmages in Caldon. He had also served as Name Master longer than anyone could remember.

Smiling, Cato walked to the edge of the dais, then spread his arms out wide in a dramatic theatrical gesture. "Welcome! Welcome, everyone, to the monthly Name Day Celebration. Where girls become women. Boys become men. And all become citizens. And where some—a lucky few—*might* become mages!"

The audience erupted in wild applause and foot stomping. Alyse joined them, but more politely than enthusiastically. Unlike Mora who apparently would clap and stomp until her hands and feet turned raw. Rill, she noted, was clapping just as madly as Mora.

Cato waited for the tumult to subside before continuing. "Magic is the cement that holds our society together. Magic is the great equalizer. It doesn't limit itself to the noblesse alone. Magic can be found in commoners too. With magic, a commoner—with great effort and the help of the One Goddess—can become noblesse. And, alas, without magic, a noblesse can become common, but not a commoner."

Cato called out, "Names keepers, come forward."

The noblesse and commoner names keepers walked down their respective aisles and went up the steps onto the dais.

"How many celebrants do we have this month?" Cato asked.

Each names keeper responded in turn as he handed his parchment list to Cato.

"Eighty-seven noblesse."

"Two hundred and seventy-nine commoners."

"Three hundred and sixty-six celebrants." Cato pushed his bottom lip forward with his tongue. "Unlike Gaetan, we have no king. Hundreds of years ago, we drove out Toran the Usurper when he overthrew the queenship and crowned himself king. We declared

Caldon a republic governed in the name of the people by magestrates who are elected by noblesse and commoners alike. Ours is an open society in which everyone has the opportunity to advance herself, if the Five Sisters have woven that strand into her tapestry of life."

Cato held up the two parchments, waving them back and forth. "On these sheets are written three hundred and sixty-six names. The names of your children, grandchildren, and great-grandchildren. Of your nieces and nephews who are sitting here in the Hall of Naming. A few of these celebrants will be named mages. Right here. Today. In front of you. On this dais."

Cato handed the lists back to their respective names keepers, then went to the table and slowly, as if he were deliberately teasing the audience, opened the casket. "But none of that will happen without . . . *this!*" Cato lifted a golden star-shaped charm by its chain, from the box.

The intakes of breath that surrounded Alyse sounded as a single long gasp and merged with the other gasps throughout the amphitheater as Cato held up the talisman for everyone to see. Surprise jolted Alyse as she realized her own indrawn breath was part of that huge amphitheater-wide gasp. Yet the sight of the charm created a hollowness in her chest followed by an urge to flee the building. She resisted the impulse because she could manipulate the Naming charm like Priestess Sybil had taught her. She *had* to.

"Yes!" Cato said, his voice rising to a fevered pitch. "The Naming charm. The most important treasure in Caldon. Only one other exists, in Gaetan. With an enemy, who this very moment, is striving to destroy our state and our way of life. One day a month—twelve times a year—we take this charm from its vault deep in the bowels of the Treasury Building so it can tell us which of our children has the potential to become mages."

Cato returned the charm to the casket. "You all know how it works. Each of the charm's eight points has a different-colored jewel. And each jewel, except for the top one, represents one of the seven kinds of magic. I hang the charm around the celebrant's neck. If all the jewels remain blank, she has no potential for magic. If one of the jewels lights up, she has the potential to become a mage. The lit jewel indicates which type of magic she can master. And if all seven light up, she is an archmage."

Cato paused, using his tongue to push his bottom lip forward while his dark-gray eyes slowly swept across the audience. "For every girl and boy in Caldon, her Name Day Celebration takes place on the last day of the month in which she turns sixteen." He looked pointedly at each celebrants' sections, noblesse first. "And for those of you who turned sixteen this month, that time is . . . *now!*"

To Alyse, Cato seemed to have cast a spell on the audience as an awed hush settled over the amphitheater. She tossed a quick look at Rill. Like everyone else, he appeared to be holding his breath as he focused expectantly on Cato.

A smile flitted across Cato's lips while his gaze wandered back and forth across the ocean of faces. Obviously, he relished this moment. "As always," he said, breaking the spell, "noblesse first."

The noblesse candidates' names keeper consulted his list. "Marta Arath!"

The spectators glanced toward the far left section, but no one stood up.

"Marta Arath!" the names keeper called again.

From somewhere in the center left section, a woman's voice called out, "Marta!"

In the back row, a tiny girl with short black hair meekly got up.

Cato motioned for her to come forward, then smiled indulgently at the audience as she rushed down the aisle and scurried onto the dais. "The first celebrant is always the most nervous."

The audience tittered, and Marta's cheeks turned the color of the red painted on her lips while Cato positioned her to face him.

Alyse empathized with Marta, while dislike for the way Cato was using her as a comic foil flamed like a hot-burning torch. *I'm not the first, like that poor girl. But I think I'm the most nervous. Goddess, I wish this were over!*

Cato lifted the Naming charm from the casket and attached the chain around Marta's neck, taking care to make sure the back of the charm was resting against her skin, just above the top of her cream-colored gown's modest neckline.

When Marta bent her head to look at the charm, Cato lifted her chin with a finger. "No peeking."

Cato turned her by the shoulders to face the audience. Disappointed groans came from the noblesse sections. This time, Cato didn't stop Marta from glancing down to see the charm's decision. She let out a dismayed squeak.

"Too bad, Marta," Cato said. "The Five Sisters didn't weave a magic strand into your tapestry of life."

Her face a deeper crimson than her lip paint, Marta raced off the dais and flew to her seat faster than a blink. Moments later, Alyse heard a whisper of sobbing from way behind her. *That's me if Priestess Sybil's plan doesn't work.*

The next two noblesse celebrants weren't named mages either. The results didn't surprise Alyse because, as Cato had said, few children had the potential for magic. And because commoners outnumbered noblesse, usually five, six, seven, or more commoners were named mages to every one noblesse.

While noblesse candidates with last names beginning with A through C went up and down from the dais, doubts swept back and forth in Alyse like s heavy sea crashing against a rocky shore. *What if I can't control the power? What if all eight jewels light up? Goddess help me if that happens!* She shifted uncomfortably on the hard bench. Applause from the noblesse sections brought her out of her thoughts as the audience greeted the first noblesse candidate who was named a mage. Alyse joined in the clapping for form's sake. Then she dove back into her mind. *I can't let fear control me. If I do, all is lost. Center myself! I have to center myself.*

Closing her eyes, Alyse opened herself to the magic plane . . .

And was startled out of it by a sharp elbow jab from Mora. "Alyse, wake up! Cato just called your name."

Alyse sprang to her feet.

"Goddess, you're *so* weird," Mora said. "How could you fall asleep at a time like this?"

Alyse strode confidently down the aisle. Her centering exercise had worked. It had kicked all doubts from her head and replaced them with the conviction that she could succeed. *I'm a euloghe. I control my power, not the Naming charm.*

As she walked up the steps to the dais, she pictured each char as an open doorway with five sets of strong brackets fastened into the wall on either side of the doorway. Next, she imagined seven iron-bound doors made from single slabs of thick, solid oak. Each door had a strong lock and five sets of brackets that lined up with those on the walls. Using sturdy hinges, she attached the doors to the seven doorways she wanted to block. Then she shut and locked the doors. Finally, she pushed a strong iron bar through the brackets on every door. Now, only the doorway to the heart char—the healer's char—remained open. The Naming charm could only access that char. So she hoped. No, not hoped. She *knew.*

Facing Cato, Alyse concentrated on keeping the seven doors shut as he placed the Naming charm around her neck. As soon as the charm's back touched the skin above her gown's neckline, a powerful jolt of energy pierced her body, splitting into eight streams that raced toward the eight chars.

Alyse reeled when seven of the streams smashed against the closed doors, and only Cato's hands on her shoulders kept her from falling. Losing all sense of her surroundings, she concentrated on keeping the seven doors shut against the unrelenting pressure striving to break through them. After what seemed like an eternity, her strength began to seep from her body, and the doors shimmered in her mind.

Stay shut, all of you!

Then something odd happened that took her by surprise, almost distracting her from defending the seven doors. She sensed magic energy flowing through her heart into the magic plane and back again into her heart in one continuous stream. Her own personal energy blended with the magic energy, but her heart remained strong and serene, unaffected by the siege on the other chars.

Elation did a victory dance in her head. She could sense the other chars, their access blocked, reversing and heading toward her heart. Now they struck it at almost the same instant and passed through—

Alyse gasped and staggered, but Cato's firm hands held her up. It took a moment for Alyse's dazed brain to become aware of the clamor rocking the amphitheater as Cato turned her toward the audience. The rows of benches swam into focus with the noblesse, adults, and candidates alike, on their feet clapping and cheering.

Even stodgy old Cato was grinning. "Here she is, citizens!" he shouted jubilantly. "Alyse Dejune. Our second mage of the day. A healer."

Exhausted, Alyse stumbled up to her seat, then watched Mora hurry onto the dais to be named a mindbender. Relief flowed through Alyse's veins and arteries, causing her body to relax and slowly sink against the back of the bench. She had maneuvered safely to shore between two dangerous reefs. She was a healer, which meant her marriage would be postponed until after her fledgling training. And, thanks to Priestess Sybil, she had avoided being named a euloghe.

Only Priestess Sybil knew she was a euloghe.

Now Alyse had to guard that secret from everyone else, including Kate.

# # #

Rill squirmed on the bench, impatient to be called up to the dais. Cato had finished with the noblesse celebrants and was calling up the commoners now. Only thirteen noblesse had been named mages. Last year Jedd had told Rill that the celebrants at his Name Day Celebration had reacted differently to the Naming charm. He was right. Those thirteen noblesse celebrants had displayed a huge variety of reactions. And the five commoners who'd been named mages had added to the mix.

Rill still couldn't get over the Dejune twins' responses though. Theirs been at opposite ends of the spectrum. With Alyse, the Naming charm had seemed to suck all the energy from her body before it had named her a healer, and she'd staggered back to her bench like a weary, old woman. But with Mora, the charm had barely touched her skin before the Cat's Eye gemstone had lit up, naming her a mindbender, and afterward she had left the dais with bouncy steps.

Rill wondered what his own reaction would be.

He readjusted his position again on the bench as if he had an annoying itch that wouldn't go away. He wished he could cast a spell on Cato that would force him to move faster through the list of commoner celebrants. It seemed to have taken Cato ages to reach the D's. And there were still eight more letters to go through until he reached the L's. *Why couldn't my last name have been Acoff or Aken or Allston? Then I would of been named a mage long before now.*

Rill thought back to what he'd heard when he'd eavesdropped on the conversation in his parents' bedroom. How did his mom know he'd be named an archmage? And just how was she going to protect him? By having him look into her eyes while he was on the dais. He uttered a silent, derisive snort. A lot of good that would do! But she'd been so insistent that he figured he'd go along with it.

Then he furrowed his brows in puzzlement. What did his mom mean when she'd talked about breaking her vow? What vow? He wanted to ask all those questions to her face but knew she'd explode in anger if he did.

"Dori Kolter!" the commoner names keeper called out.

The name pierced Rill's thoughts like the prick of a sharp needle. He bolted upright. *L's are next!* He sat stiffly, his muscles quivering with excitement as a short girl with straw-colored hair hurried past him.

Maybe it was his own eagerness to replace Dori on the dais, but her naming seemed to have taken longer than any of the others to complete. *Cato, hurry up and get it over with.* Rill wanted to cup his hands around his mouth and shout the words but knew better than to give in to the urge. Finally, Cato finished with Dori. That she was named a healer hardly registered. Rill's legs tensed, his feet flat on the floorboards, ready to propel him onto the dais like a stone flung by a slinger.

The names keeper consulted his list. "Rill Larkin!"

Rill jumped out of his seat and rushed down the stairs, brushing by Dori, and bounded up to the dais.

"Whoa!" Cato said, raising his hand.

Rill stopped short just a foot from him.

Cato turned to the audience and gave them a snarky grin. "The boy thinks he's a racehorse. A bit overeager."

The audience tittered.

Rill's face, neck, and ears felt as if they were on fire. At that moment, he hated Cato.

Cato lifted the chain of the Naming charm over Rill's head.

"When Cato puts the Naming charm around your neck, look me in the eyes. Don't waver. Just look me in the eyes until the Naming charm makes its decision." His mom's words rushed into Rill's head like a flash flood. Rill held his breath, hands clenched and ready to move. As soon as Cato adjusted the charm's back against Rill's skin, Rill spun toward the commoner adults' section. His eyes latched upon his mom's like a pair of bloodsuckers. What happened next surprised him. He couldn't look away. It was as if his mom's familiar dark-blue eyes had taken on a mesmerizing power to turn him into a statue. How else could he explain the stiffness in his body that made him unable to move?

"Look toward me, boy!" Cato said irritably.

Rill couldn't have obeyed him if he wanted to.

Cato gripped Rill's shoulders to turn him around. But as soon as his hand touched Rill's chestnut-colored short jacket, energy gushed into Rill's body, split into eight streams, and sped in different directions. Rill staggered when one stream stopped short as if it had slammed into a granite barrier. He vaguely felt both of Cato's hands holding him firmly by the shoulders.

"He's an archmage!" a commoner celebrant shouted. "The first one today."

A tingling sensation swirled in Rill's chest, then swept over his whole body. *Holy Goddess, my mom was right! I'm an archmage!* In his mind, he saw himself in a magnificent compound on The Citadel as an archmage and a magestrate.

Rill was barely aware of other voices exploding into shouts, mainly from the commoner sections. "Archmage! Archmage! Archmage!"

Cato removed the Naming charm. "It wasn't done properly!" he bellowed over the voices. "The boy must face me first. We have to do it over."

Each of Cato's words struck Rill's chest like daggers.

"It wouldn't have made no difference!" a woman hollered. "The Naming charm would've named him an archmage if he was facing you or not."

"That's right!" other angry voices yelled. "Archmage! Archmage!"

The commoners began stamping their feet to reinforce their shouts. The amphitheater echoed with their screams and stomping.

In the front row with other magestrates, Jukka Bern rose to his feet. "The boy is right!" he shouted at Cato, his voice cutting through the noise like a sharp sword. "Whether the boy was facing you or not makes no difference to the Naming charm."

Cato's fingernails dug into Rill's shoulders. "Rill Larkin, archmage! Our first one today."

Cato's tone seemed grudging as if he hated to say the words. But Rill didn't care what Cato thought. He didn't care what anyone thought. He grinned at the audience as he fought the urge to dance all over the dais. *I'm an archmage!*

He was on his way to fulfilling his dream.

## CHAPTER 22

Cato's Treachery

ENERGY PULSED THROUGH RILL'S body as he bounded down the Hall of Naming's white marble stairs. He hugged the joy close to his chest like a miser with a strong box full of precious goldies. Eagerly he joined the throng of celebrants, some of them, like himself, now fledgling mages who were milling in the Public Square trying to locate their families. "We're so proud of you," one mother said to her excited daughter.

Rill hoped his mom would say that to him, and his leg muscles yearned to break into a happy jig.

"There he is!" his dad called out.

The dour expressions on his parents', Grandma Cinna's, and Aunt Tarri's faces as they navigated their way through clusters of commoners and noblesse, made Rill's leg muscles go slack.

"Congratulations, Son," Marc said, patting Rill's shoulder.

"Yes," Kendra said. "Congratulations. You got your wish." She started to say something else but apparently changed her mind and blew out a sigh instead.

Grandma Cinna and Aunt Tarri complimented him too. But like his parents', their voices lacked the enthusiasm of the other fledglings' parents and relatives.

"I'm an archmage," Rill said, more to himself than to his folks. He loved the way the word felt on his tongue. "The only one named." He wondered what role his mom had played in his naming. *She ain't no mage.* Yet in his mind he saw those deep-blue eyes holding him prisoner on the dais.

Rill walked between his parents, with Grandma Cinna and Aunt Tarri trailing behind as they crossed the congested Public Square toward River Road. By the time they were halfway there, the crowd had thinned out as families split off in different directions toward the Five Hills and the various neighborhoods.

They walked leisurely through The Kings, past vendors hawking their wares, women and men gossiping on the sidewalks, children playing, and riders on horseback. But to Rill, it seemed as if he and his family were enclosed in a cage of glum silence. When they approached Jedd's tenement, Rill saw his chance to break free. "I gotta tell Jedd the news."

Rill found Jedd in his hunting room sitting on a stool sharpening his sword. Sunlight filtered in through the two windows, illuminating his workbench, several unstrung longbows hanging on pegs along the wall, along with quivers filled with different kinds of arrows.

Rill had followed Jedd's recovery closely by visiting almost every day. Jedd had healed enough to perform light tasks, such as sharpening his sword and dagger, which he seemed to do constantly. But his face still lacked color, and he had lost weight and tired easily. Next week he was going to return to work. But Cobb the bowyer had insisted that he only work part time until he was fully recovered. Rill was glad Jedd was returning to the bowyer's shop but also relieved that Cobb wanted to make sure Jedd didn't work so hard he suffered a relapse.

Jedd's brown eyes burned with excitement when Rill told him the wonderful news. "An archmage! Imagine that." Then a shadow crossed his face. "No First or Lesser Family's matriarch is interested in having me as a backwatcher. Soon I'll turn eighteen. And if I don't find a patron by then, I'll probably be conscripted." A note of desperation crept into his voice. "I don't wanna be a legionary or a seaman. If I'm conscripted, I'll run away."

"Where to?" Rill asked.

"Over the Sharp Teeth Mountains to Annatol."

Rill pictured what would happen if Jedd fled and, trying to make his way through a pass in the mountains, was captured by Geraldo Afrius's legions stationed on the Caldonian side. A judge would issue a warrant for his arrest. If Jedd were found guilty, he'd be executed. If he succeeded in reaching Annatol . . . *Goddess help him!* He wouldn't last long, despite his fighting skills, in that barbaric, ungoddessly place.

Rill grinned to himself as an idea slipped into his mind. "I'm an archmage. They're in short supply. First and Lesser Families will compete at the bidding to have me as an apprentice. And, ya know, even apprentice mages have backwatchers. So I'll ask that you be mine."

Jedd clasped Rill's hand. "Thanks. I hope you succeed."

A warm glow filled Rill's chest as he walked with light footsteps the rest of the way home. What he'd told Jedd wasn't bragging. He'd make certain Jedd didn't have to flee to Annatol.

Rill's warm glow quickly faded when he arrived home to find his mom and dad in the kitchen sitting side by side at the larger trestle table, their expressions so grave it wouldn't have surprised him if they told him Grandma Cinna had died.

Kendra pointed to the bench on the opposite side. "Sit."

Rill obeyed, knowing they were going to stomp down his happiness over being named an archmage. *But mom, she wanted me to be an archmage.* He found the contradiction between what he'd overheard in his parents' bedroom and the heated words he now anticipated confusing. But he might be wrong. *Wait and see what they say.*

Kendra folded her hands on the tabletop and bent toward him. "You've been named an archmage. You know your dad and I were opposed to it—"

"Then why did you tell me to look you in the eyes? Are you some kinda mage?"

Kendra flinched as if a wasp had stung her. "Don't be silly. Like I said. Your dad and I were opposed to you becoming a mage. But you had your mind set on it. And I thought if you focused all your atten-tion on me, you'd make it easier for the Naming charm to determine what kind of magic was your strongest."

"We had no idea you'd be named an archmage," his dad said.

Lies. But why? Rill held his thoughts close to his chest like a card player not wanting to show his hand.

Kendra leaned even closer to him. "Your dad and I don't think you know what you're getting yourself into."

"I'm on my way to becoming noblesse," Rill said. "*That's* what I'm getting myself into. And there ain't nothin' you can do about it."

A vein in Kendra's neck bulged, and Rill braced himself to receive her fury. Fortunately, his dad placed a restraining hand on her arm. Squeezing her eyes shut, she managed to rein in her temper. "We're happy you achieved your dream," she went on more calmly. "You're an archmage. But you're not an ordinary one. That's what your dad and I were afraid of—"

"How did you know that?"

"Because you demonstrated it when you set the stable on fire."

Rill smirked as memories, admittedly now sanitized, popped into his mind. "And without using a staff. That's when I knew I'd be named a mage. But I had no idea I'd be an archmage." *Till I heard you say it.*

Kendra grabbed his wrist, her fingers tightening like a wrist brace. "You have the power, but you're not trained in controlling it."

"Umm . . . ain't that the point of fledgling training? To learn how to control it."

Kendra's fingers tightened even more, making Rill wince. "Learn-ing to control it isn't good enough. You've got to *master* the power. That will be your only defense."

Rill felt as if he'd suddenly become lost in well-known woods. "Defense. Against what?"

"Enemies who want to destroy you."

"What are ya talkin' about?"

"The noblesse," Marc said. "We've made a great many enemies among them because we turned most of the Kings dwellers against them. Made our neighbors self-reliant. Now our enemies have become your enemies."

Rill broke free of his mother's grip. "That ain't helpful." He massaged his wrist. "Just who are these 'enemies'?"

"The Estatis," Kendra said.

"The Estatis!" Rill snorted his disbelief. "You're just saying that 'cause Lord Deuth took my side so I could go to my Name Day Celebration. You lost, and now you're peeved."

"He had his reasons for doing that. And they weren't to help you."

"What reasons?"

"He wants to turn you against us."

"He don't hafta worry none about doing that." Rill spat the words. "You've both done a great job of it yourselves."

"We were trying to protect you," Kendra said. "We've had our differences with you. But your dad and I can't let you go heedlessly into danger. You're our son. We want you to live. Perhaps someday you'll be able to find your way to the right path. Just like—"

Marc placed a hand on Kendra's shoulder, silencing her.

Rill eyed his parents coldly. *They want to turn me against Lord Deuth 'cause they hate him. Well, it won't work.* "Who else can't I trust?"

"Cato Porta," Marc said. "He's gonna train you fledglings like he does every month to make them ready to find mentors. Know this: he hates you 'cause you're our son. And he'll use fledgling training to destroy you."

"But he'll do it legally," Kendra said. "So beware of him."

First, they try to turn me against Lord Deuth. And now they try turn me against my fledgling instructor. "Anyone else?" Rill asked, unable to keep cynicism from his voice.

"The Svaggas. They hate you as much as the Estatis do. Especially Brico."

Icy fingers walked down Rill's spine. He suppressed a shudder. The Svaggas! Almost every commoner hated that cruel and ruthless family. "And the Dejunes?" he said, his tone still skeptical. "Can I trust them?"

"No."

"Kendra," Marc said, shooting her a reproving look.

Kendra chewed on her lip. "Well, perhaps Alyse."

Figures. She can't turn me against Alyse 'cause of the temple raid. So they turn me against her family. Fat chance. "Why can I trust her, but no one else?"

Kendra threw a questioning look at Marc, who crooked an eyebrow as if to say that answering was up to her. "I can't tell you because you're not prepared to believe me. Perhaps someday . . . when you're ready."

Yeah. Sure. Rill glared at his mother. "So you're telling me that among all the noblesse, there *might* be just one I can trust?"

Kendra met his skeptical frown head-on. "Yes. That's exactly what I'm telling you. You chose to become a mage. And you want more than anything else to become noblesse. If you want to succeed in doing that—and to live—you can trust no one. Welcome to their world."

Rill considered her final words an overly dramatic touch. "That ain't very comforting."

Kendra's lips pressed into a bleak smile. "That's how noblesse live, Rill. Every one of them. Every day of the year. And every year of their lives. If you want to become one of them, you have to start thinking and acting like them."

She ain't scarin' me with her overly dramatic hogwash. Rill wanted to clap his hands and say, "Bravo. Fine performance." Instead, he climbed silently to his feet and left the kitchen.

His parents' gloom-and-doom lecture created a distance between him and them while he waited impatiently for the next day, the first day of the new month, when fledgling training would begin.

The next morning's sun shone as brightly as Rill's dreams of his future when he stepped out the front door. He hurried along the streets, ignoring vendors setting up their sidewalk booths and people beginning their daily routines. His objective was the Hall of Naming where fledgling training would be taught. After hurrying across the

Public Square, he raced up the marble stairs into the antechamber.

A Magesterium servant directed him toward a doorway in the left wall. Rill hurried through it into a hallway lined with several doors. Another Magesterium servant pointed him toward a door on the left. "Noblesse sit on the left," he said. "Commoners sit on the right."

Rill paused just over the threshold. He was standing in the rear aisle of a lecture hall. Ten rows of tiered desks descended to the floor. An isle split the tiers into two unequal sections, the desks on the right outnumbering the ones on the left. A table and a lectern stood on the floor, and a large rectangular slate board took up the wall behind them. A door on the left led to the adjoining room. Oil lamps set in sconces along walls threw the room into light and shadow.

Fledglings who had arrived earlier were already sitting at desks. Six noblesse occupied the left section. A girl sat by herself, well apart from the rest. The other five had split into two groups, separated by a couple of rows. Rill figured the divisions probably reflected the three noblesse factions: Noblessari, Traditionali, and Commonali. Nervous commoners scattered themselves throughout the right-hand section.

A girl's irritated voice spoke behind him. "You gonna take a seat, or stand there all day gaping?"

Rill stepped aside to let her by. "Sorry."

The tall, freckle-faced girl glanced at him, then smiled. "You're the archmage."

Pride swelled Rill's heart. "Yeah." He peered more closely at her. A memory popped into his mind of the wild applause when the amber gemstone in the Naming charm lit up. Like him, the only celebrant with that kind of magic. "You're the illusionist."

The girl flipped back a lock of long, dark-brown hair that had strayed over an eye. "Yeah. I'm Larissa."

"I'm Rill."

"Well, good luck," Larissa said and headed for a desk down front in the first row of the commoner section.

Rill chose a desk midway down the aisle but not too close to other commoner fledglings.

Alyse Dejune and her twin sister—Mora, Rill recalled, who had been named a mindbender—arrived a little later. Rill's gaze shot to Alyse like a bird on the wing.

Mora noticed him looking. Her lips twisted into a catty smile. She whispered something to Alyse, who shot her an angry look. Mora sniggered, then waved eagerly at the noblesse girl sitting alone and headed toward her.

Alyse returned Rill's look, and tossed him a warm smile.

He grinned, and hoped she might come over to chat, but she joined Mora and the other girl. Rill's shoulders wanted to slump with disappointment. *Maybe she's embarrassed to recognize me in front of her sister and her noblesse friends.* He quickly tossed the glum thought aside because her smile had told him the opposite.

Cato Porta entered after all the fledglings had arrived, his old-fashioned clothes sagging on his sparse frame. He cradled a small wooden box bound by metal bands and held parchment sheets in his hand. After placing the box on the table, he went to the lectern, consulted the sheets, and called the roll. When Rill's turn came and he raised his hand, Cato's eyes sped to him.

"Our young archmage," Cato said. "We're not often graced with a fledgling archmage. Come down to the front, boy, where it will be easier for you to learn."

Cato pointed to a desk near Larissa's. Rill's lungs expanded with pride as he switched seats, conscious of everyone's eyes on him. His lips kept wanting to twitch into a huge grin. *I'm the only archmage who was named. And now Cato's showing how important I am. In front of the entire class.* He recalled his parents' caution about Cato. This seat changing showed how wrong they were.

When he finished taking attendance, Cato tossed the list on the table and rested his forearms on the lectern. "The great mage of old, Lucas Stylish, said, 'A mage without a charm is a mage without power.' How true! Without a charm, a mage is just like an ordinary citizen. But with a charm, the mage becomes *extraordinary*."

Cato ran his tongue back and forth against his bottom lip while he scanned the sea of attentive faces. "If you pass fledgling training, where will you get your charms? For you noblesse fledglings, that question's easily answered. From your families." He turned to Rill's section. "But commoner families don't have charms. So where will you get yours?"

"From a patron," a commoner said.

"Correct. And where do you get a patron?"

"At the bidding," Larissa said.

"And what's the bidding?"

Rill spoke up before anyone else had a chance. "When noblesse bid on the commoner fledglings who graduate from our class. They always need more mages." *And they'll bid high for me 'cause I'm an archmage.*

"Correct." Cato moved out from behind the lectern and stood in front of the commoners. "Fledgling training is designed to teach you the basic fundamentals of magic. During the course of your training, representatives from the First and Lesser Families who need household mages will monitor your progress. When your training ends, the families will have the opportunity to bid to become your patrons. If you're lucky enough to get a patron, she will assign you a mentor to give you further instruction. For those of you who don't get a patron, don't worry. Both the legions and the sea service always need mages. And for those of you who get rejected by the military . . ." Cato shrugged. "Oh, well. It's back to being ordinary."

Moving to the table, Cato unlocked the box and drew out a charm by its chain. He held the amulet aloft, then briefly explained that the charm drew its power from the magic plane and that the mage, in turn, drew that power from the charm. His explanation was something Rill and every other Caldonian knew.

Cato placed the charm on the table, then wrote ACTUS on the slate board. "We call this the 'A-word' because it activates the charm. Whenever the back of your charm is touching your skin, the charm becomes part of you. So never *ever* say the A-word unless you intend to draw on the magic plane's energy to cast a spell."

Cato tossed the chalk onto the lectern. "That's one of the most important principles of magic you fledglings should know. But here's another principle that's just as important. Who controls the magic energy—the charm or the mage?"

The question stumped the class, even the noblesse fledglings. Some thought the mage, and others thought the charm. Cato stood watching them argue back and forth, a half smile on his lips. At last he picked up the charm again.

"Actions speak louder than words. So a little demonstration is in order." Cato nodded at Rill. "Perhaps our young fledgling archmage can help us. Come up here, boy."

Rill rose with feigned nonchalance that hid pride in being selected and went up to Cato, who had him face the class.

"I'm going to put this training charm on our archmage. And then, Larkin, I want you to say the A-word and tell me who controls the magic energy—you or the charm."

Rill waited impatiently as Cato fastened the chain around his neck and tucked the charm beneath his tunic, arranging the amulet's back against his bare chest. He pulled himself up taller, his lips threatening a foolish grin. The other fledglings stared intently at him.

"There's nothing to worry about," Cato whispered in Rill's ear. "It's only a training charm." He stepped away. "Now, boy, say the A-word."

Rill scanned the other faces and—he couldn't help it—his lips formed a smile all by themselves. "Actus."

Power coursed through Rill's body just like it had when he'd used the rohan's charm in his dad's stable. He fumbled with the charm's chain in a desperate attempt to whip it off over his head. But too late. Before his fingers touched the chain, the energy seized control of his body. Rill's eyes rolled back in his head, and he went into convulsions.

Rill felt his life's force being sucked out of him.

And he couldn't stop it!

## CHAPTER 23

Hollow Mage

RED-HOT COALS BURNED fiercely in Alyse's stomach when Rill went into convulsions. And Cato just stood there! Arms folded, he watched Rill with a faint smile on his lips. She looked around wildly. The other fledglings were gaping at Rill, mesmerized.

"Take off the charm!" she screamed.

Cato continued watching Rill's paroxysm as if he were examining the effects of an interesting spell from a spell book.

Leaping from her seat, Alyse sprinted to Rill and wrenched off the charm. Rill collapsed. Casting the charm aside, Alyse caught him under the arms, his weight making her stagger backward.

Rage boiled in Cato's eyes. "How dare you interfere!"

Alyse eased Rill to the floor and knelt beside him. She hurled a barbed look at Cato and wished she could cast a similar spell on Cato and watch *him* go into convulsions. "You despicable old man! You knew the charm was too powerful for Rill to control. I've learned enough from our household mages to know you need to say the Q-word to deactivate a charm. You didn't tell us that because you didn't want Rill to know how to turn off the charm."

"You forget yourself, Alyse Dejune."

Alyse stood to face Cato, pulling herself up to her full height, which barely came to his chin. "You're the one who's forgetting himself. Your role is to teach us the rudiments of magic, not to mistreat a helpless commoner. And you call yourself our teacher." She blew out a disgusted breath. "You should be removed from ever teaching fledglings again. I'll report this to my grandfather. I'm sure he'll have something to say about this."

Cato's eyes narrowed into angry slits. "How dare you speak to me like that."

Alyse imitated the contemptuous tone she'd heard Great-Grandmother Siema use so many times before she'd joined the ancestors. "I'm Alyse Dejune. My ancestors were great mages in Euloria hundreds of years before your first matriarch was born . . . in *Caldon*." She spat that last word at him as if it were some vile-tasting thing. "The blood of Ulbra Thane runs in *my* veins. Tell me, Cato Porta . . . whose blood runs in yours?"

Cato bared his yellowish teeth as if he were a rabid wolf. "I'll teach you."

He muttered "Actus" under his breath and slowly brought his arm up with his index finger pointing at Alyse.

She smiled disdainfully at him. "Go ahead. 'Teach' me. Just remember. My grandfather is Jukka Berne, sole presiding chief magestrate. And my uncle commands the Eastern Legions. What will they say about what you 'taught' me?"

Cato's arm stopped in midair as he struggled to master his anger. Then, slowly, his arm fell to his side. "There's no need to tell your grandfather about this. That charm was a mistake. I was in such a rush to get here on time that I took the wrong one."

Alyse knew he was lying because he didn't panic when Rill was convulsing. "I just hope you don't make another 'mistake' like that again."

Turning her back on Cato, she helped Rill to his desk.

"What a dumb thing to do," Mora said after Alyse rejoined her. "Now you've humiliated Cato."

Mora was right. Alyse knew she had just humiliated, in front of her fellow fledglings, one of the most powerful mages in Caldon.

By defending Rill, Cato Porta was no longer just her family's political enemy. He had become her personal enemy as well.

# # #

Rill sat at his desk, resting his head on his folded arms. Cato had called a break until after lunch because of "concern for our young archmage." But Rill had been too weak to move and had no appetite. Now his body was recovering, and his belly was beginning to growl for food. He replayed the incident in his mind. His dad had warned him against Cato, and he wondered if Cato had really taken the wrong charm by mistake. *Yeah. Mistakes happen.* So he decided to give him the benefit of the doubt. Behind Rill, footsteps came softly through the doorway into the classroom and down the aisle and stopped by his desk.

"Rill?"

The familiar voice made Rill glance up into Alyse Dejune's concerned green eyes. Gratitude for this noblesse girl diffused throughout his body like a warm mist. He straightened in his seat while she sat down at the neighboring desk.

"How are you?" Alyse asked.

"I've felt better." Rill lobbed her a tentative smile. "Thanks for pulling off that charm. I owe you a lot."

"What I did can't compare to what you did for me at the One Goddess Temple. And I never got a chance to thank you for rescuing me."

"You didn't need no rescuing. You can take care of yourself with that dagger of yours."

Alyse placed a hand on Rill's arm, the warmth of her fingers sinking through his tunic's coarse wool sleeve into his skin. "I'm thanking you anyway."

"It was Jedd that did it. And your friend Kate." Rill looked at her inquisitively. "Or is she your backwatcher?"

"She's both. How's Jedd?"

"He's much recovered. And Kate?"

"She's recovering."

"Well, isn't this the happy couple."

Alyse whipped around, removing her hand from Rill's arm as if she'd been scorched. Rill glanced toward the voice.

Mora Dejune stood in the doorway. She walked down the aisle and stopped by their desks. She squinted at them. "Why do I get the feeling you know each other?"

Rill was about to say they'd met when the One Goddess Temple was attacked, but Alyse spoke first. "I think taking the charm off his neck was a pretty good introduction."

Rill took her hint that they were strangers. "Yeah, it was." He smiled at Alyse. "And I'm glad she came to see how I am. No one else did."

Mora eyed them distrustfully. Before she could say anything else, fledglings began drifting into the room. Alyse left with Mora and returned to her desk.

Before long, Cato came through the side door and called the class to order. "This morning's accident with our young archmage was unfortunate," he said. "And I apologize for it. But it does illustrate an extremely important point about using charms. Can someone tell me what that is?"

Before anyone could answer, Cato pointed at Rill. "How about you."

"Don't use a charm that's more powerful than your own power to control it," Rill said.

"Why?"

"'Cause if the charm's more powerful, it'll suck up all your personal energy."

"Correct." Cato beamed at Rill as if he were a star pupil, then swept his gaze across the other students. "See what experiencing something firsthand does for learning? It's a lesson our young archmage won't forget."

Rill hid a grimace. *I could of learned a different way.*

Cato seemed not to notice. He placed his forearms on the reading stand and leaned toward the class, his expression dead serious. "The lesson our young archmage learned this morning, and which you learned through him, is basic to spellcasting. Magic energy and personal energy are in a constant tug of war. When you cast a spell, you expend personal energy. If you use too much of it, you won't be able to prevent the magic plane from sucking up all your personal energy. So the smart mage stops casting spells before she reaches that point."

Cato opened the side door and stepped aside. "Bring him in."

A black-clad Magesterium servant pushed a wooden-wheeled chair with a thin elderly man sitting in it into the room. The servant maneuvered the chair in front of the table, facing the fledglings. The man in the chair stared vacantly at them.

Cato placed a hand on the man's shoulder. "May I introduce Rodleen Gespar. He used to be a mage. Now he's what we call a 'hollow mage.' Can anyone tell me what a hollow mage is?"

The room went deadly silent while some of the fledglings darted uncomfortable looks at one other, and others averted their eyes from Cato.

Cato nodded at Rill. "Not even our young archmage?"

Rill's gut squirmed while a horrifying suspicion settled in the pit of his stomach.

Cato heaved a theatrical sigh. "A hollow mage is a mage who's had all her personal energy sucked out of her by the magic plane." Cato grimaced and shook his head. "Poor Rodleen is a commoner who was your average household mage. But he wasn't satisfied with the abilities the One Goddess gave him. Oh, no. Not good old Rodleen. He had *ambition* and deluded himself into believing he could become more powerful than his betters. He tried to use a charm that was too powerful for him." Cato patted Rodleen's shoulder. "This is the result."

Rodleen continued staring straight ahead through lifeless eyes, oblivious to Cato and the fledglings.

Rill's throat constricted so tightly he couldn't breathe. *That could of been me!*

## CHAPTER 24

Practice Charms

ALYSE GLANCED SIDEWAYS AT Mora, who had just sat down beside her at the dinner table. It would be just like her to mention this morning's incident between Cato Porta and Rill Larkin. But after the meal was served, Alyse was dumbfounded when Maude dismissed the servants and spoke to Jukka.

"Are you sure we have the votes to elect Deuth co-chief magestrate to replace Locien?"

"He's as good as elected," Jukka replied, his hazel eyes gleaming with malicious delight.

Pilar's eyes burned with curiosity. "Is it really feasible?"

Maude uttered a cynical laugh from the head of the table. "For a special election to replace a co-chief magestrate who died in office, the magestrates—not the people—vote. I already have agreement from the matriarchs of our allied families that their men will vote for Deuth tomorrow in the Magesterium. So, yes. The election's already won. After he completes Locien's term, Deuth will run for a full term next year, and our families will remain in control of the state."

Alyse and Mora swapped quizzical looks as Jukka ran a thumb across smirking lips. "We'll take Cato and his Traditionali cronies off guard," he said. "They think we're going to bring up the matter of Locien's replacement next week."

Maude tapped the tabletop, then pointed to Alyse and Mora. "Not a word of this to anyone."

The continual intrigue among the political factions made disgust slosh around in Alyse's belly like bilge water, and she couldn't wait until dinner ended so she could escape to see Kate.

Alyse found her cousin sitting up in bed, propped against a pair of fluffy pillows, reading a book by lamplight. Pulling up a chair, Alyse sat down and asked how she was feeling.

Kate plucked irritably at the top sheet and blanket and repeated what she'd said again and again over the past days. "I want to get out of this bed. I can't stand the inactivity."

"Lenia said you need a lot of rest."

"I guess she's right." Kate sighed. "I'm so tired all the time."

"You almost died." Alyse's lie tugged at her heart.

"But I didn't."

She wished she could tell Kate the truth about how Kendra had pulled her back from Elustra. But a promise was a promise, no matter how difficult to keep.

When Kate asked about Alyse's first day of fledgling training, Alyse told her how Cato had almost turned Rill into a hollow mage. "I'm not sure if it was intentional."

"I wouldn't trust that old codger." Kate closed her eyes. "I think I'll sleep for a while."

The next morning Alyse got up late because fledgling training was always postponed until the afternoon on the days the Magesterium met so Cato could attend the sessions.

As she and Mora were crossing the receiving hall to leave, Grandfather Jukka stormed through the front door, slamming it shut on his nine dynamae who had escorted him home, and stomped past them without a glance.

Alyse had never seen him in such a foul mood before.

Alyse followed him with puzzled eyes as he passed into the family area. "What's eating him?"

Mora sniggered. "I bet the Magesterium meeting didn't go the way he expected."

Mora's hunch proved correct. On their way down The Citadel and across the Public Square, Alyse and Mora caught snippets of excited, mirthful, or outraged conversations from clusters of people they passed. Bit by bit, they pieced together what had happened. The Commonali had joined with Cato Porta's Traditionali to hand Grandfather Jukka's Noblessari a resounding defeat by voting down Deuth's nomination as co-chief magestrate. Afterward, the factions hadn't been able to agree on a replacement, which left Grandfather Jukka as sole chief magestrate for the rest of the year. It was obvious to Alyse that the Traditionali had caught wind of Jukka's maneuver and formed an alliance with the Commonali to thwart it.

"Who do you think tipped off old Cato?" she asked.

"Probably a spy in one of the Noblessari households." Mora snickered. "I bet the old goat's gloating."

Mora shot Alyse an I-told-you-so smile when Cato entered the classroom with an uncharacteristic bounce in his step. He also had three gray-clad city watchers in tow. One watcher carried an iron strongbox that she set on the table while the others took up positions by each door.

Alyse watched with rapt attention as Cato unlocked the box with a key and took out square silver charms, which he arranged side by side in rows on the table. Then he scanned the fledglings' curious faces while he ran his tongue back and forth against his inner lower lip.

"Yesterday you learned that *you* control the flow of energy from the magic plane." Cato tossed Rill a frosty smile. "You also learned if you can't control magic energy, the magic energy will control *you*—with disastrous results."

Cato held up a charm by its silver chain. "This is an energy charm. It doesn't hold spells but it does access the magic plane. For the next few days, you will learn how to win the struggle between magic energy and your personal energy. It's called Tug of War. The magic plane tugs personal energy from your bodies while you tug magic energy from the magic plane into your bodies. The objective is to control the flow of magic energy in and out of your bodies. Once you master energy charms, you'll be ready to try your hand with practice charms that contain spells."

Alyse glanced at Mora, excitement dancing in her eyes. *I'm going to become as good a healer as Priestess Sybil.*

Cato put the charm back on the table. "The energy charms only separate those of you who can handle magic energy from those who can't. The tough part comes when you get assigned instructors who will teach you how cast actual spells with the practice charms. Each instructor has her own way of controlling magic energy. She'll teach you her personal techniques for handling it."

Alyse raised her hand.

"Yes?"

"With the energy charms and practice charms, is there any danger of having the magic plane drain your personal energy?"

"Yes," Cato said. "So none of you should become complacent. Even an energy charm can turn an incompetent fledgling into a hollow mage if she can't control the flow."

Alyse looked at Rill. Other fledglings did too. His face wore a wooden expression.

"You'll work in pairs," Cato said. "One will wear the charm while the other watches. If the charm wearer appears to be losing control, her partner will pull off the charm." He waved a dismissive hand at them. "Now find a partner. Noblesse pair with noblesse and commoners pair with commoners."

Mora raced toward a boy whose family was Noblessari, leaving Alyse surrounded by shuffling feet. She scanned the noblesse fledglings, searching for a lone Noblessari. But they all had paired off, leaving her without a partner. She spotted a Traditionali and a Commonali fledgling who remained unpaired. *There's no reason why my partner has to be Noblessari.* When she started toward the Commonali girl, the girl mouthed, "No!" and scurried toward the Traditionali girl. Alyse snorted to herself in disgust. *The new alliance between the Traditionali and Commonali includes the children.*

Alyse looked at Cato. He was staring at Rill. She groaned inwardly in dismay. Rill was standing alone, the odd commoner out.

Cato's mouth morphed into a nasty smile. "Well, boy, it looks like I'll have to be your partner."

Alyse hurried across to Rill, put a hand on his arm, and spoke to Cato in a firm tone. "I'll be his partner." From the corner of her eye, she caught relief flicker across Rill's face.

Cato pointed to a pair of noblesse fledglings. "Join them. A group of three is acceptable."

Alyse's hand tightened on Rill's arm. "I choose Rill."

"Impossible," Cato said. "We don't mix noblesse with commoners."

Alyse's muscles tensed while she held Cato's gaze. "Then it's time you did."

Cato's mouth popped open at her cheekiness, then closed with an audible *click* of teeth. "Why, you—" He swallowed whatever words he was about to say and spoke in a tone teeming with sarcasm. "How *charitable* of you. Sacrificing your own progress to help our young archmage with his."

"I believe in putting others first," Alyse responded, straight faced.

Cato glared at her, hands balled into fists, and then he turned away.

Cato's first assignment was to have the fledglings activate their charms and bring the two energy flows into equilibrium. Alyse went first. When Rill's turn came, he seemed hesitant—almost fearful. Alyse attributed his reluctance to yesterday's experience with Cato's charm. As soon as Rill activated the energy charm, relief spread across his face. Then his body went rigid, and the tendons stood out on his neck.

"My personal energy's being pulled into the magic plane!" he said, panic rising in his voice.

Speaking calmly, Alyse suggested Rill visualize the charm as a door to the magic plane, which he could open or close at will. "Open it a crack, just wide enough to let in a little bit of magic energy," she said. "And don't leave enough space for your personal energy to get out."

Rill squeezed his eyes shut and appeared to concentrate, standing as frozen as an ice sculpture. Then his body relaxed, his eyes popped open, and he grinned in relief. "I can control it!" He shook his head in wonderment. "If I didn't know better, I'd think you're already a magic user."

Alyse smiled at him.

Rill's grin faded. "What'll Cato say? We're supposed to do Tug of War."

Alyse glanced at Cato who was observing a pair of noblesse fledglings. "What he doesn't know won't hurt him."

On the last day of training with practice charms, Cato briskly dismissed five fledglings who hadn't mastered the energy glow. Alyse watched them leave, two of them sobbing. Sympathy for them flooded through her because they had so much wanted to become mages. At the same time, she renewed her vow not to wash out like them because failure would mean a choice between a quick marriage to Troy or a flight to Uncle Leoc—a decision she wasn't yet ready to make.

After the five fledglings left, Cato placed his forearms on the podium and leaned toward the class. "The rest of you learned how to activate and deactivate energy charms and how to control the flow of magic power. Your actual training starts tomorrow when you begin to work with practice charms that contain spells." Cato nodded at the door the rejected fledglings had gone through. "They're the chaff. Usually we find more. But, just so you don't grow too smug, some of you will wash out during the next training phase."

"Not me," Mora whispered excitedly to Alyse.

Cato paused to shoot Mora a disapproving look. "The next time we meet," he continued, "you commoner fledglings will break into groups according to your type of magic. I'll assign mages to instruct each group. The groups will train in different rooms. As for you noblesse fledglings, your matriarchs will select instructors for you, and you'll train at home."

The fledglings exchanged looks, their expressions a mixture of apprehension and excitement.

"Oh, one more thing," Cato said as if a thought had just come to mind. "We have a young archmage with us." He pointed at Rill. "You'll train with me, boy."

An unsettled look worked its way onto Rill's face.

Alyse wondered if he was thinking of Cato's mistake that had almost turned him into a hollow mage. She thought about mentioning the incident to Deuth Estati, but feared he'd dismiss her concern through lack of evidence. If Deuth did confront Cato over it, Cato would double down on his explanation of having taken the wrong charm by mistake.

Cato had *made a mistake, right?* Alyse wondered.

## CHAPTER 25

Wind Against Shield

A POWERFUL BLAST OF wind knocked Rill backward off his feet. His head struck the wall with a painful *thump,* and he collapsed upon the classroom's hardwood floor. Pushing himself into a sitting position, Rill shook his head to clear the mental fog before he climbed unsteadily to his feet with the help of his staff.

Rill muttered a curse. That was the fifth time in a row Cato's Wind spell had knocked him down. His eyes hurled daggers at Cato. "You're supposed to be using a level-one practice charm like me. But you're not. Yours is more powerful. So how can I defend myself against your spell?"

"Having second thoughts about training?" Cato asked, his tone mocking.

"Gimme a charm as powerful as yours," Rill said. "Then you'll see what I can do."

"Nonsense, boy! My Wind spell's level one, just like your Shield spell. The caster's focus determines the spell's strength. Put more focus on your cast. Fling it at me."

Frustration churned in Rill like molten lava in a rumbling volcano. *How can I fling a shield?* He placed himself in position again, grounded the butt of his staff, and muttered, "Sheldva."

An almost invisible wall appeared in front of him. Cato had told him that a strong Shield would appear as a semitransparent barrier. His was barely that.

"Prepare yourself, boy!"

Rill wondered how many more Wind spells he could endure. But no matter the number, he wouldn't quit.

A strong blast of wind punched through Rill's shield and knocked him over. Rill pulled himself into a sitting position and discovered Cato towering over him.

Cato wiped his fingers on his tunic as if casting the spell with them had dirtied them. "What do you think of that, boy?"

"My father's tougher."

"Prideful words, boy. Prideful words. They often come before the fall."

A voice spoke from the doorway. "Cato, you're damaging my fledgling. That will never do."

Deuth Estati.

Hope sparked in Rill.

"*Your* fledgling?" Cato said.

"Yes. My family has taken a special interest in him."

Rill squeezed his eyes shut as tears of relief welled. He was under the Estatis' protection! Opening his eyes, he quickly wiped the tears away with his sleeve.

"Which caused quite a stir among certain families." Cato chuckled.

"Then you also know Lady Ariella made me his guardian."

"Not for long. He's about to wash out."

"He is, huh?" Deuth walked down to the first row and sat on a desktop. "What spells are you casting?"

"My Wind against his Shield."

"I suppose you told Rill how to increase his spell's strength by collecting energy from the magic plane before the cast."

"That's not the point of this lesson."

Deuth rubbed his chin as if pondering Cato's response. "I see. You have a different point to make from the one I'd make if I were his instructor."

"What's that?"

"You emphasize the problems inherent in making a weak cast where I show the advantages of making a strong cast. For example, I explain that the intensity of power is a state of mind. To increase the caster's power, I recommend the fledgling visualize herself snapping up handfuls of energy from the magic plane and stuffing it into her own reservoir of personal energy."

"That's in keeping with your style," Cato said. "I believe it's called 'making a power grab.'"

"I prefer to call it 'increasing my personal power.'"

"I'm sure you do," Cato mocked.

"Wind against Shield isn't a particularly challenging pairing of spells," Deuth said. "No wonder Rill lacks motivation. Tell me, does his practice charm contain Repel?"

Cato eyed Deuth distrustfully. "Yes."

"Personally, Cato, I'd pair Wind against Repel. You know, Venta against Throba. It makes the exercise much more interesting for both casters."

"How kind of you to scatter your seeds of wisdom at our humble feet," Cato said. "Unfortunately, the boy's planted himself on barren ground. The seeds won't sprout."

"Time will tell." Deuth readjusted his position on the desktop. "But please continue with your lesson. I'll just sit here and watch."

Cato turned to Rill, his face dark with anger." Prepare yourself, boy."

Rill hurriedly cast the Shield spell. But Cato's wind punched through the still-forming barrier and struck Rill in the stomach. Rill's breath exploded from his mouth as he stumbled backward. Somehow he managed to keep on his feet.

Cato spread his hands to Deuth in a conciliatory gesture. "See what I was saying? The boy has no ability. He can't even master a first-level practice spell. I think it's time I put an end to his absurd ambitions." Cato's tone turned snide. "He should stick to being a blacksmith like his father."

Dark clouds of rage brewed in Rill's mind like a gathering thunderstorm. He turned furious eyes on Cato, who had humiliated him in front of the only mage who had believed in him. The only mage who had stood up for him against his family.

His rage burst free, and he began taking handful after handful of power from the magic plane and stuffing it into his pool of weak personal energy. "No!" Rill shouted. "Let me try again."

"Too late, boy," Cato said. "You've washed out. Go home."

"One more chance!" Rill said, still hauling in power.

"You've already had more chances than you deserve."

Rill sneered at him. "What's wrong—scared I might beat you?"

"I don't want to waste any more time on an arrogant kid who has no ability."

"You *are* scared!"

Cato laughed so hard tears trickled down his cheeks. Wiping them away, he turned to Deuth. "The boy's a comedian. He should join a theatrical troupe."

"I think he shows spunk, myself," Deuth said, standing up. "Perhaps you should accept his challenge."

"Don't be ridiculous. You're the boy's guardian. You see him out." Cato headed for the door.

"Coward!" Rill yelled.

"Perhaps Rill has a point," Deuth said. "Maybe you *are* afraid he'll best you."

Cato spun around. "Have you gone daft like the boy?"

Deuth shrugged. "Why else would you refuse a rematch, except that you're scared?"

"Because I have more important things to do."

"What could be more important than defending your reputation?"

"Against that whelp? Don't be silly."

"What will your supporters say? The mighty Cato refused a fledgling's challenge to a final rematch to prove his incompetence once and for all."

"That I was justified in not wasting my time."

"Perhaps." Deuth chewed his lip. "But consider what your detractors will say."

Cato's bushy white brows plunged into a frown. "What do you mean?"

"They'll say you were frightened of the blacksmith's son."

Cato shot Deuth a long, suspicious look. "What's your game?"

"I have none. You're Rill's teacher and I'm his guardian. You want to dismiss him for incompetence, and I want you to honor his request for a final rematch."

Cato appeared to hem and haw. "All right. Fine. One last rematch." He stalked back to his former position and stretched out his arm, fingers extended. "Prepare yourself, boy."

Rill focused on Cato's mouth, not his fingers. When Cato's lips began to move, Rill cast his spell. "Throba!"

A tremendous burst of power raced through Rill's arm into his staff and shot out the crystal faster than an arrow from a bow with a hundred-pound draw weight. The two spells clashed in midair. A mild gust of wind buffeted Rill while an invisible fist struck Cato in the chest. Cato flailed his arms to keep his balance, but his legs collapsed beneath him like a pair of broken sticks, and he hit the floorboards hard.

Rill strode to Cato's prostrate figure. "What do ya think of *that*, old man?"

Cato glared at him.

Behind Rill, Deuth clapped. "Bravo, bravo."

Rill hugged the two words to himself as if they were a warm comforter. He'd proven himself to his champions, the Estatis.

## CHAPTER 26

Tempting Future

EUPHORIA MADE RILL'S CHEST tingle as he grinned at Cato lying on the floor. *I defeated him! I knew I could do it.*

Deuth came up alongside Rill, slung an arm around his shoulder, and chuckled. "Admit it, Cato. Rill does have talent. He threw most of your Wind spell back at you."

With a moan, Cato worked himself into a sitting position. Deuth offered him a hand, but Cato slapped it away, snatched Rill's staff, and pushed himself to his feet.

"A cheap trick. That's what it was." Cato limped to Deuth and stuck his nose in Deuth's face. "And you put him up to it."

"I simply mentioned an important technique to him. One you should have taught him instead of abusing him with that ridiculous Wind against Shield combination. Rill proved his talent by taking my suggestion and defeating you with it, using a spell he'd never cast before."

"Gathering magic energy to make a stronger cast. That was going to be tomorrow's lesson."

"Oh yes. I'm sure it was." Deuth's voice hardened. "Train him properly."

"That's the blacksmith's son you're talking about. Or have you forgotten how his—"

"Watch your mouth! Keep it up, and I might have to teach you a lesson."

A smile slithered across Cato's lips. "That might be something worth experiencing."

The two archmages locked eyes for what seemed like a long time. All the while, Rill conjured up images of the two enemies flinging spells at each other, a prospect he found both thrilling and fearsome.

Deuth shrugged. "Some other time, perhaps."

"Frightened of an old man's magic?"

"Hardly. But I came here for a different reason than having a spell duel with you. Today's Rill's first day of training with a practice charm that contains spells. I suspected you might try something . . . unusual to make him wash out of fledgling training."

"What made you think that?"

Deuth tilted his head to one side. "A little birdie whispered it in my ear. What level charm were you using against Rill's?"

"Well . . . it *was* a bit higher than his."

Deuth's expression grew stern. "Treat Rill properly, Cato. The same as you would any other fledgling."

"As the instructor, I have the right to teach fledglings the way I see fit."

"To teach them, not abuse them. I don't want another Rodleen Gespar on our hands. His family still holds you responsible."

"Gespar was filled with hubris," Cato said. "He thought he was better than his superiors."

"Rill's not Gespar. He has the potential to become a powerful archmage. As one of Caldon's most powerful archmages, you have the responsibility to help him succeed."

"I can't believe you're saying this!"

"I'm his guardian. It's my duty to support him."

Cato peered at Deuth. "What's your game?"

"I have no game."

"Of course you don't." Cato snickered and patted Deuth on the shoulder. "You're right. The boy does have potential. I'll teach him the basics, and what happens after that . . . well, it will be interesting to watch."

Rill found the exchange between the mages discomforting as if they were talking about him using some secret code. Then he cast the disquiet aside. Deuth was his guardian and would make sure no harm came to him.

Cato turned to Rill. "Class is over for the day, boy. Skip along out with your guardian. I need to give these old bones you bruised a rest."

Deuth's backwatchers fell into place behind Rill and Deuth as they left the Hall of Naming.

Food vendors had set up stalls near the edge of the Public Square. Men and women crowded around them, buying meat pies, pork sausages, pastries, and other fare, then joined the throng meandering through the square.

Deuth bought Rill and himself spiced black and green olives, which the seller scooped up and poured into parchment cones. Tucking his staff beneath his arm, Deuth strolled around the edge of the square eating the olives.

Rill felt self-conscious snacking in the great lord's presence while at the same time envying Deuth's easy manner. He would act that way when he became noblesse.

"You did well today," Deuth said. "I'm proud of you."

Rill strained to keep his face from breaking into a foolish grin. "Thank you, Lord. And thank you for siding with me against Lord Cato."

"He was abusing you. Making you appear incompetent on purpose." Deuth popped a black olive into his mouth and spoke as he chewed. "I couldn't intervene because he's your teacher. But I thought if I could persuade him to give you another chance, you'd prove yourself to both him and me."

"You took a risk that I'd take your hint about grabbing energy from the magic plane."

Deuth spit the olive pit into the parchment cone. "It wasn't much of a risk. You were smart enough to take the cue from me. And it was plain to see you were furious with Cato. Anger is a powerful motivation for magic. With proper training, I think you'll go far."

Deuth's praise made Rill want to dance a happy jig and gave him the courage to ask what had been nagging him for quite a while. "Why *are* you supporting me when all the other mages despise me and hate my parents?"

"I already told you. Because you have talent."

"But you noblesse dislike my parents 'cause they organized the Kings dwellers against you."

Deuth stopped abruptly and turned to him. "I'm not supporting your parents. I'm supporting *you*. My family doesn't believe in holding the sins of the parents against the son. You deserve to have the opportunity to succeed or fail on your own merits."

Rill vowed silently to repay the Estatis' unstinting trust in him. "Thank you for your confidence in me, Lord."

Deuth selected another black olive. "There is a second reason."

"What's that?"

"Cato wants you to fail."

As if I didn't know that. "Because of my family?"

"Partly. But mostly because he and *my* family are bitter enemies. We championed you. So Cato will attack us through you."

"I won't let him."

Deuth chewed the olive as they resumed walking. "Don't be so cocky. You would've become another Rodleen Gespar on your first day of fledging training if it hadn't been for Alyse Dejune's quick thinking."

"How did you know—"

"It's my business to know."

Rill let Deuth's comment sink in while he selected a green olive from his parchment cone. "I suspected he'd given me the higher-level charm on purpose. But I gave him the benefit of the doubt."

"Don't *ever* do that again with him," Deuth said. "You'd be on your way home right now, a washout, if I hadn't stopped by."

Rill munched on the olive. "I wouldn't of gone without a struggle."

"Always the fighter. I like that about you."

Rill suppressed a grin from Deuth's unexpected praise.

"Now you can rely on Cato to teach you properly," Deuth said. "Alyse Dejune's grandfather, Jukka Berne, is sole co-chief magestrate for the rest of the year. He's my family's staunch ally and will support us against Cato. I've just put Cato on notice that he's to teach you properly, and he will."

"I'm not so sure about that."

"I am." Deuth spit his last olive pit into the cone, crushed the cone, and tossed it to a backwatcher to dispose of. Stopping, he turned to Rill. "You can trust me on that. Cato's an excellent instructor. He's good at training fledgling archmages. With Cato's help, you can become Rill Larkin, the blacksmith's son who became an archmage. Perhaps one of the most powerful in ages."

Rill's eyes opened almost as wide as his mouth as adrenaline surged through his arteries. He hugged Deuth's words to his chest as if they were precious gems.

"And who knows," Deuth said, placing a hand on Rill's shoulder, "perhaps you might get elected to the Magesterium. You'll become noblesse and found your own commoner-noblesse family. Is that something you want?"

"It's my life's dream, Lord!"

"You can achieve that dream. But it takes perseverance and the support of an influential family. Like mine. Just think of it. The world will open up to you piece by piece, like the layers of an onion. You'll gain power, wealth, and fame. It's all at your fingertips, waiting to be yours."

Rill looked past Deuth to The Citadel rising majestically above the Public Square and at the magnificent noblesse compounds dotting its sides and crown. "He has the potential to become a powerful archmage." Deuth's words made Rill giddy, and he felt close to the great lord.

"I won't let you down, Lord."

Deuth smiled. "I know you won't."

## CHAPTER 27

Rill's Miscalculation

CATO PROVED TRUE TO his word about teaching Rill properly. For the next few days, he and Rill continued practicing defensive spells with Rill's level-one charm. Rill moved up to a level-two charm. After a few more days casting defensive spells, he could control the magic energy pretty easily. He got cocky.

"I've mastered level two," he said. "When are we gonna move up to level three?"

"You'd be better off mastering your patience, boy," Cato said. "Your guardian wants me to teach you properly and that's what I'm doing. Just as if you were my own protégé."

Two mornings later, Cato held up a level-three practice charm. Rill shivered with excitement as he reached for it.

Cato pulled his hand back. "Level three is a bit of a leap. So you've got to discard your 'handfuls of energy' imagery. That's for beginners."

"What image should I use?"

"The dam. It's been used for centuries. It's also the easiest way to control the two-way flow of energy."

Cato told Rill to visualize the charm as a dam that separated magic energy and personal energy from each other. When Rill said the A-word, the dam gate would open, and magic energy would flow into his body. Rill's personal energy was heavier than the magic energy and would pool at the bottom of the dam, on Rill's side. But as increasing magic energy rushed through the gate, it would displace Rill's personal energy, forcing it through the gate into the magic plane. Rill's job was to close the gate and place just enough flashboards on the top of the dam to let in the amount of magic energy he needed to cast his spell. The more boards he took away, the more magic energy would flow into his body and the more difficult it would be to control.

"The more powerful you grow as a mage," Cato said, "the easier it will become to control a larger amount of magic energy." His lips twitched into a sardonic smile. "The trick is, you have to take control in less than a heartbeat."

"That's impossible!"

"Having second thoughts, boy?"

Smothering his anxiety, Rill put up a cocky front. "No. Let's get started."

Cato handed him the charm. "If you learn nothing else, learn this. Effectively controlling the two-way flow is what separates a first-rate mage from a second-rate one. If you can't control your energy, you can't control your spell. The spell won't have the strength you want. It also might not do what you expect it to. An incompetent mage is a danger to both herself and those around her."

For the next three days, Rill put Cato's advice to work practicing with the charm. On the fourth day, Cato tossed Rill a new charm.

"Some mages are coming in to watch you practice, boy. I thought you might want to impress them." He nodded at the charm in Rill's hand. "That should be a level four, but it's an eight. Think you can handle it?"

Cato's confidence in his ability caused a warm rush of adrenaline to sweep through Rill's arteries, pushing away all sense of caution. "You bet I can."

Cato put a hand on Rill's shoulder. "It's powerful. So whatever you do, don't lose focus."

Eagerly, Rill slipped the chain over his neck and tucked the charm beneath his tunic. Just as he said the A-word, the classroom door opened, and the sounds of multiple pairs of booted feet clomped into the room. Without thinking, Rill glanced over his shoulder. Mages were fanning out along both sides of the rear aisle. Deuth Estati was among them.

At the same time, a violent burst of raw energy from the magic plane sent Rill staggering. A cold hand of terror clutched his throat. The power was too strong for him to manage! Terrifying images assaulted his mind. Mage fire eating into the stable wall. And the figure of a man in a wheelchair—Rodleen Gespar.

Rill turned his panic-stricken gaze to Cato. Arms crossed, the archmage watched dispassionately as if he were observing the death throes of a deer.

Rill gaped at him. He should have heeded Cato's caution.

The charm's power was beyond his ability to control.

## CHAPTER 28

Fledgling Healer

ALYSE DOVE INTO HER fledgling healer training with a gusto that would have refuted anyone who dared accuse her of having an aversion to magic. As she'd expected, Grandmother Maude assigned Lenia, the family healer, as her instructor. Lenia began Alyse's training in the traditional way by sharing her method of controlling the two-way flow of magic energy and personal energy. Alyse pretended to pay attention, then used her deep-breathing exercise to go into the magic state the way the talking tube in the family archives had instructed. Her quick mastery astounded Lenia.

Alyse was taken aback when Lenia handed her an actual Healer charm instead of a practice charm to use. But Lenia cleared Alyse's confusion by explaining that fledgling healers didn't use practice charms. "Healer spells are different from all other forms of magic," she said. "Because they have to be cast on actual sick people. Think about it. A Warrior fledgling can cast a Fire Bolt on a tree to splinter or burn it. But can a fledgling healer cast an anti-anxiety spell on a tree to stop it from worrying? I don't think so."

Healing magic also differed from other types because it didn't rely solely on spells but on potions made from herbs and other ingredients that the healer cast spells on. Alyse already knew that because Lenia had treated plenty of her colds and sore throats in the past with potions she'd warmed in a kettle over a fire and then had her drink.

Alyse proved to be an apt pupil and quickly mastered everything Lenia taught her, except for healing hands, which healers used to locate and identify serious internal ailments. Only one retainer, a servant with a serious heart condition, was sick enough to require healing hands. Lenia told Alyse to move her palms over the woman's body to detect malignant energy that shouldn't be there.

Alyse tried over and over but couldn't sense any.

"It's not an easy talent to develop," Lenia said. "And, honestly, I think you need a more powerful mentor to tutor you on it."

Despite her failure with the heart patient, Lenia's mentoring filled Alyse with a satisfaction she'd never felt before. Even by healing simple ailments, she was making a positive difference in people's lives. She also could tend Kate who was still recuperating from her wounds. More than once Alyse smiled to herself, feeling like a conspirator. What better way to postpone her marriage to Troy than by helping others?

After a few weeks passed, Lenia told Alyse that she'd mastered fledgling healing. Dread formed a tight ball in Alyse's stomach. With her training over, Grandmother Maude would harp on her about marrying Troy.

"It's a shame to have my training stop here," Alyse told Lenia.

"I'm not saying it does," Lenia responded. "What you need is to study under a powerful healer who treats difficult cases."

"Like Priestess Sybil?" Alyse said quickly, breath held expectantly in her chest as she waited for a reply.

"Yes. She's the most powerful healer in Caldon." A grin began forming on Alyse's face until Lenia's next words wiped it off. "If Lady Maude approves, that is. She doesn't like her, you know."

An image of Troy dragging her to the alter in the Temple of the One Goddess in the Public Square rose up in her mind like a demon. "She *must* approve."

Lenia squared her shoulders. "I'll speak with her today."

The next morning Maude summoned Alyse and Lenia to the matriarch's chamber. Maude occupied the black oak chair on the dais while Pilar sat facing her in one of the straight-back chairs on the floor. Alyse crossed the room with Lenia following at a respectful distance. With every step she took, Alyse could feel her grandmother's sharp, flint-gray eyes boring into her like a pair of screws.

When Alyse stopped at the stairs, Maude pointed to an empty chair beside Pilar's. "Sit."

Before Alyse could turn, Maude's gaze snapped to Lenia. "What do you mean you can do no more for Lady Alyse?"

Lenia explained that Alyse had completed fledgling training in half the normal time. "Lady Alyse has the potential to become a powerful healer," Lenia concluded. "But I'm unable to give her that training. To tap her full potential, she must be mentored by an extremely powerful healer."

"Do you have someone in mind?"

"Yes. Priestess Sybil."

Maude's brows plummeted into a frown as she *ratta-tap-tapped* her fingers on the arm of her chair. The moments dragged by for Alyse like a caterpillar creeping across the road. Finally Maude made a smacking sound with her lips and looked at Lenia, her glower growing deeper. "Are you aware the Estatis despise Priestess Sybil?"

"Yes."

"And that they're unhappy I allowed her to tutor Lady Alyse in the Eulorian language?"

"Yes."

"And that fledglings can't marry until their training ends? Having Priestess Sybil mentor Lady Alyse will mean postponing her marriage to Troy Estati."

"Yes."

"Yet you still recommend she mentor Lady Alyse?"

Pulling back her shoulders, Lenia met Maude's stare full on. "I do. In fact, I think the Estatis would happily agree to a postponement if it meant their future daughter-in-law were to become an extremely powerful healer."

"How powerful?"

"At least the equal to Priestess Sybil. Perhaps even more powerful." Lenia made a sweeping gesture toward Alyse. "Lady Alyse would bring great honor and prestige to the Dejune Family. She would make your ancestors proud."

"More powerful than Priestess Sybil." Maude bit her lower lip, her forehead crinkled in thought. "Powerful enough to have brought my parents back from Elustra, the Afterworld?"

Lenia's brows arched at the unexpected question. "Not even Priestess Sybil can do that."

"There used to be a time when healers could do that."

Lenia laughed as if Maude had just told a sour joke. "Yes. And there used to be a time when there were dragons as well. Flying dragons breathing fire. But those are ancient tales told by the Eulorians to their children long before The Great Destruction. No healer has ever had such power."

"Some people say those 'ancient tales' are true."

"Lady Alyse can equal or surpass Priestess Sybil. Isn't that enough for you?"

Maude's eyes took on a calculating look while she drummed her fingers on the chair arm. Alyse held her breath, uttering a silent plea to the One Goddess to let Maude decide in favor of Lenia's recommendation.

Maude motioned to Alyse and Lenia. "Wait outside. Pilar and I need to discuss this."

In the family area near the matriarch's chamber, Alyse touched Lenia's sleeve. "When Grandmother Maude said some healers could bring people back from the Afterworld, is that true?"

"A couple of legends mention it," Lenia said. "Supposedly from before The Great Destruction. But few people believe it."

Alyse rubbed the sides of her mouth with thumb and forefinger. *Kendra Larkin brought Kate back. Where did she learn to do that?*

Before long, Pilar summoned them. Alyse's heart pounded so hard as she crossed the mosaic floor that she thought everyone could hear it. Stopping before the dais, she and Lenia looked up at Maude as if they were two condemned prisoners awaiting sentencing.

Maude spoke without preamble. "It's a Goddess-given opportunity that Alyse has the potential to become one of the most powerful healers in Caldon. So I've decided to ask Priestess Sybil to mentor her." Maude focused on Alyse. "I'm sure your training will take many, many months to complete. Are you prepared for that kind of single-minded commitment?"

Alyse's hands tingled with joy while she struggled to keep her expression neutral. *My ploy worked! I'm going to be trained by Priestess Sybil. For a long, long time. Too long for Troy to wait to marry me.* "Thank you, Grandmother, for allowing me this wonderful opportunity to help make our family great again."

"As I said, it's a Goddess-given opportunity." Maude chewed the side of her lip. "It will mean postponing your marriage to Troy—"

Alyse's heart did a joyful cartwheel.

"For a few months or so until you settle into a routine with Priestess Sybil."

Alyse scarcely managed to conceal her distress. "But custom doesn't allow an apprentice healer to marry before her training ends."

"Customs can be overlooked when necessary. Except one." Maude's gaze nailed itself to Alyse's. "That the firstborn must be the first married."

Bile billowed up Alyse's throat and into her mouth. She barely avoided gagging in front of her grandmother.

By embracing magic, she had failed to evade marriage.

## CHAPTER 29

Natural Talent

CATO'S VOICE, CALM BUT urgent, penetrated Rill's fright. "Don't panic, boy. Visualize the dam. Close the gate."

Whirling toward Cato, Rill opened his mouth to scream for him to rip off the charm.

"Are you sure you want me to rescue you?" Cato asked softly, then pointed to the mages who were lined up in the rear. "They came to watch you, boy. Do you want them to see you can't handle the charm?"

Cato's question quenched Rill's panic. He would *not* become another Rodleen Gespar! He *would* control the charm. Rill took a deep breath, squeezed his eyes shut, and pictured the dam with its gate wide open. The magic energy was gushing through, forcing Rill's personal energy over the dam into the magic plane. He'd already lost a lot and was weakening fast.

Rill focused his full attention on the gate and slowly forced it down into the gushing torrent of energy. The opposing streams—magic and personal—fought to prevent him from cutting them off, but relentlessly he pushed down against them until the gate finally struck bottom. Magic energy still spilled over the top of the gate, so he added three layers of flashboards, fumbling with their images, until the current was blocked.

Rill staggered from exhaustion.

Then fear squeezed his heart. On the other side of the dam the magic energy thrust powerfully, threatening to shatter the gate. His mind dull from fatigue, Rill had trouble concentrating. The image of the dam wavered. Fighting off panic, he imagined himself climbing down into the pool of personal energy, putting his shoulder against the gate, and shoving back against the pressure. But weariness was fast overcoming him, and cracks were appearing in the gate.

Cato's voice pricked through Rill's foggy consciousness. "The Q-word, boy. Say the Q-word."

Rill groped for the command. "Quies."

Instantly the magic energy disappeared, and the dam vanished from his mind.

Rill's legs gave out, but Cato caught him under the arms. "Well done, boy," Cato whispered in his ear, a hint of pride in his voice. "Well done."

Cato released Rill, who stood shakily on his feet. Rill became aware of a tomb-like silence encasing the room. He glanced at the mages. All were staring at him.

His gaze veered to a short, thickset man with black hair who stood beside Deuth Estati. Brico Svagga. The swarthy mage returned Rill's look with hate-filled eyes. He whispered something to Deuth, then laughed mockingly.

Anger flashed across Deuth's face, and he spat some words at Brico, who dismissed them with a flick of his hand.

"Some fledgling you've got there, Cato," Brico said with a sneer. "He can't even handle a simple charm."

Arms crossed, Cato leaned toward the bidders and smirked at them. "Actually, today he was supposed to be introduced to a level four. But I gave him a level eight instead."

Brico scoffed. "He still couldn't handle it."

"On the contrary. The boy has natural talent. He controlled the charm better than most fledglings would." Cato waved at the assembly of mages. "The problem was, you all came in before I had a chance to work with him. And your noisy entrance distracted him at a crucial moment when he was activating the charm. But even with that disadvantage, he mastered the magic energy. You all saw that for yourselves. What other untrained fledgling has ever been able to control the energy of an eighth-level practice charm without having mastered the first seven?"

Rill leaned on his staff, his lips twitching into a prideful grin and looked at Deuth.

Brico Svagga whispered into Deuth's ear, and Deuth shot Brico a withering look.

As Rill turned his attention to Brico, the hostility on Brico's face made Rill shiver. *Why does he hate me so?*

The mages began filing out of the room. They spoke among themselves, but Rill couldn't catch their words. Deuth muttered something to Brico, then nudged him toward the door. Brico hurled a final hate-filled look at Rill, and left.

Deuth walked down the steps, his expression burning with anger. "Do your job, Cato. Train Rill properly."

Cato folded his arms across his chest. "I am."

"You're not. You used that charm as a way to attack me through him."

Cato stretched his body to his full height and met Deuth's angry eyes defiantly. "Not so. The boy has the potential to become a powerful archmage. And you want him all to yourself, without any competition at the bidding. I just made sure that won't happen. Other families have now seen the boy's potential. And they'll give you a run for your gildas to secure his oath of loyalty."

Like a powerful hurricane, Cato's words swept Rill's breath away. *Natural talent and the potential to become a powerful mage. I got 'em both!* Then another thought struck him that made his nerves tingle with anticipation. *Maybe another First Family will outbid the Estatis for me at the bidding.*

Goddess, that would be something!

## CHAPTER 30

The Wasting Man

ALYSE AND PRIESTESS SYBIL left the chief priestess's office and strode along the corridor toward the House of Healing. Frustration churned in Alyse's chest like boiling water. Several weeks had passed since she'd started training, and all she'd done so far was watch Sybil treat patients. Well, maybe not just observe. On some of the more seriously ill patients, Sybil had used her "inner eye" to examine them and discover the cause of their ailments. Several times she had asked Alyse to locate where a patient's illness lay with her own inner eye using all her chars, but to Alyse's frustration, she had failed each time.

"Some healers eventually find their inner eye," Sybil had told her. "And others never do."

Alyse didn't consider that a very comforting response.

Turning left, Alyse and Sybil entered the House of Healing, going past the open doors to sick wards while priestesses and novices who were ward attendants hurried by to tend to their patients. Visitors stopped Sybil twice. The first asked what ward her husband was in, and the other wanted to know where he could find his cousin who had been brought in a couple of days ago. Alyse thought that Sybil must have memorized the patient roster because both times she named the ward without hesitating. As she and Sybil left the second visitor, Alyse wondered where Sybil was taking her. All Sybil had said was that they were going to see a "special patient."

Alyse fingered the oval bronze Healer charm, with its engraved image of the One Goddess, beneath the bodice of her dress. Before agreeing to mentor her, Sybil had demanded a preliminary meeting. "Before I make a decision," Sybil had told her, "you must agree to certain conditions."

Alyse tilted her head in puzzlement. "Conditions?"

"You're a euloghe. You don't get your magic power through a charm. So you'll wear a fake Healer charm. Agreed?"

"Yes," Alyse said.

"Good. Most healers, even powerful ones, learn to heal by rote. Like other kinds of charms, theirs contain spells for specific ailments. The healer identifies the sickness. If her charm doesn't contain a spell to cure it, she must call in a healer whose charm does contain the spell. If the cure also requires a potion, the healer mixes the potion and applies it. This sort of healer can't become a true one because she can't use the combined power of all her chars. Only a euloghe can do that."

A suspicion crept into Alyse's mind on soft, padded feet. *Priestess Sybil's a euloghe.* She hugged that thought to her chest.

"Second," Sybil said, "you must promise to use all your chars in healing."

Alyse's stomach rumbled queasily at that prospect. But she wanted to be a true healer. To help people. To make a difference in the world. So she'd nodded. "Agreed."

Smiling, Sybil had embraced her. "I welcome my new apprentice."

Now Sybil turned toward a ward whose door was closed. Inside, five beds crowded either side of the room with a narrow aisle between each row. Men and teenage boys lay in the beds. Some were sleeping, and others were staring vacantly at the ceiling. Alyse suspected they were too sick to be curious enough to watch a healer and her apprentice.

"This ward contains male patients with acute cases," Sybil said as she stopped by the last bed on the right.

An elderly man who appeared to be in his late seventies or early eighties lay in the bed. His eyes were closed, and he seemed to be sleeping. The lagged rise and fall of the sheet and light blanket reflected his shallow breathing.

Sybil pulled the sheet and blanket down to the bottom of the bed, exposing an emaciated body clothed in a flimsy linen nightshirt. She spoke to Alyse in Eulori, which they used with each other when she was mentoring Alyse in front of patients. "His daughter and young grandson brought him here earlier today. They said he was wasting away. And even though he was hungry, he couldn't keep any food down. He was starving to death, becoming weaker and weaker every day."

"Why didn't they bring him earlier?" Alyse asked, her eyes riveted on the labored rise and fall of the man's chest.

Kneeling beside the bed, Sybil slowly moved her hands, palms out, along the man's body. Her focus seemed to be on the patient, yet she answered the question as she slowly moved her hands from the man's head down to his toes. "It's a bit complicated. They're country dwellers. Just last month they moved here to Caldon."

"You mean, they waited over a month to—"

"The family consists of him and his wife, their daughter, who brought him, and their grandson, who's too young to be conscripted. The rest of the family—their daughter's husband, three of their daughter's four children, and their unmarried son—were conscripted over the past few years. He and the remaining family members tried to work the farm, but the challenge proved overwhelming. So the grandmother finally sold the farm to a large landowner who'd been pestering her for over a year to sell it. He bought it for a pittance and promised to let them remain there, but evicted them days after the grandmother signed the contract."

Indignation rushed through Alyse. *Just like that poor family I happened upon on the way to our villa.* She glared as Sybil bent over the patient, and saw the three men with cudgels evicting the family from their ramshackle farm.

"Anyway," Sybil said, "they came to Caldon and found a place to live here in The Kings. But it took them a while to get settled and make friends. Meanwhile, this poor man's condition kept getting worse. Yesterday a neighbor suggested they bring him here."

"I hope they didn't bring him too late," Alyse said.

"I think not." Sybil rose and faced Alyse. "I've located where his ailment lies. See if you can find it."

Alyse couldn't keep discouragement from her voice. "I'll try."

"I know it's been frustrating. But finding your inner eye is different for every healer. You must discover the sight for yourself, in your own way. What's ailing this man is very strong. The ailments in the previous patients you tried to examine with your inner eye were much weaker." She nodded at the man. "I'm hoping the fierceness of his sickness will make it easier for you to find it."

Alyse knelt beside the man and, beginning with his head, slowly moved her palms down over his chest toward his groin.

"Can you detect his personal energy?" Sybil asked softly.

"No. I detect nothing."

"Open your mind to the energy of your heart char. Let it flow through your body and into your hands."

Frustration gnawed at Alyse as she moved her hands over the old man's legs and feet. "Still nothing."

"Do you perform your char exercise?" Sybil asked.

"Every morning."

"Do it again. Now. Maybe your chars need strengthening."

Alyse moved out from between the two beds and settled into a comfortable sitting position on the floorboards and went through the exercise.

"You might have a subconscious aversion to magic," Sybil said as Alyse stood up. "That might be your problem."

"I want more than anything to be a healer. So I accept magic. All forms."

"Maybe consciously. But not subconsciously." Sybil gripped Alyse's shoulders and touched foreheads with her. "Remember, the heart char provides the healing power. But it's the energy from the other chars that reinforce that healing power. All the chars work together to support one another—to reinforce one another—because all the energy comes from the same source: the magic plane. That's why a charm wearer, from healer to archmage, can never become a truly powerful mage. Because the charm separates the chars from one another. Understand?"

Alyse nodded. "Yes."

"Good. Now try again."

They returned to the old man's bedside. Alyse knelt and placed her palms above his head. Slowly, she moved them down his body.

"You're going to use healing magic," Sybil said softly while Alyse worked. "Concentrate on your heart. Picture your heart as a vast reservoir already partially filled with magic energy. Then imagine that the seven other chars have conduits that divert their energy into the pool. Direct the power from those chars through the conduits into your heart. Can you feel the power gathering there, like water filling a spring?"

Amazement spread across Alyse's face. "I feel it! The energy flowing from the other chars into my heart. I feel the power building up."

"Good. Don't let it overflow. Redirect the excess back to the magic plane."

Alyse pictured another channel that funneled the surplus energy back to the magic plane. "I've done it! I can feel the power waiting to be used."

"Now, without losing your concentration, explore his body with your inner eye. Start with his head again."

"But how will I—"

"Don't doubt yourself. Trust your instincts. Give yourself over to the healing power. The energy of a healer's heart is positive. Let that energy guide you to your inner eye."

Alyse bobbed her head, not trusting herself to speak. As soon as she placed her palms over the old man's forehead, she felt an odd sensation. "My hands tingle," she whispered. "That's never happened before."

"Because you never fully surrendered yourself to the healing energy before," Sybil whispered back. "What does his energy feel like? Tell me using an adjective."

Crinkling her brow, Alyse ran through a mental list of words. "Benevolent."

"What you're feeling is his personal energy. Now explore the rest of his body, and tell me what you find."

Alyse slowly moved her palms down the old man's face and neck. She paused near his chest and glanced questioningly at Sybil.

"What are you sensing?" Sybil asked.

"Differences in energy," Alyse replied. "It still feels benevolent, but it's very weak."

"You're reading the energy emitted by his organs, bones, muscles, and blood vessels. The weakness comes from his sickness."

A sense of awe such as she'd ever experienced before spread throughout Alyse like a mist.

"Continue exploring," Sybil told her.

Alyse moved her palms down to the man's stomach—and froze.

"What is it?" Sybil asked. "Describe it."

"It's . . . out of place. Foreign. Malevolent."

"That's the source of his wasting."

"What is it?"

Sybil switched places with Alyse. "We have no name for it. We only know what it does."

"From the power the sickness gives out," Alyse said, "it feels large."

"It is. It's living in the poor man's body. Absorbing his personal energy. Living on it. Using it as food so it can keep growing. If we allow it to continue, the sickness will consume all his energy, and he'll die."

"How can it be stopped?"

"By shrinking it to nothingness." Sybil explored the area surrounding the sickness with her inner eye. "But gradually. Over the course of days. If we apply too much healing energy at one time or shrink it too quickly, the patient might die."

"How will you heal him?"

"I'll show you." Sybil placed her hands on the spot where the sickness was growing and attacked it with the power of her heart char. Afterward, she showed Alyse how to create a cleansing smoke of cedar, dried blackberries, marjoram, wood sorrel, and wolfsbane, which she cast a spell on and then directed the smoke's healing properties into the patient's body.

As she watched Sybil, a sense of weightlessness spread through Alyse, and her body felt light as a feather as if it could float away in a gentle breeze at any moment. *I've found my inner eye.* She wanted to throw her arms around Priestess Sybil and hug her. Instead, she waved the last lingering strands of smoke toward the old man.

She had become a true healer.

## CHAPTER 31

The Bidding

THE REMAINING DAYS OF training went by quickly for Rill as Cato patiently helped him master practice charms up to level nine. Rill was thrilled with his progress and begged Cato to go up one level higher, to ten, but Cato refused. "Nine's an odd number, boy," he said. "And odd numbers are lucky numbers. So don't press your luck."

Mages came to watch Rill practice. Only a few showed up at first, but as the days passed, many more appeared until sometimes thirty or forty packed the aisles. Rill longed to tell his folks about their interest in him, but he knew they would find something negative to say. So he hugged that news to himself.

Every day the spectators' presence gave Rill a heady feeling. They'd come to see *him*. Images would flit through his mind of noblesse families competing furiously against one another for him at the bidding. The prospect made him prickle all over. But Lord Deuth had been the one to champion his cause, and Rill prayed to the One Goddess that Deuth would be the one who made the winning bid. After all, Deuth had promised to help him become a commoner-noblesse by getting him elected to the Magesterium. Then he could start his own commoner-noblesse family. The prospect of achieving his life's dream made Rill giddy.

Deuth's actions fed into Rill's hopes because Deuth often stopped by to watch. Rill always became self-conscious when Deuth appeared because he didn't want to make any mistakes that might embarrass the great lord. Sometimes Brico Svagga accompanied Deuth, and other times the short, swarthy, black-haired mage swaggered in by himself. Every time Rill caught Brico staring at him through narrowed brown eyes, like a predator waiting to spring on its prey, he was thrown off his stride. So he quickly learned to focus only on Cato and not on the observers whenever Brico was there.

Rill thought Bidding Day would never arrive, but at long last it did. He woke early that morning and eagerly put on the Name Day clothes Aunt Talia had given him. Since he'd been named an archmage, his parents, grandma, and aunt had become reconciled to his becoming a mage and family life had returned to normal. This morning's breakfast was a quiet affair, though, as if no one—including himself—wanted to speak of the bidding.

Just as Rill was finishing his porridge, his mom spoke up. "You know we won't be seeing you again. Not for quite a while, anyways."

Her words, spoken quietly, caused an empty feeling in Rill's chest because fledglings who obtained patrons at the bidding went straight to their patrons' compounds and had little contact with their own families. "I know," Rill replied softly, jolted by the unexpected flash of sadness.

"We'll miss you," Marc said, his voice taut as if he were reining in some powerful emotions.

Grandma Cinna nodded. "We wish you luck."

"And may the One Goddess watch over you," Aunt Tarri said.

They all hugged Rill before he left. And Rill hugged Faith who licked his cheek. Once outside, Rill's spirits soared like birds taking flight. After stopping at Jedd's for his cousin's good-luck wishes, he raced to the Hall of Naming to join the other commoner fledglings assembled in the classroom to await Cato's arrival.

Rill sat in the last row, near the door, so he would be one of the first to enter the Bidding Hall. He did a surreptitious head count, which confirmed the rumor that besides the five fledglings Cato had dismissed, seven others had washed out during training. Most of the fledglings sat by themselves, anxiety carved into their features, while a few banded together and spoke in hushed tones.

Only Larissa Macon, the illusionist, seemed unaffected by the enormity of today. She wore a mask of studied indifference.

Rill found it easy to imitate her attitude because Cato had made it a point to emphasize Rill's natural talent to everyone who had observed him practice. Illusionists were rare. So were archmages. And Rill knew that he, like Larissa, would go for a high price. Then an unwelcome thought sneaked into his mind.

What if someone outbid Deuth? Even worse—and this prospect sent horror slithering down Rill's spine—what if Brico Svagga outbid Deuth and won? Rill quickly discarded the possibility as if it were a fire that had scorched his fingers. The Estatis had a much higher status and vastly more wealth than the Svaggas. So he had nothing to fear.

At last Cato arrived, placed himself behind the lectern, and pushed his bottom lip forward with his tongue before speaking. "As you probably know, the number of fledglings who get patrons at the bidding varies from month to month. It all depends on the needs of the First and Lesser Families. You'll be gratified to know that this month the Dejunes are looking for warrior mages to replace the ones they lost in the recent charm raid on their compound. So I expect a lot more placements than usual."

Cato paused as the fledglings' faces lit up with expectation. Most of their faces, anyway. A few of their expressions turned glum, probably at the knowledge that they would be replacing dead or seriously wounded mages.

Cato leaned forward, forearms on the lectern. "For those of you who don't receive patrons, you do have another alternative to get mentored. By joining the legions or the sea service. Representatives will be womanning tables outside the entrance to the Bidding Hall. You can enlist and receive top-notch training from them. And those of you who are healers—you girls, anyway—have another opportunity. You can receive training at your neighborhood One Goddess

Temple, if its chief priestess agrees to take you on. There's no need to become a priestess unless you want to work in the temple's House of Healing. Because once you're trained, you can set up your own private practices."

Rill squirmed in his seat. He wished Cato would stop talking, take them into the Bidding Hall, and get on with the bidding.

"And those who don't receive patrons or don't want to join the legions or sea service . . ." Cato shrugged. "Well, it's back to being a commoner and waiting to be conscripted." He stepped out from behind the lectern. "Let's see what the future brings, shall we?"

Rill heaved a silent sign of relief. *Finally!*

Cato led them out of the classroom and along the corridor toward the Bidding Hall, which was behind the amphitheater. A pair of tables had been set up a short distance from the Bidding Hall door. Two military mages sat behind each table, one pair wearing the dark-brown uniform of the legions and the other in sea-service blue. A stack of military contracts sat on each table, ready to be signed by fledglings who didn't find a patron. The mages' staffs weren't in sight, and Rill knew the mages weren't wearing charms either. Although the law forbade all active-duty military except messengers from crossing the city boundary, the Magesterium made an exception for military recruiters once a month, on Bidding Day, if they left their staffs and charms behind.

Two black-and-silver uniformed Magesterium servants occupied a desk by the door into the Bidding Hall. A stack of papers lay on the desk. They were contracts the new apprentice mages and their patrons would sign. Nine dynamae also loitered nearby, which told Rill that Jukka Berne was attending.

Rill and the others followed Cato into the Bidding Hall. Noblesse—both mages and nonmages—packed the room, their voices creating an incessant, bumblebee buzz. A dais occupied the front of the room. Several Magesterium servants stood near the steps. The fledglings followed Cato up the stairs onto the dais. Cato stopped by the lectern and motioned for the fledglings to fill in the rows of chairs behind the lectern. Each seat had a name tag on it.

Rill ended up in the last seat in the last row, next to Larissa Macon.

Peering between the heads of the fledglings in front of him, Rill spotted Deuth Estati and Jukka Berne near the back wall. They were speaking with a middle-age woman whose auburn hair was streaked with gray. Brico Svagga stood close to the dais, leaning on his staff.

Dread churned inside Rill when the stocky mage's hostile, piglike eyes latched on to his. Rill quickly averted his gaze.

Cato stood stage center behind the lectern facing the crowd of noblesse and mages. He raised his arms. "Welcome, bidders! Welcome to this month's bidding!"

Gradually the droning voices petered out.

Grasping both sides of the lectern, Cato leaned into the crowd. "You all know the rules. But for the fledglings' sake, I'll repeat them. The highest bidder wins the right to make an offer of patronage to the fledgling. If the fledgling accepts, she becomes that family's apprentice mage. The family mentors her until its matriarch determines she's ready to swear loyalty in return for her charm and staff."

Cato turned to the fledglings. "You have the right of first refusal, which means you can reject the highest bid. If you do, you must accept the second-highest bid. If you refuse that, the bidding for you is over. When you leave the Bidding Hall, you can join the legions or the sea service. They both will provide you with top-notch apprenticeship training."

He faced the bidders. "Today we have some of the usual and some of the unusual. We'll start with the usual. Our fledgling warriors. Jessie Constrain, front and center."

In the first seat in the first row, a petite girl took a deep breath and slowly got up from her chair. Cato motioned her to come forward, and she sidled up to him like a frightened puppy seeking its master's protection. Putting his hands on her shoulders, Cato positioned her a few feet in front of the lectern. Jessie faced the bidders, her arms held rigidly at her sides.

Cato consulted the top sheet of a stack of parchments on the podium. "For those of you who didn't have a chance to observe her,

Jessie is a fledgling warrior who has demonstrated mastery of a fourth-level practice charm and all its spells. She might be slow to learn, but she does show perseverance. She'll make a welcome addition to any family that needs a basic warrior. We'll open the bidding at one thousand gildas. Who will offer one thousand?"

A heavy silence filled the room.

"Five hundred gildas," Cato said. "Do I hear five? Four hundred and fifty. Do I hear four fifty?"

Bidders began chatting quietly to one another.

"Four hundred gildas?" Cato said. "Do I hear four hundred?"

Several bidders shook their heads.

Cato appeared oblivious to the bidders' indifference. "I've been told her Fire Bolt packs a mean wallop. Jessie would be a great addition to a first line of attack or defense. Three hundred gildas. Do I hear three hundred?"

No one responded.

Cato reduced his bid levels in fifty-gilda increments until he reached rock bottom. "Fifty gildas. Do I hear fifty for Jessie? At that price, she's a steal."

Still no one bid.

Cato patted Jessie's shoulder. "I'm sorry, dear. One of the Magesterium servants will escort you out. Perhaps you'll have better luck with the recruiters. Serving the state is a proud and patriotic alternative to serving a family."

Sorrow filled Rill's chest as he watched Jessie walk down the dais steps, her eyes wet with tears. He had overheard her once talking to another fledgling about her hopes to apprentice to a good Lesser Family because she feared a First Family might not be interested in her. "I might be small," she'd said, "but I have perseverance. I just need a chance to show it."

Rill sensed a change in the fledglings' mood from tense expectation to gloom as they watched teary-eyed Jessie disappear through the door. Rill's shoulders, which he didn't realize were tense, sagged in relief when the next two warrior fledglings were won by a middle-aged woman with auburn- and gray-streaked hair for two thousand gildas each.

"Awarded to Maude Dejune," Cato announced each time.

Rill leaned forward, peering over other fledglings' heads, to get a better look at her. *Alyse Dejune's grandmother.*

From then on Cato's prediction came true. The bidding for the remaining warrior fledglings turned brisk until over half received patrons. Rill noted that, like himself, all the ones who got patrons had mastered high-level spells with their training charms. He also saw a happy smile on Maude Dejune's face because she had won the bids for many of those fledglings. The reactions of the warrior fledglings who didn't receive bids ranged from despondency to anger as they left the room. Rill wondered how many of them would join the military.

Six healer fledglings went up next, but only two found patrons, one to a First Family and the other to a Lesser Family.

One by one, Cato went through the other fledglings until only Rill and Larissa were left. Even before the door closed behind the last fledgling, everyone's eyes latched on to Rill and Larissa like starving predators waiting to feast.

Ever the showman, Cato faced the crowd without speaking, letting the anticipation mount and mount until Rill thought he could pop it with a pinprick. His own heart pounded so hard he feared it might crack through his rib cage. *Come on, Cato! Start the bidding.* Rill sighed in relief when Cato finally broke the suspense.

"You've seen the usual. So now for the unusual. We'll start with the illusionist."

The audience stirred restlessly.

Rill glanced at Larissa. She smiled at him, excitement dancing in her eyes.

"Larissa Macon," Cato called out, "front and center."

"Good luck," Rill whispered as she passed by.

Pride lighting her face, Larissa wiggled her fingers at him and went to the spot where the previous fledglings had stood, drawing herself erect with her shoulders thrown back.

Cato consulted his notes. "Larissa is an illusionist. She's demonstrated proficiency with a sixth-level practice charm and its associated spells. We all know, for a fledgling illusionist to master so much in such a short time is quite a feat. Obviously, Larissa shows enormous potential. She will be of immense benefit to whichever family she serves. So let's start the opening bid with, say . . . ten thousand gildas."

"Ten thousand!"

Cato glanced around the room. "An illusionist with Larissa's potential doesn't come along very often. Will anyone bid fifteen thousand?"

"Fifteen thousand!"

Cato shook his head in mock chagrin. "Fifteen thousand? Why, that's thievery for a fledgling illusionist like Larissa. She's worth at least twenty thousand. Do I hear twent—"

"Twenty thousand!" a familiar voice said from the rear.

Cato crinkled his face in disgust. "Twenty thousand? Jukka Berne, you might be sole chief magestrate, but you're also a thief if you think you're going to pay that little to win Larissa." He made a pretense of searching the room until his gaze settled on someone else in the back. "Deuth Estati! What about you? How many families can boast having two illusionists in their households?"

Deuth waved him off good naturedly. "No thanks. One illusionist is more than enough for my household to handle, especially since she's my niece!"

His response provoked a burst of friendly laughter.

Cato sought out someone else in the hall. "Brico Svagga! How about you? Will you bid twenty thousand for an illusionist?"

Brico shook his head, his expression sour.

"Ah, well." With mock reluctance, Cato looked away from Brico. "Twenty thousand. Do I hear thirty thousand gildas for the services of this talented girl?"

Cato's ability as auctioneer amazed Rill as Cato worked the crowd into a bidding frenzy that gradually made its way up to fifty-three thousand gildas. "Going once . . . going twice . . . gone for fifty-three thousand to Jasma Sparri!"

Some in the audience cheered and applauded and called out congratulations to Jasma, while others remained silent, their expressions sour.

Rill knew that Jasma was the matriarch of the Sparris, a powerful First Family, who belonged to Cato's Traditionali faction, which explained the divided reaction to her winning the bid. He assumed the reaction to whoever bid highest for him would be similar. *Oh, please, Divine Lady, let it be Lord Deuth.*

Cato turned to Larissa. "Larissa Macon, do you accept the patronage offer from this family?"

"I do."

Cato beamed. "Go down to your patron." He motioned at Jasma as Larissa went down the steps. "Come get your family's new illusionist. And may the blessings of the One Goddess go with both of you."

After a quick backward glance at Rill, Larissa went down the stairs to meet Jasma. Rill watched them thread their way through the crowd toward the door.

"Rillyan Larkin, front and center."

Striving to conceal his eagerness, Rill approached the podium.

Cato wrapped an arm around Rill's shoulder. "Rill is the only archmage in his month's group of fledglings. I've trained him personally. And I can tell you without exaggerating that he shows amazing talent. He can skip charm levels. That's something very few fledgling mages can do. The boy has the makings of an extremely powerful mage.."

Rill struggled to keep his face impassive as memories of all the times mages had come to watch him train with Cato swirled dizzily through his mind. *I'll go for more than Larissa. But please, One Goddess, let Lord Deuth win the bid.*

"The boy's a quick learner too," Cato said. "And yes, I'll admit it. He even bested me in our Wind against Shield exercise—by casting Repel. He's tricky, this boy is. Whatever family becomes his patron, they'll have to keep a sharp eye on him."

Suspicion crept into Rill's mind at Cato's backhanded compliment, but he kicked it out as Cato continued building him up. If Cato had stoked the bidding up to fifty-three thousand gildas for Larissa, Rill figured he himself should go for a lot more. Maybe even a hundred thousand.

Cato leaned over the podium toward the crowd. "Let's start the bidding at, say, ten thousand gildas. Do I hear ten thousand?"

Silence.

A heavy lump of lead settled in Rill's stomach at the bidders' lack of response. *What's going on? This ain't supposed to happen.*

"Ten thousand," Cato said. "That's a pittance to pay for a fledgling archmage with Rill's potential. Do I hear ten?"

A few in the audience coughed nervously. Feet scuffed against the floorboards. Rill's throat tightened the way it usually did when he was about to throw up.

Cato pointed to someone in the back of the room. "Deuth Estati. You're the boy's guardian. Will you bid ten thousand for him?"

Deuth shook his head. "No."

## CHAPTER 32

Winning Bid

RILL'S MIND WENT AS blank as a slate board, and his ears barely heard the bidders' shocked gasps. Even Cato seemed taken aback by Deuth's unexpected response, his mouth opening and closing like a fish stranded on the shore. A tense hush filled the room, building in pressure, until Rill thought it might explode into an uproar.

"Is there anyone here who will make an opening bid for the boy?" Cato asked at last.

Silence.

Then, toward the front, a disdainful voice spoke out. "Fifty gildas."

Rill's gaze darted to the bidder. His heart stopped mid beat when Brico Svagga's hard, cruel eyes met his.

"Fifty gildas," Brico repeated.

"Fifty gildas!" Cato seemed genuinely shocked. "Don't be absurd. Why . . . why, that's . . . His voice trailed off as a cunning gleam lit his eyes.

Rill's heart plopped into the sole of his boot. Something dreadful was about to happen to him.

When Cato spoke again, he took on the manner of a third-rate actor who was playing to the crowd. "Fifty gildas for a fledgling archmage with this boy's talent? Brico Svagga, I'm insulted by your bid. Who will offer more? Do I hear a higher bid?"

In the rear, Deuth Estati waved a finger lazily in the air. "Fifty-one gildas."

Shock struck Rill while his eyes hopped back and forth from Brico to Deuth. Anger simmered in his chest as his mind crazily searched for a reason why they were bidding so low. And why Deuth hadn't made the first bid, one that Brico couldn't top.

Brico raised his staff. "Fifty-two."

The crowd's gaze shifted expectantly to Deuth.

"Fifty-three."

"Fifty-four," Brico said.

Deuth waved his staff. "Fifty-five."

Cato rolled his eyes in mock despair. "Fifty-five gildas! Shame on you, Deuth Estati. I'm insulted by your bid." He threw his arms out in a pleading gesture to the audience. "Please, lords, ladies, and mages. This is the blacksmith's son you're bidding on."

Rill's anger went to full boil.

"Who will bid more?" Cato asked. "The bid's at fifty-five gildas."

Everyone in the hall stared expectantly at Brico.

"Seventy-five gildas." Brico smirked at Deuth. "Let's see if you can top that."

Rill's anger exploded into rage. He had trusted Deuth, but Deuth had been playing him for a fool all these weeks. Now Deuth and Brico were toying with him—and Cato was egging them on.

Cato screwed his face up into a sour expression. "Seventy-five gildas? Brico Svagga, I'm embarrassed for you. That's hardly a bid." He addressed the crowd. "Will no one bid more for this boy? Two hundred. Who will bid two hundred gildas?" He pointed to a woman standing nearby. "Two hundred. How about it?"

The woman held up her hands as if to ward Cato off. Some people in the audience laughed good naturedly. Cato's antics had transformed the charged mood into one of playful mischievousness as he singled out one person after another to bid higher.

After a while, Cato heaved a theatrical sigh. "If I can't get a higher bid, I have no choice but to accept Brico Svagga's seventy-five gildas.

Going once . . . twice . . ."

The thought of serving the despised Svagga Family made Rill want to throw up his breakfast porridge.

"Gone!" Cato said. "Patronage of Rill Larkin goes to the Svagga Family for seventy-five gildas." He turned to Rill, his eyes twinkling maliciously. "Rillyan Larkin, do you accept the Svagga Family's patronage?"

Rill's gaze flew from the grinning Brico to Deuth, who raised his eyebrows and gave a barely imperceptible nod. *Wait! I got first refusal. But then I gotta accept the next highest bid.* Relief washed through Rill, flushing away his anger. He grinned at Deuth, who smiled back and nodded again.

Rill wiped away his smile, straightened his shoulders, and looked Brico in the eye. "No. As a matter of fact, I'd rather apprentice to Malar, Goddess of the Underworld, than to you."

His comment brought derisive hoots from the crowd and a flare of anger in Brico's brown eyes.

"You've just exercised your right of first refusal," Cato said. "Deuth Estati made the second-highest bid of fifty-five gildas. Do you accept the Estati Family's patronage?"

"Yes."

Cato clamped Rill on the shoulder and beamed. "Congratulations, boy. Go down to your patron." He looked toward the back of the hall. "Deuth Estati, see to your family's new apprentice archmage. And may the blessings of the One Goddess go with you both."

Rill hurried down the stairs, pursued by Cato's gleeful chuckle. Many bidders from all three factions—Noblessari, Traditionali, and Commonali—were laughing and some were pounding Deuth on the back, congratulating him for putting one over on Brico as he made his way to Rill. Others were slapping Brico on the back, chuckling as they told him that Deuth had really put one over on him. From the dark look on Brico's face, he didn't find Deuth's joke funny.

Deuth wrapped an arm around Rill's shoulder as the buzz of voices and laughter continued to fill the Bidding Hall. "Congratulations, Rill. Let's sign the contract and be off."

At the Magesterium table, Rill and Deuth signed three copies of the standard contract for apprentice mages. One for Rill, one for Deuth, and one for the Magesterium's records. Rill folded his copy and tucked it into his belt purse, then walked beside Deuth toward the front of the building. His chest puffed up with pride. He was Deuth Estati's apprentice mage! But he didn't forget to utter a silent prayer of thanks to the One Goddess for watching over him and to the Five Sisters for weaving this glorious life-changing event into his tapestry of life.

Rill worked up his courage to speak as they walked along the passageway toward the front of the Hall of Naming. "Umm . . . you took a chance when you refused first bid, Lord. I might not of known what you were doing."

Deuth belted out a hearty laugh. "Not at all. You're an intelligent lad. That's one reason I want to be your mentor. I knew you'd see that I was playing a joke on my brother-in-law. Lord Brico forgot that being the second-highest bidder has its advantages."

"I almost forgot too, Lord."

"But you didn't." Deuth draped an arm around Rill's shoulder. "Beginning today, your future is linked to mine. Serve me faithfully, and, when the time is right, I'll help you get elected to the Magesterium. You'll become a new mage. Just think of it, Rill. You'll be the founding ancestor of your own commoner-noblesse family."

Images swirled through Rill's head, making him giddy, as he and Deuth exited the Hall of Naming into the early afternoon sunshine and went down the marble staircase. Rill saw himself living in a huge compound atop The Citadel with servants, backwatchers, and protectors. On public day mornings, he would sit in his receiving hall and greet clients, listen to their requests, and dispense favors. Afterward, he would stroll down the hill from his home to the Public Square, accompanied by his throng of clients. People would greet him respectfully.

When Rill and Deuth reached the cobbles, Deuth's backwatchers fell into step behind them. Deuth took a roundabout way to The Citadel as if he wanted to avoid meeting friends and clients in the Public

Square. He walked up the cobblestone road to the crest of The Citadel and eventually arrived at the Estati compound. The backwatchers dispersed after everyone entered the courtyard. Deuth escorted Rill through the doorway into the receiving hall.

Rill gawked at the ancestral cupboard on the far wall. He found the sight even more awe inspiring than on his previous visit. One day his own death mask would be in his own ancestral cupboard in the receiving hall of his own home on The Citadel. The first in a long line of Larkin death masks.

Kalso entered the room.

"Kalso," Deuth said, "you remember Rill Larkin. He's my new apprentice mage."

"We've been expecting him, Lord," Kalso said. "A room has been prepared for him on the second floor, and a tailor is scheduled to come tomorrow morning to take measurements for his new livery."

Deuth rubbed his hands together. "Good, good. Now, let's see that Rill gets settled into his quarters."

"Your pardon, Lord. Lady Ariella asked that you have the boy remain here until she speaks with you in a matriarch's council as soon as you've returned."

"A matriarch's council? Whatever for?"

"I'm afraid she didn't confide that to me."

"Oh, where's my sister?" Deuth asked.

"I believe Lady Shalira is indisposed with one of her headaches," Kalso replied.

As Kalso left, Livia Estati emerged from a side room, looking at a book she held open.

Rill's eyes flew to her. He admired the striking contrast between her curly black, shoulder-length hair and the rich red of her dress.

It took her a moment for her to realize anyone else was in the hall. She stopped, surprised. "Uncle Deuth—" Then she recognized Rill, and her homely features lit up into a smile, making her plain, heart-shaped face attractive. "Well, hello again. You're the blacksmith's son." She wrapped a finger around a curly black lock and examined him for a moment with a mischievous sparkle in her blue eyes. "So tell me. Have you become an adult and a mage yet?"

Rill's face flushed, and he silently berated himself for his reaction. He didn't want to appear the country bumpkin to this girl.

Deuth hurled his niece a reproving look. "Livia, mind your manners. Rill will be living with us as my new apprentice mage."

Astonishment filled Livia's eyes. "Does Great-Grandmother Ariella know about this?"

"She authorized me to do it."

"A decision like that should have been made in a matriarch's council."

Deuth waved her comment away. "A matriarch can make decisions without council. You know that. But for your information, no one else knew about this either. Except for Grandfather Locien. And he's with our ancestors now."

"What about Troy?" Livia said. "You're *his* mentor."

"That's right. You have a problem with that?"

Before Livia could respond, an angry voice spoke out. "You're *not* going to mentor him!" Troy Estati stood in the doorway to the family area, rage incised in every line of his face.

Deuth rolled his blue eyes up at the ceiling in exasperation.

Troy strode up to him. "You're *my* mentor!"

"Correct. And your point is . . . ?"

"I'm going to talk to Great-Grandmother about this!"

Deuth made an exaggerated motion with his arm toward the door to the family area. "Be my guest."

Troy bumped hard against Kalso as they passed each other crossing the threshold to the family area.

"The matriarch's council is ready to begin, Lord," Kalso said, unruffled by Troy's ill manners.

"What matriarch's council?" Livia asked.

"The one you weren't invited to," Deuth replied. "Because you're not old enough to take part in what's going to be discussed."

"We'll see about that!" Spinning on her heel, Livia stomped away.

Deuth smiled at Rill in embarrassment. "Please excuse my niece and nephew. They both love high drama. After the matriarch's council, we'll get you settled into your room." Then he left too.

A few moments later, Kalso returned and led Rill to the same room where he'd waited the first time he visited the Estatis to ask for an interview with Lord Locien. A lot had changed in his life since then. He was now on his way to becoming a powerful archmage and, with Lord Deuth's help, a commoner-noblesse. He wanted to shout with joy and do a victory dance.

Instead, he sat down in a chair and waited impatiently for whatever was to happen next.

## CHAPTER 33

Alyse's Progress Report

ALYSE ENTERED THE MATRIARCH'S chamber and hurried across the mosaic floor toward Mora and Pilar, who were already seated facing the matriarch's dais. A low fire in the fireplace crackled and hissed as if chiding her for being tardy. Alyse composed herself. She wasn't late, because Grandmother Maude was standing beside Pilar, talking.

Her face stern, Maude watched Alyse sit down, then went up the steps to the dais. Slowly, as if she were feeling older than her fifty-five years, she sat down in the ancient black oak matriarch's chair. She motioned for Alyse to come forward.

"The elder child first," she said.

Alyse mounted the steps. Her composed demeanor concealed anxiety lurking behind it. This matriarch's council would determine her future.

"Priestess Sybil sent me her first report about you." Maude's stern expression turned into a smile. "A glowing report."

Alyse heaved an inward sigh of relief.

Maude's gaze shot past Alyse, who turned her head quickly enough to spot Pilar giving Maude a curt nod.

Maude resettled herself in her chair. "Your mother and I have been discussing your future. If you continue to progress the way you are, Maude will declare you to succeed her as matriarch."

Alyse's jaw dropped while her mind grappled to believe what she'd just heard. "W-what?"

"That's not fair!" Mora cried behind her.

A sharp slap followed Mora's outburst, along with Pilar's harsh rebuke. "Show respect for your matriarch!"

Maude ignored the disturbance, nodding at Alyse as if nothing had happened. "It's conditioned upon your showing continued progress. But already you can find illnesses with your inner eye. I'm greatly pleased about that. You're making our family proud. I expect you to continue doing so."

Alyse's brain still reeled from the unexpected announcement. She ignored the small voice in the back of her mind that questioned whether or not she wanted to be a matriarch. "Thank you, Grandmother. I will."

"You can't identify illnesses by name yet," Maude said, "but Priestess Sybil assured me that in time you will. She also informed me that she's allowed you to treat minor illnesses without supervision, using herbs and spells. That's good. Perhaps you can reinforce what you've learned by helping Lenia in her duties here."

Alyse inclined her head respectfully while she got her jumbled emotions back under control. Becoming matriarch wasn't a done deal because a lot could happen between Maude and Pilar's deaths. "I'll be happy to help her in any way I can, Grandmother."

"I'm most anxious for you to learn how to cure illnesses using healing hands." A smug look flitted across Maude's face. "Few families can boast of a healer who has such skills."

"Other families have healers who can use healing hands," Alyse said.

Maude waved the comment aside. "But none with your potential. Once you're fully trained, your skills could equal those of Priestess Sybil herself. Or even surpass them."

Pride made Alyse thrust out her chest. "Accomplishing that will take many months of intense training."

"It will be worth the investment," Maude said. "I shared Priestess

Sybil's report with Ariella Estati, and she's just as eager as I am to see that you complete your training. Having such a powerful healer as you as a daughter-in-law is in her interests too. And she's agreed to postpone the marriage until you're further along in your training. Marriage now might be too distracting for you."

Alyse's heart did somersaults of joy. Sybil's strategy had worked after all!

"How much longer must we wait?" Pilar asked. From the tone of her voice, Maude's announcement was news to her as well. "We have a couple of families interested in Mora, don't forget. And we can't marry her before—"

Maude held up her index and middle fingers. "Two more months. Until First Fruits season."

Alyse's somersaults struck ground hard. "You just said you and Ariella would wait until I was further along in training."

"Two months *will* bring you further along," Ariella responded. "The Estatis refuse to wait any longer than that. And, as your mother just said, we have a couple of families who are interested in marrying their sons to Mora. A longer wait might discourage them, and we can't afford that."

"But—"

Maude smacked the arm of her chair. "Show some gratitude! Other families are circling the Estatis like vultures, just waiting for their chance to propose an alliance if Ariella should change her mind about renewing theirs with us. If the Estatis abandon us, Goddess knows how it will affect our other alliances."

"She's right," Pilar said. "The Spicers and the Bernes are staunch Estati allies. They might consider divorces."

Alyse fumed inside. Tempers—including her own—were becoming too heated. She had to pour water on the flames. She rearranged her features into a contrite expression. "I'm sorry. It's just that I was really hoping to be even further along in my training before I married. And I was concerned that . . . well . . . what if I got pregnant?"

"You'd have a baby," Maude replied drily. "That's usually what happens."

"At the risk of not completing my apprenticeship?"

Maude glowered at her. "You'll use protection against getting pregnant."

Alyse dared press no further. Besides, a lot could happen in two months' time to change her grandmother's mind. And if nothing changed, she would flee to Uncle Leoc's camp in The Marches. Alyse bowed her head submissively. "Very well, Grandmother."

Maude motioned for Alyse to return to her seat, then crooked a finger at Mora.

Mora approached the dais proudly, obviously confident in her abilities. She wore a dress with décolletage that revealed the chain of the Mind Bender charm behind her bodice. She mounted the steps and stood expectantly in front of her grandmother.

Maude readjusted her position on the chair. "Your mentor, Ianna Caymoore, tells me you've made good progress."

Mora's hand went to her bodice, touching her concealed charm— a gesture Alyse considered affected. "Thank you, Grandmother. I find Mind Bending easy. Frankly, though, I could make even greater progress if Ianna would let loose the reins, so to speak, and give me my head."

Pressing her lips together, Maude pinned Mora with sharp, flinty eyes. "On the contrary. She hasn't reined you in enough."

Stunned, it took a long moment for Mora to respond. "W-what do you mean?"

"You have power, but you treat your gift too cavalierly."

Mora's face turned as white as a dead woman's.

"You want to learn as many spells as you can," Maude continued, "but you learn them superficially as if quantity equals quality, and you try to learn spells that are beyond your present capabilities. In your ignorance, you don't realize there's more to Mind Bending than mere spellcasting. You must understand not just how to cast the spell and control the person but when to do it and why." Maude's tone became scathing. "Our family has no room for a superficial mage. Or for a weakling who's frightened of blood and violence."

Mora stamped her foot. "I'm *not* a superficial mage or a weakling."

"Prove it."

"I will. You'll see. I'll become one of the greatest mind benders in Caldon. And I'll be strong." Mora hurled a seething look at Alyse. "You'll have two powerful mages in this family, not one. You'll never call me a weakling again."

Maude pointed to the door. "Then go. And the next time I summon you for a progress report, show me those aren't just empty words."

Mora was waiting for Alyse just outside the door. "I want to speak to you," Mora said, her face crimson with anger, "in my bedroom."

Alyse's stomach twisted at the prospect of an argument.

As soon as they entered the bedroom, Mora slammed the door shut. "Aren't you the fine one," Mora said, her face transforming into a mask of hatred. "Goody little healer, making me look the fool."

"What on earth are you talking about?"

"'Be strong like your sister.' That's what Mother told me after the charm raid. You think I'm a weakling. The entire household does because *you* told them."

"I didn't tell anyone."

"You told Kate."

"I did not."

"Liar!" Mora said through vise-tight teeth. "You tell Kate everything. She told her friends. Now the whole household knows, and they're laughing behind my back. Can you imagine how humiliating that is?"

"You're talking nonsense."

Mora stabbed an index finger into Alyse's chest. "No. You can't imagine it. Grandmother just called me a weakling and a superficial mage. Now you're going to tell Kate, and she'll tell her friends, and then the whole household will know."

Alyse brushed Mora's hand aside. "I didn't tell Kate the first time. And I certainly won't tell her or anyone else this time. What's said in a matriarch's council stays in the matriarch's council."

"Liar!" Mora glared at Alyse while a vein in her neck throbbed. "You did that to undermine me so you could become matriarch after

Mother."

Confusion reeled in Alyse's mind. She worked her mouth, but no words came out. For a moment, she even forgot what had caused this weird argument. *Grandmother said I might succeed Mother as matriarch. That's it. Now calm yourself.* Alyse took a deep breath and forced her whirling brain to slow down to a stop. "I'm just as surprised as you."

"You scheming liar!"

Alyse reached for Mora's arm, but her sister quickly backed away. "Listen, Mora. They're trying to motivate us to train even harder."

Mora glared at Alyse, arms stiff at her sides. "First, you took Troy from me—"

"I didn't take—"

"And now you killed any chance that I might become matriarch."

Alyse couldn't prevent a pleading tone from entering her voice. "Please, listen. Yours or my succession could be forty or fifty years away. Maybe even longer. A lot can happen between now and then. You could become more a more powerful mage than me—"

Mora's emerald-green eyes took on a cunning gleam. "Yes, that's it! A lot can happen between now and then." A demonic smile slid snakelike across her lips. "Like . . . Grandmother could disinherit you. Then I'd become matriarch after Mother."

"You're not serious!"

"No, no. Not disinheritance. Renunciation. You could renounce the family."

"You're talking nonsense." Alyse went to the door. "See me when you come to your senses. Then we can have a rational discussion."

As Alyse reached for the door latch, Mora whispered, "Actus."

A cold hand clenched Alyse's stomach. She spun around.

Mora was pointing her staff at her.

"Mora! What are you doing?"

## CHAPTER 34

Trio of Liars

RILL PACED THE FLOOR impatiently while memories of the other time he'd been in the room performed somersaults in his mind. Back then, the Estatis had championed him against his parents. And now, from supplicant to apprentice. Holy Goddess! Exuberance gushed through his body, from head to toe. He wanted to dance.

"You conniving, little piece of shit!"

Rill spun toward the doorway to find Troy Estati glowering at him.

Troy stalked up to him. "I knew from the first day I saw you that you intended to worm your way into my family."

"You're wrong. I only wanted to attend my Name Day Celebration."

"Don't give me that bullshit!" Troy stepped closer. "You made up that pathetic little story to get my great-grandfather's sympathy. And then you worked on my uncle right here in this room when he came to speak to you about it. You addled his brain."

Fear clawed at Rill. He started to back away, but Troy grabbed and twisted a handful of chestnut vest, pulling him in closer. "If you believe that," Rill said, "then you're the one with the addled brain."

Troy leaned into Rill until their noses almost touched. "My uncle's obsessed with you. Persuading your matriarch to rescind her decision. Becoming your guardian. Watching you practice every damned chance he could. And now making you his apprentice. What kind of spell did you cast on him?"

"I didn't cast no spell."

"Liar!"

Troy shoved Rill away, and his hand moved toward his tunic.

Anger thrust fear aside. Rill raised his fist. "Touch that charm, I'll bash your teeth down your throat."

A familiar voice made them blanch. "Stop that nonsense, both of you!"

Rill and Troy froze.

Staff in hand, Deuth Estati entered the room. His eyes blazed blue fire as they swept across both teens, then bored into Troy.

"I can't attend our matriarch's council for even a few moments," Deuth said, "and you lose your temper and threaten my new apprentice. A fine mage *you'll* make. I have half a mind to stop mentoring you. Or maybe I'll just take your charm away."

Troy's hand slapped protectively against the charm suspended behind his vest and shirt. "No, Uncle!"

"Out of my way," Deuth said. Thrusting Troy aside, Deuth stepped up to Rill, unbuttoned Rill's vest, and placed a hand on Rill's chest.

"He's not even wearing a charm," Deuth said over his shoulder to Troy, his hand warm through the white linen fabric. "You sought to best him in an unfair fight. What do you have to say for yourself, Nephew?"

"I'm sorry, Uncle Deuth."

"And you, Rill Larkin. What do you have to say for yourself? Do you always go around threatening to bash people's teeth down their throats?"

"I was only defending myself, Lord. You'd do the same."

Deuth's brows plunged downward, and Rill realized he had overstepped himself. "Forgive me, Lord," he said hastily.

"For what?" Deuth asked, his fingers tracing a lazy pattern on Rill's shirt. "For having a manly chest? I must admit, it does feel nice."

Rill's jaw fell open, and he stumbled backward.

"Uncle Deuth!" Troy said in a shocked tone.

Deuth muttered an unintelligible word and then giggled—the sound of a girl, not a man. Rill and Troy exchanged stunned glances. Then Troy's face lit up with understanding. At the same time, Deuth's body shimmered and morphed into someone else's.

Rill watched the transformation in awe.

Livia Estati fussed over her red dress. "I don't know why my skirt always gets wrinkled whenever I cast a man's illusion."

"Livia," Troy said, "Uncle Deuth told you never to cast an illusion without his permission. He said the next time he caught you doing it, he'd take your charm away."

Livia pouted at him. "And who will tell him—you?"

"You know I'd never do that."

"I'm sure he'd be just as furious to learn that you threatened to cast a spell on his new apprentice." Livia paused, then burst out laughing so hard she snorted. She pointed her staff at Rill. "Look at him. Did you ever see anyone so surprised?"

Troy laughed too. "He's a commoner. What do you expect?"

While the siblings were talking, Rill had hastily rebuttoned his vest.

Livia placed her hand on his chest. "He does have a manly chest."

Rill backed away, which made Livia laugh again. "Oh, look. Uncle Deuth's new apprentice is shy."

Rill's cheeks burned. At that moment, he hated Livia Estati.

Troy smirked at Livia. "I heard you complaining to Great-Grandmother Ariella outside the matriarch's chamber. She refused to let you in. Poor little Livia. She's almost eighteen and still not treated as a woman."

Livia propped her staff against the wall, then made a face at Troy. "And I saw you with Grandmother Yulonna before she went into the meeting. I heard what she said." Livia raised her voice in a falsetto. "'Never question your matriarch's decisions again. *Ever.*' Poor little Troy. He's almost seventeen and still not treated as a man."

Troy blushed deeply, and Livia laughed at his reaction. Then she looked curiously at Rill. "This is all about you. What is it about a blacksmith's son that makes our matriarch take such an interest in you?"

"And Uncle Deuth too," Troy grumbled.

Rill shrugged. "I wonder that myself sometimes. All I wanted was for Lord Locien to persuade my grandma to let me attend my Name Day Celebration. I never expected all this to happen."

Livia batted her blue eyes at Rill, shooting him a sultry look while she twirled a long curl of black hair around her finger. "Apprentices usually sleep in the house, not in the barracks. Where are you staying?"

"On the second floor."

"What room?"

Rill gulped nervously. "I don't know yet."

Livia ran her tongue provocatively over her lips. "When you find out, let me know. We could have some fun together. Or am I being too naughty for such a shy boy as you?"

Her forwardness made Rill blush.

Livia sniggered. "Look at him, Troy. Did you ever see such a country bumpkin?"

When Troy didn't respond, Livia glanced at him. Ashen faced, he was staring at the doorway. She followed his gaze, a sneer on her lips. The color drained from her face.

Deuth Estati stood on the threshold, his face burning with fury. "He's not for you!" He crossed the room in long strides, took Livia's chin between thumb and forefinger, and forced her face to his. "Did you hear what I said?"

"Y-yes."

"What was it?"

"He's not for me."

Deuth's thumb and forefinger dug into Livia's chin as he emphasized the first word. "*Who* is not for you?"

"Rill Larkin."

Making a disgusted sound, Deuth shoved Livia away and turned to Troy. "Leave him alone."

Troy tried to meet Deuth's eyes but failed. "Yes, Uncle."

Deuth noticed Livia's staff leaning against the wall. "Livia, what's that doing here?"

Livia, Troy, and Rill exchanged uncertain glances but no one answered. Deuth waited silently, his impatience obvious, as he looked from one teen to the other.

No one responded.

The tension mounted, and Rill's heart slammed harder and harder against his chest with each passing moment of silence until he couldn't stand Deuth's mute, fiery stare any longer. "We were talking about staffs, Lord, and I asked to see Livia's."

Deuth turned to Livia. "Is that true?"

"Yes, Uncle."

Deuth looked at Troy. "Are you going to say the same thing?"

"Yes."

Deuth snorted in disgust. "A trio of liars, that's what you are." He pierced Livia and Troy with his gaze, each in turn. "Rill saved your skins, but it won't work a second time."

Rill's body trembled as Deuth's fierce, blue eyes homed in on him. "I require honesty and loyalty from my apprentices. Don't you ever lie to me again."

"Y-yes, Lord."

"Then we'll never have to speak of this again." Deuth's stern demeanor abruptly changed into a friendly one. "I came here to tell you, Rill, that my matriarch and the other women of the family are waiting in the matriarch's chamber to receive you and to officially recognize you as my apprentice. Livia and Troy, there's no need for you to attend."

"I'm an Estati woman," Livia said. "You might have prevented me from attending the matriarch's council, but you're not going to forbid me from this reception."

"Or me," Troy said. "I'm an Estati man. I'll replace you in the Magesterium when you join our ancestors. I'm the bond in our alliance with the Dejunes. You won't keep me out."

"Well, well," Deuth said dryly, "I'm glad to see you both are taking your responsibilities seriously for a change. Come along, then." Deuth headed for the door.

Before Rill could follow after him, Livia tapped him on the back. When he glanced at her, she mouthed, "Thank you."

Rill responded with a grin. There was something about this girl he found appealing.

Kalso was waiting outside the room, and with Deuth by his side, he led them through the reception hall into the family area, which was lined on both right and left sides by doors—some open and some closed. Two rooms with closed doors were on the far side. Kalso stopped by the left-hand door.

"Lady Ariella is going to officially introduce you to the family," Deuth told Rill. "Be sure to bow deeply to her and to everyone else. Are you ready?"

His heart drumming a staccato beat against his chest, Rill adjusted his vest, straightened his jacket, and wiped the tops of his boots on the backs of his pant legs. He licked his lips nervously. "Yes, Lord."

Deuth nodded to Kalso, who opened the door and ushered them inside. "Lord Deuth and his apprentice, Rillyan Larkin."

The magnificence of the room overwhelmed Rill, and all he could do was stand and gape like a country bumpkin. At the far end, Ariella Estati sat proudly in an exquisitely carved matriarch's chair of dark aged wood that was set on a dais. The ornamental spinning wheel stood nearby with spun yarn on it, giving the impression that she actually used it.

Behind her, a fresco took up the entire wall. The scene depicted a city being destroyed. Fires raged throughout the ruins. On the left, enemy soldiers poured through the remnants of the main gate, striking down the defenders and hacking helpless men, women, and children with swords and spitting them on spears.

Overhead, a silver dragon flew in the smoke-filled sky, breathing fire down on the city. In the center, a woman and a man stood shoulder to shoulder, staffs in hand, defiantly holding back the enemy with spells to buy time for a small group of refugees to flee into the countryside through the back gate.

Rill identified the two figures instantly. The demigods, Ulbra and Ulbridge Thane. He recognized the subject too. The destruction of ancient Euloria by the Atlanders in the final days of The Great Destruction. The mural reminded the viewer of the Estatis' connection to The Twins and to Euloria.

With difficulty, Rill tore his gaze from the fresco to take in the rest of the chamber. Its rich furnishings, the frescoes on the other walls, the magnificent fireplace, and the elegantly carved beams supporting the ceiling.

A woman occupied one of the three chairs facing the dais. She glanced over her shoulder at the newcomers. Rill recalled her from his previous visit: Lady Yulonna.

Deuth gently nudged Rill forward to accompany him across the room while Livia slipped into one of the two empty seats, and Troy moved to one side, away from the women.

From his position before the dais, Rill unobtrusively took stock of Ariella Estati. Her wrinkled skin and stringy white hair made her seem ancient, but her dark-blue eyes under narrow white eyebrows burned with intense energy. Raising a bony arm, Ariella pointed to the remaining vacant chair and spoke to Yulonna in a sharp voice. "Where's Shalira?"

"I don't know," Yulonna said.

Ariella raised her voice. "Kalso!"

The head steward entered. "Yes, Lady Ariella?"

"Where's Lady Shalira?"

"She's still indisposed with her headache."

"She missed the earlier meeting," Ariella said, "but she won't miss this one. Tell her to come here immediately."

Kalso left hastily. Before long, the door opened and Kalso entered, stopping just past the threshold. "Lady Shalira," he announced, and stepped aside to let her pass.

Rill's gasp of astonishment stuck in his throat. Because it wasn't Shalira Estati who was walking toward him.

It was Aunt Talia!

## CHAPTER 35

Shalira

RILL'S THOUGHTS SWIRLED AROUND as if they'd been caught up in a whirlwind while Lady Shalira Estati crossed the room to the empty chair between her mother, Yulonna, and her daughter, Livia. With an effort, he gathered his wits together. He suspected that Shalira's family knew nothing about her friendship with his family, and that if they found out, it could spell trouble for her.

Stepping down from the dais, Ariella put an arm around Rill's shoulder. "We're gathered here to meet Deuth's new apprentice, Rillyan Larkin. As you know, last month Rill came to seek our help against his matriarch's refusal to let him attend his Name Day Celebration. We championed his cause. Deuth became Rill's guardian and followed his progress through fledgling training. Deuth is a fine judge of character and believes Rill has potential to become a powerful archmage. I agree with him. So much so, in fact, that I'm going to dispense with the normal probationary period and give Rill the oath of loyalty today."

Rill frowned at her, wondering if he'd heard right. He scanned the faces staring at him. Yulonna and Deuth were the only ones smiling. Livia wore a startled look, while Troy scowled at him. Shalira's expression was inscrutable.

"Let me make formal introductions," Ariella said.

After Rill met the family, the women settled back into their chairs while Deuth and Troy stood to one side.

Returning to the dais, Ariella smiled at Rill and spoke in a formal tone. "Rillyan Larkin, are you willing to freely give your oath of loyalty to the Estati Family and to me as its matriarch?"

Rill couldn't contain his enthusiasm. "Yes, Lady!"

Ariella sat down in the matriarch's chair. "Then approach me and kneel."

His heart thrumming like a fast-plucked lute, Rill went up the stairs and fell to his knees in front of her.

Leaning forward, Ariella placed the palms of Rills hands together, then cupped them with her own and told him to repeat the words she said.

"I, Rillyan Larkin, swear by the One Goddess to serve Ariella Estati, the matriarch of the Estati Family, faithfully and loyally. I swear never to cause harm to her or to any other Estati. And I swear to hold the Estatis' friends and allies as my friends and allies and the Estatis' enemies as my enemies. I swear by the One Goddess never to break this oath on pain of expulsion."

When Rill finished, Ariella smiled warmly at him. "And I, Ariella Estati, matriarch of the Estati Family, promise to be a loyal and generous patron to Rillyan Larkin. I promise to provide him with a charm and a staff as well as with food, clothing, shelter, and gildas. I swear this by the One Goddess for as long as Rillyan Larkin upholds his oath to me and my family."

Leaning back, Ariella said, "Let's welcome Rill Larkin, our new apprentice mage."

Euphoria made Rill so light-headed he almost tripped going down the steps to the floor. His mind had trouble grasping that he wasn't on probation but was now an actual, honest-to-Goddess family retainer. *Tomorrow I'll release a dove in the One Goddess Temple in the Public Square to show my thanks. I'll—*

The sudden force of Deuth's slap on his back almost knocked Rill over. "Congratulations, Rill."

"I . . . I never expected it to happen like this, Lord. So . . . quickly."

Deuth chuckled amiably. "As my grandmother said, I know talent when I see it. And you, my boy, have talent. All we need to do is bring it out."

Deuth's mother, Yulonna, welcomed Rill just as wholeheartedly as Deuth, while Livia appeared a bit shy, and Troy was withdrawn. Shalira expressed her congratulations just as warmly as the other adults. Every so often, though, she put her hands to the sides of her head as if she were still experiencing a headache.

"I'll send for your personal effects," Deuth said. "And we'll assign you a backwatcher. You're my apprentice now. Your not having a backwatcher would reflect on my magetas."

Rill hesitated, biting his lower lip. "If it pleases you, Lord, I . . . umm . . . I already have a backwatcher."

Deuth raised a brow. "Oh? And who might that be?"

"My cousin, Jedd." Rill explained how Jedd was Tor Euland's nephew and how Tor had trained him in the backwatcher's skills. "He's tried to find a patron but hasn't been successful," Rill concluded. "So now he's working for a bowyer."

Deuth rubbed his chin thoughtfully. "He's Tor Euland's nephew?"

"Yes, Lord."

Ariella motioned for Rill to approach.

He stopped at her chair, his body tense as an overly tight lute string, dreading a reprimand. To his utter amazement, Ariella grinned at him.

"I like your spunk, Rill. And it might be good to have your cousin in our household, under oath to us. I'm surprised some other family hasn't snapped him up already. But that's their loss and our gain." Ariella nodded to Deuth. "Send someone to Jedd to make him an offer. Tell him we're honoring Rill's personal request."

Ariella motioned to Yulonna. "Have Kalso show Rill to his room."

"I'll show him," Shalira said quickly.

"Then see to it."

Shalira grimaced, putting her fingers to her temples. A few moments later, she led Rill out of the room and through the family area.

Anger simmered inside Rill. When they reached the steps to the second floor, his anger came to full boil. He turned to Shalira. "My family lied to me, and so did you. You're not my—"

"Not here, Rill—"

"You're not my aunt. You're noblesse."

Shalira took his arm in a vise-tight grip and shoved him up the stairs. "Keep quiet, or you'll put both our lives in danger!" she whispered fiercely.

Grudgingly, Rill trudged up to the second-floor landing. Shalira brushed past him, turned left, and started down the hallway.

Sunlight spilled through slit windows along the outer granite wall, casting a patchwork of light and shadow. Even in his agitated state, one part of Rill's mind noted that the windows, which overlooked the Estatis' grounds, nearby streets, and neighboring compounds, made good defensive positions for warrior mages and archers if the compound were attacked.

Shalira turned a corner and opened the door to the second room. She gestured for Rill to go inside. The windowless room was dark, but the window slits in the corridor cast allowed enough weak sunlight through the doorway for Rill to see the space was sparsely furnished: a narrow bed in the center with a pillow at the head and a neatly folded blanket at the foot; a night table with an oil lamp, next to a set of flint, steel, and tinder; a wooden chest at the foot of the bed; a washstand with pitcher, basin, soap, and washcloth; a chair and small desk with a second oil lamp on it; a shared fireplace built into the wall, a stack of kindling nearby; and pegs running along the length of the wall opposite the fireplace.

Shalira lit the lamp on the nightstand, then closed and locked the door. Lamplight made shadows waver along the walls. Shalira pointed at the bed. "Sit."

Rill perched on the edge of the mattress. *She's full of deceit like my mom.*

Shalira stood over him in the lamplight. Her posture reminded him of the way his mother had loomed over him when he was a child and she was about to lecture him for misbehaving.

"For your information," Shalira said, "your parents and I became friends long before the animosity between our families began."

"Commoners and noblesse don't become friends," Rill said. "Not the way you and my parents have."

"You've become quite the expert in commoner-noblesse relations in your brief sixteen years of life."

"I'm expert enough to know your family wouldn't approve if they knew."

Shalira let out a deep, weary sigh and sat beside him. "Your mother and I met under unusual circumstances. My family approved of our friendship. Then differences between our families split us apart. My grandmother forbade me from ever seeing your mother again. On pain of expulsion. But our love for each other was too strong. I couldn't sever my ties with her—or with you. That's why we hid my identity from you. If my family ever found out . . ."

"You could of trusted me not to tell."

"You were a child. Would you entrust to a child a secret that could ruin your life and the lives of the people you love?"

"I ain't a child no more. I'm an adult. You could of told me."

"That's true. But it was easier to keep things as they were. Perhaps we were wrong to do that."

"But you did it and now I'm here. So what do we do?"

Twisting toward Rill, Shalira grabbed hold of his wrists. "Go home, Rill."

Rill recoiled as if he'd been stung by a shock eel. "Leave?"

"Yes. Right now."

"You're crazy! I've dreamed my whole life of becoming a mage. Of becoming noblesse. Do you expect me to walk away from that? Besides, I swore an oath of loyalty. I can't break that. And I don't wanna."

Shalira tightened her grip on Rill's wrists as if to emphasize her words. "My brother intends to destroy you."

Rill snorted scornfully. "Now you're sounding like my parents."

"You should have listened to them."

Peeling free of her grip, Rill stood and opened his chestnut short jacket. "You gave me these clothes. You took my side against my family when they didn't want me to go to my Name Day Celebration. And now you're telling me to toss it all away and go home?"

"Yes." Shalira stood and faced him. "If I'd known you'd end up here, I would never have given you those clothes. And I would have sided with your parents. But now it's too late. The harm is done." Shalira's voice became softer as if she were talking more to herself than to Rill. "I've already asked the One Goddess's forgiveness for that."

"And I *thanked* Her."

Shalira's lips trembled. She swallowed hard and put a hand to her breast. Her body shuddered.

Distress seized Rill. "Aunt Talia . . . Lady Shalira, are you all right?"

"Is there any way I can change your mind?"

"No."

"Then promise me one thing."

"What?"

"Keep our secret. Whatever else I am, I'm an Estati. I can't stand the thought of being expelled. Of being stateless. Of not joining my ancestors when I die."

Anxiety made Rill bite his lip. If he kept the secret, he'd violate his oath of fealty after he'd barely pledged it. But whether she was Aunt Talia or Lady Shalira Estati, he loved this woman, and he couldn't live with himself if something he did caused her harm. "Of course I will."

Shalira blinked watery eyes. "Thank you, Rill. And may the One Goddess protect you." She hurried from the room as if she feared she would break down in front of him.

Rill's eyes lingered on the closed door for a long time. The encounter with Shalira had unsettled him and set puzzling questions fluttering through his head. What was the connection between the Estatis and the Larkins? Why did the Estatis hate his family so much?

And in what kind of a web of deceptions had he become entangled?

Mind Bender

"COMPEL!" MORA SAID, CASTING the spell.

Alyse's senses turned numb as Mora's eyes zeroed in on Alyse's. "You will renounce your family."

Mora had barely finished speaking when Alyse was seized by the urge to find Grandmother Maude and formally renounce each and every Dejune. I don't belong here. Not with this family. No! What am I thinking? I don't want to . . . Alyse struggled against the compulsion but couldn't overcome it.

Mora stepped closer to her. "You hate the Dejunes. You will sever all ties with the Dejunes, including Kate."

I hate each and every Dejune. Especially Kate. Alyse twisted and turned as if she were struggling against an invisible rope wrapping itself around her, forcing her to move wherever it wanted to take her.

"Now say it," Mora ordered.

Alyse's mind forced her lips to obey. "I hate the Dejunes. I want to have nothing to do with them." No! This is wrong. I don't hate my family. And I love Kate as a sister. Especially"—Alyse strove to not say the last word but couldn't resist—"Kate."

"Go to Grandmother and tell her."

Find Grandmother. Tell her. Renounce my family. I hate them all.

Alyse stepped toward the door.

Mora laughed with a combination of triumph, glee, and malevolence. The tones sparked outrage in some part of Alyse's brain that still resisted the spell's power. With a sharp cry of fury, Alyse instinctively booted the compulsion from her head, hurling it back at Mora.

Clutching her temples, Mora howled in pain, staggered backward into a wall, and collapsed to the floor. She writhed and groaned.

Alyse's legs threatened to collapse beneath her, and she gripped the door latch to steady herself. A dull ache throbbed in her head. Alyse stared saucer-eyed at Mora, whose thrashing began to ease. A jagged blade of fear sliced into her. One Goddess, help me! What have I done?

The latch to the door connecting Mora's and Jade's bedrooms rattled and started to open. "Mora!" Jade called.

Alyse staggered to the door and threw her weight against it. "What do you want?"

"I heard Mora scream."

Alyse turned the key in the lock. "Everything's all right."

Jade pushed against the door.

"I said everything's all right," Alyse said.

"I'm her backwatcher. I need to see for myself."

"You're a Dejune retainer. Remember your place."

"I want to see for myself."

It took all of Alyse's strength to summon enough energy to speak with an imperiousness that would make Grandmother Maude proud. "How dare you question me! If you say one more word, I'll have you expelled."

After a few tension-laden moments, Jade's footsteps moved away.

Jade's sneaky. You can't trust her. Alyse raced to the door to the family area and locked it. She wilted against the door, eyes closed, while the tension seeped from her body. The headache went with it.

Mora had pushed herself into a sitting position by the time Alyse crossed the room and towered over her, hands on hips.

Her face drained of color, Mora met Alyse's frigid gaze fearfully.

"W-what did you do?"

Alyse swallowed to loosen her tight throat. She had repelled her sister's Compulsion spell but had no idea how she'd done it. It was as if her euloghe power had acted on its own to save her, which meant she couldn't control her own magic. The realization infused her with horror. But she couldn't reveal that secret to Mora because the knowledge would give Mora power over her. She had to make Mora fear her.

Alyse put her hands on her hips and spoke the first words that came to mind. "Healing also involves Mind Bending. Making the patient believe certain things. Because I can bend someone else's mind, I also can prevent someone from bending mine. It's a power only the most powerful healers have. You're lucky I didn't compel you to renounce our family. I could have, you know."

Mora's expression turned even more fearful.

"I can destroy a spell-caster's mind. Did you know that?"

Mora shook her head.

"Don't you ever use a mind spell on me again. And don't go tattling on me to Mother or Grandmother or anyone else. Because if you do . . ." Alyse let the words dangle.

"I . . . I won't."

The terror in Mora's voice almost made Alyse's rock-hard exterior crumble. She offered a hand to Mora. "And don't go tattling to Jade. This is a secret between just you and me."

Alyse forced herself to walk to the door with a self-assured step. She turned the key, then, her hand on the latch, she turned to Mora. "I'm first in birth and first in magic. Don't you ever forget it."

As she stepped over the threshold into the family area, Alyse was gripped by the urge to race to her bedroom, lock the door, and scream as loud as she could in sheer panic. Instead, she made herself walk nonchalantly through the door into the rear courtyard and watch Kate practice sword fighting with her sparring partner, Freya.

There would be time for hysterics later.

## CHAPTER 37

Morning Greeting

RILL'S FIRST AFTERNOON WITH the Estatis passed in a whirlwind of introductions as Kalso took him to meet key servants and retainers. Faces, names, and roles became a blur in his mind. But two people, the mage Magnus Roeback and the bladesman Yall Throwstarr, stood out. Both had accompanied Deuth when he had escorted Rill home to persuade his parents to allow him to participate in his Name Day Celebration. Magnus, Rill learned, was one of Deuth's personal backwatchers and Yall was Troy's personal backwatcher. Everyone greeted Rill cordially, except for one man.

Milco Barr, the head backwatcher, was a grizzled, old veteran with a turf of salt-and-pepper hair that fell to the tops of his ears. His left earlobe was missing, and the thick scar that ran from behind it to the corner of his mouth had turned his lips into a perpetual sneer. When Kalso introduced Rill, Milco looked Rill over with piercing brown eyes, giving Rill the impression that he was being scrutinized by a bird of prey. Milco wiped a calloused hand across his misshapen lips and spoke in a gruff tone that reminded Rill of a bear. "You're the blacksmith's son."

Rill stomped down his irritation. He was getting tired of being called that. "My name's Rill," he said politely. "Rill Larkin."

"Rill it is," Milco said, then turned his back and walked off.

When Rill went to his room after the introductions, he found that his personal effects, including his sword, dagger, bow, and quiver of arrows, were on his bed. Rill unpacked the bundle of belongings and put them away, either in the chest or on the wall pegs. He half expected to find a note from his parents in with his things and was disappointed when he didn't. Another sign of their disapproval.

At dinnertime, Rill was still in his room with an empty, growling stomach. He wondered where he should go to eat but felt too insecure to ask. Just as Rill had worked up the nerve to seek Deuth's advice, Deuth knocked on Rill's door and informed him that as his apprentice he was expected to take his meals with the family in the dining room.

Everyone else was already seated when Rill and Deuth arrived. Ariella occupied the matriarch's position at the head of the long oak table while the women sat along one side and the men along the other. On the men's side, Yulonna and Shalira's husbands, Tolf Belkon and Alger Berne, were sitting next to each other, leaving an empty chair between themselves and Troy. Deuth motioned for Rill to take the chair, while he sat at the opposite end from Ariella, in the "magestrate's chair."

Surrounded by members of one of Caldon's most preeminent First Families made Rill want to pull his head down inside the collar of his white linen shirt. He was deathly afraid of doing or saying something stupid to embarrass himself. To his relief, most of the family went out of their way to draw him out. Deuth, Ariella, and Yulonna asked him about himself while Tolf and Alger listened attentively. Livia peppered him with questions about what it was like living in The Kings, which he answered a bit evasively because of the Kings dwellers' hostility toward the noblesse. Shalira, though, spent most of the time picking at her food. And Troy wore a sullen expression, which earned him a few sharp glances from Ariella and Deuth.

Later that evening as Rill was going to his room for the night, the door of the corner room next to his opened, and Yall Throwstarr stepped out. Rill smiled and greeted him cordially, but Yall turned an indifferent face to him. Rill kept his puzzlement from showing. This reception was far different from the earlier one Yall had given him.

"Your room was put next to mine for a reason," Yall said. He pushed his face closer to Rill's. "So I can keep an eye on you."

Tor Larkin had cautioned both Rill and Jedd about men like Yall, ones who tried to intimidate people through fear. "Sometimes it's all swagger," Tor had said. "But other times it ain't. Be cautious of people like that, but don't let them know you're scared. They thrive on other people's fear."

So Rill kept the friendly smile on his face and said, "Thanks, Yall. That's kind of you to keep an eye on me because I'm new here. I appreciate your thoughtfulness. And I'll be sure to let you know if I have any questions or need anything."

Yall appeared confused. He opened his mouth to say something but apparently thought better of it and marched off.

Early the next morning, Rill was awakened by a servant knocking on the door. Climbing out of bed in his nightshirt, Rill lit the oil lamp and padded to the door, which he opened to find an elderly, gray-haired woman with clothes draped across an arm.

She handed the clothing to him. It was a spare set of Estati livery that should fit him, she told him. He should wear it until the tailor made him his own livery. Before she turned to leave, the servant added that the family expected him at the breakfast table shortly.

Rill spread the clothes out on the bed and stared at them pensively. A black tunic with purple trim around the collar, cuffs, and bottom, along with black pants and a pair of polished black boots made of costly soft leather. He ran his fingers over the expensive, finely spun wool, hardly believing he had come so far in achieving his lifelong dream.

The breakfast conversation flowed more naturally than the previous evening's, and Rill actually found himself more comfortable taking part in it. When Ariella asked him how he was getting along after his first day, Rill replied that everything seemed strange, but he'd get used to it in time.

"Before long," Ariella said, "all this will be normal to you."

Toward the end of the meal, Kalso came in and whispered in

Ariella's ear. After he left, Ariella said to Deuth, "Our clients are waiting in the front courtyard."

This morning was a public day, so Deuth was wearing the black tunic with gold trim and the black pants and boots of a magestrate. Heaving a sigh, he got to his feet.

"The morning greeting . . ." he said. "A patron's work is never done."

Troy stood too, and took a last sip of watered wine.

Deuth motioned to Rill. "Come with me."

Troy choked on the wine. "Why is he attending?"

"Because I told him to."

"He hasn't been here even a full day—"

"Rill's my apprentice. Just as you are. I require both my apprentices to attend the morning greetings."

Troy's eyes shot angry blue sparks. "That's not fair. I had to wait six months before I could attend."

Deuth started to reply, but Ariella spoke first. "You overreach yourself, young man. Remember your place. I'll have no more outbursts like that."

Troy lowered his eyes, his face reddening. "Yes, Great-Grandmother."

Deuth turned to the door. "Kalso!"

"Yes, Lord."

"Call 'em in."

Rill followed Deuth and Troy out the door into the family area and headed for the entrance to the receiving hall. Five backwatchers and five protectors lingered near the doorway. Two other men waited as well. One was short with curly brown hair and held a ledger. Rill had met him yesterday and recalled that he was Deuth's secretary. A heavyset man Rill hadn't met stood beside the secretary.

When Deuth stopped, the backwatchers and protectors sorted themselves into two columns, one of protectors and the other of backwatchers. Milco and the head protector placed themselves at the head of their respective files.

Rill glanced uncertainly at Deuth, not sure what he should do.

"Rill's with you," Deuth told Milco.

Milco motioned for Rill to take up the rear position in his file.

What happened next worked like a well-drilled legion. At a nod from Deuth, Milco stepped through the door, turned right, and stopped four feet from the receiving chair. The remaining backwatchers formed a line to his right, with Rill at the end. Then the protectors copied the alignment on the other side of the chair, with Troy at standing at the end.

Rill's gaze swept across the receiving hall.

Clients, commoners by the cut of their clothes, packed the room but left a large gap between themselves and the receiving chair. Kalso stood by the door to the front courtyard. The secretary came out next and took up a position to the right of the receiving chair, and the heavyset man placed himself behind the chair.

A table and two chairs had been set up outside Deuth's study. A bottle of ink and a white quill pen were on the tabletop. A servant carrying a ledger emerged from the study, set the ledger on the table, and sat in one of the chairs. A second man carrying a heavy, iron-bound strongbox followed him out, placed the chest on the table, opened the lid, and sat in the other chair.

At last, Deuth strode through the doorway, his figure straight and his face solemn. Upon seeing him, the clients put a hand on their chests and bowed. Deuth stopped in front of the receiving chair, faced his clients, and opened his arms wide. "Welcome, friends."

A chorus of voices replied, "Greetings, Lord."

Deuth sat down. "Let those who wish to speak come forward."

A man separated himself from the crowd and approached Deuth. Deuth welcomed him by name and asked about his sick daughter. The man replied that she was better and thanked Deuth for sending the Estatis' family healer to treat her.

"I'm happy to help you," Deuth responded.

With a last thank-you and a bow, the man turned and went to the two servants at the table.

The man with the ledger checked off the client's name, and the other servant handed the client some coins from the strongbox.

Then the client went into the front courtyard where he would wait to accompany Deuth down to the Public Square.

Another client approached. Deuth turned his head ever so slightly to the heavyset man standing behind the chair. The man whispered in Deuth's ear. When the client stopped, Deuth greeted him by name and asked how he liked living in The Oaks after having spent his life in the country.

Rill glanced at the heavyset man again as recognition dawned in his brain. The names keeper, who would prompt Deuth with names and information about clients if Deuth couldn't recall it.

Rill's eyes and mind soaked up every detail of the morning greeting as one client after another approached Deuth and greeted him, or asked him for help, or thanked him for assisting with a problem before going to have their names checked off in the ledger and to receive their "weekly gildas."

Rill also detected a pattern to the clients' appeals for aid. The poorer ones asked for help with food, clothing, or some other basic necessity. The middling clients sought loans from Deuth for various reasons. Some merchants wanted to expand their businesses or buy goods to sell, while craftsmen wanted money to buy materials. Others thanked Deuth for purchases his family had made that had helped their businesses succeed. The wealthier clients tried to interest Deuth in joint ventures or, if he wasn't interested in doing that, in lending them money for their enterprises.

A pair of clients approached Deuth together, asking him to settle a dispute between them. A few clients asked him to defend them in lawsuits, which Deuth agreed to readily. Rill wasn't surprised at Deuth's willingness to defend them. Everyone knew that the noblesse attacked their enemies by suing their enemies' clients. After all, if a noblesse couldn't defend his clients, those clients would abandon him for a patron who could. All the while, Deuth's secretary recorded the requests and promises in his ledger.

Sometimes Deuth would chide a client for not following through on something he'd been asked to do. Or he would put the screws to one for not repaying a loan on time. But the exchange between

Deuth and Alain Develle, an overweight, middle-aged spice seller, stuck in Rill's memory because of the sharp way Deuth spoke to him.

"I've asked you two times already to repay the loan."

"I've had expenses, Lord," Alain said, sweat rolling down his forehead. "More than I anticipated."

"You've given me that excuse twice already. I don't want to hear it a third time."

"But it's true. I need one more extension, Lord. Just for a few weeks. *Please.*"

Deuth's brow creased into a frown while he considered the request. "Very well. I'll give you another extension. But after that, no more excuses."

"I won't fail you again, Lord."

"You'd better not," Deuth said, holding Alain's eye. "I'd hate to have someone visit you."

Fright crawled across Alain's face. "That won't be necessary, Lord," he said hastily. "I promise."

"Promise noted," Deuth responded.

As Alain scurried off, Deuth told his secretary to record in large letters Alain's extension. "He won't put me off a third time," Deuth muttered.

Rill watched Alain scurry into the front courtyard. What power! He would have that same power when he became noblesse. Some people might complain that Deuth had treated Alain too harshly, but Deuth had treated him fairly. Alain had broken his promise to repay the loan twice. If Deuth hadn't threatened him, other clients might think they could get away with not repaying their loans. Tough but fair. That was how Deuth operated. Rill vowed to be tough but fair too.

Rill's fascination with the proceedings made time slip by quickly. Before he knew it, midmorning had arrived along with the last two clients. The next-to-last one—a fat, prosperous-looking man—went up to Deuth and greeted him.

Standing up, Deuth clasped the man's shoulders and said, "Congratulations on your daughter's engagement. It will bring benefits to both your family and the groom's."

The man's face sparkled with happiness. "Yes, Lord. Two business rivals will become partners—"

The front door burst open, almost knocking Kalso over, and an elderly mage stumbled into the hall. Clutching his staff, eyes wild with terror, he raced toward Deuth. "Deuth, you've got to help me!"

"Fenn," Deuth said, his expression filled with concern, "whatever's wrong?"

"It's Cato Porta. He's going to ruin me."

Deuth headed toward Fenn.

Shouts erupted from the front courtyard. A man in gray livery ran through the open doorway and skidded to a stop when he spotted Fenn. "Murderer! He's not Lord Lodestone. He's an archmage—an assassin! He murdered Lord Lodest—"

A Fire Bolt streaked out of Fenn's staff and stuck the man in the stomach. Then, spinning on his heel, the assassin pointed his staff at Deuth.

## CHAPTER 38

The Assassin

CHAOS BOKE LOOSE AS Deuth's clients screamed in panic and scattered in all directions. Most headed for the door to the front courtyard, creating a logjam of frightened, desperate people struggling to escape outside first. Milco Barr knocked Deuth to the ground just as a slim Fire Bolt sped through the spot where Deuth had been standing. Magnus cast a Fire Bolt on the assassin and Yall flung a dagger.

But the man ducked the knife as he blocked Magnus's spell with an Ice Shield. Her sword drawn, the head protector charged the intruder. Yall rushed at him too. Magnus started another cast, but Yall and the protector crossed into his line of fire, and Magnus bit off the last letters of the spell. The killer cast a hail of daggers at the protector. They struck her in the chest and stomach, and she was dead before her body hit the tiles. The mage grinned, an insane fire dancing in his eyes, as he turned to face Yall. A blade sprung out from the end of his staff.

The attack had caught the other backwatchers and protectors by surprise. Now they dove into the fray. Laughing like a madman, the assassin charged them, using his staff as a quarterstaff.

Rill dashed to help Milco assist Deuth to his feet. Angrily, Deuth shook them off and looked at the fighting just as the murderer's blade sliced open a backwatcher's belly. The man fell close to the body of a protector whose skull had been shattered.

Two mage protectors had been slow to react to the attack. Now they hovered near the receiving chair, glancing uncertainly from the fighting to one another.

Deuth shoved the mages toward the melee. "What're you waiting for? Damn it!"

"The fighting's too closed in for spellcasting, Lord," one of them replied.

"Then use your staffs as quarterstaffs, you dolts!"

They raced to join their comrades.

Rill watched the fighting, frustration wrapping its coils around him like an octopus because he had no weapon. He gnashed his teeth at the sight of the mage laughing madly and moving with the agility of a young man while he parried his opponents' swords and slashed and butted and stabbed with his staff. The man was a skilled fighter. He kept just enough distance between himself and his attackers to prevent them from getting close enough to use their swords effectively, and at the same time maneuvered to keep them packed so close together that their bodies shielded him from spells.

Rill glanced at the two protector mages who had joined the melee. They fought like timid children, uncertain when to swing or parry or lunge with their staffs. Finally, one of them stepped toward the assassin and swung hard. The assassin ducked. The mage lost his footing, and the assassin bashed the man's head in with the orb of his own staff.

"I'll take him down," Milco said and stepped toward the fighting.

Deuth seized his arm. "No. You're too valuable to lose."

"Stopping him is my job."

"You'll stay here."

Milco grumbled but remained in place.

Just then a group of protectors charged through the front door to reinforce their comrades. A few more who had been stationed in the rear courtyard raced in from the family area.

The assassin met them head-on.

Tor Euland had taught Rill how to study an opponent's moves before committing himself to a fight. Rill did that now. He watched as the assassin gradually maneuvered himself into a corner, where the walls protected his back. His moves were like an impromptu dance. But his basic steps had a pattern to them, and he had a tendency to spin around a bit too much. He also used his staff to keep his opponents just out of sword's reach until he had an opportunity to strike.

But not out of staff's reach.

Rill eyed the discarded staffs lying on the mosaic floor, but the battle ranged back and forth over them, making it impossible for him to retrieve one.

Troy had hung back and was watching the fracas.

Rill strode over to him, snatched the staff, and strode toward the fighting.

"Hey, that's mine!" Troy cried and started after him.

"Troy, let him be!" Deuth shouted.

Rapid heartbeats pounded in Rill's ears like a pair of beating drums as he cautiously approached the assassin from the left. The mage spun right with his staff, the blade ripping into a protector. The backwatchers near Rill edged forward and hastily backed off when the assassin whirled toward them, lashing out with the staff. He pivoted right again.

Rill dashed in and swung Troy's staff at the man's knee. The orb smacked into skin and bone. Uttering a sharp cry of pain, he stumbled. Rill swung the staff again, striking him in the cheek. The man staggered against the wall. Dropping Troy's staff, Rill grabbed the killer's staff and struggled to wrest it from him.

Two protectors seized the man's arms, and Yall put a dagger to his throat.

"Don't kill him!" Deuth yelled. "I want him alive."

Yall removed the blade long enough for a protector to yank the mage's charm from his neck. The assassin still held tightly on to his staff, refusing to surrender it to Rill.

Deuth stopped in front of the assassin. "Release your staff."

The man smiled mockingly at him.

"I'll ask one more time. Then I'll have my man cut your throat."

The intruder spat blood and a tooth fragment at Deuth. "Slice away."

Yall sent Deuth a questioning look, but Deuth held up his hand. "You don't fear death," Deuth told the man. "So perhaps you fear life." He nodded to Yall. "Cut his hamstrings."

When Yall stepped toward him, the assassin let go of the staff. The sudden release of pressure on the staff made Rill stumble.

"He's not a threat anymore," Deuth said. "Release him."

The protectors holding the mage let him go, and Yall sheathed his dagger. The assassin crossed his arms over his chest and eyed Deuth, a taunting smile on his split and swelling lips.

The four Estati women hurried in from the family area, pushing their way through the press of retainers who were helping the wounded or gawking at the captive, and stopped by Deuth.

Confusion dominated Ariella's face when she took in the bloody scene. "What's going on? I was told there was an assassin here."

Deuth pointed to the mage. "That's him."

"Fenn?" Ariella said in disbelief.

"Fenn's dead," Deuth said.

"But . . . but he's—"

"An archmage," Deuth said. "He murdered Fenn, cast an illusion of Fenn on himself and came here to kill me."

"Which family is he working for?"

"That's what we're about to find out," Deuth said grimly. He pointed his staff at the man and cast a spell.

Astonishment leaped upon Rill's face when the assassin didn't morph into his true self.

Deuth cast several other spells on the man, but none worked. "What's the counterspell?"

The archmage lifted his chin defiantly. "You'll find that out only in death."

Keening erupted in the front courtyard. Rill turned toward the wide-open front door. The wailing grew louder as two women staggered into the hall. They appeared to be mother and daughter. The daughter supported the mother with an arm around her shoulder while the mother gave one last pitiful wail.

"Sarra!" Shalira said and dashed toward them.

"Celia!" Livia cried and hurried after Shalira.

"Give her to me, Celia," Shalira said, relieving the younger woman of her burden.

Celia seemed ready to drop, but Livia wrapped an arm around her waist, propping her up. Sarra leaned heavily against Shalira. She spotted the assassin through a gap in the press of bodies and pointed at him.

"Murderer!" she shrieked. "You murdered Fenn! You murdered my husband!"

The assassin watched her impassively, arms still crossed.

Tears gushed down Celina's cheeks. "Why did you murder him? My father was a harmless old man. He was no threat to anyone. You didn't need to kill him to assume his shape. All you needed was something that belonged to him."

Shaking free of Livia, Celina ran up to the man and slapped him across the face. Her hand left a red imprint. "You bastard! Why couldn't you have chosen someone else to impersonate?"

His eyes brimming with contempt, the assassin unfolded his arms and swept his gaze across noblesse, backwatchers, and protectors as if he were cutting them down with a scythe.

"He was noblesse. That made him fair game."

"Fair game?" Celina said incredulously.

The assassin snorted his contempt. "You noblesse make me puke." He gestured at the corpses and the wounded on the floor. "This is the life you created for yourselves so you could rule the roost. You're quick to kill other noblesse to get charms and power. But then you think it unfair when they kill you for the same."

"My father was never a magestrate," Celina said. "He kept out of politics."

The assassin shrugged. "In that case, he should've become a commoner. Then all he would've had to worry about was fawning over people like you for favors or becoming spell fodder for your fucking wars."

"Enough of this!" Ariella said. "Who sent you?"

The mage's eyes glinted coldly like a pair of ice cubes. "That you'll never learn. Not even in death."

"A mindbender will make short work of your braggadocio." Ariella turned to Deuth. "Fetch Ianna Caymoore—"

In a quick movement, the assassin raised his hand to his mouth. The under part of a ring glimmered on his finger.

"Stop him!" Deuth shouted.

Dropping the staff, Rill tore the man's arm from his mouth. An emerald ring sparkled on his finger. The gemstone had sprung open on a hinge, revealing a secret compartment.

An empty compartment.

The assassin grinned triumphantly at Ariella. "Not even in death."

Then his eyes rolled up in his head; his body twitched; his legs folded beneath him, and he collapsed facedown on the floor.

Kneeling, Yall rolled him over and checked his pulse. "He's dead."

"What spell did he use to impersonate Fenn?" one of the mages asked.

"We'll that find out shortly," Deuth said.

Everyone stared at the corpse, waiting expectantly. Slowly, the man's body transformed into a different one.

"Goddess in Elustra!" Rill gasped. "He's a woman."

Petite and young—no more than in her early twenties—with light-brown hair framing an unlined face, she stared blankly at the ceiling. The blue pants, vest, and white linen shirt she wore were new. In death, she seemed frail and innocent.

Deuth prodded the corpse with a booted toe. "She cast a special Death spell on herself. It's impervious to counterspells. Only in death would her body revert to its true form."

"She musta known she was on a suicide mission," Rill said.

Milco pointed to her finger. "The ring proves that."

"I've never seen her before," Ariella said.

Deuth turned to his retainers. "Any of you recognize her?"

No one spoke up.

"I thought as much," Deuth muttered.

"Is she a Gaetanian?" Magnus asked.

"We won't discuss those questions here," Ariella replied. She turned to the Lodestones. "Come, poor ladies. Come inside with us."

Closing ranks around Sarra and Celia, the Estati women escorted them into the family area.

Deuth watched them leave, his expression dark. He motioned to Milco. "What's the butcher's bill?"

"Five dead. Seven wounded."

"Five dead, seven wounded." Deuth raked a scornful glance across his backwatchers and protectors. "A fine group you are. Trained fighters. That's a laugh."

Shamefaced, no one dared look him in the eye.

Deuth clamped a hand on Rill's shoulder and turned him to face the retainers. "Rill Larkin hasn't been here a full day but he stopped the assassin. Unlike the rest of you. He served my family well today. Unlike the rest of you. He lived up to his oath of fealty. Unlike the rest of you."

Backwatchers and protectors shifted their feet uncomfortably.

Deuth scanned the group. "Where's Troy?"

"Here, Uncle," Troy said, emerging reluctantly from behind a couple of retainers.

"What kind of charm do you wear?" Deuth asked.

"An archmage's."

"Where were you during the fighting?"

"It all happened so fast," Troy said.

"'It all happened so fast,'" Deuth mimicked.

Troy's face turned deep red.

"You're an Estati." Deuth picked up Troy's discarded staff and shook it in front of Troy's face. "This is the sign of your power. And with this power comes responsibility—to lead, not hang behind. I'm ashamed of you."

"I'm sorry," Troy said. "It won't happen again."

Deuth thrust the staff at him. "It better not. Otherwise, I'll take this staff back, and you'll have to find yourself another mentor. One who doesn't mind training cowards. And I'll devote all my attention to training Rill. He's someone I can rely on."

Deuth gave Troy a long, withering look, then transferred it to the retainers. "Clean up this mess and return to your duties."

As Rill turned to leave, he cast a glance at Troy. The hate-filled look Troy hurled back at him told Rill what he'd already suspected.

Troy had become his unforgiving enemy.

Settling In

DEUTH AND ARIELLA QUICKLY restored order to the household. Deuth followed his slightly delayed routine of going down to the Public Square for the Magesterium meeting accompanied by his clients and backwatchers while the protectors returned to their posts or resumed their off-duty activities. The wounded were taken to the infirmary to be treated by the family healer, and the dead were returned to their families for burial with their ancestors. Ariella comforted the Lodestone women, then summoned a matriarch's council. And Livia, who wasn't invited, visited the wounded.

Abandoned by everyone, Rill was left at loose ends. To pass time, he wandered the compound grounds and finally climbed the granite staircase to the wall walk. Forearms on the parapet, he leaned forward and let his gaze wander over the neighboring compounds and the private dwellings and the government buildings in the Public Square spread out across the bottom of the hill. He let his mind drift like a cloud scudding across the sky . . .

A hand on his shoulder made him start. Turning, he found himself staring into Livia Estati's dark-blue eyes.

"Sorry," she said. "I didn't mean to startle you."

"My fault, Lady," Rill responded. "My mind was elsewhere."

"This has been an interesting first full day for you. A family friend murdered. An assassination attempt made on my uncle. And you a hero—"

"I ain't no hero," Rill muttered, recognizing his false modesty as soon as the words left his mouth.

"And now you're left to fend for yourself." Livia smiled tentatively at him. "Not very welcoming."

"I've had worse days," Rill said, thinking of the attack on the One Goddess Temple.

"Will you walk with me?"

"Of course, Lady."

"I used to come up here as a child," Livia said as they strolled along the wall walk. "I was too little to look over the parapet, so my nurse or my mother would lift me up so I could see over it." Her voice turned low. "I saw a whole world spread out before me. The tenements, temples, and homes. The statues and monuments. The Public Square. My nurse told me once that they all belonged to me. To us, the Estatis. I'm still not certain if she was joking, but I like to think she was."

Rill thought it odd that this noblesse girl he hardly knew was confiding her memories to him, a commoner. Yet he listened attentively, grateful for her trust.

Livia stopped to rest her elbows on the top of the granite wall and let her gaze drift across the vast expanse of the city. "This is my favorite spot. Do you know why?"

"No."

"See there?" Livia asked, and pointed.

Rill followed the line of her finger. "The Mother Goddess Temple?"

Livia nodded. "Seeing it makes me feel good because I know She loves me. She loves all Her children. Everyone, noblesse and commoner alike." Her tone hardened. "No matter how badly people treat them."

Rill hesitated, fumbling for a response.

Livia must have sensed his embarrassment because she laughed nervously. "Please forgive me. I can become maudlin sometimes."

"I don't think so."

She put a hand on his cheek, making Rill sensitive of her warm palm and fingers, and smiled at him. "You're just being kind."

They strolled along again, side by side in silence. Livia brushed against Rill's arm, and he wasn't sure if she did it by accident or by intent.

For some strange reason, Rill found himself attracted to her. Yet he had to keep his distance because of Deuth's warning yesterday. "He's not for you." Wariness crept through Rill. He couldn't afford to get entangled with Livia Estati if he wanted to retain her uncle's patronage.

To break the silence, Rill said, "Have they found out anything about the assassin?"

"No," Livia replied. "And they can't figure out who was her patron."

"She could of been a dagger woman for hire in The Slums."

"Dagger women aren't mages."

Livia ceased talking as they approached a protector, then stopped out of earshot a short distance away. She rested her forearms on the parapet and looked at the compounds across the street. "Maybe I shouldn't tell you this. But I feel I can trust you." Livia's eyes searched his. "Can I?"

"Yes." Rill leaned his forearms on the wall and idly watched noblesse men and women, many accompanied by backwatchers, ambling along the road. Livia sidled closer to him until their shoulders almost touched, making him more keenly aware of her presence.

Livia hesitated a moment as if still uncertain whether she should actually confide in him. "They are pretty certain about one thing."

"What's that?"

"A First or Lesser Family probably isn't behind the attack."

Curiosity made Rill turn to face her. "Why do they think that?"

"Because we only attack one another for charms. And the assassin wasn't after Uncle Deuth's Peer charm. She was after his life, in a very public way."

"Why?"

"Because she was a malcontent."

Rill scratched his head in bewilderment. "A malcontent?"

"Yes."

"Like a rohan?"

Livia shook her head, making her black curls do a slow dance. "No. They're part of society. The malcontents are people who can't fit into society. In fact, they want to do away with our way of life."

"I ain't never heard of no malcontents."

"Neither had I until today. But I overheard my mother talking to my grandmother about them. Apparently, malcontents do things to stir up trouble. To set noblesse against commoners. They like chaos."

Rill's thoughts flew to his parents. Could they be malcontents? They had turned the Kings dwellers against the noblesse. But the Kings dwellers kept to themselves and didn't do anything to stir up the other neighborhoods against the noblesse. And even though the noblesse didn't approve of the Kings dwellers' refusal to become their clients, they seemed to go along with it.

Rill chewed his lip while he gathered up courage to contradict her because he wasn't sure what her reaction would be. "You know what I think?"

"What?"

"That she was a Gaetanian cut-throat. I ain't never heard of no malcontents."

Amusement twinkled in Livia's eyes. "You're so sweet . . . but *so* naïve."

"Um, thanks for the compliment . . . I think."

Livia turned serious. "I've told you more than I should. Promise not to tell anyone, or I could get into trouble."

"I promise."

Livia scurried away without looking back.

Rill stared after her, wondering why he was so attracted to her.

# # #

Rill lingered on the wall walk after Livia left. Sometime later, magestrates living on The Citadel began returning home from their Magesterium session, surrounded by their retinues of backwatchers and clients.

A lone figure rounded the corner and headed up the street. He wore a sword and dagger belted around his waist and had a rucksack strapped to his back, with a quiver of arrows slung over one shoulder and a bow bag over the other.

Rill's heart thrummed with excitement. He cupped his hands around his mouth and yelled. "Jedd! Hey, Jedd!"

Jedd spotted him and waved.

Rill rushed down the staircase, raced out the front gate, and started to hug Jedd, then hesitated, wondering how he'd get his arms around Jedd's accoutrements. Instead, he grinned and slapped him on the shoulder. "I'm sure glad to see you."

"Me too," Jedd said, beaming back. "I couldn't believe it when Milco Barr came to our door yesterday and invited me to serve the Estatis as your backwatcher."

"It's 'cause I asked for you."

"That's what he told me. Thanks."

Together they headed for the Estati compound.

"There's another thing Milco told me," Jedd said. "About Uncle Tor."

"What's that?"

"The two of them were sword companions."

Astonishment spread across Rill's face. "What?"

"I was just as surprised," Jedd said. "Uncle Tor never talked much about his work."

They resumed walking.

"Milco told me if I accepted, he'd mentor me. How could I refuse *that* offer?" Jedd readjusted the straps of his backpack. "Mom and Grandma weren't so pleased about the offer though."

"They try to stop you?"

"Naw. They said it was my decision. But they did say something odd this morning before I left."

"What was that?"

"Not to act surprised if I met someone here I know. I asked them who, but they said she'd prefer to meet me in her own way. Whoever 'she' is."

Rill slapped his forehead. "By The Sisters, I forgot." He told Jedd about Shalira passing herself off as Aunt Talia.

"Holy Weavers!" Jedd said. "How'd she get to be friends with our families?"

"Beats me. But I do know if Lady Ariella finds out, she'll expel her. And we can't let that happen."

"Don't worry. I'll keep my mouth shut."

They went through the gate and stashed Jedd's backpack and weapons by one of the front barracks, then went up to the parapet to watch Deuth return with his retinue. After stopping outside the front gate to thank and dismiss his clients, Deuth entered the compound with the backwatchers.

Rill hurried down from the parapet with Jedd in tow.

"What have we here?" Deuth asked, his gaze going from Rill to Jedd.

Before Rill could answer, Milco spoke up. "By your leave, Lord. That's young Jedd Euland, Tor Larkin's nephew."

"Ah, yes." Deuth smiled at Jedd. "Thank you for accepting Lady Ariella's invitation. Milco, see that Jedd gets settled in. Lady Ariella will inform you when she wants him to take the oath. Rill, you go with them. Afterward, come to my study and we'll discuss your training."

Milco conducted Rill and Jedd upstairs to the empty room on the farther side of Rill's. As Jedd shrugged out of his knapsack, Milco explained that the Estatis liked to keep their personal backwatchers close by. "In case there's a charm raid," he said.

Milco turned to leave.

"Oh, wait," Jedd said.

Milco faced back to him.

"Can you tell me about Uncle Tor?" Jedd asked, almost pleadingly. "I ain't never met no one who served with him. And the both of you were sword companions."

Milco thought for a moment, passing a hand over his misshapen mouth. "He was loyal to his patron and to me. And to those he served with too. He didn't kill for the joy of it. He gave no quarter when necessary, but never killed no one who didn't deserve it. And he was fearless, but not rash. Those are good qualities, and not many backwatchers have them."

Jedd's shoulders slumped. "I was hoping you could tell me stories about my uncle."

"Yeah," Rill said. "I'd like to hear them too."

Milco's expression darkened. "You'll have to ask someone else," he said and left.

Jedd's gaze lingered on the closed door, hurt reflecting in his eyes. "He was Uncle Tor's sword companion and said he'd mentor me. But when I ask him about Uncle Tor, he shuts up tighter than a clam. What's wrong with this fresco?"

"I guess only The Sisters know." Rill slapped Jedd on the back. "To Shelar with him. Let's get you settled in."

It didn't take them long to unpack and put away Jedd's few belongings. Then they headed for the stairs. Yall Throwstarr stood blocking their way at the landing. His face devoid of emotion, he looked Jedd up and down with deliberate slowness that verged on contempt.

"So you're the great Tor Larkin's nephew."

Scowling, Rill started to say something but Jedd cut him off. "That's right." Jedd tossed Yall a friendly smile. "And you are . . . ?"

Yall puffed out his chest. "Yall Throwstarr. I'm sure you've heard of the Throwstarrs."

"Sorry," Jedd said. "Ain't never heard of them."

"Your uncle must've mentioned us."

"My uncle never talked much about his work."

"My family's line of backwatchers goes back nine generations," Yall said, tapping his chest for emphasis. "I know yours goes back only two, beginning with your uncle."

Jedd shrugged. "We all hafta start sometime. Even the Throwstarrs."

Jedd tried to pass, but Yall blocked him again. "I've got nine notches on my kill stick. How many you got?"

Jedd's face turned rock hard. "I ain't got no kill stick. And Tor Larkin never kept one neither. He told me the quality of a backwatcher ain't measured by the notches on her kill stick, but by how well she protects her patron. Now, if you'll step aside, we got our duties to tend to."

Jedd pushed by Yall and started down the stairs. Rill followed behind him. With every step he took, he could sense Yall's fiery eyeballs burning deeper and deeper into their backs.

## CHAPTER 40

Rill's First Lesson

AFTER HIS FIRST WEEK, Rill settled into a routine with Deuth, and the uncomfortable feeling he'd experienced during the first few days gradually faded as the Estatis accepted him into their fold. Even Troy's attitude went from hostile to civil. Ariella and Yulonna continued to treat him warmly, and Shalira carried on as if she'd never known him before he'd arrived as Deuth's new apprentice.

Livia was the only one who welcomed him into the household without reserve, would talk to him animatedly, and tease him playfully. Rill responded cautiously. His wariness was reinforced by the disapproving looks he sometimes caught Ariella, Yulonna, and Deuth firing at Livia. Day by day, though, he and Livia eased into a guarded friendship.

On public days, after Deuth returned from the Magesterium, he would instruct Rill in the basics of spellcasting. There was more to it than Rill thought. Breathing and relaxation exercises to put himself into the proper mind frame to cast the spells. Pointers on how to exert the least amount of personal energy to cast the most powerful spell. Tips about how to comport himself as a mage among noblesse and commoners. Afterward, Deuth would go with Troy to Mages' Field outside the city walls to supervise his spellcasting. Rill envied Troy. While Troy was actually casting spells, Rill was stuck inside the compound doing breathing exercises, and not a single mention from Deuth of when he'd receive his own charm and staff or cast his first spell.

Milco fulfilled his promise to mentor Jedd. Off duty, he trained Jedd. On duty, he treated Jedd the same as everyone else. He was blunt in his manner, generous with his criticism, and stingy with his praise. He also demanded discipline and expected unquestioned obedience. But he treated everyone fairly. Although some backwatchers grumbled about the hard workouts Milco gave them, they all respected him.

Oftentimes, Rill found himself envying Jedd's relationship with Milco and resenting his own with Deuth. His vexation finally reached a breaking point one afternoon when Deuth summoned him to his study for yet another breathing exercise.

Deuth was sitting behind his ornate, polished cherrywood desk, rays of sunshine cascading through the window onto a sheet of parchment on the writing stand in front him.

Behind him, busts of Ulbra and Ulbridge Thane flanked an alcove that contained shelves lined with old leather-bound books. On the opposite wall was a striking fresco of the murder of Ulbridge Thane. Ulbridge was on his knees, propping himself up with his staff, while Malvo Daugan plunged a dagger into the mage's back.

Everyone in Caldon knew the story of The Twins: how they'd rescued Ulaire Gaetani, the first queen of Caldon, during The Great Destruction and taken her across the Rocky Strait with the other refugees; how they'd served as Queen Ulaire's regents during her infancy and opposed her marriage to Malvo Daugan; how, in the Thanes' old age, Malvo had persuaded the queen to remove them as her advisers and convinced her to demand that Ulbridge surrender his Brother charm to her; how no one had dared to enforce the order when Ulbridge refused; how Malvo had murdered Ulbridge and stolen his charm; how Ulbra had avenged her brother, recovered his charm, and buried it with him in a secret tomb, probably somewhere beneath the city.

Both the story and the fresco fascinated Rill. Every time he came into the study, he would pause for a moment to look at it. Pleased with Rill's interest in the painting, Deuth indulged him in his whim. This time, though, Rill strode up to Deuth's desk without glancing at the fresco.

"Ah, there you are," Deuth said, looking up from his writing. "Not even time to admire the fresco? You seem like a man with an important mission."

"I do have a mission," Rill said curtly. "And it *is* important."

Tossing the white-feathered quill pen aside, Deuth focused his attention on Rill. "All right. Let's hear it."

Rill took a deep breath, his heart pounding against his ribs, fearing his mentor's reaction to what he was about to say. "With all due respect, Lord, I've spent all these weeks learning how to breathe and relax and comport myself. Which is fine. I ain't complainin' about that. But when am I gonna get a charm and staff? And when am I gonna start learning to cast spells?"

Deuth's lips curled into a sardonic smile, which made Rill's heart pound even harder. "Well, well. My apprentice has found his voice at last. It took you long enough." Then Deuth smiled. "Congratulations on completing your first lesson."

Rill's jaw unhinged in surprise. "Huh?"

"Lesson One," Deuth said, raising a well-manicured index finger. "If you want something, either ask for it or take it—even if it's from a noblesse. But if you take something, make sure you don't get caught, especially in this house."

Rill's mind grappled with the lesson. Asking for something, he understood. But taking something—stealing it—was a different matter.

Picking up the quill pen, Deuth toyed with it. "The expression on your face tells me stealing goes against your nature."

"I was taught not to steal," Rill said. "Everyone knows it's wrong."

"Those are morals for commoners, not for noblesse." Deuth pointed the quill's feathered end at Rill. "If you want to become noblesse, you have to scrap the scruples you learned from your family. You know there aren't enough charms to go around. That's why we have charm raids. To take them from families that have charms we want. And that's why you'll have to steal a charm to prove yourself."

Rill's stomach churned at the unexpected news. "But not all apprentices steal charms to prove themselves."

"That's because we have a superabundance of Warrior charms. But not of Archmage charms."

"Then why not go to Euloria and get more? I bet The Twins left plenty behind."

Deuth hesitated before speaking. "Do you *really* expect me to respond to a statement as stupid as that? You know the answer as well as I do. The Great Destruction unleashed evil forces, and The Twins forbade us ever to return to Euloria or any other city there. That's why the whole continent is called The Forbidden Lands."

"But that was a thousand years ago," Rill said.

"Do you want to go there? If so, I'll be happy to give you a boat. You can cross the Rocky Strait today."

Rill's muscles went rigid, and the hairs on the nape of his neck stood on end.

Deuth made a derisive sound. "I thought not. Even I wouldn't violate The Twin's injunction." He paused. "But others have."

"What?"

"Over the years, some of the more reckless mages have crossed over. Individually and in groups. But none of them ever returned."

"Not even one?" Rill asked in a half whisper.

Deuth brushed the quill feather across his chin thoughtfully. "Well, one did. Years ago. The foolish son of an allied family. He came back half-dead and out of his mind. Kept muttering about dragons killing the others in his party. Dragons flying in the sky breathing fire."

"Did he ever recover?"

"No healer could help him. His family kept him locked away until he died." Deuth fixed Rill with a steady look. "So that's why you'll need to steal a charm."

Rill spoke with a tremble in his voice. "What if I hafta kill someone?"

Deuth shrugged. "Then you kill her."

"In cold blood?"

"If that's what it takes."

The prospect of killing in cold blood to take a charm made Rill's stomach do a queasy somersault. His reluctance must have been plain to Deuth.

"Oh, my," Deuth said sarcastically. "I see we have a lot of work to do on those pesky scruples of yours."

Rill's face burned with embarrassment.

Chuckling, Deuth opened the lid of a box on his desk and pulled out a charm by its chain. He tossed the talisman to a startled Rill, who caught it.

"It's a Warrior charm. I've been keeping it here for the day you came to confront me."

Rill's pulse quickened. "Thank you, Lord."

With eager, fumbling fingers, Rill attached the chain around his neck and slipped the charm beneath his tunic. His skin tingled from the charm touching it.

Deuth leaned back in his chair. "How does it feel, knowing you have all that power at your command?"

Rill grinned at him, his insides vibrating with excitement. "Awesome!"

Deuth asked for the charm back, and Rill returned it reluctantly.

"Don't worry," Deuth said. "Before long you'll be wearing your own charm. Do you know why?"

"No, Lord."

"Because you're a man I can count on. Someone I can trust."

Rill's heart sang at the compliment.

Deuth clamped a hand on Rill's shoulder. "We begin lessons tomorrow."

## CHAPTER 41

Livia's Humiliation

THE NEXT DAY DEUTH took Rill to a special practice range he had set up in the side courtyard. After handing him the Warrior charm and a staff, Deuth taught Rill how to cast a Fire Shield spell to create a protective barrier downrange to prevent a poor cast from damaging the compound's wall. Then he taught Rill how to cast Fire Bolt, which was one of the simplest Fire spells. Deuth made the first cast. His Fire Bolt was a short sliver of red flame, no thicker or longer than an arrow but just as deadly. Rill recognized the spell as one the assassin had used. A thrill of excitement coursed through him as he anticipated casting the spell himself.

From that day on, the practice sessions began and ended the same way. At the beginning of the practice, Deuth would hand Rill the charm and staff and stay for a while to critique him before leaving to tend to his own affairs. At the end of the practice, Deuth would return to help Rill with any problems he'd encountered and to collect the charm and staff for safekeeping. Each time he handed them over, Rill did it reluctantly.

Day after day, Rill practiced casting Fire Bolts on a target, the hard and sometimes frustrating work making his initial thrill quickly fade into monotony that was sometimes punctuated by the excitement of mastery. He began close-up, aiming at a large mark. Rill's bolts were shorter and thinner than Deuth's, obviously less powerful, and didn't fly as quickly to their target.

Deuth told him not to worry. More powerful Fire Bolts would come as he increased his strength and became more experienced in spellcasting. "And don't forget," Deuth added, "my own charm is the Peer charm—one of the most powerful Archmage charms in existence." He didn't need to add that his personal energy and his ability to control magic energy were much greater too.

After Rill could hit the mark nine out of nine casts, Deuth had him move back a few paces and start all over again until he could strike the target another nine out of nine times. Day after day, Deuth had Rill repeat the "nine out of nine" exercise until he could strike the target nine out of nine times from sixty paces. When the ninth spell finally struck the mark, Rill beamed triumphantly at Deuth.

Deuth laughed. "You've only just begun with Fire Bolt, not finished with it."

To Rill's dismay, Deuth had him return to his original casting distance, exchanged the large target for a smaller one, and told him to repeat the process all over again until he could hit the smaller target nine out of nine times from sixty paces. With a chuckle, he patted Rill on the shoulder and said, "Three smaller targets are waiting for you after you master casting Fire Bolt on this one."

One day an odd thing occurred late one morning during practice. When Rill cast a Fire Bolt, nothing happened. Fortunately Deuth came by just then, and Rill told him about it.

"You must be tired," Deuth said, relieving him of his charm and staff. "You'd better take a break till midafternoon."

When Rill resumed practice, the spell worked.

At first Rill felt self-conscious practicing because household retainers, especially mages, would drift over to watch. After a few days, though, he grew used to them, and before long most of them stopped observing because his practicing had become commonplace.

Things were different with Troy and Yall. Rill hated it when those two showed up. They dropped by pretty often too. Initially, their unwanted presence set Rill's nerves ajar, disrupting his concentration and casts. Once he even forgot to invoke the spell and stood gaping stupidly at the target wondering why nothing had happened. Troy's and Yall's snide laughter made his cheeks burn. Gradually, through hard concentration, Rill learned to shut his mind to everything but the spell, cast, and target.

Except for Deuth, the one person Rill couldn't ignore was Livia. The first time she stopped by, Rill expressed his concern. "What if Lord Deuth should happen by and find you here?" he said. "You'll get in trouble."

Livia eyed him teasingly. "You mean *we'll* get in trouble. But don't worry. I checked to make sure he wasn't around before I came."

From that day on, Livia became his most ardent fan. Often she would come once or twice a day to watch and praise him when he made a particularly good cast or commiserate with him if his cast was off. Her enthusiasm was contagious, and Rill found himself grinning or grimacing at her on those occasions. Every so often she would brush her fingers against his arm. His body tingled with pleasure when she did that, and he kept having to remind himself of Deuth's warning. But he couldn't help himself because he was coming to like her, and she appeared to feel the same way about him. Sometimes she would pop up when Troy and Yall were there jeering him, scold them for mocking Rill's abilities, and order them to stop. Troy always obeyed and made sure Yall did too.

Jedd would drop by whenever his own practice schedule allowed. If Livia was there alone, the two of them would chat pleasantly like longtime friends. But if Jedd encountered Troy and Yall, he and Yall would eye each other as if they were enemies instead of backwatchers sworn to serve and protect the same family.

"Yall and I both pledged our fealty to the Estatis," Jedd told Rill once when he'd mentioned Yall's latent antagonism toward him. "But he's Troy's man. I'm yours."

One afternoon, Rill was working on his second spell, Fire Burst, which sent a blast of fire at the target. Because it was a higher-level spell than Fire Bolt, the spell required more magic energy and more personal energy. Rill had been casting one burst after another to see how many he could cast in the shortest possible time. The exercise drained so much personal energy that Rill's legs felt shaky.

Suddenly Cato's admonition about becoming a hollow mage popped into his head, along with the image of Rodleen Gespar in his wheeled chair. The memory caused a tremor of fear to rumble through Rill's body, and he immediately took a break. Now, leaning on his staff, he knew why so many mages did the same, especially after casting a lot of spells.

Livia appeared and feigned disbelief. "You're not stopping, are you? You've hardly begun."

"I've been here casting spells all morning and half the afternoon," Rill said. "My personal energy's low. I gotta take a break before it all drains out."

Livia's homely face lit up in a grin. "I know what *that* feels like."

"Oh yeah?" Rill returned the grin, not caring if it showed how much he liked her. "Then tell me."

Livia put a thumb to her lip, thinking. "Like . . . you're really, really thirsty but your water jug is empty, and you can't drink till it's re-filled."

"Not bad," Rill said, nodding appreciatively. "Does it feel like you ain't eaten for two days and hafta wait another before you can get a meal?"

"*That's* descriptive." Livia chewed her lip, searching for another simile. "Does it feel as if you've been traveling all day but still have to go half the night before you reach the inn?"

"Yeah."

Livia stepped closer and put a hand on Rill's arm. He felt the warmth of her fingers thorough the fabric. A shiver of excitement danced across his shoulders. Livia smiled as if she'd sensed his reaction, her dark-blue eyes on his.

"Does it feel like—"

"What's this?" an angry voice demanded.

Rill's throat muscles froze as he and Livia spun to face Deuth.

Livia drew herself up to her full height of slightly over five feet, her arms straight at her sides and her hands balled into fists. Nearby, protectors suddenly found things to occupy their attention. A few, though, cast furtive, sympathetic glances at her.

Enraged, Deuth glared at Livia. "Never *ever* disturb my apprentice again when he's practicing."

"She wasn't disturbing me, Lord," Rill said. "I was just—"

Deuth whirled toward him. "Was I talking to you?"

"No, Lord."

Deuth turned to Livia. "I'm waiting for an answer."

"Rill was taking a break because his personal energy was low. We were comparing notes about what that felt like."

Deuth dismissed her excuse with a scoff. "When have *you* ever had occasion to experience that?"

"You know I've had intensive training," Livia said, her tone spiked with indignation. "I have the potential to be a powerful illusionist. I proved that when I was being mentored: 'She has the instincts and talent of a natural-born illusionist.' That's what my mentor said. But since then you've hardly given me a chance to increase my skills."

"I don't give a damn what your mentor said. You're useless to the family."

"That's not true. Illusionists can be very useful."

"You want to be useful?"

"Yes."

"Then do what the assassin did. Go out, kill one of our enemies, and bring me her charm. Or pass yourself off as a friend of Cato Porta and stick a dagger in his belly."

Livia's face turned pale.

"That's why you're useless," Deuth told her. "Because you're too tender hearted."

"Not all mages have to be cold hearted and ruthless like you."

"If the Estatis weren't cold hearted and ruthless, this family would have declined generations ago. But we didn't. We remained preeminent. Because we're"—Deuth thrust his face close to Livia's—"cold hearted and ruthless."

Livia didn't flinch. "I can help the family in other ways besides killing."

"How? By making yourself look like Grandfather Locien come back from the Afterworld?"

"No. I could—"

"Become an actress. You'd have a great career on the stage. You wouldn't need makeup to change your appearance."

"Why do you hate me so?"

"Because you shame our family. And you're useless to us. We need to form alliances, but not even a second-rate Lesser Family wants a slut like you married to their son, even if you are an Estati."

Tears trickled down Livia's cheeks, and she angrily wiped them away with the heels of her palms. Deuth watched her, an expression of pure hatred on his face. Livia returned the look, her eyes piercing his like a pair of sharp-pointed flints.

"Even if Great-Grandmother Ariella did marry me off to some second-rate Lesser Family or even to a fat merchant's son, this house is where I belong. That's more than I can say for you." Livia lowered her voice, infusing it with contempt. "Everyone in Caldon knows you belong in the Svaggas' house, not here."

Deuth's hand balled into a fist, and Rill feared Deuth would strike Livia. The urge seized Rill to intervene before things got out of control, but he resisted it.

Livia leaned into Deuth. "I'm an Estati," she said, her voice seething with contempt. "My children will be Estati. But your son isn't. Garth is a Svagga. And he always will be."

"You slut!" Deuth bared his teeth at her like a rabid wolf aching to attack a defenseless victim. "You throw yourself at every boy you lay eyes on. Even my apprentice. You're a whore. Just like your mother—"

The veins in Livia's neck throbbed. "How dare you say that about my mother!"

Deuth made a choking noise as if something was caught in his throat. "I . . . I'm sorry. I shouldn't have said that. Now, get out of my sight!"

Turning, Livia strode away, head high.

Deuth watched her, his face dark and pensive. Then he turned to Rill. "And as for you—"

"Lord Deuth!" Yall Throwstarr cried, running up to him.

"Can't you see I'm busy?"

"Your pardon, Lord. But Lord Troy wants to see you at once."

"Tell him to wait."

"With all due respect, Lord, he can't. It's urgent."

"Everything's always 'urgent' to him." Deuth heaved a resigned sigh. "Well, what is it this time?"

Yall whispered something to him. Whatever Yall said made Deuth's body twitch and his eyes bulge. Then Deuth and Yall hurried toward the house.

Rill watched Deuth leave. He hated himself for not standing up to Deuth for Livia. But doing that would have made matters worse, especially for himself. *Coward!* a small voice jeered in the back of his mind. He shut out the voice while at the same time the memory of Deuth's hateful treatment of Livia and of her distress rattled him. For a fleeting moment, Rill wondered if he'd made the right decision by getting involved with the Estatis. But he shrugged the thought aside. Most First Families were like the Estatis—wealthy, privileged, and arrogant. He vowed never to become like that when he became noblesse.

The disturbing exchange between Livia and Deuth left Rill unable to concentrate on spellcasting. So he decided to go to his room. Unfortunately, he couldn't return the charm and staff to Deuth because Deuth was preoccupied with Troy's problem. Not wanting to be accused of being irresponsible, Rill decided to take the implements with him and return them to Deuth later.

Rill went into the house. While he was walking toward the second-floor stairs, the same elderly, gray-haired servant who'd given him his borrowed livery bumped into him and slipped a small piece of folded parchment into his hand, apologized, and moved on. Masking his surprise, Rill closed his fingers around the scrap and went up to his room. After shutting the door, he unfolded the parchment.

Beware of YT. Search your room!!!

Rill scowled at the words. Was this some kind of joke? He was about to toss the parchment away when he had second thoughts. The Estatis weren't a joking family. *Better safe than sorry.*

Rill searched the wooden chest at the foot of the bed but found everything in place. Nothing was missing from his desk or from the wall pegs either. Standing in the middle of the room, Rill pondered the words in the note. Nothing had been stolen *from* his room. But what if something had been hidden *in* his room?

Rill's eyes drifted to the bed—the only place in the austere chamber where an object could be concealed.

He searched the pillow and pulled down the blanket and sheets. Nothing. He lifted the edge of the mattress and ran his hand along the rope mesh beneath it. He let out a startled breath when his fingers touched a thin length of chain. He pulled it out and held it up.

Holy Goddess!

A charm dangled from the chain.

He gaped at the talisman while fear coiled in his chest like a poisonous snake preparing to strike.

In the hallway, someone's boots hurried along the floorboards. They stopped outside Rill's door. Rill's heart jumped in panic. Before he could hide the charm, someone lifted the latch and entered.

Jedd. His face turned pale when he spotted the charm. He quickly shut the door. "Is that yours?"

A chill brushed across Rill's shoulder blades. "No. I just found it here. Under my mattress."

Horror flashed across Jedd's face. "That's Troy's charm! And it's just been reported stolen."

## CHAPTER 42

Deserters

ALYSE AND KATE STRODE through the crowded Public Square toward River Road on their way to the One Goddess Temple. They wore cloaks and dresses of coarsely spun wool and cheap brown shoes made from low-grade leather. Commoners' clothes. Priestess Sybil had insisted they dress like commoners so Alyse would be more readily accepted by her patients who would all be commoners. Alyse felt like a hypocrite doing that as if she were hiding who she truly was. She also wished they'd left their cloaks at home because already the early Sowing season air was mild, and the day promised to be warm.

"You've been unusually quiet this morning," Kate said.

"I was thinking about the deserters."

"What deserters?"

"The ones who slipped into the city yesterday." Alyse unfastened her blue cloak and slung it over her shoulder.

"Where did you hear that?"

"At breakfast this morning. From Uncle Jukka. He said there were three of them. One's wounded. He got shot in the leg by an arrow while they were sneaking out of Uncle Leoc's camp. Legion trackers followed them here to the city boundary, but couldn't cross it."

Kate was silent for a moment and then said, "I think I might have seen them."

Alyse paused in mid-stride to face Kate. "Really?"

"Yes. Three men went through the kitchen yesterday just before we left for the day. Priestess Gilda was with them."

"Was one of them limping?"

"I couldn't tell. Priestess Gilda blocked my view."

"I don't see Priestess Gilda getting mixed up with deserters." Alyse resumed walking. "Besides, if those men were the deserters, they would've sought sanctuary in the temple, by the One Goddess statue."

"You're probably right." Kate unclasped her dark-brown cloak and draped it over her shoulder. "If they sought sanctuary, they'd have to stay within touching distance of the statue. And if they did that, they wouldn't be able to slip away because the City Watch would place guards around the temple complex."

Alyse readjusted her cloak across her shoulder. "Most likely the deserters are lying low and hoping to slip out of the city unnoticed. Maybe cross over the Sharp Teeth Mountains into Annatol."

Alyse lapsed back into silence, remembering the conversation at breakfast. It wasn't the adults' talk about the deserters that she found so distressing but their general attitude toward deserters and commoners.

After Uncle Jukka had mentioned the deserters and how they'd been tracked to the city limits, Degas had pursed his lips in disapproval. "No active-duty soldiers allowed beyond the city boundaries. Foolish rule. Trackers should be allowed to enter Caldon and arrest them. They're deserters. Take them back for execution. Make an example of them."

"Leoc wrote me that the desertion rate is increasing," Pilar said, knocking the top off a soft-boiled egg. "Mainly the conscripts, not the volunteers."

"The commoners hide the deserters." Maude looked at Jukka and rapped the tabletop with her knuckles. "The Magesterium should pass a law that punishes deserters' matriarchs. Hit them where it hurts, in the heart of the family. I think I'll suggest that to our allied matriarchs. They'll support it. And I'm sure the other factions' matriarchs will too. This is one thing we can all agree on. You can introduce the legislation."

But Jukka had shaken his head. "The rabble won't stand for it. Push them too hard, and we'll have a second Revolt of the Commoners on our hands." He'd paused to sip his watered wine. "The answer to the problem is an all-volunteer legion. Thankfully, we're partway there already."

Alyse was still brooding over the conversation when she and Kate reached the One Goddess Temple. While Kate headed for the temple entrance, Alyse passed through the House of Healing's double doors. Each morning when they split up, guilt nibbled at Alyse like a mouse nipping at cheese. Because Priestess Sybil didn't think it appropriate to have a backwatcher shadow her apprentice healer all day, she'd asked Kate to stay clear of the House of Healing. So every day, Kate passed the time by watching the religious ceremonies, helping out in the kitchen, and reading in the library.

It doesn't seem fair. Kate spends the day killing time while I learn healer's skills. Once Alyse had mentioned to Kate about how she felt, but Kate had shrugged it off. "I like to read, and I've made friends with the kitchen staff. Besides, waiting is part of what backwatchers do."

When Alyse went to report to Priestess Sybil, Priestess Gilda—the middle-aged assistant chief priestess—told her Sybil had gone outside the city to help a desperately sick woman who couldn't be transported to Caldon. "Priestess Sybil left late yesterday afternoon, just before you went home," Gilda concluded. "Apparently, she forgot to tell you in her rush to be off. I expected her back early this morning. But I guess the emergency was more serious than she thought. So you're on your own till she returns."

Alyse experienced an uncomfortable moment of self-doubt. She'd never worked without Priestess Sybil being within calling distance to advise her if problems arose. Then she kicked her uncertainty aside, reminding herself that she had to work independently sometime, and now was as good a time as any to start. Clinging to that thought,

Alyse set out to work.

She spent the first part of the morning treating new patients who had arrived the previous evening or earlier that morning. The majority of their ailments and injuries were minor, and Alyse had little trouble treating them. Most of the patients she sent home after tending to them, but a few with more serious conditions, she assigned to wards.

After that she went from ward to ward, visiting patients. She saw her own first, hoping Priestess Sybil would return by the time she finished those rounds. But Sybil didn't. So Alyse dropped in on Sybil's patients.

Alyse finished her rounds toward noon and went to the kitchen to grab a bite to eat. She found Kate there eating a bowl of lamb stew, and joined her. They chitchatted for a while. Afterward, Kate asked her what she was going to do next. Alyse usually performed her char exercises and afterward, if time allowed, went to the temple library to study medical texts and ancient scrolls. But she decided against working on her chars. With Priestess Sybil gone, she was responsible for the patients and could get called at any time, perhaps when she was doing the exercises. It wasn't good to stop the chars partway through.

Around midafternoon, Alyse was with Kate in the library reading when she sensed someone in the doorway. Looking up from her medical text, she saw Priestess Gilda standing on the threshold.

Worry lines creased Gilda's forehead while her apprehensive gaze shifted from Alyse to Kate and back again to Alyse. Then Gilda's shoulders slumped, and she let out a long, deep breath.

Alyse put the book aside. "Priestess Gilda, does someone need my help?"

Gilda looked at Alyse with troubled eyes. After a long hesitation, her eyes cleared, and she threw her shoulders back. "Yes. Someone is in dire need of help. One of Priestess Sybil's special patients. He arrived yesterday, after she'd left to make the call outside the city. He has a very serious injury. I'm afraid if he's not treated soon, he'll be dead by morning."

Alyse strode up to her. "Take me to him. At the very least, I can stabilize his condition until Priestess Sybil returns."

Gilda fiddled with her green sash. "I . . . I'm not sure you should."

"I'm a healer. Of course I should."

Gilda held up a hand as if to wave Alyse off. "No, no. You shouldn't. I was wrong to even think of asking you."

Gilda turned to leave, but Alyse slipped her fingers through Gilda's green waist sash. "Take me to him."

"No." Gilda removed Alyse's fingers. "I can't allow it. You could get into serious trouble by seeing him."

Alyse fixed her with a haughty look. "You *will* take me to him."

Gilda struggled to make up her mind, clearly torn between two horrible choices. "If I do, you must promise me something."

"What?"

"Never to tell the authorities what you see or do."

Gilda's demand sparked Alyse's suspicions. "You're talking about the wounded deserter."

Gilda looked stunned. "How did you know?"

Misgiving settled in Alyse's stomach like a heavy weight. Now that her hunch had turned into fact, she wondered if she really wanted to become involved with the deserters. What would her family say if they found out? Even worse, what would Uncle Leoc say? She couldn't bear his condemnation or the disgrace she would bring to her family. But she was a healer. It was her Goddess-given duty to help the sick and injured, no matter who or what they were. She inhaled a deep breath, settling herself. "You can rest easy," she told Gilda. "No one else knows—"

"Except me," Kate said, putting her book of religious sayings aside as she rose from her chair. "And my promise is as solid as Alyse's."

Alyse told Kate to wait in the library, then followed Gilda to a locked room in the rear of the House of Healing. Gilda unlocked the door and went inside.

A pair of oil lamps, each on a separate table, cast the room in light and shadow. By one wall, a young man with a short beard, who was hardly out of his teens, lay in a bed, covered with a sheet and blanket that rose and fell in time with his rapid breathing. His face was dirty as if he hadn't washed for days. Two other grimy-faced men, one short and one tall, hovered over the young man. Fright spread across the tall man's face when he spotted Alyse. The catch in his breath alerted his companion, who swung around to confront the women.

"Who's she?" the short man demanded, his voice cracking from fear.

The tall man swallowed nervously. "And where's Priestess Sybil?"

"Priestess Sybil hasn't returned yet," Gilda said, shutting and re-locking the door. "Hilbrand's condition is critical. If we wait any longer to treat him, he'll die. So I've brought Priestess Sybil's apprentice healer to see him."

"Bring a lamp." Alyse went to the bed and pulled down the bed-clothes while Gilda held the oil lamp over Hilbrand. Alyse wrinkled her nose at the foul stench. The right leg of Hilbrand's dirt-stained pants had been slit almost to his buttock, and his thigh was wrapped with a soiled, smelly bandage. Alyse's stomach reeled, but she suppressed the urge to throw up as she knelt beside Hilbrand. Gently, she unwrapped the dressing to expose black flesh and a wound that oozed thick yellow pus.

Gangrene. Panic gushed through Alyse's arteries. She knew nothing about treating such a wound. But she did know the discoloration was ominous. She glanced up at the two men. "How long has his leg been this color?"

The short man's gaze examined her up and down. "You dress like a commoner yet speak like a noblesse."

"I'm neither commoner nor noblesse," Alyse said. "I'm a healer. Answer my question."

"Since yesterday," the man responded.

"He cut himself with a scythe," the tall man said. "A farming accident."

"Don't lie to me," Alyse told him curtly. "I know an arrow wound when I see one."

The men swapped terrified glances.

"You're the three deserters," Alyse said.

Their bodies stiffened.

"But that's none of my business," Alyse said. "I'm a healer. Healing is all I'm concerned about."

They relaxed and looked at each other as if transmitting silent messages. The tall one turned to Alyse. "We're farmers," he said. "But we were conscripted—"

"Against our will," the other added.

"So we deserted. Hilbrand was wounded when we were leaving camp. We bandaged his thigh as best we could. But we had to keep running. After a few days, his wound turned red, then brown, and now it's black."

"We couldn't abandon him," the short man said. "He's our friend. We come from the same area."

Alyse put a hand on Hilbrand's brow. It was burning with fever. She ran her palms slowly over his body, exploring him with her inner eye. She detected a dangerously rapid heartbeat and malevolent energy, the gangrene overpowering everything else. That rot, which was the core of Hilbrand's sickness, was gobbling him up. She sensed that he had even less time to live than Priestess Gilda thought. That knowledge sparked desperation in Alyse.

Closing her eyes to concentrate better, Alyse focused her healing energy on the gangrene. If she could shrink the foulness even a little, perhaps she could prolong Hilbrand's life until Priestess Sybil returned. Panic clutched Alyse when she realized her healing energy had no effect. *What should I do now?* She struggled to keep her expression confident as she headed for the door. "I need to fetch something. I'll be right back."

Alyse raced to the library. Kate had left, but Alyse had no time to wonder where as she hurriedly pulled out one medical text after another to search for a way to treat gangrene. Suddenly Kate raced into the room. "City watchers!"

Alyse glanced up from *Serious Ailments and How to Treat Them.* "What about them?"

"They're *here!*"

Alyse's fingers twitched, and the book slipped from her hands to the floor. "But the House of Healing is part of the temple. It's inviolable."

Kate blew out an angry breath. "Not to them."

"They're after the deserters."

"That's what I figure."

Images of Hilbrand, who was tottering on the brink of death, being hauled out of his bed and dragged back to Uncle Leoc's camp tore a jagged path through Alyse's mind. "Come on."

She and Kate raced into the House of Healing. As they were passing one of the wards, Alyse heard Priestess Gilda angrily demanding to know who had authorized the city watchers to violate the temple's sanctity by invading the House of Healing. The cousins managed to reach the deserters' room without being seen. But when Alyse tried the latch, it refused to move.

Locked!

Alyse rapped softly on the door. "It's Priestess Sybil's apprentice. Let me in."

A panicky voice—Alyse couldn't tell whose—came through the wood. "Priestess Gilda locked us inside and left to deal with the city watchers."

Alyse ground her teeth in frustration. "Do you have the key?"

"If we did, we wouldn't still be here."

Alyse turned to Kate. "Find Priestess Gilda and get the key."

As Kate ran off, Alyse fidgeted as the sounds of the searchers drew closer and closer. A coil of dread wrapped itself tighter and tighter around her chest, like a boa constrictor winding its coils around its prey. At last, Kate returned. Alyse grabbed the key, fumbling until she finally slipped it into the keyhole and opened the door. The lamplight revealed both men crouching by Hilbrand's bed.

"Thank the Goddess!" the tall man said.

They began lifting Hilbrand up from his bed.

Alyse shut and locked the door. "Don't move him."

"We hafta get outta here," the short man said, his voice laden with panic. "And we ain't leavin' Hilbrand behind."

Alyse nodded at Kate. "Stop them."

Brushing her cloak aside, Kate drew her sword. "You heard her."

The short man turned to Alyse, his face radiating scorn. "You said you wanted to help. I should of known we couldn't trust a noblesse."

Outrage and fear darkened the other man's face. "You brought the watchers here."

"You *can* trust me," Alyse told them. "I didn't bring the watchers."

Both men eyed her suspiciously.

Alyse wanted to scream at them. Instead, keeping her voice calm, she said, "I'm a healer, and Hilbrand's my patient. I won't let anything happen to him or to you."

"Fine words," the tall man said. "But you got nothing to back them up with, even if you are noblesse. The watchers are backed by the power of the Magesterium."

Alyse put all the authority she could muster into her voice. "I won't let them arrest you. I give you my word. Just let me do the talking." Even as she spoke, apprehension crawled along her skin. *They're Uncle Leoc's soldiers. If I lie, I'll be committing treason. And what will Uncle Leoc think of me?* The thought of his condemnation made her muscles quiver as she looked at the men. *But these men are poor farmers. And I bet they just want to return to their farms. If they still have them. Maybe some noblesse bought them for a pittance, just like they did to that poor family I met on the way to our villa and with the family of the poor man I treated for the wasting disease.* That last thought decided her. Even if it was treason, she would protect these men.

Alyse spoke forcefully while her mind raced to determine how to best handle the impending confrontation with the watchers. "I won't let them arrest you, I promise."

The deserters glanced at each other, then reluctantly nodded their agreement.

Kate positioned herself in the shadows in the opposite corner from the bed, her sword and dagger concealed beneath her cloak. Just then someone tried the latch. When it didn't work, a fist pounded on the door.

"Open up! By the authority of the Magesterium, open up!"

Alyse unlocked the door and quickly stepped away.

The door burst open, and three watchers barged into the room. Two women—a blonde and a brunette—and a man.

The brunette pointed at the deserters by Hilbrand's bed. "There they are."

The deserters cowered against the wall.

Alyse placed herself in front of the watchers' path and used the most imperious tone she could summon. "How *dare* you violate the sanctity of the temple and of this House of Healing?"

"These men are deserters from the Eastern Legions," the brunette responded. "Interfere, and we'll arrest you too."

"You have no right to be here. The temple and its House of Healing are inviolable."

The brunette motioned to her companions. "Take them."

The two watchers started forward.

Alyse put up her hand. "I order you to stop. These men are farmers. I'm a healer." She pointed to Hilbrand. "And he's my patient."

"You're a liar," the brunette said.

Fury burned in Alyse's green eyes as they locked upon the brunette's. "You don't want to tangle with me."

The brunette shrugged. "If that's the way you want it." She spoke to her companions. "Take her along as well. Interfering with our official duties. That's a treasonous offense."

Alyse stepped into the brunette's personal space. "I'm Priestess Sybil's apprentice healer. And I'm in charge of this House of Healing until she returns."

"Congratulations," the brunette said in a snide tone that made Alyse's blood boil.

A deep scowl knit Alyse's brows together, and she injected haughtiness into her tone that would make her deceased Great-Grandmother Siema proud. "I'm also Alyse Dejune. My grandfather, Jukka Berne, is sole chief magestrate. *And* I'm the niece of Leoc Dejune, Commander of the Eastern Legions. Do you honestly think I'd harbor deserters from his legions or undermine my grandfather's authority as chief magestrate?" Alyse's stomach clenched at the thought that they might, indeed, think just that.

The blonde and the man traded uneasy looks, then glanced at the brunette, who suddenly appeared hesitant.

Kate pushed herself off from the wall and swept open her cloak, revealing her weapons. "And I'm Kate Dejune, *Lady* Alyse's backwatcher."

Even in the weak flickering lamplight, Alyse could see the color drain from the faces of all three watchers. The brunette's gaze danced from Alyse to Kate and back to Alyse.

Alyse silently cursed the woman's obstinacy. "I swear these three men are farmers," Alyse said, hoping the watchers didn't notice she hadn't sworn by the One Goddess, which would have made the oath binding. She nodded at Hilbrand. "He's my patient. He injured himself in an accident with a scythe."

The brunette held Alyse's gaze, trying to intimidate her to back down.

"If you take them," Alyse said, "I'll have you all expelled from the City Watch. You'll join the rabble in The Slums."

The brunette cleared her throat as if a lot of phlegm were in it. "Well, if we can't believe the word of a Dejune, whose word can we believe? Obviously, our informant was wrong. We'll have to look somewhere else."

She led the watchers out of the room.

Alyse stifled a burst of relieved laughter. Then she trembled as she also realized that she'd crossed what she'd always thought was an uncrossable boundary. She had lied to city watchers, preventing them from carrying out their legal duties, but also had interfered with her uncle's authority over his legionaries. She had committed treason. If Uncle Leoc or the Magesterium learned about it, she'd be in serious trouble. Expulsion from her family would be a lesser consequence, and execution would be the worst.

Hilbrand groaned. His eyes fluttered open.

Tossing her own fears aside, Alyse knelt beside him and put a comforting hand on his forehead.

His gaze drifted to her, his gray eyes half focused. He shivered. "Who . . . are . . . you?"

Alyse gently stoked his brow. "Alyse. Priestess Sybil's apprentice."

Hilbrand shivered again. "So cold. I'm . . . so cold."

Alyse tapped Kate's shoulder. "Get some blankets for him."

Hilbrand's friends approached the bed. Tears brimmed in the short one's eyes while the tall one choked back sobs.

Hilbrand stared blankly at them for several heartbeats before recognition dawned on his face. The tips of his lips arced into a weak smile. "Ebar. Ord. Did we make it?"

Ebar nodded, not trusting himself to speak.

Ord wiped tears away with his knuckles. "We're in the One Goddess Temple. In The Kings. We're safe."

"I . . . I'm sorry I held you back."

"Oh, you didn't hold us back," Ebar said in a quivering voice.

Powerlessness washed over Alyse like an incoming tide. Hilbrand would be dead soon, and she couldn't prevent it. She dug her fingernails into her palms. Some healer she was!

A sharp rap on the door startled everyone. They relaxed when a voice said, "It's me. Kate." Alyse hurriedly unlocked the door. Kate entered with an armful of blankets, which she and Alyse spread over Hilbrand. He fell into a fretful sleep before they finished.

Alyse placed a finger on Hilbrand's neck. She could barely detect a heartbeat. She considered her two options, both of them equally bleak. She could return to the library and flip through pages of medical books, searching for spells and herbs to use. But poor Hilbrand would probably be dead by the time she discovered a treatment. Or she could simply do nothing and let him die. Alyse bit her lip. She couldn't let him die.

Ord mopped more tears from his cheeks. "He ain't gonna make it, is he."

His words—a statement, not a question—summoned Alyse back to the present. She fired Ord a look so fierce that he jerked backward. "If I can help it, he will!"

At that moment, Gilda returned. "The city watchers have left." She nodded at Hilbrand and Ord. "And if I hadn't locked the door, you would've tried to escape and been arrested by now."

"Never mind that," Alyse said. "There's still time to save Hilbrand. Don't let anyone move him till I come back." She touched Kate's arm. "Come on."

Where are you going?" Gilda asked.

"To find a cure for Hilbrand."

## CHAPTER 43

Stolen Charm

RILL'S TERRIFIED GAZE HELD Jedd's. "Stolen! But I just discovered it here, under my mattress."

"Someone stole Troy's charm," Jedd said, his voice taut with urgency. "That's why I'm here. Lord Deuth just summoned the entire household to the receiving hall."

Rill pulled the parchment from his belt purse and thrust it at Jedd. "I've been set up by Troy. He had Yall put it here."

Jedd scanned the note. "Where'd you get this?"

"Don't matter. We gotta figure out what to do."

"Show Lord Deuth the note."

Rill shoved the parchment back into his purse. "No. I ain't gonna get whoever sent it to me in trouble."

"You gotta get rid of the charm."

"I know, I know." Rage exploded inside Rill like a volcanic eruption. He knew how to get even with Troy and Yall. "Come on."

As Rill reached for the door latch, footsteps hurried along the hallway toward his room and stopped at the door. Rill thrust the charm behind his back.

Yall Throwstarr barged inside and stopped short when he spotted Jedd. "You should be in the receiving hall."

"I came to tell Rill," Jedd replied.

"That's my job, not yours."

"I'm his backwatcher. So I thought I should do it."

"Next time, don't think. Just obey Lady Ariella's orders."

Jedd put on a sheepish expression. "I didn't mean no harm—"

Yall waved them into the corridor. "Get going. Hurry! Lady Ariella will be furious if you're late."

"We're right behind you," Rill said. "Lead the way."

Turning, Yall headed back the way he had come.

"Get Yall downstairs," Rill whispered to Jedd. "Tell him I went back for the staff Lord Deuth lent me and I'll follow right along."

"What're ya gonna—"

"Just do it."

Jedd nodded and hurried after Yall.

After grabbing the borrowed staff from his own room, Rill entered Yall's bedroom and quickly shoved the charm under the mattress. Then he dashed down the hallway, took the stairs two at a time, and entered the receiving hall chasing Jedd's and Yall's heels.

The entire household assembled in front of Ariella who sat in the receiving chair staring grimly at them. Deuth stood on one side and Troy on the other. The Estati women were lined up behind her, partially blocking the ancestral cupboards.

Tendrils of apprehension wrapped themselves around Rill as he stopped beside Jedd and faced the Estati Family. But they loosened and slipped off when Troy stared at him, the ghost of a smile on his lips. Rill set his features into an impassive mask that hid a grin. Troy was in for a shock.

Ariella brushed cold blue eyes across the women and men gathered before her. "I summoned you here to tell you something." She paused dramatically. "Lord Troy's charm is missing."

"Stolen!" Troy said. "Not missing."

"Misplaced or stolen," Ariella said, "it makes no difference. The charm is missing. My question to you all is this. Has anyone seen the charm?"

Some women and men glanced nervously at one another while others looked stiffly ahead. But no one spoke up. A long silence crept by.

Ariella grasped the arms of the chair and leaned toward her retainers. "I'll ask one more time. Has anyone seen Lord Troy's charm?"

To Rill, the silence seemed to press down oppressively on everyone. Retainers cleared their throats or bit their lips or rubbed the backs of their necks. All avoided eye contact with Ariella.

Ariella's white-haired head bobbed in a decisive nod. "You've had your chance. Now every room in this compound will be searched. You'll all stay here until the charm's found."

As if on cue, Deuth headed for the door, with Kalso, Milco, Magnus, and the new head protector behind him.

When Troy started toward them, Ariella caught him by the sleeve. "Not you."

Clearly unhappy at being left behind, Troy resumed his original position beside Ariella.

With Deuth in the lead, the searchers went upstairs to hunt. Time dragged by as feet *clomp clomped* on the ceiling above Rill, moving along the hallway and back and forth through rooms. Despite knowing that the charm wouldn't be discovered in his room, Rill's nerves felt like lute strings stretching to the snapping point. Every so often he noticed Troy and Yall exchanging smug looks, and each time Rill would grin to himself as he imagined the shocked expressions on their faces when they learned where the charm had been found. Finally the searches returned, a dour-faced Deuth at their head and Troy's charm in his hand.

"You found my charm!" Troy said. "Where was it?"

Ignoring Troy's outburst, Deuth approached Ariella and whispered into her ear. She flinched as if stung by a wasp, then stood up. "You all are dismissed. The family will meet in the matriarch's chamber."

"B-but wait . . . w-who's the thief?" Troy asked, confusion swirling on his face as the family retainers began leaving. "You have to punish him."

"Oh, we will," Ariella said. "Yall Throwstarr, you will attend the meeting too."

Rill lingered long enough to enjoy watching Troy's eyes open as wide as an owl's and Yall's body freeze, and he found the bewildered looks they shot each other delicious.

That'll teach 'em to set me up. He chuckled to himself as he and Jedd headed for the second-floor stairs.

Upstairs, they sat down on Rill's bed.

"That was a close one," Jedd said. "Troy must really hate you to try to frame you for theft. Especially of a charm."

"He's jealous 'cause Lord Deuth is mentoring me." Rill tapped the end of the staff he was holding between his legs on the wood floor. "But I still ain't returned this staff and the charm to Lord Deuth. Guess I'll hafta do it later, after they expel Yall."

"You think they'll really expel him?" Jedd asked.

"Don't see why not. They found the charm in his room. And the noblesse ain't got no use for charm thieves." Rill laughed softly. "I'd sure love to know what's going on down there in the matriarch's council."

"Good thing someone warned you."

Rill rubbed his cheek. "Yeah. I wish I knew who though."

"But the note—"

"Wasn't written by the person who gave it to me." Rill paused as two images formed in his mind: Shalira and Livia. But which one had warned him?

Jedd got up from the bed. "Hafta go. Got a training session—"

Someone knocked on the door. Rill opened it to find himself staring at a grim-faced Kalso. "Lady Ariella requires your presence in the matriarch's chamber."

Rill and Jedd traded quizzical looks. Then Rill's stomach churned as a horrid thought crept into his mind. *Troy must of convinced them that I stole his charm. Now they're gonna expel me. But how could he—*

"Immediately," Kalso said.

Still holding the staff and conscious of the charm resting against his skin under his black tunic, Rill followed Kalso into the matriarch's chamber.

Ariella sat in her cherrywood chair, her short, rectangular body rigid with anger as she watched Rill approach. The women occupied straight-back chairs facing her. Deuth, Troy, and Yall stood clustered by the dais near the bottom step. The coldness in Deuth's blue eyes matched his grandmother's. Troy and Yall glowered at Rill, outrage darkening their faces.

Rill's heart galloped like a runaway stallion, making his chest ache. Something had gone terribly wrong in his attempt to return Troy's charm to the actual thief.

Ariella crooked a finger at him. "Come."

Rill stopped at the first step.

"Yall claims that you stole Troy's charm and put it in his room to frame him," Ariella said.

Rill shook his head. "That ain't true, Lady. I had nothing to do with stealing the charm."

Yall started to object but Troy spoke first. "That's a lie!"

Rill locked eyes with him. "Where's your proof?"

"You're jealous of me," Troy said. "You stole it to make me look bad."

Rill brushed Troy's accusation aside with a scoff. "It's just the opposite." He turned to Ariella, hesitated, and ran his tongue nervously over his lips. *Should I make the accusation? What if they don't believe me?* He wrinkled his brow into a determined scowl. *But I ain't gonna let them two destroy my chance to achieve my dream.*

Throwing his shoulders back, Rill looked directly at Ariella. "It's true. I planted the charm in Yall's bedroom—"

Troy let out a loud whoop of triumph. "I knew it all along! He set Yall up—"

"'Cause I found it under the mattress in *my* bedroom."

"Liar!" Troy shouted.

Rill spun toward him. "How could I steal your charm? You keep it in your room when it ain't around your neck. You gave it to Yall to place in my bedroom."

"Why would Troy do that?" Deuth asked in a quiet voice.

Rill strove to keep his tone even. "'Cause he's jealous that you're mentoring me. He wants you all to himself."

Troy blew out a disgusted breath. "Another lie."

Deuth tapped Yall's shoulder with his staff. "Did you put Troy's charm under Rill's mattress?"

"No, Lord," Yall replied, straight faced.

"But Rill says you did put it there."

"Damn right he did." Rill couldn't keep his anger from lacing his words. "When I found the charm under my mattress, I knew right away who put it there. Probably on orders from Troy. So I turned the tables around by stashing it under *his* mattress."

"He's a liar!" Yall stepped toward Rill, but Deuth blocked him with his staff.

Ariella smacked her lips. "Looks like we're at an impasse. Either Rill's lying, or Troy and Yall are lying." Her gaze slid to Deuth. "What can we do to learn the truth?"

"Bend some minds," Deuth said.

Ariella's lips compressed into a taut smile. "Yes. Deuth will cast mindbending spells on all three of you. You will be compelled to tell the truth. Whoever's lying will be expelled, including Troy."

Rill caught Troy and Yall swapping unsettled looks, and hid a grin.

"One last chance before we start," Deuth said. "Whoever took the charm speak up. Otherwise the consequences will be harsh."

"*Extremely* harsh," Ariella said.

A suffocating silence pressed down on the room, making it difficult to breathe. Rill looked directly at Ariella while Troy and Yall stared at each other as if trying to decide how to respond. Finally, Troy's shoulders slumped.

"I . . . I gave Yall my charm."

"What for?" Deuth asked.

"To plant in Rill's room."

"Why?"

Troy looked down at the floor. "So you'd expel him."

Ariella glowered at Troy. "I'm ashamed of you. Trying to frame an innocent retainer just because you're jealous he's being tutored by your uncle. You're not fit to have a charm and staff, so I'm taking them from you."

Troy stepped back impulsively. "No!"

Ariella slammed her fist on the arm of her chair. "Yes! If you want them back, you'll have to go from here to the Temple of the One Goddess in the Public Square and ask Her forgiveness . . . on your knees." She jabbed her index finger at Yall. "And you, Yall Throwstarr, tried to destroy Rill by planting Troy's charm under his mattress. That's an act of disloyalty to me and my family. You broke your oath to us. I'm going to expel you."

Troy rushed up the dais steps and stopped before Ariella. "Great-Grandmother, no! He'll become a rohan."

"He should have thought of that."

"But . . . but he wasn't disloyal. He was following my orders. You can't expel him for doing that."

Deuth scratched his scalp. "Troy does have a point, Grandmother. He gave Yall an order, and Yall carried it out."

"Against your apprentice mage," Ariella said.

"Please be reasonable," Deuth responded. "If Yall had to choose between obeying an order from you or from Troy, of course he'd obey yours. But in this case there wasn't any conflict. Only Troy gave him an order, which he obeyed like a good retainer. So how can you—"

Ariella sliced her hand through the air. "He conspired to put Rill in jeopardy. He set up an innocent boy to be punished for something he didn't do. If Rill hadn't discovered that charm—"

"But he did discover it," Deuth said. "Besides, I think we should commend Troy for displaying such initiative. Even though misplaced in this case, it shows he has the makings of a true Estati. Our ancestors should be proud of him."

"They wouldn't be if his 'initiative' had gotten Rill into trouble."

"But Rill didn't get into trouble," Deuth said. "Everything worked out. And no one outside this room suspects what actually happened."

"Except for the members of the search party."

"Their silence is beyond question. I made sure of that before we returned with the charm."

Ariella stroked her wrinkled neck thoughtfully. "Yes. Troy did show initiative."

"And so did Rill." Deuth wrapped an arm around Rill's shoulder. "He also showed he has a devious mind. We need more retainers like him."

Rill's mouth popped open. *Me, devious? Lucky is more like it. No. Not lucky. Someone's watching over me. Either Shalira or Livia. And the servant. She was involved in this too. Who does she serve? Probably Shalira. So it has to be Shalira who wrote the note—*

Ariella's next words broke into Rill's thoughts. "You're right. He could end up playing an important role in this house." She shook a finger under Troy's nose. "Our family—*your* family—pledged Rill our patronage in exchange for his oath to serve us loyally. 'Food, clothing, shelter, and gildas.' You were there when I made that oath. Those words imply protection." Her voice became sharp. "I will not tolerate you, Yall, or anyone else in this household threatening Rill's welfare or breaking our oath to him. Is that clear?"

"Yes," Troy said, avoiding Ariella's eyes.

Ariella pointed at Yall. "As for you, your ultimate obedience is to me and to no one else. You should've known what Troy ordered you to do was wrong. And you should have come to me about it."

"Yes, Matriarch," Yall said meekly.

As everyone left the room, Deuth took Rill aside to collect his charm and staff. Rill hated giving them up.

"You did well today," Deuth said. "I'm proud of you. But things could have turned out differently if you hadn't been so quick thinking." He clamped a hand on Rill's shoulder. "Lady Ariella and I have great plans for you. And we won't let anyone, even Troy, ruin them."

Exhilaration sped through Rill. *They believe in me, and I swear by the One Goddess I won't let them down.*

"I'm proud of how you handled yourself today," Deuth said. "So proud that I can say this." Deuth held up the charm and staff. "Before long, you won't have to return these. They'll be yours."

Rill smiled, and he felt proud of himself too.

## CHAPTER 44

Kendra's Aid

ALYSE RACED OUT OF the House of Healing and across the temple courtyard. Kate kept pace beside her.

"Where are we going?" Kate asked.

"To see Kendra Larkin, Rill's mother."

"What for?"

Because she healed you, Alyse almost said but recalled her promise. She wished again she could tell Kate the truth. Instead, her only response was to slow down to a trot before she was completely out of breath.

Even though she had been to Kendra's house just once through a web of unfamiliar cobblestone streets, the way Rill had led her was imprinted in her memory like the identity of a duckling's mother was stamped in the duckling's brain. Now she led Kate down narrow streets lined with tenements, craft shops, taverns, and corner shrines and pushed her way through crowds of women, men, and children on sidewalks and in the streets, who were running errands, haggling with merchants, gossiping, working, and playing. When Alyse recognized the blue-brick façade of the Eulands' tenement, she moved in a final burst of speed. A block later she turned into the Larkins' courtyard. The *clang, clang, clang* of hammer on anvil came from the smithy.

Alyse's legs and lungs gave out halfway across the courtyard. She doubled over, hands on knees, gasping for breath. Kate was almost as winded.

"What're you two doing here?" Marc Larkin stood in the smithy's doorway, his expression harsh and a cross peen hammer in his hand.

Alyse gulped down several more breaths as she straightened up to answer. "I need to see Kendra."

"You need to be on your way."

"Please! I *must* see her. It's a matter of life or death."

Marc pointed the hammer at the street. "Get out."

Alyse slipped on her disdainful mask. "I *will* see her."

She stepped toward the house, but Marc quickly blocked her way. Kate pushed herself between the two of them, her hand on the hilt of her sword.

Marc hefted his hammer. "Oh, girl. You don't know what you're doing."

The front door of the house banged open, and Kendra strode into the courtyard. "What's going on here?"

Alyse stepped around Marc and ran to her. "Kendra, I must talk to you."

Kendra studied Alyse, her expression stony. She shifted her gaze to Marc who gave a slight shrug as if to say, *It's your call.*

"Come inside," Kendra said brusquely.

She led Alyse and Kate into the kitchen. A burst of heat from the hearth greeted them. Cinna was bending over the flames stirring a kettle of what smelled like vegetable stew. Surprise registered on her face when she recognized Alyse.

Marc folded his arms as he took up a position by the door, the hammer still in his hand.

"All right," Kendra said. "What do you have to talk to me about?"

"I'm Priestess Sybil's apprentice healer," Alyse said.

Alyse expected some sort of response, even if just a nod, but Kendra's flint-hard eyes and unfriendly face remained unchanged. Ignoring her quivering heart, Alyse explained that Priestess Sybil had been called away yesterday and hadn't returned yet and that today

Priestess Gilda had asked her to treat a man with a gangrene leg. "If I don't stabilize his condition," she concluded, "he'll die by tomorrow morning. But I can't find a treatment for it. If you could only help me—"

Kendra flinched as if she'd been nipped by a dog. "No! Absolutely not."

Alyse's body shook from frustration. She *had* to make Kendra understand. "He's a deserter from my uncle's legions."

Kendra's granite façade shattered. "And you're *treating* him?"

"I'm a healer. That's my job, no matter who the patient."

"Priestess Sybil should be treating him, not you."

"She left the city last night on an emergency call in the country. I don't know when she'll be back. Hilbrand's condition needs to be stabilized now or he'll die."

"You don't know what you're getting mixed up with. If your family finds out—"

"They're farmers. All they want to do is return to their farms."

Kendra looked at Alyse as if she'd gone insane. "They?"

Alyse nodded. "Hilbrand and his two friends."

Kendra seized Alyse's shoulders, her fingertips digging so hard into her flesh through the cotton of her blue dress that Alyse thought the nails might draw blood. "Leave it now. Before your family finds out—"

"It's too late. The city watchers have already been to the House of Healing looking for them. They saw the deserters. But I told them they were farmers and they believed me. Especially when I told them who I was."

Kendra shook Alyse by her shoulders. "Alyse, you don't know what you're getting yourself involved in."

Wrenching free of Kendra's grip, Alyse drew herself to her full height while her ribs tightened inside her chest. "I know full well what I'm involved in. I've committed treason by convincing the watchers the deserters are farmers." She expelled a despondent breath. "They only want to return to their farms."

Kendra exchanged worried glances with Marc and Cinna.

"It's not right," Alyse said. "I saw another family evicted by a noblesse. And I treated a farmer who'd moved here after losing his farm to another noblesse." She described the two incidents. "It's criminal," she said, raising her voice in passion. "The state conscripts a farmer's children, which leads to the farm's failing. And then some noblesse buys it for a pittance."

"Be careful what you say," Marc told her. "The watchers might mistake you for a malcontent."

Alyse swatted Marc's comment aside with a wave of her hand. "Is it wrong to want to treat someone fairly?" She touched Kendra's shoulder. "Please help me. I want Hilbrand to live so he and his friends can return to their families. *Please.*"

Kendra stared hard at her, and Alyse met her look head-on. "You're a surprising noblesse, Alyse Dejune," Kendra said, her voice almost a murmur. Perhaps I've misjudged you." She turned serious. "What do you want of me?"

Alyse nodded to Kate. "You'd better wait outside."

"You too, Marc," Kendra said.

When the two of them had left, Kendra stepped closer to Alyse. "What do you want?"

"Can you cure gangrene?"

Kendra crossed her arms. "Tell me what you want first."

"Hilbrand is dying from the gangrene. He won't last the night."

"How do you know that?"

"My inner eye told me. And curing Hilbrand's gangrene is beyond my skills. I need you to—"

"Cure him." Kendra pulled herself up straight as a mage's staff. "No. I swore to the One Goddess never to use my powers again. I broke the oath once, for Kate. I won't break it a second time."

"I don't want you to break your oath."

"Then what *do* you want?"

"For you to tell me the cure. What spell to cast. And if the cure requires a potion, tell me the ingredients and how to mix them."

"I'll not break my oath by becoming your assistant."

Alyse wanted to stamp the floorboards in frustration. "Not my assistant. My adviser."

"You're splitting hairs."

"She's proposing a reasonable compromise," Cinna said, leaving the hearth to stand beside them.

"Whenever I hear someone say 'reasonable,'" Kendra told her, "I sense something unreasonable will be suggested."

"Don't let magic confuse your logic," Cinna replied. "You support Priestess Sybil's work with the underground trail—"

Kendra gasped in alarm. "Mother!"

"Goddess agory," Cinna said. "If the Magesterium finds out that Alyse is harboring deserters, they could condemn her as an enemy of the state."

Alyse's heart pounded so hard her chest hurt, but she ignored the sensation.

"She showed us where she stands," Cinna continued. "With us."

Alyse wished she knew what "with us" meant. Or what Kendra and Cinna, and probably Marc, were involved in.

Cinna wagged a finger under Kendra's nose. "If Priestess Sybil asked you to help that poor man, you'd be at the temple now. Ain't that true?"

"Yes. But I wouldn't help by using magic."

"Alyse is acting in Priestess Sybil's place. And she ain't askin' you to use magic."

Kendra squeezed her lips together truculently.

"Telling her the ingredients in the potion and the spell to cast on them ain't the same as doin' it yourself."

Kendra remained silent.

"Daughter, we can't let that poor man die. Him and his two friends need to be kept safe so they can take the trail as soon as possible."

Alyse concealed a frown. That was the second time since entering the kitchen that they'd mentioned an underground trail. She wanted to ask what it was but realized they wouldn't tell her.

Kendra said nothing for a long time, her blue eyes troubled. Alyse's nerves twisted so tightly waiting for Kendra's response that she felt they'd snap.

Kendra let out a sigh so deep it seemed to come up from her toes. "You're right, Mother. I can't not help." She turned to Alyse. "Gangrene can be difficult to cure. I hope you have the power."

Alyse hoped so too.

# # #

As soon as she entered Hilbrand's room at the House of Healing, Kendra took charge by ordering Priestess Gilda, Ebar, and Ord to leave. She sent Kate out as well. Then she knelt beside the bed and visually examined Hilbrand's thigh.

"Wet gangrene," she said, looking up at Alyse. "This is the worst kind to cure. Healing hands don't work on it. The treatment requires a potion and a spell."

"And I was using healing hands," Alyse said. "No wonder nothing I did helped."

"You'll need herbs from the apothecary and then a fire for making the potion."

Alyse left Kate to stand guard outside the room, then she and Kendra hurried to the apothecary. On the way, Kendra rattled off a list of herbs and their proportions required for the potion. At the apothecary, Alyse asked the herbalist for the herbs. When Alyse got them, she and Kendra went through a side door in the apothecary into the small courtyard set aside for brewing potions. Alyse lit a fire, hung a kettle of water over it, and waited impatiently for the liquid to simmer.

Before Alyse added the herbs, Kendra told her the spell to cast on the concoction. While Alyse waited anxiously for the potion to brew, Kendra told her to bathe Hilbrand's wound four times during the daytime and another four during the night, once at the beginning of each watch. When the potion was ready, Alyse lugged the pot to Hilbrand's room. Kate followed them inside and placed herself in the shadows at the far end of the room. Kendra locked the door while Alyse set the kettle beside the bed.

Alyse pulled down the bedclothes. Hilbrand's chest barely moved up and down with his frail breathing. Alyse dipped a clean cloth into the warm potion and gently bathed Hilbrand's thigh. She waited awhile to let the treatment take effect, then explored Hilbrand with her inner eye. What she sensed numbed her body. "We're too late. He's not strong enough to make it to the next cleansing. He's going to die."

"Lend him your strength."

Alyse wrinkled her forehead. "What do you mean?"

"Transfer some of your personal energy to him."

Despair threatened to smother Alyse, making it difficult to push words from her mouth. "Priestess Sybil . . . hasn't taught me . . . that yet."

"It's not easy to learn," Kendra said. "Only competent healers can master it. But I think you can. Want to try?"

"Yes."

"Good," Kendra said, smiling her approval. "Instead of using your healing hands to direct the healing energy into Hilbrand's wound, use them to transfer your personal energy into his heart. But don't give him an excessive amount, or you'll weaken yourself too much."

Alyse clenched her hands into tight fists, then opened them. *Kendra has faith in me. I won't let her down. I won't let myself down.* Bending over Hilbrand, she placed both hands over his heart and summoned her personal energy. She stifled a groan of dismay when nothing happened.

"Visualize it," Kendra said.

Kicking dismay from her mind, Alyse visualized her personal energy flowing into Hilbrand. Still nothing happened. *I can do this.* She pressed her lips together, determined to succeed, and invoked her personal energy again as if she were casting a spell. She pulled in an abrupt breath when she felt energy streaming through her body, down her arms to her hands and into Hilbrand's body. She found the sensation comforting and, closing her eyes, gave herself over to it.

A jerk on her shoulder startled her. "That's enough."

Alyse blinked in confusion. "Huh?"

"You've given him enough personal energy."

"It feels like I just started." She let out a sigh and her shoulders drooped. "But I also feel drained."

"I know," Kendra said. "One danger of doing a transfer is that you can put yourself into a trance and give up all your energy."

"Phew!" Alyse said. "I'll keep that in mind for the next time."

Kendra nodded at Hilbrand. "How's he doing?"

Alyse's tiredness vanished when she saw that Hilbrand was breathing more deeply. She examined him with her inner eye. What she sensed made her heart tingle. She grinned at Kendra. "The transfer worked. He's gained enough strength for me to use the potion."

"Good. I'll say now what Priestess Sybil will tell you. Don't make a practice of transferring personal energy. It's too dangerous. Use it only as a last resort, when all else fails. And until you're experienced enough, make sure someone is with you to intervene, if necessary."

Exhausted, Alyse sank to the floor and rested her head against the side of the bed. She and Kendra stared at each other.

Kendra's blue eyes shone with approval. "You have the makings of a fine healer, Alyse Dejune."

Alyse smiled back tiredly. Then after a short while, she climbed to her feet. "I suppose we should let the others back in."

Kendra opened the door and stood aside as everyone entered.

Ebar and Ord approached Hilbrand hesitantly. "Will he be all right?" Ord asked.

Alyse glanced at Kendra, who shrugged. "You're the healer, Alyse. Not me."

Alyse nodded. "Yes. But it will take a long time for the wound to heal and for him to recover his full strength."

The two deserters swapped relieved looks.

"Thank you, Lady Alyse," Ord said. "Till today, I thought all you noblesse were scum. But you proved me wrong."

"That's right," Ebar said. "You knew we're deserters, yet you defended us against the city watchers. If they'd arrested us, they would of sent us back to be executed."

"Why did you desert in the first place?" Alyse asked. "We're at war. Don't you want to defend your country?"

Ebar snorted in disgust. "My country!"

"Say no more!" Priestess Gilda said in near panic. "Don't involve these girls any further."

Alyse put a hand up, warding off Gilda. "No. I want to hear what he has to say."

"I forbid it!" Gilda said.

Alyse put on her haughty face. "I'm a Dejune. You can't forbid me anything."

"I think what Alyse means," Kendra said in a more reasonable tone, "is that she's earned the right to hear what these men have to say. So has Kate."

From the sour look on Priestess Gilda's face, she disagreed.

Alyse turned to Ebar. "Go on."

"We're farmers," Ebar said. "Our families have owned and worked our farms for generations. In the past, our ancestors have left their plows many times—and willingly—to take up their swords and fight for Caldon."

"That's right," Ord said. "But things have changed. There ain't no respite from conscription. My two brothers and my sister were taken. Only my matriarch, my mom and dad, and me were left to work the farm. My brothers . . . they were killed in battle and my sister . . . she died in camp from sickness. Then the state took me. A few months ago, my dad left to work his matriarch's farm. His family's having the same problems as mine. But that left only my matriarch and my mom." He spread his hands in a gesture of helplessness. "How can I leave them on their own?"

Ebar nodded vigorously. "The same thing's happening with my family's farm."

"That's horrible!" Alyse said. "The Magesterium must be told about this. It can—"

"The Magesterium!" Ord laughed bitterly. "They make stealing our farms possible."

A chill passed through Alyse's skin into her chest and expanded into her inner core. She gawked at Ord, her mind refusing to believe what he'd just said. "How?"

Ord's eyes narrowed into angry slits. "By using conscription to make our farms fail. Without the sons and daughters to work their mothers' farms, the farms will fall hopelessly into debt."

"Then the noblesses' agents come calling," Ebar said, his voice steeped in outrage. "They offer to buy our farms for the price of a bale of hay. Two months ago one came to our farm. His offer was so low it was an insult. That's why I deserted. To help with the farm."

"My matriarch refused an offer last year," Ord said. "Now that my dad's gone, I don't know how long she can hold out."

A sense of injustice cut through Alyse like a ripsaw. Then she recalled how Kate had found bills of sale for two farms Siema had bought. Guilt replaced injustice. She took a deep breath. "Who are these noblesse?"

"We won't know their names until after their agents have bought our farms."

Alyse turned to Ebar. "But you *do* know the names of noblesse who bought your neighbors' farms."

For a moment, the two men hesitated, then glanced at each other. An unspoken message passed between them.

Ord reeled off names Alyse recognized as both allies and enemies of her family. Then he mentioned names that hit closer to home. "Svagga. Berne. Spicer. Estati." Ord paused, then spat another name at her. "Dejune."

Guilt flowed into Alyse as if it were filling a water skin the size of her chest. "I'm so sorry." Even as the words left her mouth, she realized how inadequate they were.

"You're not old enough to be concerned with your family's properties and finances," Kendra said, softness in her voice. "That's mainly the business of your matriarch and your chief steward."

"Why do the noblesse need so much land?" Alyse asked.

"Noblesse don't work," Kendra replied. "Their wealth comes from the land. From the cattle, sheep, and pigs raised on it and from the vegetables and other produce grown on it. They sell the wheat to the state for exorbitant prices to use for the dole. Their wealth also comes from owning craft shops, taverns, tenements, and even brothels in the city and paying others to work them."

Without thinking, Alyse asked, "Is your family's smithy—"

"My matriarch owns our property." A fierce blue light shone in Kendra's eyes. "Almost everyone in The Kings owns their own property or has taken it back from the noblesse. We won't let those bastards gain a foothold in our neighborhood again."

Alyse's head spun from the incredible revelations. "Is that why Hilbrand deserted? Because his family might lose their farm?"

A bitter smile crossed Ebar's face. "No, Lady. He deserted 'cause his family had already lost it."

"Forced to sell it for a pittance," Ord said.

"His mother and his sister came here to the city for the free wheat," Ebar said. "When we deserted, Hilbrand planned to join them. Me and Ord were gonna return to our families' farms. But then Hilbrand was wounded, and we knew he'd never make it to Caldon on his own. So we brought him here. We'll return home afterward."

"So that's why so many country folks are coming here to live on the dole," Alyse said. "It's awful that Hilbrand and his family have to join them. But how can they? Only a male can become a client. Hilbrand's a deserter. If he tries to find a patron, he'll be arrested. How can his mother apply for the dole without him?"

"She won't," Ord replied. "Hilbrand's too proud to join the ranks of the poor on the wheat dole."

"I don't understand. How can his family survive without free wheat?"

Ord's gaze swung to Ebar, who nodded. "By traveling—"

"Ord, no—" Priestess Gilda cried.

"—the underground trail."

The underground trail. This was the third time today Alyse had heard those forbidden words. She had an unpleasant feeling she might not like where this tale was going, but she already didn't like where it had been. She took a deep breath, afraid to ask Ord her next question but needing to know the answer. "What's the underground trail?"

"The path—"

"No!" Priestess Gilda screamed.

"—to freedom."

"To a new life without noblesse," Ebar added. "Where we all can live as free women and men."

Gilda glared at both men, her eyes smoldering like a pair of glowing coals. "You fools! You just signed Alyse's and Kate's death warrants."

Enforcer

AS THE WEEKS PASSED, Rill's spellcasting abilities increased. After Rill mastered the spells contained in the first Warrior charm Deuth had lent him, Deuth gave him a Warrior charm that held spells too powerful to be cast in their makeshift practice area in the family compound. So they began going to Mages' Field, which was outside the city gates, for their spellcasting sessions. As before, Deuth would teach Rill a spell, supervise him for a while, and then let him practice on his own for the rest of the day. As Rill's backwatcher, Jedd always accompanied Rill to Mages' Field.

The routine never varied. Rill would collect the charm and staff from Deuth in his study and then give them back when he returned from Mages' Field. Rill was proud of the trust Deuth placed in him to act responsibly and also loved the deferential way the commoners treated him when he and Jedd passed by in their Estati livery on the way back from Mages' Field.

One morning, when Rill went to Deuth's study to collect his charm and staff, he saw Yall Throwstarr and Magnus Roeback talking with Deuth by his desk. *Goddess curse him!* Rill had tried to avoid Yall ever since he had planted Troy's charm in his room.

And there he was, laughing along with Magnus at something Deuth had said.

Rill hurled a dark look at Yall, who threw one back just as dark.

Deuth smiled at Rill. "No practice for you today."

"Lord?"

"You've shown remarkable progress in your lessons."

Pride exploded inside Rill's heart, dispelling his anger at Yall. "Thank you, Lord."

Deuth leaned back in his chair and crossed a black-booted leg. "I think it's time you got some real-life experience. And also begin earning your keep. I have an errand for you. Do you remember Alain Develle?"

Rill frowned, vaguely recognizing the name but unable to picture the face. "No, Lord."

"On the day the assassin attacked me," Deuth said.

An image popped into Rill's mind. A fat, middle-aged man. Short. With a prominent Adam's apple. "The spice seller."

"Exactly. Do you recall the nature of our conversation?"

"Something about a loan."

"Yes." Deuth put his elbows on the desktop and leaned forward in his chair. "His business was prospering, and he came to me wanting to borrow money so he could buy the building next to his. He wanted to expand his shop into it. My family gave him the loan, and now it's way past due. I've asked for repayment three times. And each time he claimed he needed *more* time." Deuth mimicked the wine seller's voice. "'I've had expenses. More than I anticipated.'"

Yall and Magnus snickered at Deuth's imitation.

"Now it's high time to collect." Deuth heaved an unhappy sigh. "Extracting payment isn't something my family enjoys doing. But we have no choice. Just think what would happen if our other clients thought they could get away with breaking their agreements with us. They'd think they can walk away from repaying their lawful debts."

"What does this hafta do with me, Lord?" Rill asked.

"I'm sending you, Magnus, and Yall to collect the debt." Deuth paused. "I'll send Jedd too. He's your backwatcher and should accompany you. He also can use the experience." Standing, Deuth picked up a tightly rolled-up sheet of vellum. He pointed it at Rill and Yall. "I know you still have bad feelings against each other for the incident with Troy's charm. It's high time to put the affair behind you. If you think you can't, you can leave our service now, without being expelled."

"We can work together, Lord," Yall said quickly.

I ain't gonna jeopardize my future over it. Rill nodded. "We can."

"Good." Deuth handed the vellum scroll to Magnus. "You know what to do with this."

"I do, Lord," Magnus said cheerfully, tucking the parchment under his belt.

"I'm depending on all of you to uphold the Estati honor." Deuth gave Rill the charm and staff he'd come to collect. "And remember. No undue violence. He is my client after all."

The Sisters, which bordered The Kings along Road of the One Goddess, was more prosperous than The Kings. The gray, clay-brick sidewalks and cobbled streets were wider than in The Kings and allowed in additional sunlight, so everything wasn't in perpetual shadow. The tenements were more solidly built too. And the stores offered higher quality merchandise, the wine shops and taverns costlier wines and better dressed customers, and the street corner shrines were cleaner than in Rill's neighborhood.

Shoulders thrown back, Rill strutted along the sidewalk behind Magnus and Yall and, with feigned nonchalance, used his staff as a walking stick the way Lord Deuth did. He loved how commoners showed respect for him by stepping aside or bowing deferentially. Some even cast him wary glances, which showed they feared him. He found their reactions intoxicating.

Jedd, though, wasn't interested in making an impression.

"Tell me again," he said in a voice too low for Magnus and Yall to hear, "why we're going to the spice seller's."

"I told you already," Rill replied. "To collect a debt he owes the Estatis. He's failed to pay it three times."

"But why send you and three backwatchers? Why not his secretary or steward? Or sue him in court?"

Debt collection was something Rill was unfamiliar with. So all he did was shrug. "It ain't for us to question our patrons' motives."

Magnus stopped by a two-story building that contained a shop on the first floor and living quarters on the second. The sign over the door said ALAIN DEVELLE—SPICES AND HERBS.

"Here we are." Magnus put his hand on the door latch, then said to Rill and Jedd, "Hang back and watch how it's done."

Inside, Rill caught the mingled scents of cinnamon, cloves, mint, rosemary, and sage along with the pungent smell of fermented fish sauce. Several customers were examining spices and herbs in large, bulging burlap sacks. Tall, wide-mouthed earthenware crocks were arranged in various locations on the floor. A girl barely in her teens was pushing a mop whose handle was twice as tall as her across the floor. Behind the counter on the far side, a middle-aged woman was chatting with a customer while she weighed the contents she had scooped out from one of the small jars of mixed herbs and spices that lined the walls. A welcoming smile for the newcomers blossomed on the woman's lips. But when she noted their livery, the smile wilted.

Magnus and Yall stopped at the counter.

"Good morning," Magnus said pleasantly. "Is your master here?"

Apprehension broke out like pimples on the woman's face.

"Alain Develle," Magnus said. "Is he here?"

"My husband?"

"Yes."

The woman's eyes flicked to a closed door on her left. "I . . . I'm not sure. I'll go see."

"No need for that," Magnus said, blocking her with his staff. "We'll find him."

Magnus and Yall crossed to the door, opened it, and went inside.

Rill stopped at the threshold with Jedd and peered in after them.

The soft, shivering glows from several oil lamps on wall shelves revealed a room filled with large burlap bags and sealed crocks. The wax seal on one jar had been broken, and a tall boy, who appeared to be in his mid-teens, and a short, dumpy man were scooping out its contents and emptying it into smaller bags. Both turned to face the door.

The man's Adam's apple bobbed as he swallowed uneasily.

"Alain Develle," Magnus said heartily.

Alain whispered to the boy, who immediately scurried toward the door. Yall blocked his path.

"H-he's my son," Alain said. "P-please let him go. Lord Deuth's quarrel ain't with him."

Magnus nodded to Yall who stepped aside. The teenager shot out of the room, like a rock hurled from a catapult. Magnus returned his attention to Alain, his attitude suddenly cold and businesslike. "You know why we're here."

"I t-told Lord Deuth I needed more time."

"And he gave you more time, didn't he."

Alain remained silent.

Magnus put a sharp edge in his voice. "Didn't he?"

"Y-yes."

"You haven't kept your word. You lied to Lord Deuth."

"N-no, I didn't! I swear by the One Goddess—"

Magnus thumped his staff's butt on the wooden floor. "Liar! Three times you promised to repay him, and didn't."

Beads of sweat broke out on Alain's forehead. "I-I'll repay the loan. B-but I haven't taken in enough profit yet."

"Another lie."

Magnus stepped toward Alain, who backed away hastily and stumbled into a crock. His legs gave way, but Yall caught him under a shoulder and set him back to his feet. Alain's breath came in rapid, fearful gasps.

Magnus tapped Alain's chest with his staff's silvery crystal orb. "Perhaps we should cut off your hand as a reminder to pay."

Yall drew his dagger. Lamplight glinted off the razor-sharp blade.

Alain's gaze fell on the knife, and his face turned as white as the goose feathers on an arrow.

Rill found himself captivated by Magnus's display of raw power and its effect on the spice seller.

"You agreed to repay the loan on time or forfeit your shop," Magnus said.

Alain fell to his knees, clasped his hands together, and extended them to Magnus. "P-please don't take away my livelihood. For my family's sake, I beg of you."

Magnus gazed down at him for a long time while he fingered the silver ring in his left earlobe.

"I'll repay the loan," Alain said. "It will mean extreme hardship for my family, but I'll repay it. I swear!"

Magnus motioned for Yall to sheath the dagger. "You're lucky the Estatis aren't heartless like so many other patrons. They're generous. Even to scum like you who don't deserve their generosity."

A weird combination of hope and dread fluttered in Alain's eyes.

Magnus tugged the parchment from his belt, unrolled it, and waved it in front of Alain's face. "This is a contract between you and the Estatis. It says that you are signing over fifty-one percent of your business to them. You can keep the other forty-nine percent. You split the profits the same way. Fifty-one, forty-nine."

"Forty-nine percent!" Alain wailed. "We can't live on that. I hardly make enough profit as it is for my family to survive."

"We both know that's a lie." Magnus shrugged indifferently. "But if you prefer that the Estatis take your entire business, so be it." He stroked his gray beard. "Of course, that means you and your family will be thrown into the street. You'll probably end up living in The Slums. Fortunately, you have an attractive daughter and a strapping son. She can bring in money for you by being a prostitute. And he can become a dagger man. I do hope he's not too squeamish though."

In the lamplight, Rill could see Alain's lips and chin quiver. *I ain't never seen no one that scared before.*

"Oh well . . ." Magnus covered his lips with his hand as he yawned. "If you prefer that the Estatis take your entire business, so be it. I'm just the messenger. Goodbye." He headed for the door but stopped short of the threshold and turned. "By the way. This is a one-time offer. When I leave this room, the deal is off the table."

Fascinated with the scene, Rill held his breath, his eyes on Alain, waiting for the man's response. Agitation, fear, and anger vied for dominance on Alain's face.

Magnus stepped toward the threshold—

"Wait!" Alain shouted, his voice cracking. "I'll sign! I'll sign!"

Magnus turned back with a friendly smile. "Now, you're being reasonable."

After they left the shop, Magnus told Rill and Jedd that dealing with Alain had been an easy task. "He was timid and susceptible to fear tactics," Magnus said. "Others can be harder nuts to crack. That's where Yall comes in."

Magnus led them out of The Sisters and along Road of the One Goddess toward the Public Square.

While Rill and Jedd followed, Rill kept thinking about the scene with Alain Develle. "Did you see that?" he said to Jedd. "The spice seller was more than scared of us. He was so petrified. That's power!"

When Jedd didn't respond, Rill glanced sideways at him. Jedd's face was set in a deep frown. "What's wrong with you?" Rill asked.

"What we did to that poor man was despicable."

"What do ya mean? He didn't pay back his loan, so he got what he deserved. I think Lord Deuth let him off easy. He got to keep his business."

"Less than half of it."

"Almost half of it."

"Which means he can't feed his family."

"He was lying about that. You heard what Magnus said."

"Maybe it was Magnus who was lying."

Rill stopped and faced Jedd. "What's wrong with you? We both have good positions with one of the most powerful families in Caldon."

Jedd said nothing.

Rill poked a finger against Jedd's chest. "I'm the one who got you your position with them, remember."

"So now I hafta kowtow to you too?"

"No. But you're my backwatcher. What you do reflects on me."

"I'll keep that in mind."

Rill took a deep breath to calm his anger. "Look. I don't wanna argue with you. It's just that we're on our way up in the world, and you're complaining."

"I ain't complainin'," Jedd said. "I'm just saying that I'm a backwatcher, not a thug."

"You're an Estati retainer who swore an oath of fealty to them. Just like I did. So we hafta do what they tell us. That's how things work. Sometimes we might not like what we gotta do, but we do it anyways. That's the way to get ahead."

"Uncle Tor never intimidated or harmed helpless people."

Rill made a dismissive sound in his throat. "He just never told you about those things 'cause he thought you'd change your opinion of him."

"Uncle Tor taught me his backwatcher values. And doing what we just did goes against every single one of them."

Rill stood nose to nose with Jedd, the anger burning on his face matching Jedd's. Magnus's impatient call from up ahead broke the tension.

"Come on!"

The summons broke Rill's fury. He waved his hand in acknowledgment, then turned back to Jedd. "You're my best friend. Let's not argue."

Jedd chewed the inside of his cheek, then said, "All right."

Rill hurried up the road to join the others. He glanced over his shoulder. Jedd was taking his time catching up.

Rill mumbled a curse at Jedd. *He ain't gonna ruin my chances of becoming noblesse 'cause of his surly attitude. If he keeps it up, Lady Ariella will expel him. And I don't wanna choose between the Estatis and Jedd.*

'Cause if I hafta choose, I'll pick the Estatis.

The Underground Trail

EVERYONE JUMPED WHEN THE door latch lifted and Priestess Sybil walked in. She took in the tableau with a sweep of her silver eyes. "Priestess Gilda," she said, "what's going on here?"

In a no-nonsense manner, Priestess Gilda explained about the three deserters and how Alyse had insisted on treating the one with the gangrene leg. "And then the city watchers barged in searching for them—"

Priestess Sybil gulped an outraged breath. "City watchers . . . here?"

Gilda nodded. "Into this very room. But Alyse made them leave."

Sybil's cheeks reddened with anger. "Good Goddess in Elustra! I leave the city to tend a patient overnight. And while I'm gone, you get Alyse involved with deserters *and* with the watchers? She's the chief magestrate's granddaughter and the niece of the Commander of the Eastern Legions. Think of the scandal, not just to our temple but to Alyse. She could be prosecuted for treason. What were you thinking, woman?"

Apprehension trickled down Alyse's spine. *But nothing will happen if we all keep the secret.* She hoped they would. Especially the deserters if they were captured escaping the from city.

Throwing her shoulders back, Gilda looked Sybil in the eye. "You put me in charge of the temple and the House of Healing. I did what I thought was right."

Sybil glared at Gilda, her mouth drawn into a tight line. "And put Alyse in a compromising position. The noblesse would like nothing better than to close us down because we serve the Kings dwellers. Only the high priestess keeps them at bay. Think of the innocent novices and priestesses—not to mention the Kings dwellers—who would suffer if your actions make her change her mind."

"The watchers violated the sanctity of the temple by entering," Gilda said, indignity saturating her voice.

"The Magesterium might view that differently."

"They won't if we all keep our mouths shut," Alyse said.

"That includes Kate, I suppose." Sybil crooked an index finger at her. "Come on out. I see you lingering there in the shadows."

Kate stood beside Alyse. "It does include me."

Sybil shifted her gaze to Gilda, her eyes flaming with anger and her lips pressed together so tight not even a strand of Alyse's thin chestnut hair could pass between them.

"Priestess Gilda made the right call," Alyse said. "Hilbrand was at the point of death. We had no idea when you'd be back. And if we'd waited till now, not even your healing skill could have saved him."

"That's your professional opinion?" Sybil asked.

Alyse nodded curtly. "Yes."

"Alyse is right," Kendra said.

Sybil heaved a sigh as if she had no choice but to accept what had already been done. "Alyse, we both know gangrene is beyond your skills. I supposed Kendra helped you."

"I didn't help," Kendra said. "I merely advised."

"And your oath?"

"Remains unbroken."

"Frankly, Kendra," Sybil said, "I find it difficult to believe that, given your oath, you'd even 'advise.'"

"I find it difficult to believe myself. But Alyse persuaded my mother, who persuaded me." Kendra's lips worked themselves into a wry smile. "And perhaps I'm willing to admit that I was wrong about at least one noblesse girl."

Sybil turned to Alyse. "Tell me what did you do to heal him."

Alyse pointed to the kettle on the floor beside the bed. "I mixed the potion. Kendra told me the herbs to use and the spell to cast on it. Then I bathed Hilbrand's wound with it. But the potion wasn't enough. So I gave Hilbrand some of my personal energy."

The flesh color drained from Sybil's face, turning it as pale as a dead woman's. "You *what?*"

Alyse hugged Sybil's reaction to her chest. "I gave Hilbrand some of my personal energy," Alyse said as if doing that was an everyday event.

"But . . . but I haven't taught you how to do that yet. And I've never given you a case that required it. You're not ready."

"I had no other choice. Kendra told me how to do it."

Sybil lapsed into silence, and Alyse imagined her brain struggling to take in everything that had happened. "Well," Sybil finally said, "it looks like I underestimated you." She stepped closer to Alyse. "What do you think the outcome will be?"

"He'll live."

"Hilbrand owes his life to Lady Alyse," Ord said.

Ebar nodded vigorously. "We all owe her our lives. If the watchers had taken us . . ."

"Well," Sybil said, "let's just hope it doesn't get out that we harbored three deserters."

Alyse tapped her fingers against her thigh, hesitating over what Sybil's reaction would be to what she was about to ask. But she had to know. "There is one other thing."

"What's that?" Sybil asked.

"What's the underground trail?"

Sybil put her hand to her chest as if she were having a heart attack. "*What?*"

Ebar coughed and cleared his throat. "I'm afraid me and Ord mentioned it."

Sybil gawked at him as if his confession had sent her mind reeling drunkenly.

"I want to know," Alyse said. She nudged Kate. "*We* want to know."

Kate nodded. "We already know it's a trail to freedom and to a new life."

Alyse crossed her arms and sent Sybil a challenging look. "I lied to the city watchers and saved Hilbrand and the others. If I'm arrested and executed for doing it, Kate will be too because she assisted me. So I think we both have earned the right to know."

Sybil's gaze bounced from Gilda to Kendra, but they kept their expressions neutral. *You're on your own with this one,* they seemed to be saying. Sybil licked her lips, then squared her shoulders. "It's a secret route to Annatol, beyond the Sharp Teeth Mountains. For quite some years now, the Annatolians have allowed deserters and their families to live there, in their own towns that they built. There are stops along the way, like here, where like-minded Caldonians take in and feed the 'walkers.' Hide them too, if necessary. Some of the deserters even enlist in the Annatolian legions to prevent our Western Legions from fighting their way through the Sharp Teeth."

Numbness spread over Alyse's body while she and Kate exchanged stunned looks. "Does the Magesterium know about this?"

"They know people take in deserters," Sybil replied. "But they don't realize how widespread the underground trail movement is. And they don't know about the deserters' towns. Each town is populated by ex-legionaries, many with their families. Including mages who brought their charms and staffs with them. Parents train their children to fight. They want to live free from this perpetual war with Gaetan. And they'll defend their new homeland to their last breath."

Alyse looked blankly at Sybil as if her mind had turned itself off, like a waterwheel whose river had dried up. She finally managed to slip her gaze to Kate, who appeared equally stunned.

Sybil eyed Alyse somberly. "You wanted to know. So now you do."

"I . . . I had no idea," Alyse whispered, more to herself than Sybil.

"Of course not," Sybil said. "It's a secret. One that you and Kate must keep. If the Magesterium should learn that there's an organized movement to help deserters . . ." She let the sentence dangle.

Alyse rubbed the back of her neck. "Well, I guess I learned more than I expected."

"It's too late for regrets."

"I have none." Alyse read Kate's expression. "And neither does Kate. This endless war is destroying Caldon and its people. And the way the noblesse are taking advantage of it to steal the farms of the women and men who fight for their country. It's unconscionable."

It's more than unconscionable," Kendra said. "It's—"

Hilbrand groaned.

Alyse knelt beside his bed. Ord and Ebar came up behind her and looked down at their friend. Hilbrand's eyes blinked open and slowly focused on Alyse's face. She put a hand on his forehead. It was hot with fever. "How do you feel, Hilbrand?" she asked softly.

Hilbrand grasped Alyse's wrist in a weak grip. "I had a vision. Neg, the Goddess of Death, told me the Five Weavers ain't finished with my tapestry. She said my time ain't up yet."

Alyse shivered as awe fluttered up her neck. Kate had heard a voice—Kendra's—calling her back from the Afterworld too! Behind her, Alyse heard Kendra's gasp. Hilbrand's astonishing words resonated with her as well.

Alyse gently detached Hilbrand's hand from her wrist. "You were dreaming. Rest easy. The crisis has passed. You'll recover."

Hilbrand's hand motioned weakly under the covers at his two friends hovering over him. "Are you still here?"

Ord smiled, his gray eyes watery. "We couldn't leave till we knew you'd get better."

"That's right," Ebar said, wiping away tears with his dirty knuckles. "Now that we know you're in good hands, we can return to our farms and help our families."

"I'm sorry I held you back," Hilbrand said.

"Friends don't abandon each other," Ebar responded.

Alyse put a hand on Hilbrand's shoulder. "You should rest."

Hilbrand closed his eyes and was asleep before Alyse had gotten to her feet.

Ord turned to Priestess Sybil. "We hafta leave before the city gates close. We got a long way to travel."

"If you value your families' safety," Sybil told them, "going back to your farms is out of the question."

Ebar's forehead wrinkled. "What do ya mean?"

"The trackers didn't find you here. So now a detachment of legionaries will go to your farms. A mindbender will accompany them. If they don't find you at your farms, the mindbender will question your family." Sybil's expression darkened. "A mindbender can get the truth out of them pretty easily. If you're hiding out anywhere on your farms or in the general area, they'll find you. And you won't be the only ones to suffer. Your families will too."

Fearful looks passed between Ebar and Ord.

Ord swallowed noisily. "What can we do, Priestess?"

"You must walk the underground trail with Hilbrand."

"But our families!" Ord cried.

"Our farms!" Ebar said.

"If your families are forced to sell their farms, they'll come here," Sybil told them. "I'll make sure they're sent on the trail to join you."

"But our families will think we're dead," Ebar said.

"That belief will protect them."

Ord's shoulders sagged. "We have little choice. Not if we value their safety."

Ebar nodded unhappily.

"You can stay here with us until Hilbrand is ready to travel so you can walk together. We have a safe place where you can hide." Sybil turned to Priestess Gilda. "Take them to it now. We'll move Hilbrand there too."

Alyse followed the two deserters with her eyes until Gilda closed the door behind them. Then she felt Hilbrand's forehead again. She detected no change in his fever but could tell he was resting more comfortably. She smiled at Kendra and said, "Thank you for helping me. Hilbrand would've died without your assistance."

"He would've died even with my help if you'd had less skill and power," Kendra said.

Alyse watched Hilbrand while a tiredness spread through her like a heavy mist, a sensation she found more fulfilling than exhausting. *I cured him.* Reluctantly, she turned to Priestess Sybil. "Now that you've returned, I suppose you'll want Hilbrand under your care."

"It might be better if Alyse saw Hilbrand's treatment through to the end," Kendra said before Sybil could reply. "It would be good training for her. And probably safe enough. I don't think the city watchers want to tangle with the Dejunes."

The suggestion numbed Alyse's mind.

Sybil's brows furrowed into a pensive frown. "Kendra might be right. But if you should be caught hiding deserters and treating one of them—"

"I'm a healer, and Hilbrand's my patient," Alyse said. "I'll see this through."

"And I'm Alyse's backwatcher," Kate said. "So I'm in on this too."

Sybil nodded her agreement.

I've committed two treasonable offenses already. The realization bit into Alyse with the sharpness of a wolf's teeth. And now she would oversee Hilbrand's healing. *A third treasonable offense.* But the way the Magesterium—and her own family—treated the women and men who fought for their country in the legions and the sea service sent outrage sweeping through Alyse like a tornado. She had to do something to oppose it even if to simply heal Hilbrand and send him and his friends off on the underground trail, no matter the consequences to herself.

Then another thought struck Alyse, trapping her breath in her lungs and making her light-headed. *Have I become a malcontent?*

If so, she'd accept that label.

## CHAPTER 47

Livia's Party

A HAND CLAPPED OVER Rill's mouth woke him from a sound sleep. Before he could struggle, a voice hissed urgently in his ear.

"I'm not going to harm you. Honest. I need your help."

Troy's voice!

His body rigid, Rill looked up. Glimmering candlelight from the night table transformed Troy's face into a dark oval against a darker background.

"I'm going to take my hand away," Troy whispered. "Please don't make a commotion. For Livia's sake."

Livia's name sent apprehension streaking through Rill. He really liked her and feared something had happened to her. As soon as Troy removed his hand, Rill sprang into a sitting position.

"What about Livia?"

The rope mattress sank as Troy sat. "First, I want to make it clear that you're the last person I'd come to for help."

"Then why are you here?"

"Because my mother asked me to. She said there's no one in the household we can trust except you." Troy paused and shot Rill a curious look. "Why would she say that?"

Suspicion made Rill's chest tighten. "You set me up once already by planting your charm under my mattress. Why should I believe you now about Livia?"

"Mother thought you might distrust my motives. So she told me to tell you this. That she likes your Name Day clothes."

Rill's chest loosened. Livia *was* in some sort of trouble. He scrambled out of bed and fumbled for his clothes. By the time he had put on his pants and tunic, his sight had adjusted to the gloomy light provided by the candle Troy had brought with him and placed on the nightstand.

Troy had a dark cloak wrapped around him. Worry lines creased his face. He pointed at the sheathed sword hanging by its belt on a wall peg. "You know how to use that?"

Rill glowered at Troy as he pulled on his black leather boots. "If you don't tell me about Livia right now, you'll see how well I can use it."

"She's in danger."

Dread shimmied up Rill's spine. "What kind?"

"We have to rescue her."

Rill wrapped his fingers around the front of Troy's linen shirt and pulled him close. "What danger—"

Troy pried Rill's fingers loose. "You have to swear to keep this secret. Only you, me, and my mother can know."

"I swear," Rill whispered, wanting to scream the words at Troy but knew the noise would wake up Yall and Jedd. "Now tell me what danger she's in."

Troy was silent as if he dreaded answering the question, which ratcheted up Rill's fear for Livia. Finally, Troy spoke. "She's at a party."

Rill's fear exploded into rage. "At a party! You sneaked into my bedroom and scared the living crap out of me by saying Livia's in danger. And she's just out partying?"

"Lower your voice!" Troy hissed. "Yall and Jedd might hear."

"I don't believe it!" Rill whispered. "Is this some kinda joke? If it is, it ain't funny."

"Let's get something straight." Troy's voice rasped like a file across metal. "I don't like you. But I love my sister." Troy stood and faced Rill, his expression distraught in the pale candlelight. "Look. Livia has a reputation for being wild. She does things just to spite the adults. She keeps pushing the boundaries of what she can get away with. Mother and I do our best to protect her. But tonight she's gone past the limit. If the adults find out, Great-Grandmother Ariella will expel her for sure. And my uncle and grandmother will cheer her on."

"For going to a party?"

"Not just a party. A *wild* party." Troy paused, then said, "In The Slums."

Goose bumps rose like pimples across Rill's shoulders. The Slums. The most notorious neighborhood in Caldon. A place where no respectable citizen ventured except to visit sleazy brothels or to hire dagger women and dagger men who had no scruples about who they murdered. Rill had never visited The Slums and would never risk stepping into it, especially at night—not even on a dare. He wasn't that stupid.

"What's she doing there?" Rill asked as he buckled his sword belt around his waist.

"She's gotten involved with an unsavory lot of noblesse and commoners. Mother's been keeping it secret from the rest of the family. And from me until tonight." Troy bit his upper lip, hesitating. "Livia's never done anything this extreme before."

"Why didn't Lady Shalira stop her?"

"She didn't know Livia had left the compound. I think Livia must've used Illusion magic to get out without being seen."

"Then how did Lady Shalira find out Livia's at the party?"

"From a spy she planted in another family. Someone who's loyal only to Mother. She got word to Mother just a short time ago."

Rill threw his cloak around his shoulders and fastened the clasp. "What's the plan?"

"We're going to bring her back. By force, if necessary."

"How? We can't leave the compound without the protectors on the walls and at the gates knowing. Unless you cast an Illusion spell on us."

Troy shook his head. "I haven't dealt with illusions yet. Uncle Deuth doesn't think much of them. But Mother's going to show us a secret way out." Troy picked up the candleholder and started for the door. "Mother just told me about it. A secret matriarch's tunnel in the matriarch's chamber. She said that many First and Lesser Families have one. In case they need to escape from a charm raid. But only the women know about them. You're sworn to secrecy about that too. Mother told me if Great-Grandmother Ariella learns that she told us about it, Grandmother would expel her."

Slipping out of the room, Rill and Troy stole along the shadowy hallway lit only by a weak moon and starlight filtering through the narrow window slits and then crept downstairs to the matriarch's chamber. Shalira was waiting anxiously inside, holding an oil lamp. She wore a dark-blue cloak over her thin white linen shift. Her ginger-colored, nape-length hair was disheveled from sleeping.

"Hurry!" she said. "We have no time to waste."

She led them up onto the dais and then to the fresco on the back wall depicting the destruction of Euloria. She depressed the image of a tiny stone fragment hidden within a pile of rubble from a destroyed building. Rill started at the sound of a sharp *click* as the fragment moved inward, and a rectangular section of the painting, half the height of a door, moved outward slightly. Shalira pulled the door open the rest of the way to expose a set of narrow stairs leading down into pitch blackness. Two unlit torches lay on the top step. Shalira picked them up and thrust them at Rill.

"Light these after you leave the tunnel," she said. "But do it well away from the door to the outside."

Troy picked up his staff, which was propped next to the doorway, and muttered a Light spell. The orb flared to life, emitting a bright, whitish glow. He bent to go through the opening and then went down the stairs. When Rill started past Shalira, she clutched his arm and whispered fiercely in his ear. "Bring Livia back."

"I will," Rill said and hurried down the staircase.

Troy was waiting impatiently by the bottom step. The white mage light revealed the beginning of a tunnel, its smooth sides wide enough for three women to stand abreast of one another and its ceiling high enough for a tall woman to stand upright.

"Let's go," Troy said.

Rill walked alongside Troy down the passageway, which ran straight for a short while, then curved right. He figured they were moving parallel to the back wall of the rear courtyard. Before long, the tunnel turned left and angled down in a gentle incline that became steeper before gradually leveling off and ending at a closed, iron-bound oak door.

Troy took hold of the latch and murmured an inaudible spell. The light from his staff winked out, plunging the passageway into blackness. Then a faint *click* sounded as Troy lifted the latch. The door swung inward noiselessly to reveal a thick screen of bushes blocking the opening. Troy plunged into the shrubbery, pushing his way through scraggly branches and leaves.

Rill followed on his heels.

They emerged halfway down the slope of The Citadel, on an isolated section that was too steep for buildings to be erected. Above them, the cresent moon cast amber light down on them, and stars sparkled in the sky, like tiny diamonds sprinkled across black velvet. Below them, The Oaks and The Sisters stretched out on either side, both neighborhoods deep in shadows except for occasional pinpricks of bobbing lights—the torches of noblesse and commoners walking along unlit streets on nocturnal ventures of their own. Glancing over his shoulder, Rill saw only bushes and the rocky hillside.

"What happened to the door?" Rill asked.

"Mother told me it's hidden by a powerful Concealment spell," Troy replied. "Let's go. We're entering by Ulbra's Road."

Rill followed Troy around the side of the hill to a secondary street where they paused for Troy to light the torches with a spell.

As they continued, Rill's heart pounded in his chest, the torch in his left hand pushing the darkness back by only a few strides. Most Caldonians, if they went out at night, traveled in armed groups of five or more because nighttime was the most dangerous part of the day-night cycle. The City Watch provided scant protection for the citizens, which was one reason the noblesse relied on backwatchers and protectors to keep them safe. During daylight, the city watchers patrolled only the seven city gates and the area around the Public Square, and during the four nighttime watches, they guarded only the city gates.

From the corner of his eye, Rill noticed Troy was just as tense, gripping his staff in a way that would let him cast a spell in any direction at a instant's notice. Their shared unease gave Rill a strange satisfaction. Troy's nerves weren't any better than his own.

Every so often, they encountered groups of noblesse men and women, accompanied by backwatchers, who were returning from banquets. Rill and Troy would pull their cloak hoods over their heads and cross to the opposite side of the road. A few times, they heard boisterous shouts and bawdy songs from drunken roisterers who were out of sight up ahead. At the first sounds, Rill and Troy would extinguish their torches and scurry into the shadows until the carousers staggered by on their way home from drinking parties, brothels, or gambling dens, their torchlight lurching just as drunkenly as the revelers.

Their route took them past The Slums, sprawled out below them in a scattered patchwork of light and blackness. At last they reached the street that led down to the base of the hill. Rill's quick-thumping heart missed a beat as he stepped upon the cobbles of Ulbra's Road. On the left side, the buildings that formed a border of The Tombs sat in darkness and silence.

The right side marked the edge of The Slums. The windows on the first floors of the dilapidated tenements, crafts shops, and stores facing the road were shuttered while pale candlelight shivered in open second- and third-floor windows. The harsh glare of lamplight burning in the windows of taverns and bars made those buildings stand out like beacons for lost sailors. An incessant clamor of voices came from inside—ribald songs, raucous laughter, and shouting.

Rill wondered how the Tombs dwellers across the road could sleep at night with all that rumpus. Ahead of Rill, clusters of laughing, drunken men and women—their faces thrown into faint detail by the torches they carried—plunged into the dark, narrow streets that led into the heart of The Slums or emerged from those shadows onto the thoroughfare.

From somewhere close came a faint plea for help that was suddenly cut short. Rill stopped and glanced around apprehensively. "What was that?"

Troy shrugged indifferently. "Probably the last sound some poor slob will ever make."

Rill gulped down one breath after another.

"Have you ever killed anyone?" Troy asked.

"No. Have you?"

"Yes. More than once. And let me tell you something. Life to the scum who live here is cheaper than a pail of seawater. If you need to use your sword, don't hesitate. Your enemy won't." Troy resumed walking. "When—not if—we meet someone, act tough. Even if you're shitting in your pants. They don't respect softness here. Watch me and follow my lead."

Cautiously, they walked block after block along Ulbra's Road, passing rowdy groups of noblesse and commoners and spotting silhouettes moving furtively in the darkness. Troy paused at a side street that was wide enough for a horse-drawn cart, and then, with a slight nod to himself as if in confirmation, turned into it. Rill got the impression Troy either knew where he was going or had been given excellent directions.

Like the tenements and craft shops on Ulbra's Road, closed shutters protected the first-floor windows of the buildings on this street while many of the higher-story windows were open to the warm night air of early First Fruits season. Many windows were dark, but some emitted mellow glows. Several times, doors opened quickly and men stole out with their heads bent low and scuttled away like rats returning to their holes. The alleyways were narrow, and the light from Rill's and Troy's torches hardly made a dent in the utter blackness between the buildings. Rill's stomach churned at the stench of rotten garbage mixed with urine that pervaded the air.

An intersection lay ahead. When Rill and Troy were halfway to it, three dark figures appeared from around a corner and sauntered toward them.

"They don't have torches," Troy said softly. "That's not good. It means they're from here. Prepare yourself. Make eye contact. And, whatever happens, don't flinch."

Rill hardened his features and moved his right hand closer to his sword grip. His heart banged so hard against his chest he feared it might burst through ribs and flesh. When the men entered the fringes of the twin torchlights, Rill noted their dirty, tattered clothes.

Troy activated his charm in a voice loud enough for the men to hear. "Actus."

Rill exchanged looks with one of the strangers, a burly man who was a little taller than himself, and hoped he projected a convincing display of toughness. The man's gaze was so cold and fearsome that Rill's first instinct was to look away. It took a great force of will for Rill to maintain his pose. The burly man intentionally shoved Rill as he passed, and Rill pushed back equally hard. After the trio went by, Rill and Troy turned to follow them with their eyes until the three turned onto another street and disappeared from sight.

Relief seeped out of Rill in a long sigh.

Troy resumed walking. At the intersection, he took a right and then a left at the crossway of four narrow streets. Rill followed Troy down one of them, which ended at a wide road lined with dilapidated houses, three-story tenements, taverns, and pubs. Spirited lamplight danced in open windows on many of the first and upper floors, illuminating the street.

This area was more lively than the others Rill had passed through. Bursts of raucous laughter, music, and rowdy singing came from drinking places along the road. "Painted ladies"—girls and women in short, flimsy shifts and wearing heavy makeup—stood in entryways or sashayed up and down the street. Rill guessed their ages ranged from the teens to the forties or fifties.

A pair of girls in their mid-teens approached Rill and Troy with expectant smiles, but a sharp word from Troy made them veer away. One of the girls made an obscene gesture at them. From a doorway across the street, a young woman blew Rill a kiss.

Rill's discomfort must have shown on his face because she laughed and sent him another kiss. Something seemed odd about her. Rill peered more closely at her. His eyes popped out and he nudged Troy. "That woman . . . she's a man!"

Troy regarded him for a moment, an amused smile on his lips. Rill's face flushed from embarrassment. Why hadn't his parents ever told him about things like this? Now he really looked like a country bumpkin compared to Troy.

After going through a couple more intersections, Troy stopped by a two-story house that stood apart from the other buildings. Its façade and sides were clean and freshly painted. Troy extinguished his torch and placed it on the ground near the doorstep.

"What's this place?" Rill asked as he placed his dead torch beside Troy's.

"A pleasure house," Troy replied. "It's for people who want to have parties, but don't want to be seen having them."

He rapped smartly on the front door with the orb of his staff. A young servant girl in a clean lavender dress answered the knocks. Her gaze quickly took in Troy's expensive clothes and Rill's livery. She made a slight bow to Troy.

"Welcome, Lord, to—"

Troy brushed past her, and Rill followed him into a vestibule that was brightly lit by expensive-looking oil lamps set in sconces. A staircase opposite the entrance led to the second floor. A corridor ran past the stairs and disappeared deeper inside the house.

"A girl came here for a private party with friends," Troy said briskly. "She's petite and plump, with black curly hair that comes down to her shoulders. Dark complexion. Heart-shaped face. Dark-blue eyes."

The girl's expression became guarded. "I'm sorry, Lord. There's no one here who fits that description."

Troy scowled at her. "Don't play games with me."

"I'm not, Lord. I'm being truthful."

"You're lying."

"Even if she is here, the names of our clients are confidential."

Troy banged his staff on the floor. "Bring me the mistress of the house—now!"

One of the side doors opened, and two men stepped into the vestibule. They were of normal height, one thin and wiry and the other brawny, with muscles bulging under his expensive tunic. Both wore swords. The hard glint of their eyes told Rill they were ruthless and would maim or kill without compunction.

The wiry man looked Troy up and down while Troy stood in frosty silence, contempt on his face. "Are these boys bothering you, Nellar?" the man asked.

"They've come inquiring after one of our clients."

"I asked to see the mistress of the house," Troy said in a commanding tone.

"What business do you have with our clients?" the man asked.

"That's between me and your mistress, not her hirelings."

"We don't tolerate uppity noblesse here."

"And I don't tolerate uppity servants." Troy jerked a thumb at Rill. "Take a look at his livery. Do you really want to anger the family he serves?"

The man's gaze moved to Rill. "Fetch the mistress," he told Nellar.

Nellar scooted through another doorway and a short time later returned with a fat, middle-aged woman who wore a stylish dress. The woman made a signal to the men, who returned to the room they'd been in. Nellar scampered away too.

The woman introduced herself as the mistress of the house and asked how she could help. Troy answered that he was looking for a girl and described Livia to her. "Her friends rented a room here for a private party," he concluded.

"You must realize, Lord," the woman said with a polite smile, "that we keep the names of our clients private."

Troy's smile matched hers. "You can rest assured that I'd like to keep this matter confidential among the three of us. If I have to involve the girl's family in the matter, the consequences could be extremely bad for your establishment, and for you. Her family has a long reach."

The woman turned her gaze to Rill, letting it linger on his livery. "She's upstairs. Last door on the left. And please don't make a scene."

"I'll keep things as undramatic as possible," Troy said.

Upstairs, Rill and Troy went to the end of the hall, passing closed doors through which came moans and grunts of women and men making love, and stopped by the left door at the end of the hallway. A sudden burst of raucous laughter erupted on the other side. Turning to Rill, Troy put a finger to his lips, ordering silence. He gently lifted the latch—and kicked the door open.

Low flames from oil lamps kept the large room in perpetual gloom. Pillows and mattresses were strewn all over the floor. Thirteen or fourteen men and women in their late teens to early twenties were on the mattresses in various stages of undress. They gawked at Troy.

One of the men climbed off a pair of women he'd been kissing and climbed unsteadily to his feet. "Whas da meanin' of this?" he said in a drunken, muddled voice.

Troy aimed his staff at him, muttered a spell, and an invisible force hurled the man backward against the two women.

Some partiers glanced at staffs that were propped against a wall. Troy uttered another spell, which sent the staffs flying to the far side of the room.

Rill spotted Livia sitting next to a young man. Her eyes appeared glazed as if she were drunk or drugged. She wore only her white shift, which clung to her plump body. "There she is."

"I see her," Troy said. "If any of these bastards move, cut them down."

Rill drew his sword. "Gladly."

Troy went to Livia and hauled her to her feet. She tried to pull away, but he held her fast by the wrist.

"You have no right coming here," she said, slurring her words.

"I have every right." Troy shoved her toward a pile of clothes by the rear wall. "Get dressed."

The force of Troy's push made her stagger and tumble onto the clothing. Kneeling, she pawed through tunics, shirts, pants, and dresses until she found her own dress.

"Help her," Troy told Rill. "Then get her outside."

Troy turned to confront the partiers.

Sheathing his sword, Rill helped Livia pull the dress on and laced up the back. She leaned heavily on him for support while she put on her shoes.

"Come on," Rill said, grabbing her hand and helping her into the hallway. The smell of wine on her breath was strong in his nostrils.

Troy picked up Livia's staff from the ones he'd scattered. Then, keeping his eyes on the partiers, he backed to the doorway. They watched him with a mixture of inebriated anger and wariness.

Pausing on the threshold, Troy raked his raging gaze across their faces like a scythe cutting through hay. "The party's over for Livia," he said. "Her association with you is over too. You know who I am. And I know who each and every one of you is." He paused to let his words sink in. "This is my promise to you. If any of you speaks to my sister again, your family will answer to mine for it. And you personally will answer to me."

Troy swept his staff across the partiers, and an invisible wind hurled them backward across the floor. Then he seized Livia by the arm. "Watch my back," Troy told Rill as they left the room, and Troy dragged Livia down the hallway.

Dropping a few paces behind, Rill followed them out of the pleasure house. In the street, Troy passed a wobbly Livia over to him. "Take this too," he said, handing Rill Livia's staff. "I need to keep one hand free to use my staff if we come up against anyone."

After relighting their torches, they headed back the way they'd come. Rill found it awkward supporting a drunken, staggering Livia with his left arm while he gripped both her staff and the torch in his right hand. He worried constantly about what he would do if he needed to draw his sword. He'd have to drop all three—Livia, staff, and torch. Not a good reaction to danger. To make matters worse, he and Troy had to adjust their pace to Livia's, which slowed them down considerably.

"I hate you, Troy," Livia mumbled. "I was havin' fun."

"Do you think they'll follow us?" Rill asked, shifting Livia's weight on his arm and readjusting his grip on the torch and staff.

Livia kissed Rill's cheek as he dragged her along. "I like you, Rill," she murmured. "Ever since I met you, I have."

"Of course not," Troy said. "They're already back to partying. I want to get out of The Slums fast. Being weighed down with Livia makes us easy prey."

Livia pressed her body against Rill. "I really, *really* like you."

"You're drunk," Rill told her softly, in a kind voice.

Rill's adrenaline was in a constant rush, and Livia's weight on their progress was a constant drag. It seemed to take forever before they reached the wide street where Rill had seen the "pretty boy." But at last they passed through that road and then the other dark and narrow streets until they were only a few blocks from Ulbra's Road.

Livia moaned. "I don't feel so good."

"We hafta keep going," Rill said.

She made a gagging sound. "I have to throw up."

Troy stopped abruptly. "Well, hurry up and do it."

Livia fell to her hands and knees and vomited on the cobbles.

Bending down, Rill lay the torch and staff on the ground and held the front and back of Livia's head with his hands, the way his mom did whenever he was sick and throwing up.

When she finished, Livia managed a weak smile. "You're a good person, Rill. That's why I like you so much."

"Umm . . . thanks," Rill said. He wished she had said that when she was sober because he liked her a lot but dared not say it because he feared her family's reaction. Rill picked up the torch and staff, then reached down to help Livia to her feet.

Troy's words, spoken low, made him freeze. "Trouble ahead."

Rill looked past Troy. Three shadowy forms stood in front of them at the beginning of the block. Two held swords and the other hefted a battle-ax. The men sauntered toward them.

"I'll handle them," Troy said. "You take care of Livia."

Rill helped Livia the rest of the way up. Despite her inebriated condition, he sensed tension in her body.

The whisper of leather on cobbles sounded from behind. Rill glanced over his shoulder. A pair of men had emerged from an alley half a spear's throw away and were heading toward him. One held a sword, the flat of the blade resting over his shoulder. The other gripped a long, heavy cudgel.

"They're behind us too," Rill said.

"You'll have to handle them," Troy responded.

Rill dropped the staff and then eased Livia back to the ground. Switching the torch to his left hand, he drew his sword with his right.

The men approached into the torchlight. Rill recognized the cudgel bearer as the burly man who'd bumped into him earlier. His companion was tall and had a short beard. His arms were longer than Rill's, which meant he had a longer reach.

Rill hoped the swordsman wasn't proficient with his weapon.

The burly man charged and swung his cudgel.

Rill parried the blow with the flat of his blade, then shoved the torch in the man's face. The man screamed and dropped his club, his hands clutching at seared flesh. Rill thrust his blade into the man's stomach.

"Rill, watch out!" Livia screamed.

Rill spun around just in time to block the bearded man's sword swing to his head. The force of the blow against his blade knocked Rill off-balance. The man shouldered him against a tenement window. Rill struck the windowsill hard. Quick as a striking snake, the man's sword lashed out at Rill. Clumsily, Rill parried the stroke, but the sword flew from his hand.

The man brought his sword back to deliver a killing strike. A mage's staff struck the elbow of his sword arm. With a howl, he dropped his weapon. Moments later, the mage's staff swung past him and struck Rill on the knee.

Pain seared Rill's leg, and he collapsed to the ground. As he fell, he caught a glimpse of Livia, her staff still in her hand, with a horrified expression on her face.

She raised her staff to swing again at the man, but he ducked under it and punched her in the stomach. Livia dropped the staff and doubled over.

"Bitch!" the man said. Picking up his sword, he raised it to strike Livia.

Ignoring his pain, Rill jumped to his feet and flung himself at the man, who crashed backward against the wooden façade of the tenement and fell to the ground.

Rill went down with the man, and rolled on top of him.

The man kneed Rill in the groin.

Rill howled, fell backward, then painfully pushed himself to his knees.

But the man was already towering above, intertwining his fingers and locking his elbows. He clubbed Rill on the side of the head.

The strength of the blow knocked Rill sideways to the ground. Groaning, he rolled onto his back.

The man picked up his sword, clasping the handle in both hands and stood over Rill. He raised the sword and made ready to plunge it into Rill's belly. "Bastard!"

"Troy, help!" Livia screamed.

A sliver of red struck the swordsman in the back, pitching him onto the clay-brick sidewalk.

Livia crawled to Rill. "I'm sorry! I didn't mean to hit you. I was aiming at him."

Rill moistened his mouth to speak.

Livia wrapped her arms around him and put her head on his chest. "I would never ever hurt you. Never!"

Rill grinned weakly at her and stroked her curly black hair. "I'm alive, thanks to you."

Troy's legs appeared in front of Rill. Then an arm reached down and helped him to his feet. "Lucky for you I just finished with the third man." Troy grinned at Livia who was on hands and knees beside Rill. "It looks like a little excitement sobered up my sister."

"Oh!" Livia said. "I . . . I'm going to puke . . . again." She spewed her stomach's contents on the dead man. When she finished, Rill helped her to her feet, and she leaned against him for support. Her body felt warm against his own.

Troy's torch had been hacked to pieces and Rill's was just about burnt out. "We'll use mage light," Troy said and cast the spell that set his staff's orb glowing white. "Let's go, Livia. Mother's waiting for us."

"I'm in for it now," Livia muttered.

Troy led the way. As Rill limped by the bodies of the three men Troy had fought, he noticed two had died from Fire Bolts, but the third had been stabbed in the chest. Troy's staff had a spring-loaded blade. Rill's respect for Troy grudgingly increased. He could do more than just cast spells in a fight.

By the time they reached the entrance to the matriarch's tunnel, Rill was walking normally again, and Livia had stopped only once more to vomit. They hurried through the passageway, eager to return and put the night behind them.

When they emerged on the dais, Shalira was there waiting anxiously for them. She pulled Livia into a hug. "Thank the Goddess you're safe!" She noted Rill's dirty clothes and scrapes. "Are you all right?"

Rill smiled tiredly. "I'm fine."

"I'll bring bandages and ointments for cleansing wounds to your room when I finish with Livia."

Troy laid a hand on Rill's shoulder. "Thanks."

Livia groaned. "I don't feel so good."

"Let's get her to her bedroom," Shalira said.

Rill reached for Livia's arm, but Shalira stopped him. "Troy and I can handle it." She put a hand on his cheek and smiled warmly at him. "Thank you, Rill. You'll never know how much this means to us . . . to *both* of us."

Rill sneaked back to his room, where he sat on his bed in the darkness and thought about what had happened. He'd killed his first man. He found it strange that he didn't feel sick or remorseful about it. Perhaps the fight with the rohan in the cave had hardened him. Or maybe he simply considered Livia's life to be much more valuable than a cutthroat's, which it was.

And Troy had thanked him for helping. In fact, he'd actually sounded grateful.

Then Shalira's parting words echoed in his head: "You'll never know how much this means to us . . . to both of us." Rill scratched his head, perplexed. *What did she mean by that?*

## CHAPTER 48

Revelation

WHEN LIVIA DIDN'T APPEAR for breakfast the next morning, Shalira informed the family that Livia wasn't feeling well. "It's that time of month," she said.

Ariella crinkled her brow in thought. "Livia's sacred time of the month seems off. I recall her having it less than a month ago. Is something wrong with her?"

Shalira glanced quickly at Troy and Rill. "Grandmother, please! Let's not discuss Livia's personal matters in front of the boys. It would embarrass her if she knew."

"As if 'the boys' don't already know about these things," Ariella said. "Well, we can't have her lollygagging about all day. Have Jocelynn see her."

Shalira inclined her head in acknowledgment, but Rill knew she wouldn't follow through by having the family healer discover Livia was suffering from a hangover.

That afternoon when Rill returned from practicing spellcasting in Mages' Field, Livia intercepted him as he headed for the second-floor stairs. She gave him a warm smile, which he returned with one just as warm. Concern flared up in him, though, when he noticed her bloodshot eyes.

"How are you feeling?" Rill asked.

"Much better, thanks."

"I'm glad to hear it."

Livia took hold of Rill's hand, sending a tingling sensation coursing through his body. "Come with me."

"Where?"

"Just come."

She led him downstairs into a room that was partially lit by the late afternoon sun burning through a single window. Taking hold of Rill's other hand, Livia turned to face him. "I just want to thank you for what you did last night. What I was doing in that place was stupid."

The image of Livia in her flimsy linen shift popped into Rill's mind, and he blushed. "That's all right. I'm glad you didn't get into any trouble . . . other than, uh . . . you know . . . drinking too much."

Livia's warm, dark-blue eyes stared into Rill's. "I remember what I said to you last night. Do you?"

'I like you, Rill. Ever since I met you, I have.' "Yeah."

"I meant what I said. You're a good person. That's why I like you so much. So *very* much."

Her words set Rill's heart thumping. "I like you too. For a long time. But I've been afraid to say it."

"Don't be." Livia moved her face closer to his, and then their lips met. They wrapped their arms around each other, pressing their bodies together. Rill closed his eyes as Livia parted her lips—

And was brutally torn from his embrace and flung across the room. Livia screamed when her body smacked against the wall, and she collapsed to the floor. Fear ripped through Rill like jagged lightning as Deuth Estati towered over him, tall and furious.

Deuth turned to Livia, eyes crackling blue fire. "You slut! I told you he wasn't for you."

Livia picked herself up and confronted him just as angrily. "Nothing I do satisfies you. I can never meet your oh-so-high standards. Whatever I say, you think is stupid. I'm eighteen now, and you don't think I'm good enough to marry an ally—"

"Because you're not."

Livia took hold of Rill's arm. "I've found a boy I like, and you're not going to take him from me. Not like you did the others. I don't care if—"

Deuth forced them apart violently. "I said Rill isn't for you."

Livia stumbled, then, catching her balance, turned toward Deuth,. Her eyes spat blue sparks at him. "Give me one good reason. Just one."

A vein on Deuth's throat throbbed. "You really want to know?"

"Yes."

"If I tell you, you'll have to keep it to yourself. On pain of expulsion." Deuth's gaze hopped to Rill. "Both of you."

Rill nodded his acceptance, just as anxious as Livia to know Deuth's reason.

Deuth's raging eyes met Livia's head-on. "Because he's . . . your brother."

Stunned, Rill's brain froze.

## CHAPTER 49

Livia's Story

RILL GAWKED AT LIVIA while his thoughts swirled as if they were flotsam and jetsam caught up in a whirlpool. He glanced at Livia. Her dull blue eyes told him that Deuth's words had blown her mind away too. He tore his eyes away from hers and moved them to Deuth, working his mouth to speak, but his tongue was frozen in his mouth.

"My brother!" Livia backed away from Deuth. "No. That's not possible."

Livia's response quickly thawed Rill's tongue. "You're crazy!" He shook his head back and forth as if he were punch drunk. "She ain't my sister."

Deuth's gaze slipped from Livia to Rill, fury stretching his lips into a long, tight line. "You're half brother and half sister."

Livia rubbed her forehead, her eyes squinched in confusion. "How can Rill be my half brother?"

"Through your mother."

"Shalira?"

"No." Deuth paused as if he were having trouble dislodging the next words from his mouth. "Through Carolyn."

Livia's black eyebrows squished together into a puzzled frown. "Who's Carolyn?"

"My older sister."

Livia's frown deepened. "What older sister? My mother's your only sister."

Deuth ran a hand through his cinnamon hair. "Shalira's my younger sister. Carolyn was my older sister. She's your mother, not Shalira."

Livia stared at Deuth, eyes and mouth wide open. "That's impossible!"

"It's true."

Livia chewed her lip while she digested the information. "Then . . . Shalira is—"

"Your aunt."

"You said Carolyn *was* my mother. She's dead?"

"Yes."

"If Shalira's my aunt," Livia said, "how can Troy be my brother?"

"He's not," Deuth replied. "He's your cousin."

"My cousin!" Anger turned Livia's body rigid. "Damn you! All my life, I've been living a lie, and you knew it. The entire family knew it."

"Not Troy—"

Livia stepped toward Deuth until only a hand's width separated them. "How could you do this to me—"

"Not *to* you. *For* you."

Rill had listened to the weird exchange between Livia and Deuth, while inside his head, the world as he knew it had shifted around in confusion, like pieces of colored glass in a kaleidoscope. Now the pattern in Rill's mental kaleidoscope settled into place, but he couldn't discern how his own piece fit into this weird new design. "What does this . . . this Carolyn hafta do with me?" he asked Deuth. "I ain't never heard of her before neither."

"That's because she changed her name." Deuth looked pointedly at Rill. "To Kendra."

A sudden dizziness struck Rill, and he staggered backward. He shook his head in disbelief like a dog refusing to give up a beloved toy clenched in its teeth. "My mom's a commoner. How can she be an Estati?"

Livia peered at Deuth through slitted eyes. "You owe us both an explanation."

Deuth massaged the back of his head as if the confrontation had made it ache. "Yes. I suppose I do."

"Then start talking," Rill said, not caring if his harsh tone angered Deuth.

Deuth pulled up a chair and sank into it, then motioned for Rill and Livia to sit too. They remained standing in front of him, Rill's arms crossed and his stance wide and Livia's fists on her hips.

It took Deuth a long while to assemble his thoughts. "Carolyn had a natural gift for magic," he said. "She could've been one of the most powerful archmages ever. Perhaps even as powerful as The Twins, Ulbra and Ulbridge Thane. But she turned against her own kind, the noblesse, and took up with a commoner. A . . . blacksmith."

A blacksmith! The revelation sent Rill's mind whirling in confusion again. "My dad!"

"Yes." Deuth rubbed a thumb across his cheek and seemed reluctant to continue.

Rill uncrossed his arms and bent toward Deuth. "Go on."

"Carolyn changed her name to Kendra. The blacksmith's matriarch adopted her. She married the blacksmith, and she bore him a son." Deuth looked at Rill, dark-blue eyes meeting dark-blue eyes. "You're that son."

Rill opened his mouth into a gigantic O as a single thought whirled around in his head as if caught up in a twister. *My mom's an Estati and an archmage. And I inherited her power.* His chest tingled.

Deuth's lips tightened, and his expression turned inward as if recalling a bitter memory. "Carolyn disgraced our family and we expelled her," Deuth said. "She was no longer an Estati. So we erased all mention of her from our family records. She can never join our ancestors in the Afterworld. To all Estati—past, present, and future—Carolyn Estati never existed."

Deuth's words made the twister in Rill's head vanish. *She ain't an Estati. Not no more. But the Estatis support me. They'll help me become noblesse*. Rill felt his connection with the Estatis tighten.

"Who's my father?" Livia asked.

"Brico Svagga."

Livia put a hand to her throat, white faced. "Goddess preserve me!"

Deuth gave a disdainful snort. "Fortunately for you, we're a matrilineal society. So kinship is through your mother, not your father."

"The thought of Svagga blood in my veins makes me want to puke!"

"Your blood is Estati, not Svagga," Deuth said. "And Shalira has been more of a mother to you than Carolyn. Your birth mother discarded you, the fruit of her womb, to take up with a commoner. An uneducated blacksmith who stinks of sweat and horses."

"How does my mo . . . Shalira fit into this?" Livia asked.

"Carolyn's betrayal created the worst scandal among the noblesse in generations," Deuth said, staring into the empty space between the siblings. "The First Families, allies and enemies alike, forbade anyone to ever mention her name again."

Suddenly restless, Deuth stood and paced around the room. "But you were an Estati, not a Svagga. You needed a mother. So Shalira and Alger Berne offered to bring you up as their own." His voice turned bitter. "You can't imagine the scandal Carolyn caused among the noblesse. Her betrayal threatened our alliance with the Svaggas because she left Brico, her lawful husband, without a divorce, for that . . . that *blacksmith*." Deuth lapsed into silence, clenching his teeth so hard the muscles in his cheeks bulged.

"There's more to this story, ain't there," Rill said.

Deuth nodded. "I was engaged to marry Altonia Portia, Cato's younger sister. It was an opportunity to have Portia switch from the Traditionali to our Noblessari faction." Deuth's face took on a faraway look and his features softened. "We were in love, Altonia and I. Can you imagine that—two noblesse marrying for love?" Deuth's distant look morphed into a sour expression. "But Grandmother forced me to marry Adele Svagga instead to keep our alliance with the Svaggas intact. Altonia ended up marrying a rabid Traditionali."

Deuth's story caused a jumble of emotions to swirl through Rill. Surprise. Anger. Bitterness. Disbelief. Pity. Curiosity. "You never saw her again?" he asked softly.

"We tried once," Deuth replied. "Secretly. But her husband learned about it. He told his matriarch, and she told Malia, who's Altonia's matriarch, and Ariella. Ariella ordered me to keep away from Adele. And Malia told Altonia if she even so much as spoke to me again, she'd expel her. I couldn't let that happen. So I've never seen her since." Deuth's expression became fevered and tense. "Your mother deprived me of my happiness so she could have hers."

Rill squirmed inside, embarrassed by Deuth's openness. Yet an ugly flower of doubt blossomed inside him, and he had to know the answer. "Is that why you championed my cause—to get even with my mom?"

Deuth's face radiated surprise. "No, no. It's just the opposite. To give you the chance you never had. To become a mage and noblesse. To found your own noblesse commoner family."

Rill breathed out a silent sigh of relief while appreciation for Deuth's and his family's generosity expanded his heart.

Livia glared at Deuth, arms still rigid and hands clasping and unclasping. "All this time, the noblesse have known about my real mother, and I haven't."

Deuth swatted her accusation aside as if it were a troublesome fly. "Not all of them. Just the older generations. Once they join their ancestors, no one will know. The secret will be safe."

"And that's why the noblesse keep calling me the 'blacksmith's son,'" Rill said. "'Cause they know the truth. I bet everyone in The Kings knows too."

"Only the older ones," Deuth said with a shrug. "But, like us, those commoners will die off too."

Rage blew through Rill with hurricane force. Everyone in Caldon knew the truth about their parentage but him and Livia. That knowledge drew him closer to his new-found sister.

Deuth turned to Rill. "You were cheated."

"Cheated. How?"

"You were born after we expelled your mother. If she had become pregnant with you—even by the blacksmith—before she was expelled, you would have been born an Estati instead of a Larkin because kinship passes through the mother. You would have been noblesse—"

Rill's legs wobbled beneath him. He gripped the top rail of a chair to steady himself. "I could of been born noblesse?"

"Yes. And it's your mother's fault you weren't."

Rill's fingers tightened on the chair rail while anger ravaged his mind and body. He wanted to pick up the chair and slam it against the floor.

Deuth put a hand on Rill's shoulder. "My family's been keeping an eye on you all these years. Your determination to become a mage impressed all of us. That's why Lady Ariella agreed to champion your cause and had me take you on as my apprentice. If you fulfill our expectations, we'll adopt you into our family. You'll become an Estati."

Joyful tears rolled down Rill's cheeks. The Estatis had faith in him and his abilities. Whatever Lord Deuth wanted him to do to become a mage, he'd do without question. Then anger hot as a volcano's lava bubbled inside him, sweeping aside the joy. "My parents tried to destroy my life. Almost before it had begun."

Deuth nodded his agreement. "They tried to stop you from occupying your rightful place in the world."

"And if it hadn't been for you, Lord Deuth, they would of succeeded." Outrage sparked a wildfire inside Rill. "It's time I had it out with them."

"That's right," Deuth said. "Tell them what you think."

That was exactly what Rill intended to do.

## CHAPTER 50

Showdown

THE BURNING AFTERNOON SUN matched Rill's temper as he crossed the cobblestone courtyard of his family's house with long, angry strides. The *clang, clang, clang* from the smithy assaulted his ears. Faith bounded toward him, barking happily, but Rill shoved her away when she came alongside him. "Git. I ain't got no time for you."

The hammering in the smithy stopped, and Marc appeared in the doorway in his brown leather blacksmith's apron. "Rill, come here! I wanna speak to you."

Ignoring him, Rill went up to the house and barged into the kitchen. The door slammed against the wall with a loud bang.

Kendra, her back to him, had just started to put a tray containing several loaves of raw sourdough bread into the beehive oven built into the wall beside the hearth. She spun around, the tray in her hands.

Rill stopped by the preparation table and glowered at her.

Kendra slid the tray into the oven, closed the iron door, and turned to him again. Anger shimmered across her face while she wiped her hands on a towel. "My, my, ain't you the lofty one," she said, taking in his black uniform. "All decked out in your Estati finery. And ready to do your master's bidding, no matter who you hurt."

Behind Rill, the front door opened and closed quietly and footsteps crossed the floorboards. Passing through Rill's side vision, Marc stopped beside Kendra, folded his arms, and regarded Rill sternly.

"We heard what you did to Alain Develle, the spice seller in The Sisters," Marc said. "You're becoming quite the Estati henchman, depriving an honest man and his family of a living."

Rill's eyes cast fireballs at his father. "Shut up . . . *blacksmith!*"

Marc tensed, the muscles exposed by the rolled-up sleeves of his sweat-stained linen shirt. He stepped toward Rill, but Kendra put a hand on his arm.

"He didn't come here to talk about that."

"I just learned the truth about you," Rill said through gritted teeth.

Kendra tossed the hand towel onto the preparation table and brushed flour off the apron protecting her plain, homespun dress. Then, hands on hips, she looked Rill in the eye. "Go on."

"You're Deuth Estati's sister."

"*Was*, not is," Kendra said. "I'm a Larkin now."

"I could of been born noblesse if you hadn't married this"—Rill gestured angrily at his dad—"*blacksmith.*"

"Who told you that?"

"Lord Deuth himself."

"He's lying."

"He ain't!" In a voice trembling with fury, Rill related what Deuth had told him.

Kendra's body became more rigid as he spoke, and her frosty blue eyes slowly morphed into two balls of dark-blue fire. "Lies! All lies! He's using you to take his revenge on me. I feared he'd do it. That's why I didn't want you to go to your Name Day Celebration. If you weren't declared a mage, you'd be safe from his corrupting influence." Kendra slammed a fist on the preparation table, making the dirty bowls and cooking utensils jump. "It's high time he and I had it out." She spun toward the door.

Marc gripped her arm and pulled her back around. She bared her teeth at him like a raging female wolf protecting her cub from a predator. Marc put his hands on her shoulders and looked her in the eyes. "Calm down. Anger ain't gonna get you nowhere. Just make things worse."

Kendra tried to wrench free, but he held her firm. "No, by Goddess! He won't harm my boy."

"He ain't a boy no more. He's a man."

"We have to protect him."

"There ain't nothin' we can do." Marc tenderly rearranged a loose lock of scarlet hair that had fallen near Kendra's eye. "He's gotta make his way on his own now . . . or lose it on his own. It's part of growing up. You had to go through it too." He lowered his voice to a whisper and spoke three words which Rill could barely make out. "Remember little Kendra."

The blue fire in Kendra's eyes died into ashes, and her shoulders slumped. "How can I forget her." Leaning into Marc, she buried her face in his chest and let out a muffled sob against the leather apron.

Rill watched them, his eyes blue ice, his muscles quivering from anger, and his heart as hard as the granite monuments in the monument-maker's front yard next door.

"He should know the truth," Marc said gently. "Maybe it was wrong for us to have kept it from him."

Marc guided Kendra to the eating table, and she slumped onto the bench. He motioned for Rill to join them, but Rill moved to the opposite side of the table. He didn't want to be anywhere near them. Marc sat beside Kendra and slung an arm around her trembling shoulders.

Kendra sucked in a huge lungful of air and eased it out in a long, ragged sigh. "It's true. I used to be Carolyn Estati. Shalira's older sister. I was also a mage."

"An archmage," Rill said in a tone as if he were accusing her of a crime. And he felt as if she had committed a crime, keeping this information from him.

Kendra nodded. "Yes. An archmage. The most powerful one in generations. I wore the Peer charm. Did my former brother tell you that?"

Peer charm. Rill blinked at his mom while the name of one of the most powerful charms in existence spun dizzily in his mind like a child's top. As much as he tried, he couldn't visualize his mom wearing the Peer charm or casting its spells.

"My grandmother, Ariella, gave it to me," Kendra said. "I was the oldest child and an archmage. So wearing it was my birthright. But I gave up the charm. My former brother wears it now."

Rill's mind scrambled to understand why any archmage would give up such a powerful charm, but couldn't. "Why did you give all that up?" he asked.

"Because I hurt people," Kendra replied.

Rill stifled a laugh of disbelief. *My mom hurt people? She's gotta be making all this up.*

Kendra must have read his thought because her mouth formed into a bitter smile. "I was wild back then. And I had a temper, which you inherited, unfortunately. I became addicted to my power. I was ruthless, arrogant, cruel, and self-centered. And I did terrible things to people. Sometimes to further my family's interests and other times . . . well, other times just for the enjoyment. I didn't care who I hurt or how they suffered."

"And you hurt quite a few people," Marc murmured.

"Yes," Kendra said, a choke in her voice. "I still see them in my sleep. Their faces haunt me. And nothing I do can bring me peace."

Breathing heavily, Kendra gripped Marc's hand till her knuckles showed white. Marc seemed not to notice the pressure. He smiled encouragingly at her.

Kendra ran her tongue across her lips. "I formed a group of young rowdies. Noblesse, like myself. The commoners were our targets. We ransacked neighborhoods for fun. Set buildings on fire. Cast spells on people. Stole things. The commoners were petrified of us. We frightened our families as well. But they were too scared to discipline us. After all, I wore the Peer charm and I was powerful. We did all this while Marc was with the Eastern Legions. But when he came home, things changed."

Rill's jaw dropped open. "You fought them?"

"No." Marc gave Rill a crooked smile. "I sued the Estatis in court."

"And lost," Kendra said. "Because the noblesse control the courts. They take care of their own. Even wild, brutal ones like me."

Marc's brown eyes darkened with anger. "We Kings dwellers were the noblesse's clients, but they bribed the court to find against us. We'd sworn fealty to them in return for aid and protection, but they broke their oaths to us. So we ceased being their clients. Instead, we armed ourselves and organized our own defense—"

"And elected your father as their leader," Kendra said with a glint of pride in her watery eyes.

"After all," Marc said, "a well-placed arrow can cut down any mage, no matter how powerful a charm she wears."

"I was outraged with Marc for suing us and for turning the Kings dwellers against us," Kendra said. "So my friends and I decided to pay the Kings dwellers a visit and put them in their place. But we hadn't counted on Tor Larkin being home visiting his family. When Marc and his band of neighborhood defenders confronted us, I thought they were bluffing. And I called his bluff by casting a spell on him. But before I could finish invoking it, Tor shot an arrow into my leg." Kendra pulled her skirt up to her thigh to reveal a thin, white slash.

Rill couldn't hide his surprise at the revelation. He'd seen the scar several times before, but she'd told him it was from a childhood injury. *Another lie.*

"I thought my family would punish Tor for assaulting me," Kendra said, lowering her skirt. "But he had too great a reputation for even an Estati to take on. I couldn't believe it! My family was afraid of him. Afraid of a commoner. But Tor Larkin didn't scare me. So I decided to deal with him myself. I kept my eye on him and bided my time until he visited his mother's house again. Then I set out to kill him." Kendra fell silent, reluctant to continue.

"Go on," Marc said softly.

Kendra inhaled a ragged breath and continued speaking, but now in a tight voice. "Tor and Milco Barr were sword companions. Somehow Milco learned about my plan and rushed to Tor's house to warn him. But Tor had come over here to visit Marc. When Milco learned that, he raced here, every moment fearing he might be too late. But he wasn't. He entered the courtyard when I was halfway to the front door. He called out for me to stop. Marc and Tor heard the commotion and went outside to see what was going on."

Kendra turned her head away, deep lines of pain etched into her face. "I can't go on!"

"Yes you can," Marc said, tenderly stroking her hand. "You must. For Rill's sake."

Kendra swallowed loudly and turned haunted eyes toward Rill. "I was so filled with rage at Milco that I forgot all about Tor. I cast a Fire Bolt at Milco. But Tor pushed him out of the way. At the same time, Tarri's little daughter ran out of the door into the courtyard. The bolt went between Milco and Tor and struck her down." The muscles on Kendra's throat quivered. "Little Kendra died. I murdered an innocent child!"

"Aunt Tarri was married!" Rill said.

"No," Marc responded. "She had a 'love child' by a close friend. The child's name—my niece's name—was Kendra."

His mom's confession jumbled Rill's mental image of his aunt, who always seemed so prim and proper. And altered his feelings about Grandma Sorah and Aunt Marvis. *They all knew about this, but kept it from me. And from Jedd too. I can't trust them either.* "You never told me about Aunt Tarri's daughter."

Kendra struggled to compose herself. "It was before you were born."

"You could of told me anyways."

"Both our families saw no point in raking up the past. And there was no reason for you to know. Little Kendra's joined her Larkin ancestors. Let her rest in peace."

Fury flared up inside Rill like the fierce flames in a blacksmith's force. *What other secrets are they keeping from me?*

Kendra swallowed hard, making her Adam's apple bob, then wet her lips with her tongue. "I was married to Brico Svagga then. Our marriage was loveless, like all noblesse marriages. But I'd had a child by Brico. Livia. She was six months old at the time. Livia was the only living thing I truly loved. When I saw what I'd done to little Kendra, Livia's image burned itself into my brain. I was horrified and fled. The next morning . . ." Kendra choked. "The next morning . . ." Kendra pressed her face against Marc's chest. "I can't go on."

"The next morning," Marc said, wrapping a protective arm around Kendra's shoulders, "I carried my niece's little body in my arms to the Estati compound and demanded justice. But they rallied around Carolyn, and I got none."

Kendra's shoulders shook from weeping, her face nestled against Marc's apron.

"What happened?" Rill asked, spellbound despite his anger.

"She was racked with guilt," a familiar voice said.

Rill twisted around to the doorway to the family area. Cinna and Tarri were standing on the threshold. He wondered how long they'd been eavesdropping.

Cinna and Tarri went to Kendra, who threw herself into Cinna's arms and continued to weep while Tarri placed a comforting hand on her back. Cinna stroked Kendra's brilliant-red locks and cooed to her as if she were a baby.

"Carolyn went to Priestess Sybil for spiritual guidance," Cinna said after a while. "And with the One Goddess's help, she had a religious experience. She vowed never to use her magic powers again. And she also vowed to make amends for taking my granddaughter's life."

"By marrying my dad?" Rill asked.

"No," Cinna replied. "By offering herself in little Kendra's place. I had my doubts about the offer at first. She seemed sincere, but I feared the offer might be part of some trick she and her gang were gonna play on us. But I searched my heart and prayed to the One Goddess for guidance. I felt She wanted me to give Carolyn a chance to redeem herself. So I agreed to a trial period. The next day she publicly renounced her family. I knew then she was sincere 'cause there's no going back from a public renunciation."

Kendra looked at Rill through red, tear-drenched eyes. "They forgave me. Both the Larkins and the Eulands. Can you believe that? They forgave me."

"She earned our forgiveness," Cinna said. "And even though I feared seeing her every day would bring us pain, it didn't bring none. Only love. So we adopted her, and she changed her name from Carolyn to Kendra." Cinna smiled wryly at Rill. "I'm sure you've figured out by now that your mom and dad fell in love and married."

Kendra sat down on the bench at the eating table opposite Rill. She rubbed her knuckles on teary eyes.

"Your mom still has a problem with that temper of hers though," Cinna said. Her brown eyes zeroed in on Rill. "Just like you."

Rill ran their story through his mind, examining every detail. It was so different from Deuth's that it didn't add up. *They're lying.* "Lord Deuth said his family expelled Carolyn."

"'Twas the other way around," Cinna responded. "*She* renounced *them.*"

"Either way," Rill said, "I could of been noblesse if Mom had remained in the family. They wouldn't of cared if my dad was a blacksmith, as long as my mom remained an Estati."

Cinna made a scoffing noise.

"It's true!" Rill said. "Lord Deuth told me so himself. His family would of accepted me as an Estati. They—"

"He's lying," Kendra said, angrily swatting away the rest of her tears. "Deuth would never allow a child mothered by a commoner to be adopted into his family. Especially if he were my child. And Ariella certainly wouldn't either."

Deuth's words spun around in Rill's head. *If she had become pregnant with you—even by the blacksmith—before she was expelled, you would have been born an Estati instead of a Larkin because kinship passes through the mother. You would have been noblesse.* "You're the one who's lying!"

"Oh, Rill," Kendra said. "You're so much like me. You have bad blood in you. My blood. Estati blood. I'd hoped to bring you up away from the temptations of magic that almost destroyed my life. That did destroy the life of a poor, sweet, innocent child and hurt so many other innocent people. But I failed. The lure was always there, no matter how hard I tried to keep you away from it."

"I could of been noblesse," Rill said, anger shooting each word from his mouth, like arrows from a longbow. "But you denied me my birthright by marrying a blacksmith."

Kendra jumped up from the bench, crossed to the other side of the table, took hold of both Rill's shoulders, and shook him. "Rill! You're letting your anger confuse your reason. You never had a chance of being born noblesse because you were conceived *after* I was adopted and married Marc. Not before."

Rill pulled free. "You're lying! Lord Deuth told me himself they would of accepted me as an Estati."

"He's the one who's lying! He's—" Kendra stopped and heaved a dispirited sigh. "Oh, what's the use? You won't believe anything I say."

Hatred of his mother boiled in Rill's chest and spewed out as words from his mouth. "I got news for you. Lord Deuth told me the Estatis will adopt me if I prove myself to them." He derived intense satisfaction from the distress that bloomed on his mother's face. "I can still become noblesse, and there ain't nothin' you can do about it."

"Deuth's using you—"

"He's not!"

The force of his anger made Kendra flinch but she recovered instantly. "He is! He's getting back at mc through you."

"No, he's not."

"The Estatis will never let you become noblesse because—"

Lies, lies, and more lies. "You're lying!" Rill flung the words in Kendra's face.

"Listen to me," Kendra said. "The Estatis' allies will turn against them if they make you noblesse—"

Another lie. "I'll become a magestrate too. Lord Deuth will support me. He told me so himself—"

"The Estatis will never let you step foot inside the Magesterium."

"You denied me my birthright and tried to turn me against my true family. But Lord Deuth—my uncle—is gonna set things straight."

Kendra gripped his arms so hard her nails seemed to bite through the black wool, and shook him. "You've got it all wrong." Frustration and anger vied for domination of her voice. "All I've ever wanted is to protect you."

Lust for revenge against his mother—against his whole family—for denying him his birthright seized Rill. He twisted free of Kendra's grip and hurled a barbed look at her. "I hate you!" Then he raked the four adults with his eyes. "I hate *all* of you. I renounce you. You're no longer my family." Rill turned to leave.

Kendra held out an arm, imploring him, but Cinna pulled it down. "Let him go. There ain't nothin' we can do for him. He's lost to us."

His mom's sobs sent a wave of delicious satisfaction coursing through Rill's veins as he slammed the door behind him. He strode across the cobbles toward the road. *I'll show them. I'll become one of the most powerful archmages ever. And I'll make sure they never forget that they tried to deny me my birthright as an Estati.* Yet, somewhere deep inside his soul, he felt a twinge of guilt at disowning them.

Which he ignored.

He'd tell Lord Deuth what he had done. His renunciation would prove his unquestioned loyalty to the Estatis and his resolve to do whatever it took to have Lady Ariella adopt him into the family.

## CHAPTER 51

Cousins Split

RILL CLUTCHED HIS STAFF for sheer life, trying to prevent the bootmaker from ripping it from his hands. The bootmaker kneed Rill in the groin. Pain shot through Rill like a jagged knife blade. He released the staff. The sudden freedom made him stagger backward, crashing against shelves holding rolls of shoe leather. Grasping between his legs, he fell to the wooden floor. His mind barely registered Magnus struggling with one of the bootmaker's apprentices for control of his own staff.

Rill rolled over onto his side, still clutching his groin.

On the opposite side of the shop, three apprentices had cornered Yall with assorted weapons. One had picked up an oak chair and used it to back Yall into a corner. Yall slashed at the chair, but at the same time another apprentice slammed an ax handle at the blade. Yall's sword went flying. The third was threatening Yall with a long-bladed dagger that he appeared to know how to use.

"Jedd, for Goddess's sake—help me!" Yall shouted.

Rill peered around as the pain between his legs began to fade. He spotted Jedd standing by the front door, near a display of boots, watching.

"Jedd!" Yall screamed.

Jedd went slowly to Yall's aide. He seemed reluctant to help.

Rill got onto his hands and knees. Magnus was still struggling to wrest his staff from the apprentice. But now the bootmaker had Rill's staff and had stopped behind Magnus.

Rill pushed himself onto his feet but ducked as the bootmaker slung the staff over his shoulder, winding up for a swing at Magnus. Rill grabbed the staff just under the orb and yanked it from the bootmaker's hands.

The bootmaker spun around in shock just as Rill shoved the orb into the man's belly. The bootmaker stumbled backward into the counter and slid to the floor.

Turning toward Magnus, Rill quickly activated his charm and cast a Paralyze spell on the apprentice. He wished he could have used a Fire Bolt, but he feared Lord Deuth would disapprove. "Rough them up however much you want, but don't kill anyone," he'd said. "Serious injuries are bad for my clients' morale." Next, Rill cast Paralyze spells on the other three apprentices, ending the fight.

Magnus, his silvery eyes glittering dangerously, approached the bootmaker, who had worked himself into a sitting position, his back against the counter. Magnus stood over him, his legs spread wide apart over the man's legs, like an outraged god peering down at a wayward mortal. Magnus pulled out the now flattened parchment that was tucked behind his belt.

"You're way overdue repaying your loan." Magnus waved the contract at the bootmaker. "The Estatis were going to be magnanimous and let you keep fifty-one percent ownership of your business. But now . . ." He scowled at the bootmaker, the tips of his gray eyebrows plunging so low they almost touched the bridge of his nose. "Now the Estatis are taking full possession of your business—blade, grip, and pommel—for failing to repay your loan."

The bootmaker's eyes opened so wide Rill could see the whites that surrounded his yellowish-brown irises.

After the bootmaker left the shop with his wife, three children, and four sacks full of pitiful belongings, Magnus turned to Jedd. "I'm not at all happy with your performance today. You stood by and watched the bootmaker and his apprentices attack us. You've become increasingly surly and unsupportive with each contract we've enforced. This one takes the prize. You stood aside while three men attacked Yall. Lady Ariella and Lord Deuth won't be happy when I tell them."

On the way back to the Estati compound, Rill took hold of Jedd's arm and stopped so that they fell a few spear lengths behind Magnus and Yall. Ever since he had told Deuth that he had rejected his family, to their faces, the Estatis had become even more approving of him. But Jedd's actions threatened Rill's standing with them. "Why didn't you help us back there? We all were in trouble."

Jedd shrugged indifferently. "I thought you could handle it. Two mages and a backwatcher against a bootmaker and four apprentices."

"That's what you said the last time. When you stood aside while Magnus, Yall, and me had to contend with the swordmaker and his apprentices. Except you held back longer this time. What's wrong with you?"

"I'm a backwatcher—"

Anger at Jedd, mixed with concern with his own status with Deuth, pulled at Rill's guts. "You're my backwatcher. What you do reflects on me."

Jedd, his face empty of emotion, said nothing.

Rill swore at him under his breath. "This attitude of yours is gonna get you in trouble with Lord Deuth. And it's gonna lower his opinion of me."

Jedd snorted, and Rill thought he detected contempt in the noise. "You don't hafta worry about Lord Deuth's opinion of you. He's real pleased with the way you carry out his orders. Taking over clients' businesses. And now kicking the bootmaker and his family out into the street. You're gonna turn into an archmage who will make the Estatis proud."

Jedd quickened his pace to catch up with the others.

Rill watched him go while worry wormed itself into his brain. Jedd had sworn loyalty to the Estatis. If they didn't like his performance, they would expel him. Then he'd become a rohan. And Jedd seemed to be doing all he could to become one.

Rill batted the thought aside as he hurried after Jedd. He had his own objective. To be adopted by the Estatis. And he wouldn't let anything or anyone get in his way.

Not even Jedd.

# # #

A few weeks after the incident with the bootmaker, Rill and Jedd went to Deuth's study to pick up Rill's charm and staff so he could practice in Mages' Field.

They found Deuth at his desk going over some documents. He pushed the parchments aside. "You're not practicing today."

Rill couldn't keep his disappointment off his face. "Why not?"

"Because I have an errand for both of you. You've been on five already, with Magnus and Yall. Magnus has given me good reports about you, Rill."

Rill clasped the praise as if it were a precious jewel. "Thank you, Lord."

Deuth's gaze shifted to Jedd. "Too bad I can't say the same for you. Magnus told me you act surly on the errands. On the last one, you held back from supporting Yall when he needed it." Deuth rubbed his clean-shaven jaw. "The jury is still out on you. You took your time pitching in to help Magnus with the swordmaker. And you took even longer with he bootmaker. Your heart doesn't seem to be in your work."

Rill silently cursed Jedd. He'd told Jedd his uncooperative attitude would get him into trouble. Then pride swelled Rill's chest. *But Lord Deuth ain't criticizin' me 'cause he knows I'm trustworthy.*

"My heart is in backwatching, Lord," Jedd said politely.

"Your heart should be in serving my family," Deuth said. "You gave us your vow."

"To serve as Rill's backwatcher."

Deuth picked up a quill pen and ran a finger along its vein while he studied Jedd. To Rill, the tension in the room mounted, twisting his nerves tighter than a bow bent to the breaking point. At any moment, he expected Deuth to dismiss Jedd.

Jedd, though, waited calmly, with no outward sign of apprehension.

Deuth tossed the pen onto the desk. "My family took you on in deference to Rill. And we're keeping you on for the same reason. But don't think our patience has no limits."

"Thank you, Lord. I'll keep that in mind."

"You'd better."

Deuth handed Rill a rolled-up parchment and explained that Dayson Florens, who owned a wine shop in The Oaks, had borrowed money to expand his business into a combination wine shop and bar and to invest in a wine shipment from overseas, and now Dayson refused to repay the loan. "Pay him a visit. And don't return without either the money or the signed contract," he said.

"You can count on us, Lord," Rill responded as he slipped the contract under his belt.

"I know I can count on at least *one* of you." Deuth's blues eyes glided to Jedd.

Rill waited until he and Jedd were walking along the cobbles on Citadel Road to the Public Square before confronting him. "What were you doing back there? You practically begged Lord Deuth to expel you. Then you'll become a rohan."

"I was reminding him about my duties as a backwatcher."

"You swore an oath—"

"To protect you and the Estati Family. Which doesn't include beating people up to make them sign over their property. That's stealing."

"It ain't stealin'."

Jedd scoffed at Rill's justification. "It is to me. The Estatis are making a mockery of their obligations to their clients."

"That ain't true. Those people refused to meet their obligations to their patron. Other families do the same thing with their clients."

"And they're bad patrons too," Jedd said, his words laced with anger. "A good patron helps her clients. She doesn't use debt as an excuse to take their livelihoods from them."

"They still can keep a share."

"Not the owner's share."

"How much they keep is none of your business."

Jedd kicked at a stone, sending it flying over the cobbles. "Maybe I should make it my business. Yall and Magnus are nothing but thugs. That last time was disgusting. We beat up that poor bootmaker and his apprentices so he'd sign the contract, giving the Estatis over half his business. And then we took over his entire business 'cause he refused. That whole affair made me feel dirtier than the other times." Jedd's tone deepened. "The Estatis are nothing but thieves. And you're becoming just like them."

"I am not!"

Jedd kicked another stone, his anger making it travel farther than the first. "You don't see Milco Barr doing what Yall and Magnus are doing. I bet none of the Estatis even dare suggest he do it."

"You better be careful what you say and do," Rill said. "The Estatis' patience has its limits, and you're wearing it thin."

"My patience has its limits too. I gotta respect myself. That's something you don't seem to be concerned about since you got so chummy with the Estatis."

Rill spun toward Jedd. "If you're gonna say something, come out and say it."

"All right," Jedd said. "You're acting like a trained puppy dog. Lord Deuth snaps his fingers, and you do exactly what he says."

Love for Jedd and his own ambition vied for dominance inside Rill. Jedd was his cousin and his best friend but was angering the Estatis. What if Lord Deuth and Lady Ariella began blaming him for Jedd's bad conduct? And what if they decided that Jedd's conduct reflected so badly on him—Rill—that they wouldn't adopt him into the family? That prospect sent horrifying images of what his failed life would be like afterward, swirling through his head as if scattered by a windstorm. Rill wished he could tell Jedd about his agreement with the Estatis. But he couldn't because he was sworn to secrecy.

Rill stopped and faced Jedd. "What else can I do? I'm Lord Deuth's apprentice. He's gonna help me become a powerful archmage. And a magestrate too."

Jedd rolled his brown eyes skyward. "As you've reminded me over and over."

"Look. Collecting debts is like an initiation. We won't be doing it for long. We just hafta prove our loyalty."

Jedd let out a surly snort.

"Come on," Rill said and started walking down the road. For a moment he feared Jedd wouldn't follow. But Jedd took a few long strides and settled into step beside him.

Dayson Florens's wine shop was in The Oaks, on a street near the foot of Oak Hill. The place was buzzing with the conversations and laughter of women and men, who sat at tables drinking wine. A woman in her mid-to-late thirties with light-brown hair went from table to table refilling clay mugs. Several customers stood along the bar at the back of the room.

A skinny old man, who was mostly bald except for a few strands of white hair, stood behind the counter chatting with a customer while he poured red wine into a large clay jug from one of the wooden barrels that lay on its side in a wall rack. Rill recognized him as Dayson Florens.

Up till now, a mixture of excitement and apprehension had been twisting Rill's stomach into knots at the prospect of confronting Dayson, especially if he proved recalcitrant. At the sight of the weak old codger, his anxiety vanished. *This will be easy.*

The hum of voices faded into heavy silence as the customers became aware of a mage and a bladesman in black Estati livery standing inside the doorway. Their reaction filled Rill with a thrilling sense of power. Suddenly aware of the charged atmosphere, Dayson looked past the customer to Rill and Jedd. His face clouded over.

Rill went up to him. "You're Dayson Florens."

"Yeah."

Aware of customers' hostile eyes drilling into his back, Rill lowered his voice. "I'm here on an errand for the Estatis. I'd like to speak with you in private."

Dayson filled a customer's wine cup, then set the wine jug on the bar. "Whatever you gotta say, say it here."

"Tell your customers to leave."

Dayson crossed his arms and sent Rill a challenging look. "I will not."

Rill's heart quivered like a frightened bird facing a hungry cat. This wasn't going the way he'd anticipated. He nodded at Jedd. "Make them leave."

Jedd drew himself up to his full height and his muscles tensed. For a moment Rill feared Jedd would refuse. But Jedd turned and shouted, "Everybody out!"

People turned from the counter, and others rose from their seats.

Throwing up his hands, Dayson yelled, "Stay, friends! There's no need to go."

Panic shot through Rill as he pictured himself returning to Lord Deuth in defeat. He pressed his lips together in a thin, tight line. *I won't let that happen!* He banged his staff on the floorboards. Then, raising his voice, he said, "Actus."

The customers glanced nervously at him and then at one another. Rill made a show of touching the charm beneath his black tunic. The man Dayson had been speaking to scurried for the door. Others quickly followed him until the bar was empty except for Dayson and the serving woman. Relief gushed through Rill as he turned back to Dayson. But his entire body was trembling, which made him angry. He hoped Dayson wouldn't notice.

The serving woman came and stood beside Dayson. He smiled lovingly at her and said, "Go on upstairs to your mom, honey. I gotta talk to these . . . hirelings."

The woman hesitated, but Dayson motioned for her to go. She left with obvious reluctance.

"The loan the Estatis gave you is long past due," Rill said. "I've come to collect it in full."

Dayson wiped a clay wine mug with a rag. "I'll tell you the same thing I told Lord Deuth. I used part of the money to expand my shop into this here building. Made this part into my tavern. I invested the rest of the money in a cargo of wine. The ship sank in a storm, and the entire consignment was lost. Now I'm barely keeping my head above water."

"You look prosperous enough to me," Rill said.

"I'm not. In fact, I'm just about breaking even. I figure another six months, and I'll make a profit. You tell Lord Deuth that if he waits till then, I can start repaying his loan in installments."

"Lord Deuth wants the money now."

Dayson placed the mug on the bar. "As I said, right now I got no way of repaying."

"Yes you do." Rill tossed the parchment onto the bar. "That contract gives the Estatis fifty-one percent of your business. Sign it, and the loan will be considered paid."

"What—turn over my shop to him?"

"Only fifty-one percent."

"That'd make the Estatis the owners."

"It would repay your loan and give you forty-nine percent." Rill pointed to the parchment and spoke with an edge in his voice. "*Sign the contract.*"

Dayson put his hands on his hips. "I will not."

Dayson's pigheadedness made Rill's arms and legs shake. Dayson *had* to sign the contract. Rill gave him what he hoped was an intimidating look, like the one Magnus gave clients the previous times. "I've got the power of the Estatis behind me. You'll sign . . . or I'll make you sign."

Dayson jeered at him. "Look at yourself. You're quivering all over like a scared rabbit. They sent a boy to do a man's job."

Dayson's humiliating dismissal made Rill's anger surge. "Is that your last word?"

Dayson nodded, hands still on hips. "It is."

Rill motioned to Jedd. "Break one of his legs."

Jedd's lips drew back in disgust. "I will not."

Rill's pulse galloped. "I said break his leg!"

Jedd drew himself up, body straight, and eyes burning defiance. "Do it yourself."

A sardonic smile played on Dayson's lips. "Full of piss but no vinegar, eh."

Rill glowered at Jedd while his heart's pace burst into full gallop. He spoke through gritted teeth. "You swore an oath of fealty to the Estatis."

"To be a backwatcher, not a thug."

A horrid image popped into Rill's head. Him returning to Lord Deuth in defeat. A failure. Thwarted by a skinny old man and by Jedd's disobedience. He pictured condemnation in every crease on Lord Deuth's face. Then he imagined an appalling scene that made his chest so tight he couldn't breathe: Lady Ariella withdrawing her offer to adopt him.

No! Something snapped inside Rill. He swung his staff at Dayson. The crystal orb struck him on the side of the head. Howling in pain, Dayson stumbled backward into the rack of wine barrels and collapsed to the floor. Rill raced around to the other side of the bar and beat Dayson's prostrate body with the staff. Over and over and over.

"You won't send me back empty handed! Sign it, damn you! Sign it, sign it, sign it!"

Suddenly the staff was torn from Rill's hands. He spun around, furious.

"Stop it!" Jedd said. "Do you wanna kill him?"

"No! I want him to sign the damned contract!"

Groggily, blood staining his white hair, Dayson tried to push himself into a sitting position with one hand but collapsed back upon the floor. His other arm hung useless. Blood dribbled from Dayson's mouth.

Rill snatched up the contract from the countertop and thrust it in Dayson's face. "Sign it!"

Dayson shook his head.

Rill reached for his staff to whack him again, but Jedd refused to release it. Turning, Rill kicked Dayson in the side. Once, twice, thrice. "Sign it!"

Dayson groaned in pain. "All right, all right, I'll sign."

Jedd refused to search for pen and ink. Fuming at Jedd's insubordination, Rill found them himself and propped Dayson up into a sitting position so he could scratch his name on the parchment, then let him fall back onto the floor. Rill rolled up the parchment and stuck it under his belt.

"Thanks for nothing!" he said to Jedd as he seized the staff from him and strode angrily through the door.

Many of the customers were milling around outside on the sidewalks and in the street, their voices creating an angry buzzing like wasps whose nest had been disturbed. Other Oaks dwellers were emerging from stores and taverns on either side of the road to find out what the ruckus was about. When they were told, their expressions turned hostile.

Several people pushed by Rill into the shop.

Jedd came out and stopped beside Rill.

The sight of Jedd made Rill wish Jedd had never been born. *Jedd wanted me to fail.* "Come on," Rill said angrily. "Let's get outta here."

He started walking toward River Road but stopped when he realized Jedd wasn't with him. He turned and saw that his cousin hadn't moved.

"Come on," Rill shouted.

Jedd shook his head. "I ain't goin' back. What you did in there was the final straw."

"I was doing my job. Unlike you."

"Beating up an old man to make him sign away his business. That's your job? That's what you're gonna do to become a mage?"

"I'll do whatever it takes."

Jedd looked at Rill, then heaved a sad sigh. "You've changed, Rill. I don't know you no more. And you know something? I don't wanna know you." Jedd strode toward Rill, brushed by him, and continued up the street.

"To Shelar with you!" Rill yelled. "I'll do just fine without you."

Jedd raised a hand into the air and made an obscene gesture.

Behind him, a woman dashed out of the shop into the middle of the street. "Someone get Dayson to a healer. He's hurt real bad." She turned to Rill, her face blazing with outrage. "You Goddess-damned bastard!"

The buzzing voices around Rill erupted into angry shouts. He slid his gaze across a multitude of rage-filled faces. Some people started toward him.

"Actus!" Rill said and waved his staff at the crowd.

People backed off.

All the way back to the Estati compound, Rill kept imagining all sorts of worst-case scenarios about how he had handled his assignment. Sure, Dayson had signed the contract. But he'd had to beat him up to do it. And Jedd had stood by watching. Doing nothing. Oaks dwellers had almost attacked him—Rill. And Jedd had walked off. *Lord Deuth is gonna blame me for that.* But Deuth's reaction to the news stunned Rill.

"You did well," Deuth said, smiling. "You persuaded Dayson to sign the contract. And you showed the other Oaks dwellers my family won't tolerate clients who don't fulfill their end of an agreement. As for Jedd." Deuth shrugged indifferently. "Who needs him? He was a bad influence on you. Lady Ariella will expel him in absentia."

"He deserves it." Guilt nibbled at Rill as he said the words, but he pushed it away. *It's Jedd's fault, not mine.* "He almost made me fail."

Deuth gave Rill's shoulder an affectionate squeeze. "But you didn't. And I'm very pleased with your progress. Lady Ariella is too. Keep up the good work, and you'll become Rill Estati."

Rill Estati. The name spun round and round in his head, making him giddy. His efforts were paying off.

Pride swelled near to bursting as he left the study. He'd thought how he'd handled the assignment would bring him condemnation. Instead, it had brought the opposite. All the work he had done since becoming Lord Deuth's apprentice mage was finally paying off. He couldn't wait to finish his training. He had proved to Lord Deuth and Lady Ariella that he would make an Estati they would be proud of. And he would continue to prove it over and over and over until they adopted him.

And as for Jedd. *Who needs him?*

## CHAPTER 52

Alyse's Ultimatum

LIGHT LEAPED DOWN FROM oil lamps along the walls and danced among the beds, chairs, and tables in the secret underground chamber. The interplay of light and shadow made Hilbrand's thin body appear like a scarecrow dressed in old, well-worn clothes.

Hilbrand bowed to Alyse, then spoke with heartfelt sincerity. "Thank you, Lady Alyse, for all you've done."

Hilbrand's words warmed Alyse's heart. "I'm glad I could help you. But you must thank the One Goddess too. It's through Her I receive my healing powers."

On either side of Hilbrand, Ord and Ebar inclined their heads to Alyse. Like Hilbrand, they wore nondescript tunics and pants. Pouches filled with gildas hung from their belts and study boots were on their feet.

"You did more than heal Hilbrand, Lady," Ord said. "You saved us from the city watchers." He sent a smile to Kate, who stood a little away from Alyse. "And you did too. If it wasn't for both of you, we'd be dead by now."

Ebar nodded solemnly. "If you ever need our help—"

"Or our swords—" Ord said.

"Just send us word. We're your men forever."

Alyse laughed lightly to hide her embarrassment at their deep show of gratitude. "I wouldn't know where to find you to send word. But thank you. I sincerely appreciate your offer. And I wish you the best of luck. May the One Goddess's blessing go with you."

"Come on," said a fourth man, who watched impatiently nearby. "If we delay much longer, the crowds in the Public Square will thin out, and we won't have much cover."

Ord and Ebar crossed to join their guide for the underground trail. As he turned to follow them, Hilbrand said to Alyse, "Thank Priestess Sybil for us too."

"I will," Alyse said. "I'm sorry she isn't here to see you off."

"She has more important matters to tend to than the likes of us," Hilbrand said. "Goodbye, Lady."

Then Hilbrand was gone, walking with the others up the stone staircase that led to the area between Priestess Sybil's office and the library. From there they would mingle with the worshipers in the temple, becoming anonymous Caldonians returning to their homes.

Alyse sighed. "I'll miss them."

"Me too," Kate said. "They're good men."

After extinguishing the oil lamps, Alyse picked up the finger lamp from the table and went upstairs with Kate. They paused by the corridor leading to the temple, ready to go their separate ways, Alyse to the House of Healing and Kate to the temple kitchen, when a novice rushed up to them.

"Lady Alyse, come quick!"

"What's the matter?"

"A patient was just brought in. He has a serious head injury."

Alyse and Kate followed the novice at a fast walk to the ward where a thin, elderly man lay unconscious on a bed. His head was wrapped in a bloody bandage, and an arm was bent at an unusual angle. A gray-haired woman around the same age was kneeling over him, sobbing. A woman in her mid-thirties with light-brown hair, eyes reddened by weeping, hovered by the older woman's side. Two younger men stood nearby watching, concerned expressions on their faces.

"What happened to him?" Alyse asked.

"A mage and a bladesman came to collect a debt my husband owed the Estatis," the elderly woman said, her voice shaking with anger. "He didn't have the money. So the mage tried to make him sign a contract giving fifty-one percent of our wine business to the Estatis. When my husband refused, the mage beat him up with his staff."

Outrage billowed through Alyse. "That's terrible!"

"It's criminal!" the brown-haired woman said.

"The bladesman wanted to have nothing to do with it," one of the men said. "Some of us gathered outside Dayson's shop. The bladesman broke his oath to the Estatis and walked off. Right in front of us." He pointed to his companion. "Brefor and me saw him do it."

"We brought Dad to our temple healer in The Oaks," the younger woman said. "But she said caring for his head wound was beyond her skills. She told us to bring him here to have Priestess Sybil treat it."

Kneeling beside Dayson, Alyse carefully unwrapped the bandage to expose a battered bald head. The healer in The Oaks had cleaned the blood from Dayson's head, but flecks of dried blood remained on the fringe of white hair. Alyse explored Dayson's skull with her inner eye. Then examined the rest of his body.

"His head wound is extremely serious," she said to Dayson's wife and daughter. "His arm's broken, and the bone's sticking out of the skin. He has some nasty bruises all over his body too." She looked up at the men. "Do you know the name of the thug who did this?"

Brefor nodded vigorously. "Rill Larkin."

Alyse twitched as if shocked by an electric eel. She glanced at Kate, who appeared equally astonished. "Rill Larkin. Are you sure?"

"I'm positive."

"And the other?" Alyse asked. "The one who broke his oath?"

"Jedd Euland."

Alyse sneaked a quick look at Kate whose eyes beamed relief.

After shooing everyone from the room, Alyse shaved Dayson's hair, applied healing hands and salve, and re-bandaged his head. Then she reset his arm and put it in a splint and treated his bruises. When she finished, she called The Oaks dwellers back in.

"He'll recover," she said. "But it will take a while. He'll have to stay here for several days, so we can continue to treat his head wound."

When Priestess Sybil returned, Alyse and Kate told her about Dayson. Sybil shocked her by saying she'd already heard about the incident. "Bad news travels fast throughout the neighborhoods."

"I can't believe Rill beat up that poor old man," Alyse said.

"It's not like him," Kate said.

"Unfortunately, Rill's under Estatis influence now," Sybil told them.

Concern filled Kate's dark-brown eyes. "What about Jedd? He broke his oath."

"Yes," Sybil responded. "And he rid himself of the Estatis."

"But they'll expel him. He'll become a rohan."

Sybil smiled reassuringly at Kate. "Many backwatchers idolize Tor Euland. Jedd's his nephew. If the Estatis expel Jedd, I don't think anyone will touch him."

"Thank the One Goddess for that!"

"Of course, no First Family will take on a rohan. And he'll probably be conscripted next year."

Kate's expression went from happy to apprehensive.

"Does Kendra know what Rill did?" Alyse asked Sybil.

"Yes. And she's heartbroken over it. His whole family is upset." Sybil cast out a deep sigh. "But Rill's a man now. He's responsible for his own actions."

Alyse hadn't seen Kendra since the incident with Hilbrand. But ever since then she'd felt a connection with her. Alyse thought if she herself was upset about Rill beating up Dayson, Kendra must be devastated. "I've got to see Kendra."

"Do you think that's wise?" Sybil asked.

"I'm not sure. But I have to do it. Rill's a good person. He saved me when the temple was attacked. He's chosen a dark path to walk. But deep inside I know he's still a good person. He's just . . . gone astray."

"If you go," Sybil told her, "you might be getting into something that's over your head."

"What do you mean?"

"I think it would be better if you didn't—" Sybil broke off as if a thought had suddenly entered her mind. "No. That's Kendra's decision to make, not mine. If you feel you should see her, then go."

As Alyse hurried out, Kate fell into step beside her.

"Stay here," Alyse said, fearing she and Kendra might reveal information Kate shouldn't know. "This doesn't involve you."

"Of course it does," Kate said. "Jedd and I fought together at the One Goddess Temple so you and Rill could escape. That means I am involved. Besides, I'm your backwatcher. You go nowhere without me."

Alyse threw on her lightweight cloak. By the time she had finished fastening the cloak pin, Kate was beside her, adjusting her own cloak to conceal her sword and dagger. They went out into the afternoon heat. Because of her healing work, Alyse had become well liked by many Kings dwellers. They thought well of Kate too. But many First Families had spies in all the neighborhoods, including The Kings. Alyse knew if anyone spotted her going to the Larkins, word would get back to her family about it. She couldn't afford that to happen. So she pulled the cloak's hood over her head to conceal her face. Kate did the same.

As Alyse approached the Larkins' courtyard, she heard the rhythmic ring of Marc's hammer from the smithy. She crossed the courtyard and knocked on the house door.

Kendra opened the door. She drew in an astonished breath when she recognized the faces inside the hoods. "What are you girls doing here?" she asked in a less-than-friendly tone.

"We came to see you," Alyse replied. "Is this a bad time?"

Someone stood in partial sight behind Kendra. Alyse peered around Kendra, but Kendra shifted her position, blocking Alyse's view. "Yes, it is."

"Then we'll go."

"That would be good."

A scream came from the smithy.

"Marc!" Kendra cried. She brushed past Alyse and sprinted toward the blacksmith shop.

Whirling around, Alyse and Kate raced after her.

They found Marc kneeling, clutching his cheek with both hands and groaning in pain. Kendra dropped to her knees beside him.

"Marc, what happened?"

"A piece of red-hot metal snapped off and hit me in the cheek. Goddess, it hurts!"

Kendra put an arm around his shoulder and helped him to his feet. "Come into the house."

Someone came running across the courtyard and into the smithy. Out of breath, the person stopped behind everyone. Alyse glanced over her shoulder.

A young woman in a dark-gray cloak, its hood pulled back, returned the gaze. The gasps that escaped both their lips came at the same instant. "Alyse!"

"Livia! What're you doing here?"

"I was about to ask you the same question."

Marc groaned. "Oh Goddess, this hurts."

"Oh, don't be such a baby," Kendra said. "Come on. Let's get you into the house."

In the kitchen, Kendra helped Marc onto the bench at the eating table. "You're the healer," she told Alyse. "You treat him."

Alyse applied healing hands to Marc's wound. "The area will be sore for a few days. He'll also need to apply an ointment to the spot once a day for a week. I can have some sent to you from the temple."

"We have plenty," Kendra said. "He's had worse burns than this."

"And Kendra always refuses to treat them," Marc grumbled in a tone that showed he was ribbing her. "She always sends me to Priestess Sybil."

Marc's joking fell flat because the three girls were giving one another perplexed looks while Kendra was frowning at them. As if on cue, the girls shifted their eyes to Kendra. She shot an inquiring look toward Marc, who arched a brow as if to say, *It's up to you.*

Kendra pointed at the table. "You girls might as well sit down."

Alyse and Kate sat beside Tarri and across from Kendra, Livia, and Marc. Cinna sat at the head of the table.

Kendra's expression turned dead serious as her gaze moved from Alyse to Kate. "If word gets back to the Estatis that Livia was here," she said, "they'll probably expel her."

"You can trust us not to tell," Alyse responded. "We like Livia and don't want to get her in trouble, let alone expelled. Besides, if my family finds out Kate and I were here, we'd get into serious trouble too."

"This is weird," Livia said to no one in particular. "Really, really weird." She looked at Alyse, bafflement etched into every line on her face. "You're the last person I ever expected to see here. What's your relationship to Kendra?"

"My relationship?" Alyse said, her dark-brown eyebrows creased in puzzlement.

"I mean . . . are you cousins, or—"

"Cousins?" Alyse laughed. "Don't be silly." She told Livia how she and Kate had met Rill and Jedd when the One Goddess Temple was attacked and how Rill had brought her to his home for safety. "My family doesn't know about it. They think I was at the temple the whole time. So please don't tell anyone."

"I won't," Livia said.

Alyse stared at Livia, curiosity burning hotter and hotter in her brain. "But what are you doing here? And what did you mean about my 'relationship' to Kendra?"

Kendra put a hand on Livia's wrist. "Livia and I have a secret." Pain and joy battled each other on her face. "I've lost a son but gained a daughter."

Alyse's forehead crinkled in bewilderment. "Huh?"

"Livia's my daughter," Kendra said.

"And Rill's half sister," Livia added.

Alyse felt as if Kendra had just punched her in the belly. Her reaction swiftly turned to disbelief as Kendra recounted her wild days as an archmage and the horrible events that had taken her down a path to repentance and salvation, which had led to her marrying

Marc Larkin. At that point, Livia took over and explained how she had put her uncle in a position where he had to reveal the family secret when he'd caught her making a pass at Rill.

"At first," Livia said, "I was furious with Kendra for abandoning me. And at my family for keeping the information from me and letting me live a lie all my life. I was outraged at Shalira too. How would you feel if you suddenly discovered your mother is really your aunt, and your brother is really your cousin? Or that your uncle's new commoner apprentice is actually your half brother? I was so enraged that I decided to have it out with Kendra."

"And she did," Marc said. "It was a real screaming and sobbing match between them. I don't know who won."

"I don't want to go through something like that again," Livia said. "But in the end, I sensed Kendra actually cared about me even though she'd abandoned me when I was a baby." She rested her head against Kendra's shoulder. "How's that for a contradiction? And I didn't know it, but Shalira visits her every so often and keeps her up to date on what I'm doing." Livia paused, tears watering her cheeks.

Kendra stroked her hand.

"Now I know why my family hates me so much. Because I'm Kendra's daughter." Livia gave a bitter laugh. "After all, kinship goes through the female, not the male. So they had no choice but to keep me."

"At least you know," Alyse said quietly.

Livia sniffed and wiped a tear from her cheek with her forefinger. "Yes. That's something." She settled back with a sigh. "Anyway, my mother and I decided to keep meeting so we could get to know each other." Livia looked reprovingly at Kendra. "But I still haven't gotten over my anger. To have my whole life upended like this . . . it's a difficult thing to take."

"And the guilt for doing it is difficult to take too," Kendra said softly.

Livia sniffed again and blew her nose with a handkerchief she drew from her sleeve. "The bad thing is that Uncle Deuth ordered Rill and me not to tell Troy. So now Troy's the only one in the family who's still living this terrible lie. I feel awful about keeping it from him. Except for Shalira, he's the only one in the family who cares for me. I don't know how long I can go without telling him."

Troy! Alyse's heart ached for him, and for Livia too. Then guilt stirred in her chest like a snake awakening from sleep at her refusal to marry Troy. But guilt was self-inflicted, and she wouldn't let herself fall into that trap. She cleared her throat. "What about Rill? Do you think he can keep the secret?"

"Sure," Livia replied. "He wants more than anything to become a mage. So he'll do whatever Uncle Deuth tells him."

In the late afternoon, Alyse left for home with Kate and Livia. When they neared the crest of The Citadel, Livia headed toward her compound while Alyse and Kate continued to theirs and then went to their respective bedrooms to change.

Alyse had just finished putting on a clean blue dress when Lothar, the head steward, knocked on the door and told her that Lady Maude wanted to see her in the matriarch's chamber immediately.

"Now, what?" Alyse muttered to herself.

Maude was waiting in the black oak matriarch's chair, her fingers drumming on the polished arm, and Pilar and Mora were seated in straight-back chairs in front of the dais. Before Alyse could sit down, Maude beckoned her forward.

Alyse stopped at the dais steps.

"I have wonderful news," Maude said.

"What's that?"

"Your wedding day is set for two weeks from today."

Dread clutched Alyse with freezing fingers and the room spun dizzily. "Two weeks?"

"The Estatis have grown impatient. They want our alliance renewed immediately, as do I."

Delay, delay, delay! The words shot through Alyse's head like a hail of arrows. "I can't be ready in two weeks. I haven't even thought about a wedding gown."

"I don't care if you wear your nightshift. As long as you get married."

"But all the preparations. Guests to be invited. Food to be cooked. Musicians—"

"Are being taken care of as we speak."

"But—"

"No more excuses!" Maude shot up from the chair and thrust a finger at Alyse. "You'll marry Troy in two weeks. You will spend that time preparing for your wedding. After the wedding, you will continue your training with Priestess Sybil, but as a married woman. And let me make this perfectly clear to you. I expect you to produce a baby within ten to twelve months after your wedding."

Anger blurred Alyse's vision. "What do you think I am—a piece in a game to be moved around on the board any way you want?"

Maude stomped down the steps and slapped Alyse across the face.

Alyse stumbled backward, a hand on her stinging cheek.

Maude spat words at her. "No! You're a Dejune. My firstborn granddaughter. I expect you to fulfill your role as firstborn by re-cementing our alliance with the Estatis and by giving me a grandson who will be a mage. We need to regain our seat in the Magesterium. And it would be helpful if he was an archmage too, so we could access our charm vault."

A spiteful retort rolled down Alyse's tongue but she clamped her teeth on it. Giving vent to her outrage would only make her situation worse. Alyse forced herself to lower her eyes and make a dutiful submission. "Very well, Grandmother. I'll do as you say."

"See that you do."

Alyse hurried from the matriarch's chamber, eager to escape the hateful place, while Maude's repellent announcement slopped back and forth in her head. Two weeks! She rushed across the family area to the refuge of her bedroom, slamming the door shut, tears of frustration drenching her eyes. As she waited for her agitated breathing to return to normal, Uncle Leoc's face slid into her mind along with his offer of refuge.

But his camp in The Marches was such a long, long distance away through places she'd never traveled. She thought of all the obstacles she could encounter—brigands, wild animals, thunder and lightning storms—which sent sharp slivers of apprehension through her body. She dismissed them with an angry growl deep in her throat. She would overcome the hazards, no matter what.

She would run away to Uncle Leoc's camp in The Marches.

## CHAPTER 53

Alyse's Flight

THE NEXT MORNING BEFORE breakfast, Alyse went into Kate's bedroom and told her about her decision. "You can come with me to The Marches if you want—"

"Of course I'll go," Kate said.

Frustration settled on Alyse's face. "I spent all last night trying to think of how to sneak away, but couldn't. And I'm sure Grandmother has ordered the household staff to keep an eye on me."

"I wouldn't doubt it." Kate stroked her chin thoughtfully with thumb and forefinger, then grinned at Alyse. "How about if you embrace your wedding?" Before Alyse could disagree, Kate explained her scheme.

Alyse put the first part of their plan into action the next morning during breakfast by announcing she was going shopping to buy shoes for her wedding.

Maude's gray eyes beamed approval. "I'm glad you've finally come to your senses. But you can't leave the compound without an escort."

"I'll take Kate with me," Alyse said.

Maude put down her cobalt-blue wine glass. "Your wedding's being announced today. Now our enemies will be looking for any way they can to prevent it. One teenage backwatcher is hardly adequate protection. I'll send a couple of adult ones along as well."

Does Grandmother Maude suspect anything? If she did, Alyse would have to prove her wrong.

From then on, Alyse played the dutiful child and dove into the wedding arrangements with gusto, which lulled Maude into believing her granddaughter had indeed truly come to her senses and accepted her role as firstborn twin. Alyse also made it a point to go shopping frequently for "wedding things." Two additional backwatchers always accompanied her and Kate on the shopping jaunts. But they varied on each trip, depending on who was available at the time. Alyse figured she and Kate could steal away from them pretty easily when the time came to flee.

While Alyse performed her role like a consummate actress, Kate made their escape preparations. She rented two horses and stable space from a stable in The Oaks, just a few blocks from the Public Gate that led to the eastern part of the country. Then she secretly purchased commoner clothes and supplies they'd need for their journey and hid them in the stable.

Nine days crept by with agonizing slowness for Alyse as she lulled her family into believing she was going through with the wedding. And each day she wished time would speed up so she could run away.

Alyse woke up on the tenth day consumed by excitement and apprehension. Today she and Kate were fleeing. During breakfast, Alyse complained that she had no jewelry suitable to wear at the wedding and was going shopping to find some. Then the worst possible thing happened.

Mora announced that she would go along with her. She added that Jade would accompany them too. "Alyse can rely on my impeccable taste in jewelry to find exactly what she needs," Mora said.

Alyse wanted to strangle her sister.

Unfortunately, both Maude and Pilar were delighted at Mora's display of sisterly harmony when so often she and Alyse were at odds with each other. Alyse, though, could barely keep her distress from showing. She and Kate could still pull off their plan. But they would have to be extra careful . . . and clever.

Alyse cagily chose the shop she would visit. The store was popular with both noblesse and rich commoners. The owner was one of the top jewelry makers in Caldon, and his exquisite works were highly sought after by noblesse and wealthy commoners alike. The shop was in The Oaks, on a street that boasted a number of high-end craft stores. It also just happened to be a couple of blocks from the stable where the horses and gear were waiting.

Mora botched up Alyse's cleverly laid plan from the start. Right after breakfast she decided to change into a different outfit, which took her a while to select. Then, to Alyse's increasing frustration, Mora used one excuse after another to fritter away the first part of the morning, all the while, Alyse silently cursed her for wasting precious time. When Mora finally announced she was ready to venture outside into the warm morning sunlight, Alyse was ready to throttle her.

Alyse's legs ached to break into run as she walked down Citadel Road and crossed the Public Square with her little procession. Instead, she forced herself to go at a leisurely pace and engage Mora in mindless chitter-chatter. When they reached The Oaks, Mora insisted they stop at a couple of stores so she could see what new items they had in stock.

Alyse complied because she thought if she refused, Mora would become suspicious. Frustration roiled in her like wild waves in a stormy sea. *At this rate, I'll never be able to run off.* At last, around late morning, they arrived at the jewelry shop.

Alyse had been so focused on her frustrations over Mora's dillydallying that a new problem snaked into her mind as she entered the jewelry store. She couldn't figure out how she and Kate could break away from Mora and Jade. It seemed that Mora would stick with her all the way home. *Does she suspect this trip is just a ruse?* That thought made her nerves twist so tight she thought they'd snap like a frayed rope.

It took all of Alyse's willpower to act like a giddy future bride as she explained to the jeweler that she was looking for a necklace and earring combination for her wedding. When the jeweler asked if she wanted them to match her green eyes or her lavender wedding dress, Alyse replied she wasn't sure. She silently thanked the man for the question. Going through a wide assortment of selections would allow her time to figure out how to give Mora and Jade the slip.

The jeweler placed several sets of necklaces and matching earrings on the counter, each set containing beautiful gemstones. The late-morning sunlight burning through the windows made the gems sparkle. Alyse tried on the various sets and took her time examining herself in the mirror, asking Mora, Kate, and Jade for their opinions and discussing their opinions in as much detail as possible.

The last two sets of necklaces and earrings contained emeralds whose green almost matched Alyse's eyes. Mora picked up one of the necklaces. "These sets are so nice, Alyse, I don't know why you saved them for last."

Alyse took the necklace from her and pretended to examine it, along with the earrings. She shook her head and handed them back to Mora. "The green isn't an exact match with my eyes."

Then try on these." Mora handed Alyse the other set.

Alyse heaved a deep, despondent sigh. "This green isn't good either. I want to look at more."

"Don't be silly," Mora said. "The green matches your eyes perfectly. Try them on."

Alyse put on the earrings while Mora attached the necklace around her neck. She studied Mora's image in the mirror, and smiled. She wanted more than anything to pummel her twin for shoving a wrench in her plans. "You really think Troy will like the earrings?" she asked, striving to keep her tone light.

"Oh yes," Mora replied. "And the necklace."

Alyse made a display of pondering, and examined herself again in the glass while her nerves screamed at her to shake off Mora and Jade. But how?

Mora cut into Alyse's thoughts. "She'll buy this set," she told the jeweler. "How much?"

"A thousand gildas," the jeweler said.

Alyse opened her mouth to tongue-lash Mora for butting in when a plan slipped into her head as if it were sliding on grease. "A thousand gildas!" she said, feigning indignation. "Why, that's roadway robbery."

The jeweler's lips tightened as if offended by her statement. "Lady Alyse, I make the best jewelry in all of Caldon."

"You could give it to her for free," Mora said, a malicious gleam in her eye. "As a wedding gift."

The jeweler spread his hands in apology. "Lady Mora, with all respect, if I did that for every noblesse bride who came in here, I'd be bankrupt inside of a week."

"I'll give you five hundred for it," Alyse told him, knowing Mora would become suspicious if she didn't haggle.

"Why . . . that's an insult," the jeweler responded, a hurt expression on his face. "Eight hundred."

Alyse pressed her lips into a thin, defiant line. "Six hundred."

"Seven fifty." The jeweler's eyebrows furrowed into a scowl. "And for that price, I'll hardly make a profit."

Alyse folded her arms across her chest. "Seven hundred."

Tears formed in the jeweler's eyes, and Alyse thought he might burst into sobs. "Seven twenty-five."

Keeping her arms crossed, Alyse pasted a look on her face that said she wouldn't back down. "Seven hundred. Final offer."

The jeweler made a display of hemming and hawing. "All right. For you, Lady Alyse, it's seven hundred. Just don't tell anyone you bought my jewelry so cheaply."

Alyse forced her lips into a smile and promised. She turned to Kate, praying to the One Goddess her cousin would recognize her own unspoken role in this desperate scheme. "Pay him the seven hundred gildas."

When distress sprang upon Kate's face, Alyse wanted to cheer. "Lady Alyse, your mother only gave me four hundred. I don't think she thought you'd buy something this expensive."

"Oh no!" Alyse wailed in mock dismay.

She turned to Mora, who instantly threw up her hands to ward her off. "Don't look at me! I just came along for the pleasure of spending quality time with you."

Alyse turned back to the jeweler and told him to send the bill to the Dejunes on The Citadel. As she expected, he replied that he only took cash, not credit. Alyse asked Mora to send Jade back home to ask Grandmother Maude for more money.

Again, as she'd anticipated, Mora refused. "Carrying your money is Kate's responsibility, not Jade's."

Alyse turned to Kate. "You'll have to go home for the money."

After Alyse promised the jeweler she'd be back later with the payment, she and the others left the shop. Taking Kate aside, Alyse gave her instructions about going home, in a voice that carried to the other girls. Then she whispered, "I'll lose them as soon as I can. Meet me at the stables. Have the horses saddled and packed to go." Kate nodded, then strode purposefully along the clay-brick sidewalk toward the Public Square.

"What now, girls?" Mora said. "More shopping?"

Alyse squinted at the sun, gauging its angle. "It's way past noon and I'm hungry."

Mora thought lunch was a great idea and suggested going to an upscale tavern.

But Alyse preferred going to a food stall in the public market for a meat pie. "I haven't had one from there in ages."

Mora gave in with a graciousness she rarely displayed.

The three girls strolled from The Oaks to the sprawling public market that bordered the Public Square, pushing their way through buzzing throngs of commoners, liveried servants, and occasional noblesse and backwatchers who jammed the street. They worked their way past market booths shaded by awnings of plain or brightly striped canvas and butchers' stalls that displayed joints of freshly slaughtered cows, lambs, and pigs. At one booth, Alyse stopped to smile at a mutt dog that sat gazing longingly at a pig's head hanging above the counter. At other stalls, chickens squawked in cages, awaiting the indignity of having their heads chopped off and their necks bled in vats of boiling water. Fish mongers hawked fish so freshly caught that the piles were squirming. The girls passed count-less other kinds of vendors too, while laughing children dodged be-tween people's legs.

All the while, Alyse searched with increasing desperation for an opportunity to slip off unnoticed. But Mora never gave her a chance. It was as if she knew Alyse's desire to visit the marketplace was a subterfuge.

Eventually, Alyse stopped at a booth run by two brothers who were selling meat pies and ordered a couple. Jade paid for them with Mora's money. Then, pies in hand, Alyse and Mora moved on down the people-packed road munching on their pies while Jade kept a watchful eye on them. Alyse's stomach was so knotted with anxiety she felt like throwing up her mouthfuls of meat and crust as she pic-tured Kate waiting at the stable with their saddled horses worrying when—or if—she would arrive.

From farther down the street came the wail and beat of pipe and tabor. Relief swept through Alyse like an incoming wave. "Oh, listen! That's the signal for jugglers and fire eaters. Let's go watch."

By the time they reached the performers, a circle of spectators had already gathered around the troupers.

Alyse worked her way between bystanders to get closer to the front. Mora and Jade followed but couldn't find positions next to her. More onlookers shoved in behind them to form an almost solid wall of bodies. Before long, the jugglers began their performance and soon had everyone laughing and clapping. Alyse could hear Mora's distinctive chortle to her right.

Cautiously, Alyse sidestepped to the left, forcing her way through the spectators and then through the horde of pedestrians milling in the road until she broke free of the market area. Then she hurried to the livery stable. She found Kate inside, dressed in ordinary com-moners' clothes and her sword and dagger buckled around her waist partially concealed by her brown cape.

"Thank the Goddess you're here!" Kate said. "I thought maybe they suspected something and made you go home."

"No." Alyse slipped out of her red silk dress and pulled on the coarse woolen pants that were draped over her horse's saddle. "It was difficult to get away from them." Quickly she donned the linen shirt, cotton vest, and cloak that were under the pants, then took the belt and dagger Kate handed her. "We have to hurry. We've already lost over half a day's travel time."

Alyse buried her dress in a pile of hay, alongside Kate's clothes. Then, taking her bay mare's reins, she headed for the open door. Kate walked beside her leading her own mare. Suddenly Jade appeared in the doorway. Alyse stopped so abruptly her horse bumped into her, making her stumble a couple of steps forward.

"Well, well, well," Jade said. "The two little birds are flying away."

Kate dropped her reins and drew her sword.

Mora stepped into view. "Oh my. Drawing against a fellow backwatcher. Grandmother Maude will be *so* angry with you, Kate, when I tell her."

"We're leaving," Alyse said, taking hold of the reins of Kate's gray mare. "And you're not stopping us."

Mora's lips bent into a spiteful smile. "Why would I want to stop you?" She nodded to Jade, who stepped aside, opening the way out. "I *want* you to leave. Because then Grandmother will expel you, and I'll be the who marries Troy."

"You're welcome to him," Alyse said.

A smug grin settled on Mora's lips. "I knew you were up to something. Going out shopping so much. And then today wanting to buy expensive jewelry for your wedding when you have plenty at home, including emerald green, that you could use. Maybe Mother and Grandmother bought your change of heart, but I sure didn't."

Kate sheathed her sword and took her horse's reins from Alyse.

Even though Jade had moved aside, Alyse still faced Mora. "If you mean what you say," Alyse told her twin, "then get out of my way."

"With pleasure." Mora stepped aside. "I'll even delay going home to deliver the news. That'll give you extra time to put even more distance between here and wherever you're going." She eyed Alyse curiously. "Where *are* you going?"

"None of your business."

Leather creaked as Alyse and Kate swung into their saddles, then walked their horses out of the stable into the blazing early afternoon sunlight. Kate intentionally brushed her mare's flank against Jade, making her stumble. Their horses' iron-shod hooves clopped on the cobbles as Alyse and Kate headed for the Public Gate and the road to The Marches.

Alyse's arms and legs tingled. She knew Mora well enough to know she couldn't be trusted. When she turned in her saddle to look at the stable, Mora was nowhere in sight. Alyse pictured Mora racing home to tattle. Grandmother Maude would send backwatchers to capture her and Kate before they could get too far. Then Maude would expel her, and Uncle Leoc would be unaware of what had happened. Alyse had to reach her uncle's camp before the pursuit—and there *would* be a pursuit—could catch up with her.

Alyse pressed her heels into her mare's flanks. She and Kate had to put plenty of distance between themselves and Caldon before they could rest.

## CHAPTER 54

Pursuit

THE KNOCK ON RILL'S door came late in the evening, just as he was sitting down on the bed to pull off his boots and turn in for the night. Yawning, he opened the door.

"Lord Deuth requires you in his study," Kalso said. "Immediately."

"Do you know why?" Rill asked, curious about the unusual summons.

"It's not my business to inquire. Nor is it yours."

Rill hurried downstairs.

When Rill entered the study, he received another shock. The harsh yellow light of the oil lamps on shelves along the walls revealed Troy, Yall Throwstarr, and Magnus Roeback huddled with Deuth by his cherrywood desk. The two backwatchers expressed no emotion when they saw Rill gaping at them from the doorway.

"I still don't believe she did it!" Troy said to Deuth. "I love her. I even told her that. Now I feel betrayed."

"You were betrayed," Deuth told him, the flickering flame from the oil lamp on his desk exposing his face distorted by rage. "And don't talk to me about love. That's where you went wrong. Love has no place in marriage. If you want love, find it in someone else's bed."

"I know that now, damn her," Troy said, teeth clenched.

Deuth ran a hand through his reddish-brown hair. "I'm at fault too. I encouraged your grandmother to put off the marriage until she had time to enhance her healing skills. Alyse is devious. She knew we'd bite like a fish on a lure at the prospect of you having a wife as a healer who could match Priestess Sybil's skills. Lucky for us we caught onto her scheme when we did."

Deuth noticed Rill and beckoned him to join them.

Rill's neck tingled. Something unusual had happened, but what? "You sent for me, Lord?"

Troy hurled a furious look at Rill. "You're not sending *him* with us."

"Remember your place," Deuth said. "You're the reason we're here tonight."

"But—"

Deuth stabbed his index finger into the center of Troy's chest. "Do you know how to track someone?"

"No."

Deuth nodded at Rill. "Do you?"

"Yes, Lord."

"We don't need an extra mage," Troy said stubbornly, ignoring the deepening wrinkles in his uncle's anger-creased brow.

"Can you guarantee your spells will always hit their mark?" Deuth asked Troy.

"It depends on what counterspell's cast against me."

Deuth's gaze shifted to Magnus. "Can you?"

"It depends on the counterspell, Lord."

Deuth eyes skipped to Rill. "Can you guarantee your arrows will always hit their mark?"

"As long as I got arrows to shoot."

"Do you know how to use a sword and cast spells?"

"Yes, Lord."

Turning to Troy, Deuth pointed at Rill. "There you have it. Archer, bladesman, and mage all rolled up into one. He's going with you."

Troy heaved an infuriated groan. "But—"

Deuth's eyes snapped. "I'll hear no more objections. Is that clear?"

"Yes, Uncle," Troy responded unhappily.

"Excuse me, Lord," Rill said. "But where am I going with them?"

"After Troy's future bride."

Surprise tumbled through Rill. "Alyse Dejune?"

"Yes. It seems she has . . . reservations about the marriage."

"She's run away?"

Deuth flipped Rill a sour look. "That's rather obvious, isn't it? Considering I'm sending you after her. Her backwatcher went with her too."

Rill didn't know how to respond to what Deuth had said—or to the entire situation. *Why would Alyse run away from marrying an Estati? It don't make no sense.*

Troy pounded a fist on Deuth's desk. "The Dejunes are responsible for not stopping her. So why aren't they going after her?"

"They were," Deuth said. "But Lady Ariella told them we would instead."

"Why?"

"Because Alyse insulted our house, not theirs, by running away. So it's up to you, Troy, as the injured party, to bring her back. But I have included one Dejune backwatcher in your group."

"Who's that?"

"Jade Channer, Mora's backwatcher. It's only fitting that if one of the twin's backwatchers ran away with her charge, the other twin's backwatcher brings the disloyal one back."

The door opened abruptly, making everyone jump.

Livia walked in. "Hi, all," she said brightly, wiggling a hand at them.

Deuth pointed at the door. "Get out of here."

Livia strolled nonchalantly over to them, sat down in a chair by the desk, and smoothed out the skirt of her dress. She flashed Deuth a taunting smile as she settled back against the crossrails.

"Why, you arrogant bitch!" Deuth lunged toward her.

Livia held up a hand, palm out. "I wouldn't do that if I were you. Matriarch's orders."

Deuth's fingers stopped just short of Livia's arm.

Livia nodded at her uncle's outstretched hand. "Back off. Great-Grandmother Ariella would not want her messenger womanhandled."

Rill could tell it took a lot of willpower for Deuth to settle back in his cherrywood chair. "What's her message?"

The corners of Livia's mouth rose into a smirk. "I'm going with you."

Deuth squeezed his eyes shut as if to deny what he'd just heard. Then he opened them and blew out a mouthful of air. "No you're not."

"You have no say in the matter." Livia paused dramatically. "Matriarch's orders."

"What!" Deuth's half rose from his chair. "When was this decided?"

"Just now. In a matriarch's council."

"Why wasn't I invited?"

Livia raised her eyes to the dancing shadows on the ceiling, pretending to ponder. "Umm . . . because you're not a woman?"

Deuth ground his teeth, whether from anger at the messenger or at the message or at both,. Rill couldn't tell. "And exactly what brought on this decision?"

"The women of the family think your expedition is too top heavy in males."

"Jade Channer's coming. So there's no need for you."

"Jade's going along to make sure Kate Dejune doesn't act up. They despise each other. Which leaves poor Alyse in the hands of three males. One of whom is her future husband." Livia wagged a finger at Deuth as if he were a naughty child. "Now, how does that look? People might think she became 'damaged goods' on the way home."

Deuth stabbed Livia with his eyes. "Like you?"

If Deuth intended his remark to bait Livia into a hostile reaction, she didn't bite. "Yes. Like me."

Deuth's face turned red with anger, but it was obvious to Rill that Deuth had no choice. He couldn't buck his matriarch's decision.

"All right," Deuth finally said as if he hated spitting out each word. "You'll go with them."

Livia tossed him a mocking smile. "I knew you'd understand."

Deuth's hands trembled as if he wanted to wrap them around Livia's neck and squeeze the life out of her. Then he scanned the five faces in front of the desk, his blue eyes angry, frigid, and determined. "Bring Alyse Dejune back. Mora told us she left by the Public Gate. That means she's heading for her uncle's camp in The Marches. Find her before she gets there. Whatever it takes, bring that"—his eyes dug into Livia—"*bitch* back." He picked up a quill pen and fumbled with it as if he had to reassemble thoughts his anger had scattered. "You leave first thing in the morning. You'll have to ride hard to catch up with them because they left early this afternoon. So they have well over half a day's start on you."

Rill's gaze stepped across each of his new companions, one by one. *I bet they ain't hardly ever been on horseback. So it's gonna be a longer chase than Lord Deuth thinks.* But he considered it prudent not to mention that to anyone, especially Deuth.

Rill and the others left to pack for tomorrow's journey. Livia headed for her bedroom. Rill caught up with her before she got half-way there.

"Are you sure you wanna go?" he asked. "It could be dangerous."

A determined look came upon Livia's face. "Alyse is one of the few people who's never condemned me. Who's always treated me kindly. Kate too. Now I have a chance to repay them. I'm going to make sure nothing bad happens to them on the way home."

Livia gave Rill a quick peck on the cheek and strode off.

As he headed toward the second-floor stairs, Rill found conflicting emotions vying with each other at having his half sister accompany them. Excitement that he would be spending time with her and apprehension for her safety. He feared that Livia Estati, who was used to the comforts of home and who had never confronted anyone or cast a spell in a life-or-death situation, might end up seriously injured—or dead—before the journey's end.

Now that he had found his sister, Rill didn't want to lose her.

Sneak Peek

A Light in the Window

SOMETIMES A GOAL ISN'T WORTH PURSUING
OTHER TIMES, WINNING MEANS LOSING.

## CHAPTER 1

Flight

TOWARD EVENING ALYSE DEJUNE and her cousin, Kate Dejune, rode along the dirt road into a sleepy town nestled at the edge of a forest and stopped by an inn to water their horses at a trough. The settlement was close enough to Caldon, a half day's journey behind them, that the townspeople didn't pay much attention to two dust-covered teenage girls traveling through the countryside, even if Alyse wore a long-bladed dagger on her right hip and Kate had a sword and dagger belted around her waist.

Dismounting, Alyse and Kate brushed road dust off their nondescript commoners' rough woolen pants and vests and white linen shirts, and stretched to ease their aching muscles after hours of hard traveling in the saddle. While Kate watered their mares and refilled their canteens from a small circular fountain in the town center, Alyse stood beside her gazing longingly at the inn as she absentmindedly fingered her shoulder-length chestnut locks.

Already oil lamps had been lit in the inn's two unshuttered windows facing the fountain, emitting warm welcoming glows. One by one, dancing yellowish flames from candles and oil lamps in the windows of the shops, inn, and homes lining both sides of the road began appearing.

Alyse peered up the road that disappeared into the gloomy forest beyond the town. The sight of the woods sent dread slinking across her shoulders. "I wish we could spend the night here," she said wistfully, eying the inn. "Except for our trips to the family villa, we've never stayed overnight outside the city. To sleep tonight in the forest surrounded by trees and wild animals and Goddess knows what else . . ."

Kate handed Alyse a canteen heavy with water. "We can't." Her tone indicated she wished the same thing. "We've barely put a half day's distance between us and Caldon—"

"I know." Alyse unstopped her canteen and swallowed a mouthful of cool water. "Mora told us she'd delay telling my parents we'd run away. But I bet she went right home and told Grandmother Maude. I can just picture the glee on her face as she's doing it."

Kate nodded agreement.

"Then grandmother will expel me from the family and Mora can marry Troy Estati instead of me." Alyse paused, then added heartfelt words. "And she's welcome to him."

Kate wrapped her canteen's strap around her saddle pummel. "Even if Mora kept her word, and I'm sure she didn't, she knows we left by the Public Gate. That's the road to The Marches. It leads to your uncle's military camp there."

"We have to reach Uncle Leoc before they catch up to us." Alyse pushed the wood stopper into the canteen's mouth. "He'll protect us."

"You hope."

"He gave me his word."

"He might be the Commander of the Eastern Legions, but he's also subject to the Magesterium. If they order him to hand you over, he will."

Alyse tightened her saddle's cinch, suddenly eager to set off again. "He won't. Unless he crosses the border into Caldonian territory, the Magesterium can only suggest, not command. Besides, the Magesterium won't get involved because this dispute doesn't involve the state. It's between two families."

"Which happen to be among the most powerful in Caldon." Kate brushed back strands of black hair from her forehead. "It's the matriarchs who pull the strings in the Magesterium. If your Grandmother Maude and Ariella Estati—"

"The Dejune and Estati matriarchs won't involve the Magesterium. And Uncle Leoc won't hand me over to my grandmother. He'll smooth things over."

Kate looked unconvinced.

"Besides you," Alyse said, "Uncle Leoc is the only person in the whole world I trust. He'll keep his promise."

Kate shrugged. "It's too late now for second thoughts. We have to see this through and hope your uncle keeps his word."

"He will."

Kate eyed the forest, creases of apprehension working their way into her face. Alyse was relieved to see that her cousin was just as frightened of the forest as she was.

"Let's get going." Kate mounted her gray mare. "We have lots of distance to cover."

Alyse swung into her saddle, then pointed her mare's head toward the forest. She and Kate started off at a walk.

A couple of passersby eyed them curiously, but one elderly man stepped into the street, blocking their path. "You girls headin' into the forest?"

"That's *our* business," Alyse said.

"That's Malagnar Forest yonder."

"So?"

"There's brigands holed up in there. Wise travelers don't pass through Malagnar Forest except in groups. And they avoid it at night." The man pointed to the inn. "I'd stay there tonight if I was you."

"We'll keep that in mind," Alyse said.

With a shrug, the man stepped aside. "Don't say I didn't warn ya."

Moving past him, Alyse urged her bay mare into a trot. Kate kept pace beside her.

"Travel fast," the man shouted after them. "And don't stop for nothin'."

As soon as Alyse entered the forest, tall pines and trees bristling with leaves loomed up on either side of her, creating a partial canopy that threw the road into shadow. Alyse recalled the man's warning and her heart tightened with dread. She'd never been this far east before and she'd never heard of Malagnar Forest. She suppressed a shudder. The forest's name sounded ominous.

Alyse didn't go too far along the dirt road, riding side by side with Kate, before Kate suggested stopping. Alyse peered uneasily at the darkening woods. "I thought we were riding straight through."

"We are," Kate responded. "But we should eat first and give the horses more of a breather. We won't get any more food or rest until we reach the other side of the forest. And Goddess knows when that'll be."

Dismounting, Alyse and Kate led their mares behind a clump of bushes a short way off the road and tied the reins to branches. Then they unfastened feedbags from their saddles and fed the horses. Afterward they settled down on a fallen tree trunk with their own travelers' fare—a loaf of crusty bread, a large hunk of cheese, and a leather wine pouch.

They ate in silence as the sun began its slow descent behind the forest canopy. Hoots came from somewhere nearby, sending shivers down Alyse's spine. She traded nervous looks with Kate. Then, as if on cue, they both laughed.

"We're city girls through and through," Alyse said.

Kate bobbed her head in agreement. "Take some poor villager and put her in the city and she'd be just as frightened."

"Rill told me once that he goes into the woods hunting with Jedd—" Alyse stopped abruptly as memories of her last encounter with Rill Larkin flooded her mind. Or, rather, memories of what he'd done to Dayson Florens, the wine shop owner she'd treated at the One Goddess Temple.

Rill had beaten up the old man to force him to sign over the larger share of his business to the Estatis for not repaying money he'd borrowed from them. Rill's lust for becoming a mage had made him into an Estati thug.

Alyse exchanged a quick glance with Kate, who appeared just as troubled by the dark thoughts Rill's name had conjured up.

"At least Jedd had the good sense to walk away from it all," Kate said.

"Yes." Alyse couldn't hide the sadness in her voice. "And it's too bad Rill didn't walk away too. Deep down, he's a good person. But the Estatis have led him astray to get back at his mother."

Leaves rustled off to their right. Kate jumped to her feet, half drawing her sword. Alyse gripped the handle of her dagger. She held her breath, listening for more sounds and peering at the dark, dense foliage. The mares snorted and pawed the leaf-covered ground. An animal's high-pitched scream erupted from deeper in the forest. The horses snorted again and jerked at their reins, making the leaf-covered branches bend.

Alyse and Kate swapped fearful looks.

"What was that?" Alyse asked in a tense whisper.

"An invitation to be off," Kate replied.

Alyse and Kate hastily unfastened their mares' reigns from the branches, led them back onto the road, and continued on their way at a trot. Soon sunset turned into twilight and eventually into darkness. To Alyse's relief, the moon was full and the partial canopy of branches and leaves allowed its pale light to shine through, revealing the contours of the road as a barely visible carpet running between thick walls of blackness.

Even though they were halfway through First Fruits, the hottest season of the year, the air grew chilly and Alyse took her light woolen cloak from her saddlebag and wrapped it around herself. After a while she lost all sense of time and distance traveled as her body moved in rhythm to her mare's gait. The sounds of the horses' hooves on the hard-packed dirt weren't loud enough to deaden the terrifying barks, screeches, screams, and howls that continuously erupted in the woods on both sides. Fear clutched at Alyse each time she heard them.

To Alyse, it seemed as if the journey through the gloomy, sinister forest was taking forever. She was an occasional rider, not a frequent one. And she'd been in the saddle for so long that the muscles in her buttocks, thighs, and legs sent out sharp pains in time to the drumming of her horse's iron-shod hooves against the road. Alyse was about to suggest a halt to Kate when movement at the edge of the woods up ahead caught her attention. Surprised, she drew in on her reins. Beside her, Kate's horse reared up with a wild whinny.

"Brigands!" Kate shouted, drawing her sword. "Don't stop. Ride!"

Alyse dug her heels into her mare's flanks as dark figures charged into the road from both sides of the forest.

"Unhorse 'em!" a rough voice shouted.

A hand closed on Alyse's leg. Whipping out her dagger, Alyse stabbed the hand. The attacker yelped in pain and let go. Then murky figures brandishing swords and clubs surged around her mare, trying to wrest Alyse out of the saddle. Alyse slashed at them wildly. But as soon as one attacker fell away two more seemed to replace her. Frantically, Alyse tried to kick the horse into a gallop but more brigands barred the way. The mare reared, almost unseating Alyse. Suddenly Kate appeared swinging her sword at the attackers and opening a path for the mare.

"Ride!" Kate yelled.

Alyse dug her heals into the mare's flanks and the horse exploded into a gallop.

A dark form lunged at Alyse as the mare sped by. Alyse cut at the brigand with her dagger, slicing through flesh and bone. The attacker screamed and stumbled back.

And then Alyse broke free of the brigands. Her first thought was for Kate.

Galloping hoof beats sounded behind her.

"Keep going!" Kate cried.

Alyse rode furiously for a long time, with Kate chasing after her. Alyse's heart beat fiercely against her ribcage, striving to outrun the furious beating of her bay's hooves against the ground. In her mind, she felt the brigand's hand on her leg. A shudder swept through her body. *If he'd unhorsed me—* She kicked the thought from her mind. He hadn't.

Kate drew up beside her and they rode together. After a while, Kate slowed down to a trot and Alyse matched the pace. Finally, Alyse pulled in on her reins. Kate did too.

"Are you all right?" Alyse asked as she strove to get her breathing under control.

"Just a few nicks," Kate said. "I think we surprised them with our spirited defense."

"You did. Not me." Alyse raked her fingers through her chestnut hair in frustration. "I feel so vulnerable with just a dagger. I appreciate you teaching me how to use one. But when we get to Uncle Leoc's, I want you to teach me how to use a sword."

"You have your Kinesi magic."

"No!" The force of Alyse's outburst astonished even herself. She lowered her tone but kept it firm. "I won't use Kinesi magic. Or any other magic except Healing magic. Besides, I don't know how to summon the kinesi power. I can only access it in times of stress. Sometimes not even then. And I don't know how to control it."

"If you learned how to summon and control it, you could use it whenever you wanted."

Alyse shook her head doggedly. "I won't use Kinesi magic."

"Kinesi magic can be better than a sword for some things. You've shown me that."

"I won't use it."

"Why?"

Alyse urged her mare closer to Kate's and spoke in a tone teeming with determination. "Magic is the root of all that's wrong in the world. First and Lesser Families raiding and killing one another for their charms and staffs. Conscripting fledging mages who don't receive patrons at the bidding or who don't join the legions or the sea service. And this ages-long war with Gaetan. We started it because we wanted to recover the charms and staffs Toran the Usurper took with him when the Caldonians rebelled against him and he fled the city to found Gaetan. Also—"

Kate put up a hand as if to ward her off. "All right. Point made. I'll teach you how to use a sword."

They broke free of the forest a little after dawn and stopped to eat a quick meal by the edge of the woods. Both girls' buttocks and thighs were sending them agonizing streaks of fire. Alyse applied healing hands to ease Kate's aching muscles.

"I wish you could use healing hands on yourself," Kate said as they waited for the magic to take effect.

"So do I," Alyse responded. "But a healer can't heal herself. Only others."

"We'll take more frequent breaks so you can stretch your legs," Kate told her.

"But our pursuers—"

"Probably haven't set out until this morning. We have a good lead on them. So I think we can afford to go a little slower."

Remounting, Alyse and Kate continued riding.

As the sun climbed into the sky, they began passing farmers riding in wagons piled with produce or firewood or leading donkeys or mules carrying loads, and fellow travelers on foot or on horseback. The road brought them through a combination of woodlands, hills, and open land dotted with small farms, a few large prosperous ones, and an occasional inn. Every so often a crossroads split off from the main road but Alyse and Kate continued east. At one point, a brook four spear lengths wide followed alongside them, babbling over rocks and flowing under fallen tree limbs, before veering off into the countryside. Once, Alyse spotted a young teenage girl fishing by the stream using a rod made from a stick, and envied her carefree attitude.

Around midmorning they passed through a village. By this time, both girls, who hadn't slept since the night before they left Caldon, were dozing in their saddles.

"We have to take more than short breaks," Alyse said. "We need to sleep."

"Soon," Kate told her. "We've got to make sure we can't be overtaken."

In the early afternoon they entered a prosperous-looking town where they stopped to buy a flask of weak beer and a couple of cold meat pies for themselves, and grain for the horses. A short distance out of town they spotted a stand of trees and shrubs on a knoll that provided good concealment.

"Now we can sleep," Kate said.

As Alyse swung down from the saddle, she stifled a groan from the pain that lacerated her buttocks and thighs, and hobbled around to ease her aching muscles. Meanwhile Kate unsaddled and fed the horses and by the time she began brushing them down, Alyse, her muscles finally loosened up, came over to help. Afterward they greedily devoured the pies and drank the beer. Then they laid their cloaks on the ground and stretched out on them, thankful for the warmth of the afternoon sun.

Alyse fell asleep instantly . . .

And was awoken by Kate shaking her shoulder. "Get up!"

Alyse's heart leaped in panic. "W-what?"

"We overslept."

Alyse yawned and stretched. "Is that all?"

"It's almost evening."

Blinking to sharpen her focus, Alyse spotted the sun drifting down toward the horizon.

"We need to get going," Kate said.

After saddling the horses, Alyse and Kate resumed their journey. They traveled all night, the soft moonglow lighting their way like a constant beacon as they trotted through sleeping hamlets, villages, and towns. A few times fright seized Alyse's heart when she heard horses approaching and she and Kate hurried off the dirt road to find whatever concealment they could. But the riders always passed by without noticing them. When dawn broke, the cousins stopped to rest and eat. Then they remounted and kept going all morning and into the afternoon, taking short breaks and stopping once in a town to buy food.

In the evening they happened upon a large, two-story inn by a crossroads near an ancient red oak. In the faltering light, the sign swaying in the warm, gentle breeze said RED OAK INN. The unshuttered windows glowed with friendly lamplight and a plume of smoke curled up lazily from one of the two chimneys until it faded into the darkening sky. Several horses were hitched to iron rings set in stone blocks and a few wagons were parked near the stable beside the inn, their horses waiting patiently in their traces. Music, singing, and laughter drifted out through the unshuttered windows.

"This place looks cheery enough," Alyse said. "Let's stay here tonight. Besides, I can't go any farther."

"Neither can I," Kate said.

As the girls dismounted, the stableboy—who couldn't have been older than twelve—ran up to them and asked if they'd like him to take care of their horses. Kate handed him some coppers and instructed him to feed and brush down their mounts. After wiping the road dust from their clothes, the cousins put on their cloaks, slung their bulging saddlebags over their shoulders, and went into the inn.

The large common room was bustling with activity. Trestle tables were occupied by all sorts of commoner travelers, from merchants to farmers to wayfarers. A wandering bard stood near the unlighted hearth strumming a mandolin and singing a rousing song. Some guests were singing along with her, waving their beer mugs in time to the music, while others were talking boisterously or focused on eating or simply listening. Many of the men and women clustered around the square tables along the walls ignored the commotion, preferring to chat among themselves.

Opposite the front door, a heavyset man in a soiled leather apron worked behind a counter that ran half the length of the room. He filled ceramic beer mugs and wine goblets from a bank of wooden barrels and handed them to customers at the bar or to a teenage serving girl to bring to the tables. The people at the counter appeared to be familiars because they bantered good naturedly with the man, whom they called Deek. A sharp-faced woman came out of a door by the staircase to the second floor carrying two wooden trenchers full of stew topped with thick slabs of bread and headed toward a table.

"Is that man, Deek, the innkeeper or just a servant?" Alyse whispered to Kate. "I've never been to an inn before."

"How would I know?" Kate whispered back. "I've never been to one either."

Inhaling deeply to settle her jittery nerves, Alyse walked up to Deek. "Are you the innkeeper?"

Putting his elbows on the counter, Deek leaned toward Alyse, his gaze taking in her plain commoner clothes. Alyse wrapped her cloak closer to her body, but not before Deek spotted the dagger belted to her waist. Then his eyes slid to Kate and performed the same inspection, lingering on the sword and dagger partially hidden beneath her cloak.

"I am," he said.

"Ya got a room for two?" Alyse cringed inwardly at her poor attempt to sound like a commoner. She'd never tried imitating their speech patterns before. And neither had Kate who was brought up speaking like the noblesse. "A private one."

The trace of a smile plucked at the corners of Deek's lips. "A private room for two, huh?"

"Yeah."

Deek stroked the sides of his mouth with a thumb and forefinger. "Just so happens I got one private room left."

"We'll take it," Alyse told him. "Your stableboy's already tendin' to our horses. We want supper too. What ya got for food?"

"Stew. Stew. Or stew."

Alyse couldn't hide her disappointment. She didn't like stew. "That's all?"

"Bread comes with it. Is there anything else you'd like?"

"A bath. Have two tubs taken up to our room. We wanna bathe before eating."

"This here is a *public* inn," Deek said, amusement in his voice. "The washrooms with tubs are communal. One for women. One for men. You take your baths there or stay dirty."

"All right. How much?"

Deek fingered his stubbly chin again, calculating. "Let's see now. Private room for two. Baths for two, including soap and towels. Supper and breakfast for two. Stabling two horses for one night." Deek named a price, which Alyse knew was much too high. He smirked at her, a challenge in his eye.

Futile anger burned in Alyse because she knew he wouldn't budge. "Very well." She nodded to Kate. "Pay the man."

Kate took the money from her belt purse and handed the coins to Deek.

He pocketed them, then leaned across the bar, putting his face so close to Alyse's she could smell his bad breath. He spoke in almost a whisper. "A word of caution. The two of you might be dressed like commoners. And you did a fair job of talkin' like one. But you gotta work on your el-lo-cution more. Here's a tip. Only a noblesse has her servant hold her money and pay the bills."

"My mother's a merchant," Alyse said sharply.

Deek handed Alyse a wry smile. "Maybe. But she didn't teach you no common sense. You don't display a heavy purse in a public place. That can prove dangerous for two young girls traveling by themselves, even if one is a backwatcher."

"I'll keep that in mind. Now we'd like to go to our room." Alyse held out her hand, palm up. "The key."

"Key?" Deek guffawed and slapped the counter, causing nearby patrons to glance at him. He leaned toward Alyse again and spoke softly. "Here's another tip. To further your ed-u-cation. Public inns have common sleeping rooms, which ain't got no locks. But I can tell that you're used to fancier ways than us common folk. So I gave ya the one room that can be barred from the inside. When you're in the room, I suggest ya keep the door barred at all times."

"Thank you," Alyse said. "I'll keep that in mind."

Deek summoned the serving girl, who led them upstairs and down a dim hallway, which had windows at either end, to the next-to-last door on the left. Weak light from the setting sun filtering through the unshuttered window barely lit the room. The furnishings were plain and simple. A bed large enough to sleep three people. A nightstand on either side, each with an oil lamp. A clean chamber pot under the bed. A wash stand with a bowl, a pitcher of water, soap, and towels. And pegs along a wall for hanging clothes. The single window looked out onto the stable and the woods beyond. There was no fireplace, and Alyse thanked the Goddess that they were traveling during First Fruits instead of the colder seasons of Reaping, Sleeping, or Awakening.

Kate closed and barred the door while Alyse lit a lamp using flint and steel. "It's almost a two-week trip to your uncle's camp. But a few more nights at inns with prices like this one's and we'll be broke before we reach it."

"I know," Alyse said glumly.

"And only the Weavers know what other expenses we'll have to pay for before we get there."

"Like food."

"Maybe we should spend the nights in the woods from now on."

"Or try harder to pass ourselves off as commoners," Alyse said quickly. "We can work at it. Perhaps starting with our e-lo-cution."

She and Kate giggled.

"That'll take some doing," Kate said.

"We can practice while we're bathing."

After their baths, Alyse and Kate put on their extra set of clothes and went to the common room to eat. They found an isolated table in a corner and sat across from each other.

The serving girl brought them wooden trenchers of chicken stew with slices of wheat bread on top and ceramic goblets of watered wine. While they were eating, anxiety crawled up Alyse's spine on spidery legs because she sensed that she and Kate stuck out in the noisy room like a pair of signal beacons. Whenever she glanced furtively around, though, everyone appeared to be more interested in the bard's songs or in their own conversations or food and drink than in two teenagers eating chicken stew.

After chatting for a while, Alyse and Kate turned their attention to the minstrel who was singing about two ill-fated lovers whose families were dead set against their marrying. Alyse wished she had a lover who would defy his family to marry her instead of having to flee a prospective husband who wanted to make her his wife against her will. Tuning out the bard's words, Alyse imagined what her lover would be like—

Kate touched Alyse's arm, then grinned and laughed, as if Alyse had said something funny.

Alyse gave her an odd look, puzzled by Kate's bizarre behavior. "What—"

"Don't look now," Kate said, still grinning but her voice tense. "Two men at a table behind you have been eying us for some time now."

Alyse's shoulders turned into gooseflesh but she managed to giggle back at Kate. "Do you recognize them?"

"No," Kate said, laughing. "One's wearing an eye patch and the other has pockmarks all over his face. Ugh! They're definitely not anyone we want to know."

"Do you think they mean trouble?"

Kate grinned. "Well, they definitely seem interested in us. Let's finish eating and go up to our room. But don't hurry. And whatever you do, don't look at them. Let them think we haven't noticed."

At Kate's first words, Alyse's appetite had vanished. But she forced herself to continue eating, leisurely spooning her now-tasteless stew into her mouth. When she and Kate finished, they returned to their chamber. Kate barred the door.

"We'll leave first thing in the morning," Alyse said. "Before breakfast. If those men mean trouble, we'll be long gone before they wake up."

Alyse and Kate climbed into bed fully clothed, leaving only their boots on the floor, and slipped their unsheathed daggers under their pillows. Despite the anxiety that looped around her like the coils of a snake, Alyse—exhausted from two days of travel—quickly fell into a deep, dreamless sleep.

And all too soon, Kate shook Alyse's shoulder. "It's time to go."

Alyse yawned and stretched. Through the thin walls on either side came sounds of snoring. Golden light from a rising dawn trickled through the window. Kate buckled on her sword belt. Then she and Alyse slung their saddlebags over their shoulders, picked up their boots, and quietly stole along the corridor and down the stairs on stockinged feet. Sounds of someone working in the kitchen filtered through the closed door. The front door was barred. Kate quietly lifted the heavy length of wood from the slats and they stepped outside into the warm morning air.

The happy chirping of birds in the branches of nearby trees welcomed them. Alyse studied the trees and bushes, searching for telltale signs of the two men. Quick movement among some trees caught her attention. Her heart stopped. And then beat again when a fox trotted into view with a squirrel in its mouth.

Alyse sent a triumphant smile to Kate as they pulled on their boots. "We gave them the slip."

When they reached the stable, Kate opened one of the doors partway and they sidled through the gap. Fortunately the door to the hayloft was open, allowing enough sunlight inside for the girls to see. Alyse hastily saddled and bridled her mare and tied her saddlebags into place, then led the horse out of the stall.

Kate emerged from the adjoining stall at the same time. "I'll open the door all the way," Kate said, handing her reins to Alyse.

Before Kate could take a step, a hand gripped the partially open door and opened it wider.

Kate's hand dropped to her sword.

Two men came through the gap. They wore expensive but well-worn clothes. The taller man wore an eye patch. The shorter man had a pock-marked face and hefted a battle axe menacingly.

"Well, well," Eye Patch said. "The chickens are flyin' the coop."

The men stepped forward a few paces.

Drawing her sword and dagger, Kate placed herself in front of Alyse.

Just then several more figures walked through the doorway and fanned out on either side of Eye Patch and Pock Face. They were dressed in the what looked like discarded, threadbare trappings of noblesse and noblesse commoners. They were armed with various weapons.

Pock Face hefted his battle axe. "A backwatcher. As soon as I seed them two girls last night, I knowed one was noblesse and the other her backwatcher."

Eye Patch's lips curved up into an unpleasant grin. "The little noblesse'll fetch us a tidy sum."

"Run!" Kate hissed. "Go out the back while I keep them busy."

Alyse drew her dagger. "Not without you."

"Don't be a fool. Flee!"

Two men sprang at Kate with their swords. She parried their blades and the three of them danced back and forth across the floor planks fighting. Instead of helping their two companions, the others watched the three battle as if they were observing a sports contest instead of a desperate life-or-death struggle. When one of the men stumbled away wounded, one of the onlookers replaced him.

"That's right," Eye Patch said. "Wear her out. She might be young but she won't last forever."

"Tag team match," Pock Face said, laughing gruffly.

Eye Patch sneered at Alyse, then nodded at Pock Face. "Time to take the golden goose."

Pock Face walked toward Alyse. The smirk on his lips told her he thought she was easy prey. When he reached for her, she slipped under his arm and thrust her dagger into his side.

He stumbled away, clutching the wound as blood flowed through his fingers. "She stabbed me! The little bitch stabbed me!"

Alyse charged the brigands fighting Kate. She knifed one in the back. With a shout, the brigands on the sidelines raced toward her. She spun around to face them but someone came up from behind and put his arm around her throat. Another seized her knife hand and twisted. Alyse struggled, but the arm around her neck cut off her air and the fingers pressing her wrist felt like the jaws of a tightening clamp. Her hand opened unwillingly, and the dagger struck the floorboards with a *clunk*.

Unsheathing his dagger, Eye Patch went to Alyse, wrapped his fingers around her chestnut hair, and drew her head back, exposing her neck. He placed the blade against her neck.

Alyse's breath stuck in her lungs and she dared not move.

"Drop your weapons, girlie," Eye Patch called to Kate. "Or I'll slit her throat. Your patrons won't like that, eh?"

Kate's opponents stepped back out of sword range. Kate looked toward Eye Patch, keeping her sword and dagger up.

Eye Patch dragged the blade lightly across Alyse's neck, making her heart freeze. She could feel blood trickling down her skin.

Eye Patch leered at Kate. "Want more blood?" He positioned his knife to make a deeper cut.

Kate threw down her sword, her face a combination of anger and disgust.

"And the dagger."

The knife clunked on planks.

Two brigands seized Kate by the arms. A third walked up to her, sword in hand, and shot Eye Patch a questioning look.

Eye Patch nodded. "Kill her."

Thanks very much for reading *Charm Wars*.

If you enjoyed the book, please leave a comment or write a review on goodreads and other appropriate websites.

.

www.ingramcontent.com/pod-product-compliance
Lightning Source LLC
Chambersburg PA
CBHW051550100726
47898CB00001B/42